Julia Justiss

THE SMUGGLER AND THE SOCIETY BRIDE

I0650699

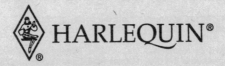

HARLEQUIN®

TORONTO • NEW YORK • LONDON
AMSTERDAM • PARIS • SYDNEY • HAMBURG
STOCKHOLM • ATHENS • TOKYO • MILAN • MADRID
PRAGUE • WARSAW • BUDAPEST • AUCKLAND

Recycling programs
for this product may
not exist in your area.

ISBN-13: 978-0-373-29604-0

THE SMUGGLER AND THE SOCIETY BRIDE

This edition published by arrangement with Harlequin Books S.A.

For questions and comments about the quality of this book please contact us at Customer_eCare@Harlequin.ca.

www.eHarlequin.com

Printed in U.S.A.

Dear Reader,

My story introduces Lady Honoria Carlow, daughter of spymaster George Carlow, Lord Narborough, whose best friend was convicted and hanged for the murder of a third colleague. Now, nearly twenty years after that tragedy, someone seems bent on exacting revenge against all the families involved in the scandal.

All Honoria knows is that some unknown enemy devised a ruthlessly effective plan to ruin her, one so clever even her family believes it was her own recklessness that brought it about. Stunned and furious with her relations for dismissing her protests of innocence, she flees to her eccentric aunt in Cornwall. Despairing, unsure what she can do with the remnants of her life, she encounters the dashing free-trader known as "The Hawk."

Gabriel Hawksworth agreed to become temporary captain of the *Flying Gull* as a favor to the army friend who saved his life. Upon meeting "Miss Foxe," he wonders immediately why such a beauty is residing on the Cornish coast instead of in London, dazzling suitors. Gabe scents a scandal… and if Miss Foxe has been banished for being less than a lady, he's just the man to tempt her to a little dalliance.

But as he delves into the mystery of Honoria, desire for a brief affair turns to fascination and then a compulsion to find the truth behind the event that destroyed her life. Even if that knowledge might mean losing her forever.

I hope you'll find their story compelling!

Julia

To my fellow "continuista" authors, Louise, Chris,
Gayle, Annie and Denise and to the editors for allowing
me to participate in the most exciting and enjoyable
writing experience of my career.

Look for these novels in the Regency miniseries

SILK & SCANDAL

Chapter One

May 1814. Sennlack Cove, Cornwall

The shriek of gulls swooping overhead mingled with the crash of waves against the rocks below as Lady Honoria Carlow halted on the cliff walk to peer down at the cove. Noting with satisfaction that the sea had receded enough for a long silvered sliver of sand to emerge from beneath its high-tide hiding place, she turned off the path onto the winding track leading down to the beach.

Honoria had discovered this sheltered spot during one of the first walks after her arrival here a month ago. Angry, despairing and brimming with frustrated energy, she'd accepted Aunt Foxe's mild suggestion that she expend some of her obvious agitation in exploring the beauties of the cliff walk that edged the coastline before her aunt's stone manor a few miles from the small Cornish village of Sennlack.

Scanning the wild vista, Honoria smiled ruefully. When she fled London, she'd craved distance and isolation, and she'd certainly found it. As her coach had borne her past Penzance towards Land's End and then turned onto the track leading to Foxeden, her great-aunt's home overlooking the sea, it had seemed she had indeed reached the end of the world.

Or at least a place worlds away from the society and the family that had betrayed and abandoned her.

One might wonder that the sea's violent pummelling against the rocky coast, the thunder of the surf, and the slap of wind-blown spray and raucous screeching of seabirds could soothe one's spirit, but somehow they did, Honoria reflected as she picked her way down the trail to the beach. Maybe because the waves shattering themselves against the cliff somehow mirrored her own shattered life.

After having been hurtled onto the rocks and splintered, the water rebounded from the depths in a boil of foam. Would there be any remnants of her left to surface, once she had the heart to try to pull her life back together?

Though Tamsyn, Aunt Foxe's maid, had tacked up the skirts of her riding habit, the only garb Honoria possessed suitable for vigorous country walking after her hasty journey from London, the hem of her skirt was stiff with sand when she reached the beach. Here, out of the worst ravages of wind, she pulled back the scarf anchoring her bonnet and gazed at the scene.

The water lapping at the beach in the cove looked peaceful, inviting, even. She smiled, recalling lazy summer afternoons as a child when she'd pestered her older brother Hal to let her sneak away with him to the pond in the lower meadows. Accompanied by whichever of Hal's friends were currently visiting, dressed in borrowed boy's shirt and breeches, she'd learned to swim in the weed-infested waters, emerging triumphant and covered with pond muck.

The summer she turned seven, Anthony had been one of those visitors, Honoria recalled. A familiar nausea curdling in her gut, she thrust away the memory of her erstwhile fiancé.

She wouldn't tarnish one of the few enjoyments left to her by recalling a wretched past she could do nothing to change.

Resolutely focusing on the beauty of the cove, Honoria considered taking off her boots and wading into the water.

With spring just struggling into summer, unlike the sun-warmed pond back at Stanegate Court, the water sluicing in the narrow inlet from the sea was probably frigid.

As she glanced toward the cove's rock-protected entrance, a flash of sun reflecting a whiteness of sail caught her attention. Narrowing her eyes against the glare, she watched a small boat skim toward the cove.

A second boat popped into view, apparently in pursuit of the first, which tacked sharply into the calmer waters of the cove before coming about to fly back toward open water. In the next instant, the following boat, now just inside the rocky outcropping that separated cove from coastline, stopped as abruptly as if halted by an unseen hand. While the first boat sailed out of sight, she saw the dark form of a man tumble over the side of the second skiff.

The boat must have struck a submerged rock, Honoria surmised as she transferred her attention from the little vessel, now being battered by the incoming waves, to the man who'd been flung into the water. Seconds after submerging, the man surfaced, then in a flail of arms, sank again.

Curiosity changed to concern. Though the waters of the cove were shallow at low tide, the man would still need to swim some distance before he'd be able to touch bottom. Had he been injured by the fall—or did he not know how to swim?

She hesitated an instant longer, watching as the man bobbed back to the surface and sank again, making no progress toward the shallows.

Murmuring one of Hal's favourite oaths, Honoria looked wildly about the beach. After spotting a driftwood plank, she swiftly stripped off bonnet, cloak, jacket, stockings, shoes and the heavy skirt of her habit, grabbed up the plank and charged into the water.

Still encumbered by chemise, blouse and stays, she couldn't swim as well as she had in those childhood breeches, probably not well enough to reach the man and bring him in. But she simply couldn't stand by and watch him drown without at least trying to wade out, hoping she could get near enough for him to grab hold of the plank and let her tow him in.

Shivering at the water's icy bite, Honoria pushed through the shallows as quickly as the sodden skirts of her chemise allowed, battling toward the struggling sailor.

She had about concluded in despair that she would never reach him in time, when suddenly, from the rocks far above the water at the trail side of the cove, a man dove in. Honoria halted, gasping for breath as a rogue wave broke over her, and watched the newcomer swim with swift, practiced strokes toward the downed sailor. Moments later, he grabbed the sinking man by one arm and began swimming him toward shore.

Relieved, she turned to struggle back to the beach. Only then did she notice the string of tubs bobbing near the cliff wall on the walk side of the cove. Suddenly the game of racing boats made sense.

Free-traders! Tethered in calm cove waters must be one of the contraband cargoes about which she'd heard so much. The first boat had apparently been trying to lead the second away from where the cargo had been stashed under cover of night, to be retrieved later.

Weighed down by her drenched clothing, Honoria stopped in the shallows to catch her breath and observe the rescuer swim in his human cargo.

Her admiration for his bravery turned to appreciation of a different sort as the man reached shallow water and stood. He, too, had stripped down for his rescue attempt. Water dripped off his bare torso, from his shoulders and strongly muscled chest down the flat of his abdomen. From there, it trickled into and over the waistband of his sodden trousers, which moulded themselves over an impressive—oh, my!

Face flaming, Honoria jerked her eyes upward, noting the long white scar along his ribcage and another traversing his left shoulder, before her scrutiny reached his face—and her gaze collided with a piercing look from the most vivid deep blue eyes she had ever seen.

She felt a jolt reminiscent of the many times when, shuffling her feet over the Axminster carpet in Papa's study after receiving a scolding about her latest exploit, she touched the metal door handle. Enduring that zing of pain had been a game, a silent demonstration to herself that she had the strength to bear chastisement stoically, despite Mama's disdain and Papa's disapproval. Though more lately, it had fallen to her eldest brother Marcus, de facto head of the family since father's last illness, to deliver the reprimands.

There the resemblance ended, for the jolt induced by this man was both a stronger and a much more pleasant sensation. Indeed, she felt her lips curve into a smile as she took in the sharply crafted face and the dripping black hair framing it, sleek as a seal.

Even had he not just recklessly leapt off a cliff into swiftly moving tidal water, his commanding countenance with its determined chin, high cheekbones and full, sensual lips, would have proclaimed him a self-confident man of action. One strongly muscled arm still towing the coughing, sputtering mariner, the rescuer strode through the shallows, carrying himself with an aura of power that, like the long scars on his chest and shoulder, hinted of danger.

A commanding man, she saw belatedly, who was now subjecting her to an inspection as intense as hers of him had been.

'Well, lass,' he said as he approached, his amused voice carrying just a hint of a lilt. 'Is it Aphrodite you are, rising out of the sea?'

Honoria's face flamed anew as his comment reminded her she was standing in ankle-deep water, the soggy linen chemise that clung to her legs and belly probably nearly transparent.

Tossing a 'well done, sir,' over her shoulder, she turned and ran. Upon gaining the shore, she dropped the plank and hastily donned her sandy cloak, her numbed fingers struggling with the ties. By the time she'd covered herself and bent to retrieve her jacket, skirts and shoes, a crowd of men was walking toward her along the narrow beach.

Accomplices of the free-traders, come to help move the cargo inland, she surmised as she chose a convenient rock upon which to perch and put on her shoes. She'd just seated herself to begin when the first of the men reached her.

Suddenly she realized their attention was fixed not on the rescuer or the cargo waiting in the cove waters—but on her. She could almost feel the avid gazes raking her body, from the seawater dripping from the loose tendrils of hair to her bare feet, the curiosity in their eyes overlaid by something hotter, more feral.

Horror filling her, she shrank back. Instead of the windswept cliffs, she saw the darkness of a London town-house garden, while the cawing of seabirds was replaced by exclamations of shock and surprise emanating from the path leading back to a brilliantly lit ballroom.

Eyes riveted on her, men closed in all around. Their gazes lust-filled, their lips curled with disdain or anticipation, their hot liquored breath assaulting her as she held the ripped edges of her bodice together. Anthony, disgust in his eyes, running up not to comfort and assist but to accuse and repudiate.

Panic sent her bolting to her feet. Boots and stockings in hand, ignoring the protest of the handsome rescuer who called upon her to wait while he deposited his coughing cargo, she pushed through the crowd and ran for the cliff path.

Gabriel Hawksworth's admiring gaze followed the honey-haired lass fleeing down the beach. After pulling the half-drowned mariner onto the shore, he straightened, breathing heavily, while the man at his feet retched up a bounty of Cornish seawater.

An instant later, some of the villagers reached them. Quickly dragging the man inland, one held him fast while another applied a blindfold and a third bound the man's hands.

Gabe shook off like a dog, chilled now that his drenched

body was fanned by the wind. To his relief, darting toward him through the gathering crowd was Richard Kessel, his old Army friend 'Dickin,' owner of the vessel of which Gabe was currently, and temporarily, the master.

'That was a fine swim you had,' Dickin said, handing Gabe his jacket. 'Mayhap ol' George will be so happy you saved his new revenue agent, he'll take a smaller cut of the cargo. Though the villagers hereabouts won't be too fond of your lending him assistance. Being a newcomer, our soggy friend—' Kessel nodded toward the man being carried off by the villagers '—is far too apt to point a pistol at one of them— and you, too, if he'd known who it was that rescued him.'

'Aye, better to have let the sea take him,' declared another man as he halted beside them.

'Well, the sea didn't, Johnnie,' Dickin said, 'so 'tis no point repining it.'

'Perhaps someone ought to give the sea a hand,' the man muttered.

'No thanks to you, the sea didn't oblige, little brother,' Dickin shot back. 'What daft idea was it to call for the cargo to be moved inland in full daylight, with a new man on patrol? 'Tis nearly asking for a scrabble.'

'I knew if the revenuer followed Tomas—not likely most times, as little as these English know the coastline—Tomas would still be able to lead him off the scent,' John defended.

'Aye—nearly drowning the man in the bargain,' Dickin said.

'What care you if there is one King's man less?' his brother replied angrily. 'Besides, I'm the lander on this venture. 'Tis *my* place to decide how, when and where the cargo gets moved.'

'If you're going to put our men and boats at risk, mayhap you shouldn't be the lander,' Dickin replied.

'Threatening to have Pa ease me out of operations?' John demanded.

'Nay, just trying to jaw some sense in your head,' Dickin said placatingly.

'Well, landing's my business, not yours, and best you remember it,' John said. Turning away, he called for the men holding the bound and blindfolded revenue agent to throw him into one of the carts.

After watching the brother pace away, Gabe said, 'Promise me, Dickin, the revenuer will get safely back to town? What happens on the high seas is up to God. I'd hate to abandon you still needing a replacement skipper for the *Flying Gull*, but I'll not be a party to murder.'

'Tis a most inconvenient conscience you've developed of late, Gabe my lad,' Dickin remarked.

'We used to share the same scruples,' Gabe replied. 'You'd never have shot a French prisoner back on the Peninsula. Nor have left one for the partisans, though Heaven knows the Spaniards had reason enough to torture the French.' Smiling anew at the irony of it, Gabe continued, 'Our former enemies…with whom you now trade for brandy, silk and lace!'

'True,' Dickin acknowledged cheerfully. 'But war is war and commerce is commerce.'

'Still, it wasn't sporting of Tomas to sail so close to the cliffs. He knows where that underwater ledge is. Our new revenuer obviously didn't.'

Kessel shrugged. 'His own fault, giving chase in daylight. If he wishes to hamper the trade, he'll have to get to know the coastline better.'

'Or try to follow us at night, when we, too, show a healthier respect for the rocks.'

'I doubt any of the revenuers wish to test the sea after dark,' Kessel replied. 'Few enough Cornishmen have your fool Irish daring. Or your expertise with a boat.'

'I'll ignore that jab at my heritage and accept your compliments on my skill,' Gabe said with a grin.

'Sure you'll not consider staying on once Conan's fit to resume command of the *Gull*?' Kessel asked. 'You've probably earned enough already from your cut of the profits to buy your own boat. We could make a good team, just as we did fighting Boney's best! Unless you've changed your mind about returning home to be your brother's pensioner?'

Gabe had a sudden vision of the family manor at Ballyclarig, windswept Irish hills—and his elder brother Nigel's frowning face. 'I'm not sure yet what I mean to do, but it won't include staying on in Ireland. I was at the point of setting out…somewhere, when you came calling.'

'Lucky I did, since with you fully recovered from your wounds, 'tis likely you and your brother would have murdered each other, if he's as self-righteous as you've described him.' Kessel clapped a hand on Gabe's shoulder. 'Though there's naught to that. Brothers often fight—look at me and Johnnie! Especially when one holds the whip hand over the other. Did you never get on?'

For an instant, Gabe ran though his mind the whole history of his dealings with the older brother who, for as long as Gabe could remember, had criticized, tattled about or disapproved of everything he did or said. 'No,' he replied shortly.

'Best that you move on, then,' Dickin said. A mischievous light glowed in his eyes and he laughed. 'Wouldn't that fancy family of yours disown you forever if they found out exactly how you've been helping your old Army friend?'

Gabe pictured the horror that would doubtless come over his brother's austere features, were the punctilious Sir Nigel Hawksworth ever to discover the occupation his scapegrace younger brother was pursuing in Cornwall. After casting Gabe off permanently, he'd probably set the nearest King's agents after him.

Shaking off the reflection, Gabe said, 'Let us speak of pleasanter things. Who was the charming Aphrodite who launched herself into the water? I've not seen her before. After her display of sympathy for the revenuer, I assume she must not be from Cornwall.'

'She isn't,' Dickin confirmed. 'Don't recall the name, but 'tis not Af-ro-dye—or whatever you said. My sister Tamsyn, who's a maid up at Foxeden Manor, says she's staying there with old Miss Foxe. Some relation or other. I've seen her on the cliff walk a time or two.'

Realizing a dame-schooled seaman-turned-soldier probably wouldn't be acquainted with Greek mythology, Gabe didn't pursue the allusion. For the first time, he felt a niggle of sympathy for the humourless cleric Papa had employed to try to beat into his mostly unappreciative younger son the rudiments of a gentleman's education.

His rule-bound tutor provided just one example of the rigid parental discipline that had sent him fleeing into the Army at the first opportunity. How would he have escaped Papa's heavy hand, Gabe mused, if Bonaparte's desire for glory hadn't pushed his nation into a war in which it was every Englishman's patriotic duty to contribute a son to the regiments? Especially a rapscallion younger son no tutor had ever managed to break to bridle.

Shaking his mind back to the present, he repeated, 'Some relation of Miss Foxe. Is she staying long, do you know?'

Dickin raised an eyebrow. 'I'll see if Tamsyn can find out. So, 'tis not enough you've all the maids hereabouts sighing over you—and barmaids at the Gull fighting each other to warm your bed. You must hunt fresh game?'

Gabe shrugged. 'What can one do when he is young, daring, handsome—' Breaking off with a chuckle, he ducked Dickin's punch.

'You'll soon catch your death of a chill if you don't get your *handsome* self into some dry clothes,' Dickin retorted. 'I'd as soon not lose my new skipper—or my closest Army comrade—just yet. Off with you, while I help the boys move the cargo inland. I'll see what Tamsyn can turn up about the lady.'

Gabe bowed with a flourish. 'I'd be most appreciative.'

'Aye, well, see that you show me how much on your next run. We'll meet at the inn later, as usual.'

Clapping Gabe on the back, his friend trotted off. Gabe made his way up the cliff walk, pausing to watch as the well-organized team of farmers, sailors and townsmen quickly freed the tubs from their temporary moorings, floated them to shore, then hefted them onto carts to be pushed and dragged up the slope to the waiting wagons. While one or two of the men nodded an acknowledgment, most ignored him as they passed by.

'Twas the way of the free-traders, he knew. Don't watch too closely, don't look a man in the face, so if the law ever questions you, you can truthfully reply that you know nothing.

At the top of the cliff, Gabe retrieved his horse and set off for what currently constituted home—the room he rented at the Gull's Roost, the inn at Sennlack owned by Richard and John's father, Perran.

The six months' run as skipper of the *Flying Gull* that he'd promised his comrade who'd saved his life at Vittoria would expire at summer's end, Gabe mused, setting the horse to a companionable trot. He had as yet not settled what he meant to do once his time in Cornwall was over.

He'd given his brother Nigel no promise of return and only the briefest of explanations before going off with Dickin, leaving Nigel to remark scornfully that he hoped after Gabe had scoured off the smudges he'd made on the family escutcheon with some honest soldiering, he wouldn't proceed to soil it again indulging in some disgraceful exploit with that seagoing ruffian.

If Nigel knew Gabe was skippering a boat for a free-trader, he would probably suffer apoplexy. How could one explain to a man whose whole world revolved around his position among the Anglo-Irish aristocracy the bond a man forms with a fellow soldier, one who's shared his hardships and saved his life? A bond beyond law and social standing, that held despite the fact that Gabe's closest Army friend had risen through the ranks to become an officer and sprang not, as Gabe did, from the gentry.

When Dickin had come begging a favour involving acts of dubious legality, Gabe had not hesitated to agree.

He had to admit part of the appeal had been escaping the stifling expectations heaped upon the brother of Sir Nigel Hawksworth, magistrate and most important dignitary for miles along the windswept southern Irish coast. After months spent cooped up recovering from his wounds, it had been exhilarating to escape back to his childhood love, the sea, to feel health and strength returning on the sharp southwestern wind and to once again have a purpose, albeit a somewhat less than legitimate one, for his life.

If he were being scrupulously honest, he admitted as he guided the horse into the stable yard of Gull's Roost, having lived on the sword's edge for so many years, he'd found life back in Ireland almost painfully dull. He relished matching his wits against the sea and the danger that lurked around every bend of coastline, where wicked shoals—or unexpected revenue agents—might mean pursuit or death.

Despite the massive collusion between local King's officer George Marshall, who complacently ignored free-trader activity as long as he got his cut from every cargo, there were always newcomers, like the fellow who'd foundered on the rocks today, who took their duties to stop the illegal trade more seriously. Although trials seldom occurred and convictions by a Cornish jury were rarer still, a man might still end up in Newgate, on the scaffold—or in the nearest cemetery, victim of revenuer's shot, for attempting to chouse the Crown out of the duties levied on foreign lace and spirits.

Still, Gabe was optimistic that his luck would hold for at least six months.

For a man unsure of what he would be doing at the end of that time, he'd considered it wise to dampen the enthusiasm of the more ardent local lasses—almost uniformly admiring of free-traders—by treating all with equal gallantry.

However, toward a lady whose tenure in the area was likely to be even briefer than his own, he might get away with paying more particular attention. While serving to discourage some of the bolder local girls, it should also prove an amusing diversion. The lass on the beach today had been as attractive as her behaviour in attempting to rescue the sailor had been unusual.

Gabe pictured her again, water lapping about her ankles while the sheer wet linen chemise provided tantalizing glimpses of long limbs, a sweet rounded belly and the hint of gold at the apex of her thighs. His breath caught, and more than just his thoughts began to rise.

With a sigh, he forced the image away. Too bad this one was a lady born rather than a hot-blooded barmaid at the Gull. He didn't think he'd try very hard to escape *her* pursuit.

Responding with a wave to Mr Kessel's greeting, and calling out for hot water as he trotted up the stairs to his room, Gabe wondered what Aphrodite's real name might be and whether she was as ignorant as his friend of the story behind the name he'd called her. Might she be learned—or wicked—enough to have understood the reference: the goddess of love rising naked from the sea?

Unlikely as that prospect was, the possibility put a smile on his face and a lilt in his step. Once inside his room, waiting for his water to be delivered so he might pull off his soggy garments, Gabe tried to keep his mind from imagining how her hands might feel against his bare skin.

All he knew thus far about his Aphrodite was that she was unconventional and courageous enough to try to swim out and save a stranger.

He intended to learn a great deal more.

Chapter Two

Shivering in every limb, Honoria rang for Tamsyn to help her out of her clinging wet clothes before hurrying to huddle over the remains of the morning fire. Some time later, no maid having yet appeared, she rang again and began divesting herself of as many garments as her reach and the numbness of her fingers permitted. After wrapping herself in her nightgown, too chilled to care if she soiled it with damp and grit, she strode to the bell pull. She was about to ring once again when, after a short knock, the housekeeper entered.

'What be you need—' the woman began, before halting abruptly, her eyes widening as she took in the heap of wet clothing, Honoria's robe-clad form and her damp, wind-tangled tresses.

'I know 'tis an odd time to request one, Mrs Dawes, but could I have a bath, please?'

After a quick roll of the eyes at the vagaries of the Quality, the housekeeper curtsyed. 'I'll have a footman bring up the tub and water, miss. I'd best add some chamomile to it to warm your joints and send along some hot tea with horehound to ward off a chill.'

Smiling through what were probably blue lips, Honoria nodded. 'Thank you, Mrs Dawes, that would be most welcome.'

Without further comment, the housekeeper withdrew. Accustomed to receiving swift chastisement for her impulsive actions, she blessed the fact that Mama and Marcus were far away in London. One—or both—of them would have had far more to say about this latest exploit than the disapproving housekeeper.

She refused to acknowledge the pang of distress and grief that thrummed through her at the thought of the family that had banished her.

She didn't need their censure—or Dawes's unspoken disdain—to realize she had once again failed to act like the gently-born maiden she was supposed to be. Honoria doubted her younger sister would ever have stripped down and flung herself recklessly into the sea, emerging later with her dripping chemise clinging to her body, a spectacle for the locals to gawk at. No, Verity would have fluttered a handkerchief and tried to summon some gentleman to come to her assistance.

Honoria smiled bitterly. Her own experience had robbed her of any belief in the existence of noble knights ready to gallop to a lady's rescue. But Verity was still naïve enough to hold tenaciously to the idea.

Nor would her paragon of a sister have been out walking the beach on a blustery day, getting her hem sandy and her curls windblown. Her sister would have remained at Foxeden Manor, her gown immaculate, nary a speck of grit marring her lovely face, decorating some altar cloth with her perfect tiny stitches and driving Aunt Foxe mad by offering, in a voice overlaid with solicitous concern, to pour her tea or fluff her cushions.

After her own disaster, she hoped Marc would keep a closer eye over her much-too-innocent sister, who would probably not recognize a sweet-talking villain for what he was until after he'd carried her off to ravish. Especially since Honoria, who had prided herself on her ability to accurately assess the character of the gentlemen she encountered, had barely escaped that fate.

A shiver that had nothing to do with the cold shook her. Verity might be a pattern card of perfection, Mama's darling who was repeatedly held up as the repository of all the feminine virtues Honoria lacked, but Honoria would never wish any harm to befall her.

She'd probably like the girl better now that she didn't have to live with her. Honoria smiled without humour. The parish priest at Stanegate, who'd often counselled her to charity during her growing-up years, would doubtless consider her exile a blessing, if it led her to think more tenderly of her sister.

Dismissing both the idea of improvement and Verity, Honoria turned her thoughts back to the scene at the beach. On the walk home, once she'd mastered her irrational reaction to the villagers' understandable curiosity, she'd begun to feel rather proud of her efforts, despite the embarrassment at the end. After drifting aimlessly this last month, trying to find something to replace the continuous round of rides, calls, teas, routs, musicales, balls and other amusements that had defined her life in London, it had felt…liberating to throw herself heart and soul into some useful endeavour. Though if the stranger had not intervened, she doubted she could have reached the struggling mariner in time.

As she brought to mind that gentleman's handsome countenance, another knock at the door interrupted her. Expecting the footmen with the tub, she was surprised when her Aunt Foxe walked in.

Looking her up and down, her aunt smiled. 'I was coming to see you when Dawes told me you'd gone bathing! I'd have judged it a bit early yet; 'twill be equally invigorating but much more enjoyable in a month. Though one must take care to bathe in a sheltered spot. The tide in some of the coves is quite strong…nor would one wish to provide a show for the fishermen.'

Wincing at the reminder of her folly, Honoria said,

'Actually, I didn't set out to sea bathe.' In a few short sentences, she described what had transpired at Sennlack Cove, then braced herself for her aunt's reaction.

'Admirable of you to attempt to help the man,' Aunt Foxe said, and Honoria felt herself exhale the breath she'd not realized she'd been holding. 'Though by the sound of it, you tried to assist a revenue agent—not an action that will win you the approval of the residents hereabouts.'

Honoria waited a moment, but her aunt added nothing else. Scarcely believing there were not to be any further recriminations, she said, 'You aren't angry with me?'

Aunt Foxe raised an eyebrow. 'Heavens, no! Why should I be? The rescue of one revenuer is scarcely going to destroy the local economy.'

The lack of criticism was so unusual, Honoria felt momentarily disoriented. As her world settled back into place, a rush of affection for her aunt filled her. Oh, her instincts had been right when they urged her to come here, rather than retreat in humiliated disgrace to Stanegate Court!

While she stood silent as this succession of thoughts ran through her head, her aunt's expression turned to one of concern. 'Is something wrong, child? Are you feeling ill?'

Impulsively, Honoria ran over and hugged her aunt. 'No, everything is fine! I'm just so glad I came here to you.'

'Heavens, you're getting salt all over me.' Her aunt laughed, gently disentangling herself from Honoria's embrace. 'I'm glad you came, too, though I might wish for you to refrain from such tender gestures until you have bathed. By the way, Dawes tells me you created the flower arrangements in all the rooms today. Thank you, my dear; they are lovely.'

'I'm glad you like them, for preparing the bouquets required such *massive* effort on my part.' Shaking her head, Honoria laughed ruefully. 'You were wise to have Mrs Dawes introduce me to the gardens. I do find it fascinating to study all the herbs' uses, and picking, drying and arranging them and the flowers helps occupy my time. I wish I might do more for you. However, I'm hopeless at mending and needlework. I could do some sketches of the coves and meadows, though, if you like.'

'I'd be delighted to have your sketches.' Her aunt paused, looking at her thoughtfully. 'It's no wonder an energetic young lady like you finds herself at a loose end here. I've been afraid you would become rather bored, marooned so far from London, with no theatres or balls or parties, no shops to browse, no friends with whom to gossip.'

Honoria felt a wash of guilt—for once the initial distress had worn off, she *had* been bored. That was certainly not her aunt's fault, however. 'You mustn't think I mean to complain! Truly, I don't miss London—except the shops, perhaps.'

That much was true. Even the name *London* called up bitter memories. She'd discovered in the most painful fashion that, far from possessing good friends, someone in London had disliked her enough to construct an incredibly intricate scheme to ruin her. So incredibly intricate, not even her own brother had believed she'd had no part in it. And so ruthlessly effective that, even after a month, the mere thought of that night still made her so sick with humiliation and distress she could not yet bear to sort out exactly what had happened.

Shaking her thoughts free, she continued, 'There may not be as many amusements here, but I love Cornwall. The cliffs, the sea, the countryside, the wild beauty of it. I can see why you decided to settle here.'

'You're sure? Certainly Foxeden, with its wide vistas overlooking the endlessly changing sea, suits me, but it's not for everyone.' Aunt Foxe chuckled. 'It is, however, a very effective location if one wishes to keep one's family from meddling in one's affairs, for which I've always been grateful.'

'As I am grateful to you for taking me in.'

Aunt Foxe gave her a fond look. 'We reprobates must stick together, eh?'

The afternoon of her arrival, Honoria had confessed to her

aunt every detail of her disaster in London, wanting that lady to fully understand the completeness of her disgrace, so she might send Honoria away immediately if she preferred not to be tainted by the scandal. After listening dispassionately, Aunt Foxe had embraced her and, to Honoria's everlasting gratitude, told her she was welcome to stay for as long as she wished.

She was tempted now to ask her aunt how *she* had ended up in Cornwall. Growing up, Honoria had overheard only bits and pieces about a forbidden engagement, a dash to the border, capture, exile, her lover's death at sea. But although Honoria had come to know her mother's renegade aunt much better over the last month, she still didn't feel comfortable baldly asking for intimate details that her aunt, a private person, had not yet volunteered.

The opportunity was lost anyway, for Aunt Foxe had started walking toward the door. 'Tell Dawes to bring tea to my sitting room once you've dried and dressed.' Pausing at the doorway, she turned back to add, 'There might even be some new fashion journals from London for you to peruse.'

A momentary excitement distracted Honoria, for pouring over *La Belle Assemblée* had been one of her favourite occupations in London. 'That would be delightful! I didn't know you subscribed!' Certainly Honoria hadn't found any fashion journals in her aunt's library when she'd first inspected the room a week or so after her arrival.

Aunt Foxe winked. 'I must have something to amuse my guest, mustn't I? I'll see you shortly.'

As her aunt exited the room, Honoria's heart warmed with gratitude. Aunt Foxe must have ordered the periodicals just for her. Once again, she was struck by that lady's kindness.

She had known her great-aunt but slightly at the time of her impulsive decision to seek refuge here. During their few childhood visits, she'd noted only that Miss Alexandre Foxe seemed to answer to no one and that her relations with her niece, Honoria's mother, seemed somewhat strained. Since her own relations with Mama had always been difficult and at the time she was sent out of London, staying with someone who had no connection to her paternal family held great appeal, Honoria had immediately thought of coming to Cornwall rather than proceeding, as directed by her brother Marcus, to the family estate in Hertforshire.

The fact that independent Miss Foxe was not beholden in any way to the Carlows was almost as appealing to Honoria as her recollection that, on one of those rare childhood visits, Aunt Foxe had pronounced Verity, already being held up to Honoria as a paragon of deportment, to be a dull, timid child.

Given the slightness of their previous acquaintance, Honoria still marvelled that her aunt had not sent her straight back to Stanegate Court, as John Coachman had darkly predicted when she'd ordered him to bring her to Foxeden.

She was deeply thankful to her aunt for taking her in and, even more, for giving credence to her story. Unlike her nearer relations in blood, that lady had both listened to and believed her, though she could come up with no more explanation than Honoria as to why someone would have wished to engineer her great-niece's downfall.

Even after over a month, it still hurt like a dagger thrust in her breast to recall her final interview with Marcus. More furious than she'd ever seen him, her brother had raged that, rash as she'd always been, he'd have expected better of her than to have created a scandal that ruined her good name at the same time it compromised her innocent sister's chances of a good match and distressed his newly pregnant wife. When he contemptuously cut off her protests of innocence, by now as angry as Marcus, she'd listened to the rest of his tirade in tight-lipped silence.

Despite their wrangling over the years, she would never have believed he would think her capable of lying about so important a matter. His lack of faith in her character was more painful than the humiliation of the scandal.

Marcus needn't have bothered to order her to quit London. She'd had no desire to remain, an object of pity and speculation, gleefully pointed out by girls of lesser charm and beauty as the once-leading Diamond of the Ton brought low. After her fiancé's repudiation and the final blow of her brother's betrayal, she'd been seething with impatience to get as far away from London and everything Carlow as possible.

Wrapping the robe more tightly about her, she walked to the window, sighing as she watched the roll and pitch of the distant sea. As for Anthony—that engagement had been a mistake from the beginning, as the tragedy in the town-house garden had revealed only too clearly.

It was partly her fault for accepting the suit of a man she'd known since childhood, for whom she felt only a mild affection. A man she'd accepted mostly because she thought that if she acquiesced to an engagement Marc favoured, her elder brother might cease dogging her every step and transfer his scrutiny to Verity. The prospect of getting out from under his smothering wing was appealing, and if Anthony proved tiresome, she could always cry off later.

She smiled grimly. Well, she no longer needed to worry about crying off—or about wedding to please her family, binding herself for life to someone who was probably the wrong man. Unless some local fisherman fell in thrall to her celebrated beauty, she'd likely never receive another offer of marriage—certainly not from anyone who could call himself a gentleman.

'Twas amusing, really. She'd chosen Anthony Prescott, a mere Baron Readesdell, over a host of more elevated contenders because she'd thought that he, having known her from childhood, would be more likely to prize her independent spirit and restless, questing mind as much as her beauty and connections. Anthony's speed in ridding himself of her after the scandal proved that a desire for a link to the powerful Carlow family and her sizeable dowry had been the true attractions.

If this boon companion from childhood who knew her so well was the wrong sort of man for her, who could be the right one?

The image of the blue-eyed, black-haired free-trader popped into her head. He certainly was handsome. Even with his hair slicked back and cold seawater dripping off that powerful chest and shoulders, he radiated a sheer masculine energy that had struck her in the pit of her stomach, setting off a fiery tingling in her core that warmed her all the way to her toes.

A resonant echo of that sensation heated her now, just remembering.

She had to chuckle. Wouldn't Marcus sputter with outrage at the mere thought of her being attracted to such a low-born brigand?

'Twas good that Papa would never learn of it; she wouldn't want to bring on another of the attacks to which he seemed increasingly prone. Mama had often rebuked her, claiming her unladylike behaviour caused him a distress that made such episodes more likely.

A familiar guilt stirred sourly in her belly. She only hoped her disgrace in London hadn't precipitated one.

Marcus hadn't allowed her to see Papa before leaving London, nor had she wished to. It pained her anew to think that her actions might harm him.

As someone had harmed her, though no one in her immediate family believed it. According to the diatribe with which Marcus had dismissed her, the entire Carlow family considered her a selfish, thoughtless, caper-witted chit without a care for the shame and humiliation her wild behaviour heaped on the family name.

On the other hand, given *that* assessment of her character, a low-born brigand was perfect for her, she thought in disgust. Though the stranger's handsome face and attractive body probably hid a nature as perfidious and deceiving as every other man's.

Except maybe Hal. A wave of longing for the brother who'd

been almost her twin swept over her. If only Hal had been in London that evening, how differently the outcome might have been! *He* would not have dismissed or abandoned her.

But with Boney now on Elba, Hal had been off somewhere in Paris or Vienna, helping secure the peace, exploring new cities, seducing matrons and parlour maids and in general having the sort of adventures which had won him a reputation among his peers as a daring young buck.

Adventures which, openly criticize though they might, Honoria believed Papa and Marcus secretly admired. Adventures denied a young lady, who would find her reputation ruined by even a whiff of the scandal that settled so gracefully about her brother's dashing shoulders.

A knock at the door was followed by the entrance of Mrs Dawes and the kitchen maid, both struggling with canisters of heated water. Wondering what had happened to the footmen who normally hefted such heavy loads, Honoria walked over to assist them. Life, she reflected wistfully and not for first time, as they poured hot water into the copper tub before the hearth, was distinctly unfair to those of the female gender.

Dawes stayed to assist her into the bath. By the time she'd scrubbed all the salt and sand out of her hair, the lady's maid turned up to help her out of the rapidly cooling water, letting the housekeeper return to her duties.

'So sorry I was absent when you needed me, miss,' Tamsyn said. 'Oh, but what a brave thing it was you done! I could hardly believe it when I seen you wading out into the water, for all the world like you was going to swim—'

'You *saw* me?' Honoria interrupted. Suddenly she understood the reason behind the maid's absence and the lack of footmen: they must all have been assisting the free-traders in moving their cargo inland. 'Tamsyn, surely you have not been taking part in illegal activities!'

'Oh, course not, miss,' the maid replied hastily, a telltale blush colouring her cheeks. 'I, um, heard all about it from Alan the footman, who met some fishermen whilst walking back from the village. But you must take care, miss! The water in the cove looks peaceful, but there be a powerful current where it runs between them rocks back out to sea. If you'd gone out much farther, you mighta been swept away!'

In the agitation of the moment, struggling in her heavy, wet clothing and desperate to reach the drowning man, Honoria hadn't particularly noticed. Now that she thought about it, she did recall how much stronger the outward tug had become as she reached deeper water. 'Luckily I didn't need to go out farther.'

'Indeed, miss. But, oh, wasn't he wonderful! Leaping off the rocks and swimming across the strongest part of undertow to haul out that worthless revenue agent! I swear, my heart was in my throat, wondering if the both of them would be sucked back out to sea,' the maid exclaimed, obviously forgetting her contention that she'd not personally witnessed the drama.

Amused, Honoria tried to resist the curiosity pulling at her as insistently as that treacherous current. Losing that struggle, she asked casually, 'Who was the young man who made the rescue?'

The maid stared at her. 'You don't know? Why, 'twas the Hawk! My brother Dickin, who's a dab hand of a captain himself, says he's the best, most fearless mariner he's ever seen! Eyes like a cat, he has, able to navigate despite tides and rough sea even on the blackest night. Gabriel Hawksworth's his real name. He's only been captain of the *Flying Gull* for a few months, but folks hereabouts already dubbed him Hawk for the way he can steer his cutter sharp into land and back out again, like some bird swooping in to seize his prey.'

'He's not local, then?' Honoria asked.

'No, miss. Not rightly sure where he hails from, though with that hint of blarney in his voice, I'd guess he's Irish.'

'Do the Irish also fish these waters?' she asked. Though the Hawk seemed too confident and commanding a man to have spent his life on a fishing boat.

'Don't know what he done before the war. He was an Army mate of Dickin's. While with Wellington's forces in Spain, far from the sea, they used to talk about sailing, my brother told me. Even took a boat out together a few times when they got to Lisbon, and Dickin said he'd never met a man who could handle a small craft better. When the former captain of the *Gull* was injured, Dickin asked the Hawk to come sail her.'

An Army man. That would explain his decisive air of command. Her brother Hal possessed the quality in abundance. 'If he is so fond of sea, I wonder he didn't end up in the Navy.'

'Don't know about the Hawk, but Dickin had no wish to be gone for months deep-water sailing. Said if the navvies ever found out how well he could handle a tiller, he'd be gang-pressed onto a frigate and never see land again! So when the Army recruiters come through, he jumped up to volunteer. Didn't mind doing his part to put Boney away, but wanted to be able to come home afterward, take care of Ma and us kids and tend the family business.'

'The *family business* being free-trading?' Honoria asked.

Tamsyn blushed again. 'Helping Pa run the inn, mostly, along with some fishing, miss. As for anything else, as folks around here will tell you, 'tis best if you don't look too close nor ask too many questions. In general, the revenuers leave everyone alone, long as old Mr Marshall gets his cut regular. That man who ran his skiff on the rocks today was a new man.'

'Who wouldn't be around to look closely or ask questions any longer, if Mr Hawksworth hadn't intervened.'

'True, but the Hawk being such a good captain, I don't think anyone hereabouts will hold it against him.'

Before Honoria could exclaim about someone being censored for saving, rather than taking, a life, Tamsyn paused to utter a sigh. 'And he's as handsome as he is skilful! So tall, with them big broad shoulders and eyes so blue, you'd think they held the whole sky inside.'

'Why, Tamsyn, you're quite the poet!'

The maid's blush deepened. 'They *are* ever so blue. All the maids—not just here, but from Padstow to Polperro, Dickin says!—have set their caps for him. Though as yet, he's not shown a partiality for any particular lass,' she added, her expression brightening.

So Tamsyn was among those smitten by the handsome captain. As for singling out one particular lady among the many apparently vying for his attention, Honoria suspected dryly that Mr Hawksworth wasn't in any hurry to make a choice.

Replaying in her mind's eye that bold dive into the swift-moving water and the tricky swim towing the struggling mariner, she had to agree that in this instance, he had lived up to the dashing image Tamsyn had described.

Recalling the intimate lilt of his voice, the admittedly intense blue of his gaze, she felt another quiver in the pit of her stomach. She sighed, unable to help sympathizing a bit with all the infatuated maidens.

Not that she had any intention of following their lead. Besides, except for that chance encounter at the beach, it was highly unlikely that the niece of Miss Foxe of Foxeden Manor would be rubbing shoulders with the captain of a smuggling vessel, no matter how locally celebrated.

As she pulled her chemise over her blessedly warm, clean, naked body, for an instant she felt again the brigand's intense blue-eyed gaze, unabashedly staring at her through that all-too-thin drape of wet linen.

A little sizzle hissed and burned across her skin.

Resolutely, she shook off the sensation. Dismissing any further thoughts of the rogue who'd inspired it, she let Tamsyn lace her stays.

Chapter Three

Two days later, Honoria accompanied Aunt Foxe to church in Sennlack. A local curate normally served the small parish, but occasionally the bishop from Exeter came to conduct the services. In honour of that visiting dignitary, an acquaintance of many years, Miss Foxe had elected to drive to town rather than remain at home to conduct her own private devotions, as she had the previous Sundays since Honoria's arrival.

Having been through the village only when her carriage halted at the Gull's Roost for directions to Foxeden Manor the day of her arrival, Honoria was looking forward to visiting the town and viewing the inside of the rustic stone church. Except for her walks along the cliffs, she'd not left the manor's grounds since her arrival.

After the service, the congregation filed out, shaking hands with the rector and the bishop before they departed or stood in small groups chatting. Honoria recognized the man currently speaking with the vicar as the innkeeper from whom John Coachman had obtained directions to Foxeden—the man Tamsyn later identified as her father. The senior Mr Kessel was flanked by two young men who bore him a striking resemblance, one of whom must be Tamsyn's fishing boat captain brother, Dickin.

The curate laughed and joked with the men, much friendlier than Honoria would have expected a clergyman would be with individuals whose true occupation, she suspected, involved activities of more dubious legality than innkeeping or fishery.

'I wonder that the vicar is on such good terms with free-traders,' she murmured to her aunt as they made their way down the aisle.

Miss Foxe laughed. 'A Welshman likes his brandy and spirits as well as the next man. You won't find any hereabouts who don't do business with free-traders. I've even heard there's a smuggler's tunnel that leads into the basement under the sacristy of this church.'

'Surely not!' Honoria replied, properly shocked—as, from the twinkle in her aunt's eye, that lady had meant her to be. *Was it true?* she wondered.

They reached the vestibule, where her aunt's attention was immediately claimed by the visiting bishop. Realizing that she would soon be introduced to him and probably a number of members of the local community, Honoria's initial enthusiasm for the excursion vanished. Hoping to postpone the moment as long as possible, she turned aside, ostensibly to allow her aunt a moment of private conversation.

Remote as Sennlack—and even Exeter—were from London, she suddenly felt sick with apprehension that the bishop might, upon being given her name, have heard about her disgrace.

Her anxiety over how to counter that possibility was interrupted by a little girl tugging at her sleeve. Having claimed her attention, the child smiled, bobbed a curtsy and held out a handful of flowers that wafted up to her the delicious odour of primroses.

'For me?' Honoria asked.

The girl nodded. Thin, with ragged blonde hair and dressed in a worn, simple gown, she appeared to be about ten years old.

As Honoria looked from the flowers to the child, she noticed with a small shock that while the girl's one blue eye stared directly at her, the other, grey in hue, seemed to be inspecting the distance beyond. The mismatched colour and wandering eye gave the child an unsettling, other-worldly look.

'How very kind of you…' As she paused, waiting for the child to supply her name, a woman hurried over.

'Sorry, miss, I didn't mean for her to bother you! Come with Mama, now, Eva,' the woman coaxed.

'She's no bother. It was sweet of her to give me flowers,' Honoria replied.

Pulling free of her mother, the girl wiggled her fingers like a flowing sea, then made a dog-paddling motion.

'She brought them because she thought you were so brave, trying to help the man who looked to drown,' the mother explained.

Giving Honoria a lopsided smile as slightly off-kilter as her eyes, the girl nodded.

Honoria felt both charmed and embarrassed. 'I'm not brave at all, but thank you, Eva. The primroses are lovely!'

The little girl patted the skirt of Honoria's gown and made another gesture, to which her mother nodded.

'She thinks *you* are lovely, too, miss.'

When the mother's fond smile abruptly vanished, Honoria glanced in the direction of the woman's gaze. One of the innkeeper's sons was bearing down on them, an angry scowl on his face.

'I thought you'd been warned not to bring her here,' he snarled at the mother.

'Sorry, Mr John,' the woman said, curtsying as she grabbed the girl's hand. 'We was just going.'

Seeming content now that her errand was discharged, the child let her mother lead her off.

Honoria watched them go, frowning.

The innkeeper's son shook his head. 'Not right for her to bring that halfwit here among normal people. Bad luck, it is.'

'She didn't seem half-witted to me,' Honoria retorted, her temper stirred by the man's harshness to the child.

He gave her a dismissive look. 'Meaning no disrespect, miss, but you're a stranger here, and probably ought not to talk on things you don't know nothing about.'

Truly angry now, Honoria was about to return a sharp remark when she heard her aunt's voice from just behind her. 'Ah, here you are, my dear. Come, let me present you to my good friend, His Eminence Bishop Richards, and the vicar, Father Gryffd.'

Dread tightened her chest as Honoria turned to face them. When Miss Foxe continued, 'Gentlemen, my kinswoman—' she found herself blurting '—Miss Foxe. Miss Marie Foxe,' she added, in deference to her aunt as an elder Miss Foxe.

As ashamed as she might be of the desperation that had produced the lie, her feelings of relief were stronger. Until she figured out what to do with her life, she'd just as lief the bishop—and the rest of Sennlack—were not aware of her true surname, in case some word of the scandal made it here from London. And with the nature of that scandal making the name Honoria sound too much like mockery to her ears, she'd might as well make the falsehood complete by using a middle name.

To Honoria's relief, after only a slight rise of her eyebrows, Aunt Foxe fell in with the deception. 'My niece is presently on an…extended visit.'

'Welcome, Miss Foxe,' the bishop said. 'Sennlack may be only a small village, but I'm sure your aunt will make you quite comfortable. The views from the coastal walk are breathtaking, her gardens lovely, and Foxeden Manor boasts a fine library.'

'Thank you, sir. I'm sure my stay will be most enjoyable.'

'Shall we tempt you to Exeter for the summer festival, Miss Foxe?' the bishop addressed her aunt. As the two began discussing this event, Honoria turned her attention to the vicar.

'Father, who is that little girl walking off with her mother?' she asked, pointing down the lane.

As if somehow knowing she was being discussed, the child paused at the bend in the road to look back and wave. With a defiant glance in the direction of the innkeeper's son, Honoria waved back.

'Eva Steavens,' the vicar replied. 'And her mother, Mrs Steavens, a recent widow. Her husband and the child's father, a fisherman, was lost at sea last winter.'

'Poor child—and poor wife,' Honoria murmured. 'Does the girl never speak?'

'Not that I know,' Father Gryffd replied.

'That still doesn't make her a halfwit—no matter what some people might think,' Honoria asserted.

'No, indeed,' the vicar agreed. 'But many of the folk hereabouts are superstitious. It's her eyes, I suppose, and that crooked smile. Fearing what they do not understand, some think it the devil's mark and avoid her. Especially…' he hesitated, as if searching for the correct word '…watermen like John Kessel, who shooed her away. It seems she gave a pretty rock or some such trifle to a friend of his, the captain of one of the local, um, fishing boats, just before he set off on a voyage. There was a storm; the ship was lost at sea with all hands. Kessel believes she possesses the evil eye and brought his friend ill luck.'

'That's ridiculous,' Honoria said flatly.

The vicar nodded. 'Indeed, but the sea is a hard mistress. One can understand that those who ply her depths would wish to avoid anything they think might increase her dangers.'

Unable to disagree with that argument, Honoria said instead, 'Is the child a halfwit?'

''Tis difficult to know for sure when one is unable to speak with her. But she appears intelligent. You must have noticed the language of gestures she has developed to communicate with her mother.'

Her newly-acquired sympathy for the innocent ignited on the girl's behalf. 'But it's so unfair! 'Tis no fault of hers that she entered life with mismatched eyes and a crooked smile.'

'It is indeed wrong for innocents to suffer for the mistaken perceptions of the world,' Aunt Foxe said, rejoining their conversation as the bishop's attention was claimed by another parishioner. 'But, alas, 'tis often the case.'

Her kind eyes and the look she directed to Honoria were so filled with sympathy, Honoria's own eyes pricked with tears.

'One waits in hope for a just God to right matters in the end,' the vicar said.

'Amen to that,' Aunt Foxe agreed.

Honoria had nearly regained her composure when a velvet-timbred, lilting voice emanating from just behind made her jump.

'Father Gryffd, Miss Foxe, good day. I heard we had a new visitor at services.'

A wave of sensation rippled across her skin. Honoria turned toward the voice that, although she had heard it only once before, already seemed familiar. Standing before her, a smile on his handsome face, was the rescuer from the beach.

Something about that smile made her stomach go soft as blancmange while little ripples darted across her nerves. Before she could figure out why a man's expression could have elicited such an absurd reaction, the man himself bowed to her aunt. 'Miss Foxe, might I have the temerity to beg an introduction?'

Her aunt hesitated. Honoria held her breath, wondering how that lady would respond. A smuggler was not a fit person for Lady Honoria Carlow to know, but snubbing a renowned local personage in so small a village hardly seemed warranted—especially on behalf of a mere Miss Foxe whose aunt was apparently on familiar terms with him.

Obviously drawing the same conclusion, with an amused smile, her aunt nodded. 'My dear, allow me to introduce Mr Gabriel Hawksworth, a…mariner lately come to our shores. Mr Hawksworth, my niece, ah, Miss Marie Foxe.'

'A breathtaking addition to our local congregation, ma'am.

I've heard Miss Marie is an admirer of gardens. Would you permit me the further liberty of escorting your niece to view the roses in the churchyard? They are just coming into bloom.'

Honoria nearly sputtered with indignation as her aunt weighed that request. Had the man in question been an eligible gentleman of rank, the inquiry would have been bold enough, but for an out-and-out rogue to solicit the company of an earl's daughter was audacious beyond belief!

Perhaps it was her certain knowledge that the Carlow men would go into fits, were they to know Honoria was strolling about with a free-trader, but Aunt Foxe nodded her head.

'I don't suppose you can involve her in too much mischief whilst walking about the churchyard in plain view, Mr Hawksworth, but I do count on you to exhibit your most gentlemanly behaviour. My dear, make the most of this opportunity to become acquainted with a local legend.'

The brigand bowed low. 'I am deeply in your debt, ma'am.'

'See that you remember that the next time you price your cargo,' her aunt replied.

Beginning to believe her aunt nearly as much a rogue as the man into whose charge she was being given, before she could think how to protest, with an elaborate bow, Mr Hawksworth claimed her hand and nudged her into motion.

Any thoughts of refusal were scattered to the wind by the little shock that leapt through her as he took her hand. Though after that jolt, her mind remained indignant over the Hawk's effrontery, her treacherous feet followed his lead quite docilely—a reaction which only increased her irritation.

'Sir, this is an abduction,' she said in an undertone.

'Hardly that! Not when I've agreed to be upon my best behaviour. I shall even refrain from detailing all the possible mischief one could get up to in a garden.'

His teasing remark doused her heated irritation as effectively as a cold sea wave. She knew all too well what mischief could occur in a garden. Because of it, she was no longer Lady

Honoria, sought-after maiden of quality allowed to maintain exacting standards about whom she would and would not grace with her company.

Still, though in truth she might now rate even lower than a plain 'Miss Foxe,' that didn't mean she had to swell this man's vanity by swooning at his feet like all the other village girls— no matter how eagerly her senses responded to him.

The best way to deal with the stranger, she decided, was to show him how unimpressed she was by his charm and dashing manner. A man who had every maid from Padstow to Polperro sighing over him could probably use a good lesson in humility.

'For that, you would need a willing partner,' she replied at last.

He paused in mid-stride and looked at her, one eyebrow quirked. 'And you think you wouldn't be?'

As he bent upon her the intensive gaze she remembered so well from the beach, a warm melting feeling expanded in the pit of her stomach. 'Certainly not,' she replied in the most disdainful voice she could summon.

He shook his head disbelievingly. 'I thought you had a fondness for mariners—or so it seemed when I saw you on the beach at Sennlack Cove. Most…intriguingly dressed, I might add,' he said, sweeping his gaze from her legs to her belly, then letting it linger at the apex of her thighs.

Honoria felt her face burn as other parts of her tingled. 'A gentleman would have forgotten my…unsuitable attire.'

He laughed, a warm, rich sound that was as engaging as his smile—drat him. 'I thought we'd already established I'm no gentleman! But unsuitable as that might make me to accompany you, I did feel compelled to seek you out. A genteel young lady who knows how to swim is uncommon enough. 'Tis even more astounding to find one who was prepared to jeopardize her safety—and dignity—by plunging in to rescue a stranger.'

His unexpected admiration, as much as his sudden dropping

of the overly gallant tone and manner, was making it difficult for her to maintain her haughteur. 'I would hope any good Christian would do the same,' she said.

'You have a higher opinion of Christians than I. So why are you so disapproving of me?'

'Of a smuggler and a law breaker?' *Who is way too attractive for my comfort,* she added silently. 'I would have deemed you intelligent enough to have already deduced the reason,' she told him, deliberately using the most formal wording she could summon to display a superior education and breeding that was meant to put him in his place.

Instead, he laughed out loud. 'Miss Foxe, you *are* a newcomer! If not upon that charge, then certainly upon aiding and abetting, you could convict half the congregation! Do you not remember seeing some of them among the group on the beach?'

A grudging honesty forced her to admit she'd noted that fact during services. 'It's a dangerous risk they all run—and for what, some bits of lace?'

Once again, he paused. After looking her up and down—setting her nerves humming wherever his gaze touched—he remarked, 'That's quite a disapproving tone for one who, if my eye for feminine finery remains true, is wearing no small bit of lace herself.'

Aghast, Honoria looked down at her pelisse. Warmer and heavier than those she'd brought from London, it was borrowed from her aunt, who was of almost the same size—and boasted a fine trimming of lace at the collar and cuffs.

With chagrin, she realized he was probably right—which made her almost as angry as the realization that, hard as she tried to will it otherwise, she was not immune to the appeal of that blue-eyed gaze or self-assured charm.

'I shall take care not to do so in future,' she said stiffly. 'I don't wish to enrich common brigands.'

To her further annoyance, his grin only widened. 'Ah, Miss

Foxe, we are not at all *common!* Those who follow the sea are a hardy lot, braving wind, tide and storm, and those who do so while eluding pursuit are more resourceful still. I don't wish to sound boastful, but 'tis a fact that quite a few ladies hereabouts admire us!'

'Ladies?' she echoed disbelievingly. 'Now I know you are joking.'

'Indeed, I am not!' he protested. 'Have you not heard of the landlady in West Looe who, when the preventives came to her establishment searching for free-trader cargo, concealed a keg beneath her skirts and sat calmly knitting until the agents departed? Indeed, even the customs collector of Penzance often calls fellows in the trade "honest men in all their dealings."'

Honoria studied his smiling face, trying to decide whether he could be telling the truth. 'I believe you are trying to cozen me,' she said at last.

'Absolutely not!' he affirmed. 'Ask anyone. Free-traders are considered quite respectable fellows hereabouts. It's even said that the church spire at St Christopher's—' he gestured upward to the building she'd lately occupied '—had its tower built by special contribution from the local landowners, to make it high enough to serve as a navigation landmark for…mariners.'

'The church tower?' she exclaimed. 'Now I know you are bamming me!'

'Since the days of running wool to Flanders, smuggling has been a part of life here. Nearly everyone is involved, either as provider or customer, from the miners who buy the cheapest spirits to the rich landowners quaffing expensive brandy. Even your aunt.'

Though she suspected as much, Honoria still didn't wish to admit it. 'Surely not my Aunt Foxe!'

The brigand chuckled. 'Do you think the local dressmaker provided the lace that trims those sleeves? Or the shop in town, the clarets that grace her dinner table—or the cognac that warms her coachman on a cold evening? If the Crown truly wished to bring illegal trade to a stop, they would abolish the tariffs.'

He must have seen the confusion in her eyes, for he continued, 'But you shouldn't think poorly of your aunt! With its proximity to France and Ireland and its abundance of natural harbours, Cornwall seems designed by the Almighty expressly to support the free-traders. One shouldn't fault the logic of folk who choose to buy the more reasonably priced goods they provide, any more than one should blame the local men who aid the smugglers. The mines are a hard life, trying to coax a living out of this rocky, wind-swept soil no easier a task, nor is extracting fish from a capricious, often dangerous sea. You shouldn't condemn men for taking an easier route to earning a few pence.'

'It's hardly easier, when those who participate may end up on the gallows or in a watery grave,' she retorted.

He shrugged. 'But all life's a gamble, a vessel buffeted by winds and tides beyond one's control. One cannot retreat; one must put the ship in trim and sail on.'

How does one meet disgrace and sail on? she wondered. Easy enough for men, who ruled the world, to urge bold action!

But her brigand was halting again. 'Ah, there are the roses. Lovely, aren't they? I'm told that, protected from the wind against this south-facing stone wall, the plants bloom earlier than anywhere else in England.'

At that moment Honoria spied them, too. With an exclamation of delight, she walked over and filled her nostrils with the rich spicy aroma of alba rose. Eyes closed, inhaling the heady scent, she was distracted for a moment from the curiously mingled sensations of attraction and avoidance inspired by the man beside her.

'They are lovely,' she exclaimed, reluctantly turning back to him. 'So at least this part of your tale is true. Is it the lilt of Ireland I hear in your voice?'

He made her a bow. 'Indeed you do. 'Tis a fine ear you have, Miss Foxe—which means it matches the rest of you.'

She felt her left ear warm, while the tendril of hair just above was stirred by his breath. Other parts of her began to warm and stir as well.

Blast the man! He made resisting his seemingly unstudied charm deuced difficult—and she had been wooed by some of London's most accomplished. No wonder all the maids from Padstow to Polperro were smitten.

'I'm convinced half of what you say is nonsense, but I'll concede you spin a good story. My brother says Irish troopers tell the best tales of anyone in the Army.'

His lazy regard sharpened. 'Your brother is an Army lad? In which regiment?'

Belatedly realizing her error, she said vaguely, 'Oh, I don't recall the number.' As if she didn't know to a man how many troopers Hal commanded in his company of the 11th Dragoons. 'I've heard you were with the Army, too,' she said, trying to turn the conversation back to him.

'Yes.'

She waited, but he said nothing more. 'That seems an odd choice for one who is…taken with the sea,' she said finally.

''Tis only a temporary occupation.'

'Until?' she probed.

'Until I choose a more permanent one.'

He was no more forthcoming than she. Was he, too, running from something or someone? The wrath of the Irish authorities over some misdeed? The vengeance of a cuckolded husband?

Though Honoria realized she should recoil from one she *knew* to be a law-breaker, she could not sense emanating from this charming blue-eyed captain a hint of anything venal or sinister. She felt no threat at all.

But then, how much credence should she put in her senses? She'd thought she could handle Lord Barwick in the garden— and had trusted in Anthony's support and loyalty.

Mr Hawksworth jolted her out of those unpleasant reflections by asking, 'What are your plans, Miss Foxe? Do you make your aunt a long visit? With summer just coming into Cornwall, it's particularly beautiful here.'

'It is lovely,' she agreed, sidestepping the question. 'By the way, how did you know I liked flowers?'

'Oh, I have my sources,' he replied.

Had Tamsyn talked to him about her? Somehow she couldn't believe that the maid, if she were granted audience with her hero, would waste it prattling about her employer's niece. 'A guess, then,' she countered, 'since most females like roses. Particularly females visiting a lady who possesses one of the finest gardens in the area. Though not this particular rose,' she added, inspecting the blossom. 'Perhaps I should take a cutting back to Foxeden. In a sheltered bed, it should thrive.'

'Under your hands, anything would thrive.'

Honoria gave him a sharp glance. He was flirting again, which given the differences in their stations, he should not. But he persisted anyway.

She should be angry, since his forwardness was almost forcing her to snub him, something she really didn't wish to do. Nor, faced with his straightforward honesty, could she seem to hold on to her anger.

Unlike other men she'd known, he didn't appear to practice deceit. He'd freely admitted who he was. If he were a rogue, at least he was an honest one.

Which made him a refreshing change from the London dissemblers who flattered to one's face while plotting ruin behind one's back.

Not that a girl could trust any man. But would it hurt to flirt a bit?

With the question barely formed, she caught herself up short. What was she thinking? Hadn't she just forfeited the life to which she'd been born for not immediately fleeing the presence of one she'd known to be a rogue?

With her treacherous inclination toward the man, the wisest course would be to remove herself from this free-trader's insidious influence.

'Thank you for showing me the lovely roses, Mr Hawksworth. But I mustn't delay my aunt's departure.' Nodding a farewell, she set off quickly away down the path toward the street and her aunt's waiting carriage.

As she'd feared, he simply fell into step beside her. 'Lovely they are indeed. But not the loveliest thing I've seen today.'

'You are a blatant charmer, Mr Hawksworth,' she tossed over her shoulder. 'I'd advise you to save your pretty compliments for those more desirous of receiving them.'

He cocked his head at her. 'And you are not?'

'Indeed no, sir. I prefer unvarnished truth.'

He laughed again, a deep, warm, shiver-inducing sound. 'Then, Miss Foxe, you are the most exceptional lady I have ever met.'

'I hardly think so,' she replied as they exited the churchyard and regained the street. 'Ah, Aunt Foxe,' she called to that lady, who stood chatting with the vicar beside their carriage. 'Were you looking for me?'

Before she could step away, Mr Hawksworth snagged her sleeve and made her an elegant bow. 'I very much enjoyed our walk. Good day, Miss Foxe.'

Politeness required that she curtsy back. 'Mr Hawksworth,' she replied with a regal incline of the head. Conscious of his gaze resting upon her back, she stepped into the sanctuary of the carriage.

A great one she was to talk of preferring *truth,* she thought disgustedly as her aunt settled onto the seat beside her. She, who'd just identified herself to the entire community under a false name. Who'd wondered what Mr Hawksworth might be hiding when she'd not vouchsafed to any but her aunt her own reason for being here.

How much do we ever truly reveal of ourselves to others?

she wondered, finding it hard to resist the impulse to look out the window and peer back at Gabriel Hawksworth.

Strangers and villains. Was he one—or both?

Chapter Four

Smiling, Gabe watched the shapely sway of Miss Marie Foxe as she entered her carriage. She was a little *too* deliberate about not even glancing in his direction as the vehicle set off.

He was reasonably confident she liked him. She most definitely responded to him, he thought, absently rubbing the hand that had been shocked by touching hers. She might not want to admit the attraction, but he was experienced enough to read, in the silent gasp that escaped her lips and the shudder that had passed through her body, that his touch had affected her as strongly as hers had him.

He grinned. Armed with that knowledge, he hadn't been able to refrain from provoking her a bit. It was much too enjoyable to watch her face burn as he let his gaze linger on those parts of her body he'd almost seen that day on the beach.

Parts he'd like to see much more clearly...and touch and caress and kiss.

Her face had crimsoned as if she knew what he'd been thinking. Had she been wishing it, too?

He sighed. Such contemplation set off quite a conflagration within him as well. What a shame Miss Foxe was not Sadie, the barmaid at the Gull whose amorous advances Gabe was having increasing difficulty dodging.

Not that he was at all adverse to the pleasures offered by an ample bosom and hot thighs. But living in an inn operated by a friend of Sadie's father, in a village where practically everyone was kin to everyone else, a maid who had three stout brothers to guard her virtue did not inspire a man to succumb to her blandishments. Even if she tempted him, which, in truth, she did not—particularly not since he'd had his first look at the lovely Marie Foxe. In any event, the enjoyment of a quick tumble with Sadie could not compensate for the trouble it would certainly cause.

Trouble or not, were Miss Foxe the lass making advances, he suspected he wouldn't resist.

He did ache for the sweetness of a woman, the bliss of release and the satisfaction of pleasing her in an intimate embrace. As he set off walking to the Gull, his thoughts drifted to Caitlyn back in Ireland, the knowing widow who'd been happy to ease the pain and boredom of his recovery with a little discreet dalliance.

He'd be better able to keep his unruly urges under control—and resist tempting young ladies he shouldn't even approach—if he paid her a visit. But he didn't want to risk having his brother discover him and piece together exactly what he was doing in Cornwall. Nor did he want to involve that lovely, compliant lady in what might be a damaging association if he were apprehended—or worse—during his sojourn in Cornwall.

With a smile, his thoughts returned to the lady who had been anything but compliant. He didn't know how well-connected the Foxe family might be, but from the arrogance of the niece, it was apparent she considered a smuggling captain to be vastly beneath her. Her irritation at his effrontery in approaching her was obvious in her haughty tone and elevated words, both of which, he felt sure, were designed to put him off.

They hadn't, of course. He found it amusing to reflect that unless the Foxe family were very well-connected indeed, by birth if not current occupation, he was probably her equal.

Even more gratifying was the knowledge that, hard as she'd been trying to resist him, she hadn't been able to mask the fact that she found him attractive.

What was such a lady doing in Sennlack? It was hardly the sort of place a lovely, unmarried miss would linger longer than the few days necessary to pay a call on a beloved aunt. Indeed, his memory was vague on the point, but wasn't the London social Season still in full cry?

He walked into the tap room and motioned Kessel to bring him a mug. Why, he continued to muse as he dropped into a seat, would a young lady whose family—if not the lady herself—should be concentrating on catching her a well-breeched husband, be wasting her beauty and her wiles on brigands like him, rather than in London, enticing more eligible gentlemen?

Perhaps her family, unable to afford the dowry necessary to marry her off, had sent her to be her aunt's companion.

Recalling her haughty demeanor—the attitude and bearing of someone accustomed to having her own desires catered to, rather than catering to others—Gabe had to laugh. She was hardly the meek, biddable sort able to adapt to living her life at the beck and call of some richer relation.

If she had been sent here by a family needing to reduce expenses, Gabe thought, frowning, they could have at least given her a maid to accompany her. Sennlack was a law-abiding town, but a luscious lamb like that needed some protection from the wolves of the world.

Like him, he thought with a grin.

Or had some mishap left her with no family but Miss Foxe? From some hitherto unknown place deep within him, an unprecedented sense of protectiveness seeped out.

The first day they'd met, he'd found the idea of pursuing the water sprite diverting. Tempting her with the attraction that ran so strongly between them might be more satisfying still.

Gabe sensed snobbery rather than fear in her reluctance

to associate with him; even for diversion, he'd never pursue a truly unwilling lady. If his instincts were mistaken and he was unable to melt that frosty demeanour, after a few attempts, he'd reluctantly abandon the game. Until then, however, he meant to apply his not inconsiderable charm into getting her to lower that ferocious guard and allow her true partiality to emerge.

He pictured her countenance, the silken texture of her face that begged for the touch of his finger, the large, expressive blue-grey eyes that could mirror the sky when she exclaimed over the roses or turn storm-cloud grey when she sought to depress his pretensions. The velvet look of those plump lips that seemed to just beg for a kiss—or two or three.

The desire she'd incited from first glance spiked, tightening his body and making sweat break out on his brow.

Just a kiss, of course, for she was a maid. Still, when the maid in question was the tantalizing Miss Foxe, even a simple kiss was a prize worth savouring.

Instead of chafing, as he usually did, at having to kick his heels in port until it was time to pick up the next cargo, now he had the charming Miss Foxe and an irresistible challenge to distract him. In these next few weeks, could he charm her out of her resistance…and into his arms?

As she'd spent the evening playing backgammon with her aunt, Honoria had tried to convince herself she had banished the dashing Captain Hawksworth from her mind. Though she was moderately successful at pretending that he was not always teasing just at the edge of her thoughts, the subject of the handsome free-trader was dragged forcibly before her the following morning when Tamsyn, who'd gone to visit her family Sunday evening, brought in her chocolate.

'Dickin tells me you met the Hawk after services yesterday. That he even walked with you in churchyard!' she said, reverence in her voice at being accorded such a high honour.

'Isn't he just the most handsome, charming man you've ever met?'

Knowing of the girl's obvious infatuation, Honoria might have expected to hear jealousy in her voice, and was struck to realize she heard none. Perhaps to Tamsyn, her brother's friend—a man with whom Lady Honoria Carlow might disdain to associate—seemed a personage too elevated to pay attention to a mere maid from a tiny village like Sennlack.

And perhaps Gabriel Hawksworth wasn't the only one who needed a lesson in humility.

'Yes, he is both handsome and charming. Though I suspect his design is to bedazzle every maid in Cornwall.'

'I figure he's already done that! He's greeted me polite enough, coming or going with Dickin, but I done never had all his attention fixed just on me. I'd probably swoon straight away!' Sighing, Tamsyn stared dreamy-eyed as she extracted Honoria's gown from the wardrobe. 'Do…do you think he might call on you?'

The tightness in Honoria's chest eased. If the maid thought he might, her deception must be safe. Even a girl from a small Cornish village, her head filled with a romantic vision of the dashing captain, would know a common smuggler would never have the effrontery to call upon someone as far above him socially as Lady Honoria Carlow.

Though still bold, for such a famous local personage to pay his respects to 'Miss Foxe' was not beyond possibility, particularly after having been introduced by the lady's own aunt.

Honoria was not sure whether to be relieved or alarmed by that fact.

In an urgent, low-toned discussion during the carriage ride home from church, her aunt had already assured her that her true identity was unlikely to be discovered. The conversation with Tamsyn had sealed her relief. She'd feared the rash announcement of a false name might backfire if the servants around whom she'd lived for the last month told a different tale.

However, as her aunt had reminded her, with her arrival being unexpected, Miss Foxe had not primed the servants to prepare for 'Lady Honoria's' visit. And having learned immediately upon her arrival of the delicacy of her situation, Aunt Foxe had been careful to refer to her as a niece or kinswoman, and to address her simply as 'my dear.'

Jerking her thoughts back to the girl's question, Honoria realized the maid's tone this time did hold a bit of an edge. Perhaps Tamsyn was not totally without hope in the captain's direction after all. Was she trying to determine whether Miss Foxe intended to set herself up as a contender for the rogue's attentions?

If so, she could speedily disabuse Tamsyn of that notion. 'I hardly think he will call,' she replied. 'He wished to politely welcome a newcomer, but I expect he enjoys feminine attention far too much to show partiality to any one lady.' Though she was piqued to discover she'd be a bit disappointed if the first assessment were true, she was quite certain of the second.

She'd met enough rakes in London to recognize a man who enjoyed and understood women. Gabe Hawksworth possessed that certain appreciative sparkle in his eye, along with an almost uncomfortably intense focus that, for the time it lasted, made a girl fancy he saw her as the most attractive and fascinating being in the universe.

Indeed, his gaze might be the most discerning she'd ever encountered. She shifted uncomfortably, hoping the rogue hadn't been able to tell just how attractive she found him.

Apparently she'd said the right thing, for the maid brightened. 'Pro'bly true, miss. Well, that gives me hope to keep trying to find the courage to flirt with him.'

Tamsyn finished helping her dress and went out. Honoria followed her, pausing to sniff appreciatively at the primroses Eva given her, displayed in a crystal bowl. She'd not seen any in Foxeden's herb garden and wondered if the plant might grow somewhere on the property. Aunt Foxe would probably enjoy having some of the fragrant blossoms in her rooms. Perhaps Honoria would go search for some.

She sighed. It wasn't as if she had any more pressing matters to attend to. But after the interlude at the beach and the excitement of meeting Mr Hawksworth, having nothing more stimulating to look forward to than picking a few posies made the day seem rather flat.

Good Heavens, why was she repining? She rallied herself immediately. Had Aunt Foxe not taken her in, she'd be at Stanegate Court, being viewed with pity or reproach by the staff and the neighbours, to say nothing of the lectures she would likely endure from Marcus each time he visited the estate. She couldn't bear to think about hearing what Mama, Papa—or her younger sister—might have to say to her.

Unexpected tears stung her eyes. How arrogantly sure she'd always been of being so much more worldly, knowledgeable and competent to look after herself than Verity! Pride goeth before a fall indeed.

No, she should sink to her knees and bless a kind Providence that she was here in Cornwall, under her aunt's benevolent eye and free to go gathering spring flowers.

After a solitary breakfast, her aunt keeping to her chamber as she usually did, Honoria went to consult the housekeeper, whom she found in the stillroom, hanging herbs to dry.

'I wanted to gather some primroses, Mrs Dawes. Are there any on this property?'

'I don't believe so, miss. If there are, they'd be growing down by the old stream bed near the copse. I've always thought one could plant a pretty wet garden there, with mints, foxglove, monarda and such. But the herb and kitchen gardens keep the boys busy enough, so I never tried anything there. The best place to find some, though, would be next to the brook that runs behind St Christopher's Church.'

That must have been where Eva Steavens had picked hers, Honoria thought. 'Thank you, Mrs Dawes. If there aren't any in the copse, perhaps I'll ride into the village and ask Father Gryffd if I might dig up a few plants from beside the brook to bring back.'

'I'm sure he wouldn't object. It's quite an interest you've taken in the plants, miss. Made some very pretty bouquets, too. The whole household is enjoying them. Now, let me find you some trugs to hold the flowers.'

After thanking the housekeeper and fetching a cloak, gloves and pattens to keep her hem and shoes dry, Honoria set out. She had a pleasant walk down the lane past the stables, its sheltered roadbed winding between lichen-covered stone walls, but upon reaching the lower meadow where an occasionally overflowing brook left the ground soggy, found no primroses. Heading back, she decided to ask Aunt Foxe if she might borrow her mare and pay a visit to St Christopher's.

Excitement fluttered in her chest at the realization that she *could* go there without fear of unpleasantness. Although she loved the cliff walk, she had confined her explorations to that solitary trail mainly because there was little chance of encountering anyone.

But as far as this community knew, she was not the disgraced Lady Honoria Carlow, but simply Miss Marie Foxe, kinswoman to a well-respected local gentlewoman. She might walk where others gathered, encounter villagers or fishermen, or converse with the vicar or the shopkeepers, safe from the dread of discovery and embarrassment.

After a month of living burdened by the weight of scandal and disapprobation, a giddy sense of freedom made her spirits soar. Laughing, she ran in circles about the meadow, whooping with the sheer joy of being alive and startling a peregrine falcon into taking flight in a reproachful flurry of wings.

Of course, she couldn't remain here hiding under a false name forever. But that harmless bit of subterfuge would provide a welcome respite, allowing her to move about freely while she figured out what to do next.

Even if 'next' was returning to Stanegate, being pressed to marry some obscure connection in the farthest hinterlands who could be induced to take a woman of large dowry and stained reputation, or living quietly on her own somewhere, forever banished from Society.

She shrugged off those dreary possibilities to be dealt with later. For now, it was enough just to anticipate the simple pleasure of a ride into town and the paying of an uncomplicated call upon the vicar.

Her buoyant sense of optimism persisted as she returned to the manor to seek out her aunt, whom she found bent over a book in her sitting room. 'Aunt Foxe, might I borrow your mare? I've so enjoyed the primroses Eva Steavens gave me yesterday, I thought to go ask the vicar if I might transplant some from a patch Mrs Dawes tells me grows by St Christopher's.'

'Of course, my dear. The ride would do both you and Mischief good. I'm so glad to see your spirits reviving! While in the village, you should shop for some trifles and stop for a glass of Mrs Kessel's cider. It's not right for a lovely, lively young girl to live in a hermit's isolation.'

Her aunt's words made Honoria wonder again why Miss Foxe—and at an age not much older than her own—had chosen to live in just such isolation. However, the inquiry still seemed too invasive of her aunt's privacy to pose at present.

'"Miss Marie Foxe" need not fear visiting the village,' she said instead. 'Thank you for allowing me that little deception.'

Her aunt nodded. 'Your name will still be yours, once you've decided how and where you wish to resume it.'

'May I ride into village immediately?' A sudden thought struck her and she frowned. 'Although I suppose I shall have to wait until later. The footmen are all occupied, and Tamsyn has not yet finished her duties.'

'Even Lady Honoria need not worry about riding unescorted here,' her aunt said. 'Especially not on my mare, which is everywhere recognized. I wouldn't advise that you ride alone after dark, or even in daylight past the kiddleywinks—the local beer halls—down by the harbour, where the miners congregate. 'Tis a hard life, and many seek to soften its edges with drink. Men whose wits—or morals—are dulled by spirits are unpredictable and possibly dangerous.'

'I shall go at once, then, and take care to avoid the harbour.'

'Could you discharge some small commissions for me? I've an order to deliver to the draper and several letters waiting at the post.'

'Of course, Aunt Foxe.'

'Enjoy your ride, then, dear. I will see you at dinner.'

Honoria set off a short time later in high good spirits. Her aunt's equally spirited mare, once given her head, seemed as delighted as Honoria to begin with a good gallop. Urging the animal on, revelling in the sweet, sun-scented air rushing past her, Honoria savoured the simple joy of being young and outside on a glorious early summer day as if she'd never experienced it before.

Perhaps, in a way, she hadn't. Until a month ago, a carefree canter through the countryside had been so ordinary an event she would never have thought to take note of it. How shortsighted she had been to prize it so little!

She slowed the mare to a trot along the route the carriage had followed yesterday, her anticipation heightening as she approached the village. Though she tried to tell herself she was only mildly curious about him, she found herself hoping that during her time in Sennlack, she would encounter one charming Irish free-trader.

Chapter Five

A short time later, Honoria pulled up the mare before the vicarage. She was about to ring the bell when she spied Father Gryffd in the distance, descending the church steps.

'Miss Foxe, how nice to see you,' he said, walking over to meet her. 'Won't you step in to the vicarage and let me offer you some tea?'

'Thank you, Father, but I have several commissions to complete for my aunt. I wished to inquire about primroses. After speaking with Mrs Dawes, I believe Eva Steavens may have found the flowers near your brook.'

The vicar nodded. 'I seem to remember a riot of them blooming there when I walked by last week.'

'If there are enough, would you permit me to carry some home?'

'Of course. Help yourself to as many as you wish. I must say, I am glad you stopped by. Might I walk along with you for a bit? It so happens that I've been thinking about you.'

Dread twisted in her gut as the prospect of discovery flashed through her mind. 'Of course,' she managed through a suddenly dry throat.

He fell into step beside her. 'I have a project in mind I've been thinking of implementing for some time. If you could lend a hand during your stay with Miss Foxe, I might be able to begin it.'

Relief washed through Honoria. 'What sort of project?'

'Since the old master retired, there's not been a school in the village. Some of the boys attend grammar school in St Just, but there's nothing for the girls. I've been wanting to establish one in which they might be taught to read and write and do simple sums. Despite what some might think, with mines and manufacturers hiring both sexes, it's as necessary for females as it is for the boys to understand the words on an employment list or to total their wages correctly. And to read their Bible, of course, should they earn enough to purchase one.'

'Why, Father Gryffd, I believe you are a Methodist!'

A light flush coloured the vicar's cheeks. 'I had the honour of hearing a disciple of Charles Wesley speak once, and was much struck by his message to do as much good to as many as one can. A directive I have tried to implement.'

'Establishing a school for girls would do much good,' Honoria said, immediately drawn to anything that would better the lot of females. 'How can I help?'

'I know you are well educated—and kind, judging by your treatment of Eva Steavens. Would you consent to helping the girls learn their letters? I'm sure they would admire you as much as Eva does and put forth their best efforts, in order to earn your approval.'

She, the bane of several governesses—to become a sort of schoolmistress? She suppressed a giggle at the thought.

Misinterpreting her silence, the vicar went on quickly, 'You might think such a task below your station, but truly it is but a variation on the service genteel ladies have always performed in making calls upon the poor.'

Given her present circumstances, not much would be considered beneath her station, Honoria thought. 'Indeed, I know it is not!' she assured him, smiling at the irony of it.

At this hour, Lady Honoria Carlow, Diamond of the Ton, would usually have been yawning over her chocolate while she flipped through a stack of invitations, all begging her presence at the most select functions offered by Society. She would have dressed, and paid calls and shopped, later stopping each evening at several events where she would be trailed by a crowd of admiring gentlemen and a bevy of ladies anxious to divert a share of those gentlemen's attentions.

If anyone had suggested that in a few short weeks she would count it a blessing to fill her idle hours assisting a bespectacled Welsh vicar to teach a passel of grubby Cornish children their letters, she would have laughed herself silly.

Even though, if one truly considered the matter, helping children learn to read was far more worthy of her time than listening to a buxom soprano sing arias or some infatuated moonling intone bad verses to her eyebrows.

As worthwhile as attempting to rescue a drowning man, she thought, feeling again the glow of satisfaction that had warmed her after that effort.

Offering village girls the gift of literacy would give them a bit more control over lives now wholly controlled by men. To females even more dependent for their welfare upon the whims of that gender than she was, that was a precious gift indeed.

She'd already decided to agree when the thought struck her. 'Will Eva Steavens be able to attend?'

The vicar considered the question. 'I don't see why not. The other children might tease her, though—or their parents might object.'

Honoria recalled the disagreeable man at church who had snarled at the child. 'Are Mr John Kessel's views widely held?'

Father Gryffd sighed. 'I'm afraid they are more widespread than a good Christian would like.'

Trying to alter deeply ingrained prejudices would be a difficult task, she suspected. 'What if Eva were to come after the other children went home?'

'We don't know that she'd be responsive to teaching,' the vicar reminded her gently.

'But you said yourself you don't believe her to be a halfwit. Certainly she communicates with her mother, albeit in a way none but the two of them understands. I think she might be very quick to learn.'

The vicar nodded. 'She might well be, and you are correct to remind me it is Eva's welfare, rather than the townspeople's prejudices, with which we should concern ourselves. I am willing to try, if you are. After you've dug your flowers, would you like to accompany me to the Gull's Roost? Eva's sister Laurie works there. We could ask her about Eva attending the school while I offer you a mug of cider as my thanks for agreeing to help with the children. And you should still have time to complete your commissions for Miss Foxe.'

Honoria smiled. 'That sounds delightful.'

And so it was, after digging up several prime specimens of primroses and having the vicar's housekeeper wrap them in newsprint for the transit back to Foxeden, Honoria found herself walking with the vicar into the tap room of the Gull's Roost.

With its low-timbered roof, wide hearth, kegs of ale by the bar and the luscious scent of roasting meat emanating from the kitchen, the inn reminded her of those she'd visited in the villages near Stanegate Court.

Mr Kessel hurried over to greet them, calling for the barmaid to bring a mug of ale for the vicar and a glass of cider for the lady. After a few minutes' chat, Father Gryffd asked if the innkeeper might spare Laurie Steavens for a moment, as he wished to speak with her.

Mr Kessel stiffened. 'If you're wanting to chastise her, I promise you, I got nothing to do—'

'No, not at all!' the vicar interrupted. 'I hope you think better of me than to believe I would take you to task for another's failings.'

The innkeeper's face reddened. 'Aye, you're right. My apologies, Father. I'll get the wife to fetch Laurie for you. Sadie,' he called to the barmaid, 'see that you keep their mugs filled.'

With a bow, the innkeeper went off to the kitchen. A few minutes later, wiping her reddened hands on an apron, a girl entered the tap room. Slender but lushly curved, with blonde hair and a matching set of bright blue eyes, there was a sweetness about her face that reminded Honoria of her little sister.

After looking Laurie up and down with a disdainful sniff, the barmaid walked out.

'You wanted to see me, Father Gryffd?' the girl asked, her face guarded.

'Yes, Laurie. I wanted to ask about Eva.'

Then Laurie's eyes widened in concern. 'Nothing done happened to her, did it?'

'No, she's fine,' Father Gryffd assured her. 'At least, she was when I saw her after church yesterday.'

Laurie sighed with relief. 'Thank goodness. Ever since the *Lizzie D* went down, I've worried about her every minute. Last week some of the village boys chased her, throwing stones.' After glancing over her shoulder, she added in a lowered voice, 'Johnnie Kessel urged 'em to it, the varmint.'

As Honoria's dislike for the innkeeper's son deepened, the vicar shook his head. 'I'm sorry, Laurie. I'll speak to him.'

The girl tossed her head. 'You do that, vicar, though it won't do no good. Thinks he knows better 'n everybody. And won't let nothing or no one get in his way, neither. So, what did you want to say about Evie?'

'I'm opening a school for the village girls and wanted your sister to attend—after the others have gone, perhaps, so she wouldn't be subjected to any unpleasantness. Would your mama agree? And do you think Eva would be, ah, receptive to learning?'

Laurie's face lit. 'Evie would love it! She's so much smarter than anybody hereabouts could credit! Ma would be thrilled to have her go—' she broke off suddenly, the smile fading '—but sorry, Father, we just can't afford it. I barely earn enough here to keep food on the table and the…other—' the girl lifted her chin, a defiant look on her face '—it don't pay regular.'

'There won't be any charge, Laurie.'

The girl stared at them. 'You'd let her come…for nuthin'?' she asked incredulously. 'Why, when Maimie Crawford went to school in St Just, her da complained every time he stopped for a brew about how it cost the trees to keep her there!'

'Fortunately, since Sennlack has so few of them, it won't cost the trees here,' Father Gryffd answered, smiling. 'With Miss Foxe's help, I think I can manage without paying a teacher.'

Laurie gestured toward Honoria. 'What does she know about my sister's…trouble?'

'I met Eva at church yesterday,' Honoria replied.

Laurie gave her a speculative look. 'And you're still willing to teach her? Why?'

'She seemed very bright to me,' Honoria replied. 'Deserving of the same chance to learn as the other girls.' She smiled. 'And she gave me flowers.'

Laurie subjected her to a hard scrutiny. Honoria returned her stare without flinching.

Finally, Eva's sister nodded. 'Don't see how you could—a rich, manor-born lady like you—but maybe you do understand. Thank you, then. You, too, Father.'

The vicar nodded. 'We're all here to help each other, Laurie. There's a place in God's heart for everyone.'

The girl swallowed hard. 'God and I ain't exactly been on speaking terms of late, Father, but if you're willing to do this for Evie, I might have to rethink that.'

The vicar smiled. 'I hope you will. And you'll speak to your mother about Eva coming to school?'

'Aye, I will. Best be getting back to work now, though.'

With another nod, the girl disappeared up the stairs. Turning to Honoria, the vicar said, 'I ought to stop and check on Mr Kessel's ailing mother. Will you be all right waiting here, Miss Foxe, until I return?'

'You needn't feel you must escort me back to the vicarage,' Honoria assured him. 'Sennlack is small enough that I'll have no difficulty finding my way back to retrieve my horse after I complete Aunt Foxe's errands.'

After proposing that they discuss the school again after services the next Sunday, Father Gryffd thanked her for her help and walked out. Watching him go, Honoria reflected with amusement that, though the vicar had thanked her, it was really *he* who was doing *her* the kindness.

Satisfaction filled her at the thought that, while she was marooned here unscrambling her future, she might use such modest talents as she possessed to help other girls—especially Eva. Something about the little girl touched her heart, even beyond the fact that they had both been cast out of the societies into which they'd been born by circumstances over which neither had had any control.

She was surprised how cheering the idea of being useful was. She didn't think herself a particularly selfish person, but for all her life up to this point, she'd filled a role—daughter, sister, gentlewoman in the country, member of Society in London. She'd always been busy with a variety of activities—but never, that she could recall, with any tasks she would describe as being truly useful to anyone.

Since her ability to choose which role she would play in future had recently been drastically restricted, perhaps she ought to seek out other ways to be useful. Once her true identity was discovered, which was bound to happen eventually, Father Gryffd might have second thoughts about employing her to assist in a school for innocent girls.

She'd like to have accomplished something towards improving Eva's situation before that happened.

Sipping the last of her cider, she was wondering over her unexpected connection to an illiterate Cornish child when a deep, melodic voice tickled her ear, stirring every nerve as the sound resonated through her body.

'Why, Miss Foxe! How delightful to see you again.'

Chapter Six

After spending the morning supervising the crew repairing rigging on the *Flying Gull*, Gabe walked into the inn to find the very woman whose voice and image had been teasing his thoughts.

She'd been playing an active part in some very lusty dreams, too, he thought with a sigh, but he'd do better to suppress those memories, particularly if he wanted to beguile her into speaking with him. Since he had nothing better to do the rest of the afternoon than read the week-old London papers, attempting to charm this luscious and resistant lady would be a welcome diversion.

Obviously not aware that he resided in one of the inn's bedchambers, as he addressed her, she gasped in surprise. He had to give her credit, though, for she quickly recovered her countenance and assumed the faintly haughty air she'd employed in the churchyard.

He barely suppressed a grin. Her reaction was like the dropping of a handkerchief at the start of a race: he couldn't wait to charge forward.

'Mr Hawksworth,' she replied with a regal nod. 'Aren't you supposed to be off somewhere robbing someone?'

'Nay, lass, 'tis full daylight. I endeavour to constrain my nefarious activities until after dark,' he replied.

She stiffened when he called her 'lass,' and he could almost see her rapidly reviewing phrases to find one biting enough to put him in his place. She looked so intent—and so indignant, he was hard put not to laugh.

He hadn't encountered a chick with feathers this easy to ruffle since leaving his brother's home.

Before she could unfurl her blighting phrase of choice, he continued, 'Mrs Kessel brews a superior cider. Won't you share one with me before you leave? It would be entirely proper, I assure you.' He gestured around the room. 'We have the whole inn to act as chaperones.'

'There is such comfort in numbers,' she replied, irony in her tone as she nodded toward the currently deserted tap room.

To his disappointment, their tête-à-tête ended practically before it began as Sadie rushed in. 'Mr Hawksworth, sir, what can I do for you? Some ale? The missus be cooking a fine roast. If you've a mind for a bite, I'll see if I can persuade her to fix you a plate now.'

Gabe suspected the persistent tavern maid had been lolling about the corridor, watching for him as she'd developed an irritating tendency to do—and was not at all interested in assisting the inn's other customer. 'Just a mug of your finest, Sadie. And a bit more cider for the lady.'

The distinctly unfriendly look Sadie cast at Miss Foxe confirmed Gabe's suspicion. 'Think she was about leaving, weren't you, miss?'

'Nay, no one could resist a wee bit more of Mrs Kessel's excellent brew. Why, 'twould be near an unforgiveable insult to that good lady's skill, and I'm certain you wouldn't wish to insult the innkeeper's wife, would you, Miss Foxe?'

The girl's expression said she was about to do just that when the lady herself walked in. 'Welcome, Mr Gabe, and you, too, miss! How go things with the *Gull*?'

'Tolerable, ma'am. She'll be ready to hoist sail by nightfall, should it be needful.'

Mrs Kessel nodded. 'Dickin said his ship'd be ready any day now and he just awaiting word. What can I get you?'

'Some ale, please. Mrs Kessel, have you met Miss Marie Foxe, Miss Foxe's niece?'

'Why, no! Excuse me, miss, I had no idea—' Breaking off hastily, the innkeeper's wife dipped her a curtsy, clearly distressed at having perhaps given offence to the relation of such an important area resident. 'A pleasure to welcome you! Your aunt's always been good enough to honour us with her custom.'

'I've just been telling her she needs another mug of your cider, which is the best on the coast. Did you not find it so, Miss Foxe?' Gabe looked at her, grinning.

'It is excellent, ma'am,' she allowed, darting him a dagger glance.

'Why, thank ye kindly, miss. Sadie,' Mrs Kessel called to the girl lounging near the bar, a sullen look on her face. 'Another cider for Miss Foxe, and be quick about it!'

There was no way now she could politely refuse, a fact of which she was well aware. Gabe watched her almost grind her teeth in frustration before her expression cleared and she gave the innkeeper's wife a smile, so unexpected that its warmth and brilliance dazzled him.

'Thank you, ma'am. I should enjoy one very much.'

Still bedazzled, he scarcely heard her reply, his brain unable to progress beyond thinking that he'd never seen her truly smile before and that, when she smiled like that, half the gentlemen on the Cornish coast would fight each other for the honour of throwing themselves at her feet.

How had she ever escaped London unwed?

Along with his realization of the feet-worshipping power of that smile came a wholly unexpected flash of emotion that felt uncomfortably like jealousy. Quite understandable, he told himself: he had seen the goddess first, and it was only natural to dislike the notion of other acolytes trying to join the procession.

Fortunately, he reflected, after mentally ticking off the possibilities, only a handful of gentlemen resided in the area, half of them already married and the other half attending the Season in Penzance or London. Unless, like some Lady Bountiful, she liked to cast her lovely smiles like coins to the poor, his only competition hereabouts for the pleasure of crossing wits with her would be fishermen, farmers and day labourers.

From Sadie's expression as she returned with their mugs, the barmaid didn't like Miss Foxe sharing her brilliant smile with him any more than he liked the idea of some other gentleman basking in its glow. The barmaid tossed Miss Foxe's mug on the table, splashing a bit of cider on her gown, then sidled up to Gabe and bent low to give him a good view of the assets bulging out the top of her tight bodice as she carefully placed his mug before him.

'Here ye be, Mr Hawksworth. Anything else you be needing, you holler.' Slowly she traced her lips with her tongue and smiled. 'Just…anything.'

Gabe might be sitting across the table from a lovely lady who possessed the most dazzling smile he'd ever beheld; he might be mindful that three strapping brothers with strong protective instincts stood between him and accepting the invitation the wayward Sadie had just tendered him—which truly didn't interest him in any event. But he was still man enough to enjoy the hip-swaying show Sadie put on as she sashayed back to bar.

He looked up to see Miss Foxe rolling her eyes. 'Don't let me keep you from pursuing more satisfying company, Mr Hawksworth,' she said sweetly.

Her knowing expression said she'd understood perfectly just what sort of offer Sadie had laid on the table with his mug. Whatever her past, she was not a total innocent, then. Her aunt might receive such information with alarm, but for Gabe, interest—and a significant part of his anatomy—stirred at that pleasing conclusion.

'What could be more…satisfying than having congress with a lady as lovely as you?' he countered, wondering whether she would catch the double meaning of those words.

Her immediate flush informed him she had. Gabe bit back a grin, certain now that some gentleman—or rogue—somewhere had played a part in her education. A reprobate brother, perhaps? Or some more intimate acquaintance? Ah, the prospect of dalliance was looking better and better!

He must have rattled her with that slightly risqué comment, for the haughty expression she'd been trying to maintain disappeared completely. 'I cannot imagine why you bother wasting your pretty words on me when there are others about so obviously more desirous than I of receiving them,' she retorted acerbically.

As blighting went, that was pretty good, Gabe thought. 'Since you have chosen to accept another cider, so as not to wound Mrs Kessel's feelings, you might as well chat with me,' he pointed out reasonably. 'By the way, it was kind of you *not* to wound her feelings, although I know you would have much preferred to depart immediately.'

She raised her eyebrows sceptically, but Gabe meant the compliment. He'd had enough dealings with the Quality, in Ireland and in the Army, to know many of them—men like his brother and the high-born witch he'd married—wouldn't have hesitated a second in refusing Mrs Kessel's offer in order to snub the man offering it. The idea of refraining out of consideration for the feelings of a lowly innkeeper would never even have occurred to Sir Nigel or Lady Hawksworth.

The sensitivity she'd just shown, along with her unusual daring in going to the rescue of the foundering sailor, her daze-inducing smile—and her obvious desire to keep him at a distance—only sharpened his interest.

Receiving honest praise rather than extravagant gallantry threw her off-stride as well, he noted. A slight blush coloured her cheeks when she realized he was sincere, and she said finally, 'Thank you. I should hope I would never wound someone merely for my personal convenience.'

'Which makes you kind as well as lovely—a rather exceptional combination, Miss Foxe. As exceptional as your swimming ability. How did you acquire the skill? That is, I'm assuming you swim, or you'd not have dared venture so far from shore, even in the cove. There's a fierce undertow.'

Wanting to encourage the sort of frank speech she'd just given him—perhaps the first uncalculated comment she'd made to him today—Gabe was careful this time to avoid needling her by making a reference to her state of undress at the time, though he pictured it lovingly as he waited for her to reply.

Miss Foxe fiddled with her mug, as if uncertain whether to snatch back her mantle of haughty reserve or simply give an honest response. Finally, with a small, wary smile, she said, 'I swim well enough. And I didn't know about the undertow.'

Miss Foxe was unquestionably one of loveliest ladies Gabe had ever seen, and he'd seen some dark-eyed charmers in Spain and Portugal. In England and Ireland, he'd witnessed many a beauty toss her perfectly coifed head, flash her luminous eyes and utter icy snubs—or come-hither comments—depending upon the social position of the gentleman addressing her. As, until now, Miss Foxe had been doing with him.

Perhaps that was why her tentative, almost shy smile struck him harder than the dazzling sunshine of her fully curved lips. Like a whaler's lance, that hint of vulnerability in so otherwise confident a lady penetrated his massive outer defences, cutting through the teasing barrier he'd donned to amuse himself and bedevil her, to strike him right in the heart.

For a moment he felt dizzy, his world knocked off-kilter, as if the *Gull* had been swamped by a rogue wave striking from out of a black night. His protective instincts began sounding like the drum beating sailors to battle, but heart-stirred and shaken, he ignored them.

'Would you have gone in anyway?'

'I don't know. Probably. I thought he was drowning. It seems strange to me that so few sailors learn to swim. Perhaps their clothing would pull them under in any event, were they to fall from the rigging? But it seems for those who pursue a life on the sea, swimming is not a simple pleasure.'

'Is it that for you?'

'It was. My older brother taught me—I used to trail after him when we were growing up, wishing I'd been born a boy who could share in all his adventures. Taking pity on me, he let me join in some of them. On a hot summer day, a dip in the pond was most refreshing.'

'I imagine your mama didn't think so.'

She laughed, and Gabe almost fell out of his seat at the electrifying flash of joy that sound radiated. He wanted to hug her and tickle her and make her laugh all day long so he could revel in the sound.

'She did not, indeed! After sneaking off, I'd invariably return with telltale mud on my stockings or a bit of weed stuck in my hair, earning me a severe scold from Mama or my governess. But you swim much better than I. You must enjoy it as well. It seems an unusual talent for an Army man. Tamsyn tells me you were an officer in the Army with her brother, Dickin.'

Ah, so she had been asking about him! Gabe couldn't help the gratification that swelled his chest. 'I was raised on the southern Irish coast and have been piloting small and large boats—and swimming—since I can remember. I love the majesty of the sea, the freedom of its vast expanses, with nothing around for miles but your ship and the elements.'

'And danger.'

He looked up sharply. Was he that easy to read? 'Yes, danger, too.'

'Yet you joined the Army?'

He shrugged. 'Having never been amenable to letting someone else command my vessel, I suppose I doubted I'd last

long enough without being either flogged to death or discharged for insubordination to rise to the position of captain.'

'So you're more a pirate than mariner?'

'I wouldn't say that, exactly. I may ignore the customs regu-
lations, but I got my fill of seeing slaughter in the Army. The sea
takes enough men; though you may not believe this, I do whatever
I can to avoid a confrontation. I'll not risk the safety of my
crew—nor do I hold with inflicting injury upon the revenuers, if
I can possibly avoid it—simply to land a cargo for profit.'

She stared at him, as if deciding whether or not to believe
him. Finally, she nodded. 'I suppose so, else you'd not have
troubled to save that revenue agent. Despite those scruples,
you've certainly won yourself a dashing reputation. One can
hardly go anywhere hereabouts without hearing tales of your
skill and daring.'

His gratification diminished a bit. Maybe she hadn't specifically inquired about him; maybe she'd just been inundated
with the sort of inflated tales that run rampant in a small town
without a lot of news to occupy the gossips. 'It's good to be
well thought of, I suppose.'

She chuckled. 'Then you must be feeling well indeed, for
you've quite a bevy of admirers—all seeming as ardent as the
young lady who brought you your ale. Tamsyn said you came
here to help her brother? I imagine the, ah, augmented income
you've been able to earn must help those back at home, too.'

Gabe had a sudden vision of his brother's perpetually disapproving face. 'Not really. I don't expect the proper home folk
would be too happy if they knew what sort of business brought
me here. In fact, it would likely create a scandal that would find
me banished from the family forever!'

She'd been smiling at his merry tone, but at that last remark,
the humour vanished from her expression as abruptly as if
he'd tossed the rest of his ale into her face.

'Thank you for conversation, Captain. Now, I must finish
some commissions for my aunt. Good day.'

Before he could even rise to his feet, she sprang up in a soft swish of skirts and half ran out of the room.

Gabe stared after her, bemused. One moment it seemed he'd coaxed her into being more open and genuine than he'd ever seen her; the next, she'd bolted from the inn. Sipping his ale, he reviewed the last bits of their conversation.

It didn't take long to pinpoint the turning point. His sister, now safely married to a baronet outside Cork, might accuse him of possessing the sensibility of a rock, but even he had noticed that 'twas after his mention of scandal—of being cast out by one's family—that Miss Foxe took flight.

Suddenly her presence in Sennlack began to make more sense. He was already convinced that no one who knew her could have believed she'd be a success as companion to an elderly relative. Appearing hastily in the middle of the Season, with what Tamsyn said had been no warning—no bedchamber ordered to be prepared for her use, nor an extra maid hired—he could see no logical explanation but that there had been some sudden, catastrophic reversal of her family's fortunes. Or a scandal.

One by one, Gabe considered the alternatives. Had her father lost all his money on the 'change, and shot himself, she might react with sensitivity to the idea of a scandal. But the remark that had turned her face pale and made her white about the lips had been his comment about being cast out of the family.

Which seemed to indicate some personal, rather than familial, scandal.

For a beautiful young lady like Miss Foxe, that could mean only one thing: involvement with some rogue and a loss of her virtue.

Might she have been sent here to rusticate after playing fast and loose with her reputation? Cornwall was certainly an ideal place to banish a young lady who had not been as prudent as she should. Gabe himself would never countenance the seduction of an innocent, be she kitchen maid or titled lady, but recalling Miss Foxe's golden hair, rounded bosom, lush lips and satiny skin, he had to feel a certain sympathy for any man who might have been wooing her. With such a prize, intoxicated by her spirit and beauty, a man might forget himself and get carried beyond the bounds of propriety.

The real question was—had *she* forgotten herself?

His much-treasured vision of her at the beach surfaced in his mind again: body outlined by her soggy clothing, the transparent linen leading the eye from her bare, foam-kissed toes up her long, long legs to a rounded swell of belly above a sweet dewy triangle feathered with gold. He could just imagine those legs wrapped around him as he drove into those golden depths.

Gabe, me lad, that's hoisting sail before hauling in the anchor. He had no proof whatsoever that she'd lost control and her virtue, only a wild conjecture based on her spirited nature and sudden appearance in Cornwall.

Still, a man could hope.

Already she drew him strongly: her smile, her sharp wit, her odd combination of pride and vulnerability. And she had tantalized his body from the start. If she were no longer an innocent maid, there would be no need to refrain from seeing if she'd be equally susceptible to dallying with another rogue. And he was just the man to find out.

Suddenly the dull days of waiting, marooned in Sennlack until the next cargo was ready to be fetched, looked more appealing.

Chapter Seven

Honoria practically ran for the door, aware of Mr Hawksworth's puzzled gaze following her, the words he'd tossed out with such levity still cutting into her heart like a sabre's slash…creating a scandal that would banish one from one's family forever.

She halted outside the door, trying to calm her racing pulse. He must indeed come from 'proper folk,' for that one phrase, obviously meant to be lightly taken, validated his good character more than anything else he could have said. A rogue comfortable operating outside the law would never have conjured up such a remark, and only one secure in the backing of one's family could speak so slightingly of losing that support.

Perhaps no one fully understood the true value of one's place within a protective, encircling clan, until one lost it.

Still, she'd acted like a looby, running off like that. She'd been trying to discourage him by assuming an overbearing, disdainful manner, not scare him away from a crazy woman.

Perhaps she'd be more successful at the latter than she'd been at the former. Her thoughts still too much in disorder to sort out, she pushed them, and questions about the all-too-attractive free-trader, from her mind and went off to carry out her aunt's commissions. By the time she'd dropped by several shops and stopped to dispatch some letters at the post, her nerves had steadied.

Her last errand took her to the draper's shop that stood on a rise to the north of town, overlooking the harbour. After handing over her aunt's order for cloth and lace—suspicious now about the origin of those items—she walked out, pausing to gaze down at the cove where a dozen ships rode at anchor. Some were obviously fishing craft, but several vessels, sleek of line and with sails reefed and ready, looked as if they were straining at their mooring lines, yearning to sprint into the freshening breeze. One of them must be the *Flying Gull*.

Unbidden, the memory of the captain's handsome face flashed into her mind. What had possessed her to speak so frankly? She was supposed to be discouraging him, an unsuitable man far below her in station. Though she was not yet sure what her eventual station would be. Was a disgraced gentlewoman still a gentlewoman? Maybe she had fallen to the level of a common smuggler.

Whatever his station, he'd not been easy to discourage.

Curiosity sparked as she considered his behaviour. Now that she thought about it, Captain Hawksworth was rather well-spoken. Much better-spoken, in fact, than any common seaman or soldier she'd ever heard.

Might he be the son of a gentleman? When she added his genteel speech to the polish of his manners with Aunt Foxe and the innkeepers, she could not help but conclude he must have sprung from the gentry.

Who was he, then? His birth could not be too elevated, certainly, or he'd never be here doing what he was doing. Though the words were meant to be humorous, the fact that he'd mentioned being banished—though not yet entirely—seemed to indicate he might be the black-sheep son of some baronet or squire. Or perhaps he was related to the peerage, but born on the wrong side of the blanket?

The natural antagonism of being raised a bastard—blood to wealth and power but barred from claiming it himself—might explain the curious dichotomy of his thinking: suffering no qualms of conscience about breaking smuggling laws, but drawing the line at inciting bloodshed to bring in his illegal cargoes.

Whoever he was, he probably was not the equal of Lady Honoria Carlow. But he might well be on a level with a Miss Foxe.

Honoria found that conclusion both disturbing and intriguing.

Still, what had possessed her to confide in him? It had been easy enough to depress his pretentions when he tried to ply her with absurd gallantries. But when he abruptly switched to sincere compliments that seemed to approve her actions, and serious inquiries that suggested he was genuinely curious about the girl behind the outward mask of beauty, then he'd succeeded in luring her to speak candidly even as his nearness intensified the strong physical pull she'd been trying to ignore.

There was just something about his smile, she recalled, that invited her to share his humour. About his eyes, so intensely blue she could understand Tamsyn's tendency to poetry. His gaze seemed to penetrate beneath the surface, to see not just golden hair and china-blue eyes, a well-curved body and smooth skin, but down to the questing, turbulent, passionate, unsettled soul within. And not just to see, but to *like* what he saw. She'd been suffused by this deep, instinctive sense of connection, this feeling that he knew and understood her as no one but Hal ever had.

In fact, Captain Hawksworth reminded her vividly of her brother: strong, dashing, going his own way independent of family, a bit of a rogue walking the fine line between propriety and disgrace. Could the Hawk become as good a friend to her as Hal had always been?

Nonsense, she thought, reining in her runaway thoughts. 'Twas sheer loneliness pushing her in this absurd direction.

She'd been away from Society too long, stripped of anyone of an age in whom she might confide. She was a candidate for Bedlam indeed if she was beginning to cast a rogue Irish smuggler into the role of friend and confidant.

Especially when he'd not only managed with embarrassing ease to level the barriers of her hauteur, but called forth from her a potent physical response that intensified each time she met him. Just an hour ago at the inn, even not knowing who or what he was, she'd been so tempted to touch his hand, to see if the mere pressure of her fingers against his would elicit another spark like the one that had blazed through her when he took her arm in the churchyard on Sunday. She'd had to wrap her fingers around her mug to resist the urge.

With her emotions still at such a low ebb and her ability to resist his charm so demonstrably weak, she must avoid casting Gabriel Hawksworth in the role of friend. She didn't think she could bear the crushing disappointment such a naïve hope was almost certain to make her suffer.

Resolutely turning away from the sea, she thrust her hand into the small secret pocket in the lining of her cloak—and felt the stone, still there where someone had put it the night of her disgrace. A bit of clear, polished glass, facetted on one side almost like diamond, smooth but unfinished on the other.

She hadn't discovered it until several days after that night, but immediately recognized the significance. She, who had been a Diamond of the Ton, now was worthless as glass.

It had to have been placed there by the same someone who had gone to such pains to set up her disgrace in the garden, someone calculating and thorough enough to make sure her ruin was complete, someone who knew her family well enough to gage their reaction.

But who? For the first time since that night, she forced herself to consider events so painful and distressing that until this moment, she'd not been able to bear examining them.

She and Anthony had had a sharp quarrel earlier that day,

he pressing her to accept as an engagement gift a heavy, ornate diamond parure that had been in his family for generations. Although supposing in the end she couldn't refuse, Honoria hadn't wanted it—especially not after having found a much finer, more delicate and intricately wrought set in the jeweller's shop. The disagreement led to harsh words: she accusing him of not caring what she preferred, he accusing her of thinking always of her own pleasure, heedless of tradition and the feelings of family.

Still angry that night, she'd looked forward to flirting outrageously at the ball they were both to attend, to punish him for speaking so unkindly. Then Anthony ruined her plans by not being present to become annoyed and jealous. So she'd been relieved—and touched—when a footman brought her a verbal message begging her to meet him in the garden, where he would show her a surprise he knew would make her happy.

Triumphant—just knowing he'd acceded to her wishes and purchased the new diamond set—without further thought, she'd left the ballroom and hurried to the rendezvous point the footman described, a small arbour at the far end of the dark trail leading from the ballroom. And found waiting for her not Anthony bearing gifts, but Lord Vickers Barwick, one of the most notorious and unprincipled rakes of the Ton.

She'd been too shocked in the first moment to speak as Lord Vickers, his eyes glazed with drink, slurred out how excited he was to discover she was interested in a little dalliance. And then he'd reached for her…

Gritting her teeth and squeezing her eyes closed, Honoria shut down the memories while a chill shook her body and nausea clawed up her throat. *Enough.* Clenching her hands together, she willed the sick feeling away and swiped at the tears that had begun to drip unnoticed down her cheeks.

Who had arranged the message that led her to Lord Barwick, knowing she would never have left the ballroom if she'd known who waited for her at the end of that dark, deserted path?

Another young lady, jealous of her place as reigning Belle of the Ton? Though Honoria believed another woman capable of such spite, she couldn't credit any of the rivals to her beauty or position with possessing either the cunning or the means to create so intricate a plan.

A rejected suitor seemed more probable. Which left her quite a list. Might there be among them some arrogant man, more twisted in character than she'd ever guessed, who'd decided if he couldn't possess her, he'd make sure no honest gentleman ever would?

She sighed. Except for satisfying her curiosity, discovering who had fashioned the trap no longer made any difference. The perpetrator had done his or her work well. Regardless of the excuse that had brought her to the arbour, as Marc acidly pointed out, only a fast young piece would have agreed to meet a man, even a fiancé, alone and unchaperoned in a midnight garden. To be discovered there by a party of gentlemen in the arms of a notorious womanizer, regardless of how fiercely she was struggling, only sealed her fate.

The architect of this scheme had been diabolically clever, using her reputation to trap her. For she had skirted the rules hemming in young ladies, earning the dubious distinction of being a dashing miss teetering on the edge of respectability, a reputation for which her brother, mother and chaperone had all chided her.

She'd never meant to become a byword. But she'd found the rules so silly and restrictive! Why such a fuss that she'd once escaped Miss Price's care and slipped down Bond Street to get a view of White's famous bow window? 'Twas morning, she'd explained when she rejoined Verity and her furious and chagrined chaperone, with no club members going in or out…though someone must have recognized her, Marcus later grimly informed her, for the news of her unauthorized visit had become the latest gossip in the men's clubs by nightfall.

Nor had she foreseen the furore that would result from her

agreeing to race her curricle in the park early one morning against a famous Corinthian who also happened to be a friend of Hal's she'd known since childhood. So, they'd scattered a few ducks and attracted a following of amused gentlemen and excited urchins. What harm was there in that?

Frowning, one by one she ticked off the series of small misadventures which had led to exasperated remonstrances from Miss Price about the deleterious example she was setting for Verity and increasingly irritated lectures from Marc about compromising her respectability.

Taken all together, she could see how the sum had been enough to position her like an apple ripe for the falling when her unknown enemy had struck. After hearing her angrily declare before the ball that if Anthony didn't care about pleasing her, she'd show him that other men did, Marcus wouldn't believe she hadn't knowingly gone to meet Lord Barwick in a foolish and disastrous attempt to inspire her fiancé with jealousy. And with Hal far away, only Marc had possessed the power and the means to track down the true mastermind behind the scheme.

Anthony's scornful words about not taking to wife a woman other men now looked upon as a common doxy still made her skin crawl with humiliation—and bruised the heart that had believed in the affection he'd avowed.

Even during his angry tirade after the event, Marc had not threatened to banish her forever. But with her character ruined beyond redemption—for even if she eventually convinced her brother to prove her innocence, the Carlow family was powerful enough that there would always be those who'd whisper the earl had simply paid well to redeem his wild daughter's reputation. No, Honoria had decided the day she quit London that whatever her future might hold, she would never return to London Society.

What would she do with herself? Helping the Methodist-leaning vicar with his school for girls might do for now—but what of the future? That unresolved question still filled her with a sickening uncertainty.

Quickly she squelched the now-familiar panicky feeling stirring in her breast, submerging it in the same dark place as her memories of that awful night. True, she still had no idea what she going to do, but she wouldn't tease herself any further about it at the moment.

Perhaps in the same 'later,' when the whole episode no longer made her feel so humiliated and hopeless, a reviving anger would come, and with it a compulsion to finally discover who or what, beside her own naïveté and vanity, had brought her to this. For now, she pushed that speculation aside like the lump of glass in her pocket.

Like she should her curiosity about the man who, so soon after her disgrace, was already tempting her to forget that no man could be trusted.

She'd just turned from the harbour to set off for the vicarage when she heard the woman's scream.

Chapter Eight

The cry resonated deep within her...an echo of the one she'd heard issuing from her own throat that infamous night. Praising the Lord it was still full daylight and certain there must be other people about, she looked around wildly, trying to find the source of the scream.

Hearing a second cry, she looked down the hill toward the port and spotted a girl outside a small stone hut, struggling in the grip of one man while another loomed close by. The girl, she realized suddenly, was Laurie Steavens, little Eva's sister.

Honoria looked quickly up and down the street again, but found it deserted. She might run back into the draper's shop, the closest dwelling to the spot where she now stood, but could she persuade the merchant to come with her to the girl's aid before the man holding her, with the help of his accomplice, carried her off?

Honoria didn't think so. All the pain and anguish of struggling vainly in a determined man's grip flooded back, and she knew she couldn't simply turn away and abandon Laurie.

Wishing herself back on the beach where she might find some wrecker's driftwood, or back in wooded country, where some convenient nearby tree might offer up a limb she could use for a club, after a moment's hesitation during which she debated whether or not to proceed with no weapon at hand, Honoria charged down the hill.

There were only two men, she thought as she hurried closer, and there must be sailors about somewhere in the port below. If she halted a safe distance away and added her screams to Laurie's, surely they could rouse someone to come to her aide.

'You, there,' she yelled as she approached. 'Release that girl immediately or I'll have the magistrate on you!'

Though the man didn't loosen his hold, he did turn toward her. 'What's it to you, wench, if we want a little sport?' he called back in slurred voice. 'Prepared to pay 'er for it, ain't we, Hal?'

The fact that one of the reprobates bore her beloved brother's name incensed Honoria even further. 'Since she does not appear to be interested in accepting your offer, let her go.'

The man called Hal, tall and skinny, squinted at her appraisingly. 'Golden-haired gel looks mighty fine, Davy. How's about I take her 'n leave you this one?'

The second man sounded as bosky as the first. In fact, he swayed on his feet when he turned, almost falling over.

If they were both cast away, a good shove on this steep slope might be enough to dispatch them. With no help yet in sight, Honoria took the chance of coming closer. 'It's the two of you that will be leaving. Come, Laurie!' She darted to the side of the girl away from the ruffian, grabbed her other hand, and jerked hard on it.

The first man held on with surprising strength, while Hal lurched in her direction. 'You come along, too, sugar-tit. Ol' Hal'll make you happy.'

'Miss, step away afore they grab you!' Laurie cried.

But Honoria hadn't grappled in impromptu wrestling matches with her older brother for naught—sessions which would have earned her a vociferous scolding if Mama or her governess had learned of them. She might not have Hal's science, but he'd taught her to give a fair accounting of herself.

So when the ruffian Hal got close enough for her to smell his liquored breath, Honoria struck him a right uppercut with as much force as she could muster.

She must have hit bone, for her fist hurt like the devil, while the ruffian went down like a felled tree. Taking advantage of the other man's surprise, she tried once again to pull Laurie free.

But the second man was stronger than his friend—or held his liquor better. After a moment's surprise at the fate of his accomplice, he snarled, 'Nay, you'll not take my woman, bitch.' Tightening his grip on Laurie, the man swung one ham-like fist at Honoria.

Resting her weight on the balls of her feet like her brother had taught her, she easily dodged the blow. But then her attention was reclaimed by Hal, who was struggling to his feet with a roar of rage.

Suddenly, Laurie's attacker was seized from behind by a man who stripped his hand from Laurie with a blow from one fist, smashed his chin with a crosscut left from the other, then pushed him backward down the steep slope. Howling, the man rolled over and over, landing against a rock some twenty feet below them.

Pivoting to face the crouching Hal, he snarled, 'Need ye my attention, too, mate?'

Babbling something incoherent, Hal put up his hands and backed away, stumbling down the slope toward his friend.

Fists at the ready and one eye still focused on the ruffians down the hill, their rescuer turned to them.

'Miss Laurie, are you all right? He didn't strike you, did he? Or you, Miss Foxe?'

'Bless you, Mr Gabe!' Laurie cried. 'No, he didn't hurt me none.'

'Nor me, Mr Hawksworth. I do thank you for the timely arrival. If you make this a habit, it's a good one.' Despite her attempt at a light tone, now that the encounter was over, Honoria found her heart pounding and her breathing shaky.

Her remark earned her only a curt nod. 'Let's get you ladies away from here. Miss Laurie, can I see you home first?'

Laurie must have been suffering an aftermath of nerves, too, for silent tears were slipping down her face. Despite her obvious distress, she shook her head. 'No, sir, I can get back home on my own. I'll just not take the short cut down by the harbour.'

She turned toward Honoria. 'Miss Foxe, I won't never forget you coming to help me, but you shouldn't have. 'Twere much too dangerous. If one of them miners had caught you—well, don't know how I could have lived with myself. But I do thank you. You, too, Mr Gabe. I best be going. Ma's expecting me and I don't want to worry her.'

After dropping them both a quick curtsy, she grabbed her shawl off the ground where it had fallen during her struggle and set off for the pathway that ran north behind the draper's shop.

Despite her calm words, Laurie still looked frightened. And the girl would almost certainly have bruises on her shoulders and wrists, Honoria thought, unconsciously rubbing her own wrists at marks long since healed.

Despite her initial success against the brigands, she was overwhelmingly thankful Mr Hawksworth had appeared when he did. Fear curdled in her belly as she remembered the un-friendly eyes she'd seen staring at them from within the stone hut. With the second rogue making a recovery, she'd have been hard pressed to fight off two of them, and somehow she knew the men within the stone structure—a beer hall, she now realized—wouldn't have come to her aid.

Like Laurie, she was more shaken than she wanted to admit. When, oh when, would she learn to think twice before leaping into a situation?

But what else was she to have done? Stand by and see Laurie molested by that drunken lout?

'Let me escort you back, Miss Foxe,' a voice interrupted

her. 'By the by, what in the name of Heaven were you doing here? I thought you were going back to the vicarage!'

'I was, when my errands were complete.'

'I'll walk you back now, then.'

She might be happy about his fortuitous intervention, but with her emotions so unsteady and given her strong attraction to him, it would be wiser not to accept Mr Hawkworth's escort. Lest she do something foolish—like throw herself into his arms and burst into tears.

Rallying her courage, she tried to put a note of belligerence in her voice. 'Thank you, but that won't be necessary. Unless the entire populace of Sennlack is full of brigands who attack innocent women?'

Mr Hawksworth sighed out a breath. 'Needs a keeper,' she thought she heard him mutter before he said, 'Miss Foxe would never forgive me if, after suffering such an upsetting experience, I didn't see her niece safely to the vicarage. I shall accompany you, whether you want my escort or not.'

She shrugged an answer and set off walking up the hill. If she kept her distance, she might buy enough time to pull herself together so she wouldn't disgrace herself in front of him.

With his longer stride, he soon caught up with her, but for a few moments said nothing. Finally, as if he couldn't remain silent any longer, he burst out, 'Admirable as it was of you to want to help, whatever possessed you to try and intervene without assistance? If I hadn't happened to be returning to the *Gull* just then, you might have been dragged away and—'

He broke off, flushed, while another wave of fear made Honoria's stomach queasy. Before she could settle it to reply, he'd continued, 'Didn't your aunt warn you to avoid the kiddleywinks by the harbour? You shouldn't ever walk that way alone, even in daylight! The miners aren't a bad lot, generally, but on pay day with some drink in them… They wouldn't care a pin for the fact that you were Miss Foxe of Foxeden Manor— only that you were a pretty wench.'

His criticism was actually welcome, for it fired an indignation that put an end to the detestable weakness that kept pulling at her. 'What was I to do, then?' she countered. 'Just stand by and watch while they made off with Miss Steavens?'

'Why didn't you call on the draper for aid? His shop stands nearest the hill.'

'By the time I could have returned there and convinced him to assist, they would have already absconded with her. We both screamed for help—there wasn't anyone else near! Don't you think I would have called on someone, used some weapon, if any had been available? Despite what you seem to think, I'm not completely witless!'

'I'd better not comment about that,' he retorted. 'You should know enough not to tangle with men full of a drink that inflames other needs.'

'I had no idea the hut was a tavern—all I saw was Eva's sister being attacked by ruffians. And having drink in them is supposed to excuse their detestable behaviour? What beasts men are!'

'I suppose we are, some of the time,' he admitted. 'But before you convict all men of being complete villains, you must know that Laurie Steavens augments her wages from the inn with…other activities. Activities that involve the exchange of coin for, ah, services of an intimate nature.'

When his words penetrated, Honoria stopped abruptly. Staring at him, she said, 'You mean she…'

'Yes, I'm afraid so.'

Heat suffused her face. Had she been a bloody fool, chasing away Laurie's clientele? She shook her head, disbelieving. 'But she…she doesn't look like a—a fancy woman.'

'You, being acquainted with so many, would recognize one,' he replied drily.

Her flush deepened, but as she ran through her mind the events that had transpired, her conviction strengthened. 'Fancy woman or not, she *was* struggling to get away. Even if she is a woman in the trade, she should still be able to refuse. No woman deserves to be forced against her will.'

He raised his eyebrows. 'Coming from a lady of quality, that's a rather charitable view of one of Eve's daughters. Most believe they get what they deserve.'

Honoria was about to reply when the memory took her. *'Need more than that cold fish Anthony Prescott, don't you? I'll give you what you want. What a fast piece like you deserves…'*

Her breath coming faster, her skin gone clammy, she stumbled and almost fell, trying to shut off the memories.

As if from afar, a voice said, 'Are you all right, Miss Foxe?' A hand clasped her elbow, steadying her.

'Y-yes, I'm f-fine,' she said, shaking off the hand and trying to still the trembling as she came back to herself.

'We're almost at the vicarage,' Mr Hawksworth said, concern in his eyes. 'Can you walk the rest of the way? I'd offer to carry you, but I suppose that wouldn't answer. If you wait here, I can fetch a gig from the inn.'

She shook her head. 'No, I'm all right now. Please excuse my—my missish reaction,' she added, almost cringing with embarrassment at having appeared so weak before him. 'You were right, I was precipitous in intervening. Thank you for coming to my aid, even though you knew…what was going on. And now you must think me ignorant as well as brainless.'

'No, you were right: Laurie was trying to break away. I, too, believe that no woman should ever be forced, regardless of her occupation. Ah, here we are at the vicarage. Won't you go in and let the housekeeper brew you some tea? If you'll forgive my saying so, you look a bit pale. As well you might after suffering such a distressing incident.'

'No, my aunt will be expecting me. I'll just get my horse and head back to Foxeden.'

'Are you sure you want to ride back? I could commandeer a gig and drive you.'

'That's most gentlemanly of you, Mr Hawksworth, but unnecessary.' All she wanted to do now was get back to the safety of Foxeden, so she might sort all this out. And escape Mr Hawksworth's company before she made any bigger a fool of herself.

To her relief, the vicar's manservant must have spied them as they approached the barn, for he came out, leading her horse. After he assisted her to mount and she'd secured the sack with the plants she'd dug earlier from the glen, she looked back at the captain, who stood watching her.

'Thank you again, Mr Hawksworth, for your assistance and…information. I shall certainly take more care in future. Good day to you.' With a nod of thanks to the vicar's servant, she urged the mare into motion.

She felt the stare of Mr Hawksworth long after she rode away.

After a mile or so, the mare's steady gait and the fresh wind blowing in Honoria's face began to soothe her nerves and settle her agitated mind. Though it still seemed so hard to believe.

Eva's sister—a prostitute! Honoria had seen Barques of Frailty on parade in Hyde Park in their fancy equipages, attended by a crowd of wild young bucks. Or flaunting their fine gowns and diamonds in opera boxes, while she giggled behind her fan with her faster friends over rumours of which rotund lord had which jewel-bedecked charmer in keeping.

Occasionally, outside the theatre, she'd glimpsed the slender figures of girls silhouetted by lamplight in the alleys near Covent Garden, before she took her seat in the carriage and the footman closed the door. They'd seemed like shadow figures, denizens of a dark and sinister world far removed from her own.

But for Laurie, sister to little Eva, daughter of that worn fisherman's widow, to be a doxy? Someone she knew, had spoken to, who had seemed entirely ordinary?

Her mother would probably faint, the priest at Stanegate

shake his head in sorrow, but Honoria could understand why a woman of great beauty and few choices might decide to take a rich lover and make the best life she could in the circumstances. But to service coaldust-grimy miners in a backwater Cornish town? The thought appalled.

What could have made Laurie choose such a path? Had she, like Honoria, been ruined by some rogue? Compromised by a lover who abandoned her to face the consequences of her indiscretion alone?

If she'd lost her virtue—and with it, her chance to make a decent marriage—those consequences would be bleak indeed. With her father dead, little work available and no other resources, how else could a girl help her family survive?

If Mr Hawksworth only knew, it was not her place to judge Laurie. After a month of fretting and bemoaning her fate, for the first time she realized, despite all that had happened, how very fortunate she was. Because save for an accident of birth, it might have been her, rather than Miss Steavens, struggling with a drunken miner outside some stone hut.

Honoria uttered an immediate—and somewhat guilty— prayer of thanks that she had been spared such a fate. Her heart twisting with grief for the reality with which Laurie's family struggled, she vowed to do everything in her power to assist them.

Chapter Nine

Honoria hadn't expected to return to town before Sunday, but two days later, she received a note from Father Gryffd asking if Miss Foxe could meet him at the vicarage the following day to consult about the school. Since a package awaited Aunt Foxe at the post and the restlessness that often drove Honoria was bedeviling her, she jumped at the chance to do a favour for her aunt and advance the scheme that might be of some practical use to Eva and her family.

With a package to collect, this time she took a gig. The vicar must have been keeping watch, for as soon as she pulled up, a servant came forward to take the horse and Father Gryffd trotted down the front steps to meet her.

After an exchange of greetings, he said, 'I've had an idea of where we might set up the school. Before proceeding any further, I wanted you to see it and tell me what you think. If you will follow me?'

He led her down a pathway into the garden and past some fragrant roses that immediately recalled to her the stroll she'd had here with Captain Hawksworth just a few days ago.

How did a free-trader pass his time, she wondered. At sea, testing his boat? Idling about the inn quaffing ale, waiting for foolish maidens to rescue?

'Just around here,' the vicar interrupted her thoughts, pointing past a hedge to a small stone building with a row of south-facing windows.

'The previous vicar, a great devotee of gardening, had this planting house constructed. It houses tools on the far side, but on this side with all the windows, he set up benches on which to start seed and propagate plants. The structure had fallen into disuse, but I recalled it when pondering where we might set up school and had the servants sweep and clean. It's large enough to accommodate a dozen children. Do you think it will do?'

Honoria surveyed the light, open space with approval. 'I think it charming! I might have received fewer raps on my knuckles if I'd had that lovely view of the woods to gaze upon while I studied French and geography.'

The vicar beamed. 'I'll see to fitting it out at once. Now, would you step inside the parlour? I'll have Mrs Wells bring us some tea.'

'I should like that. Then you can explain to me more about how you'd like me to assist at the school.'

They were walking back across the churchyard when Laurie Steavens approached and gave them a quick curtsy. 'Excuse me, Father, Miss Foxe. Robbie Lowe come by the Gull, saying he'd seen Miss Foxe's gig here. I thought you might be talking about the school, so I hurried down to tell you Ma would love to have Evie come, if you're sure she won't inconvenience nobody.'

'I'll not let anyone harm an innocent child, Miss Laurie,' Father Gryffd said gently. 'Tell your mother we thank her for sparing Eva to us for a few hours. I'll send you word at the Gull when school is ready to begin.'

Laurie nodded. 'Thank you again, Father.'

Honoria watched the conversation, not sure what to say or do. Staring at Laurie now, despite knowing of her other occupation, the girl still had a fresh-scrubbed, country maid look that made it hard for Honoria to credit she actually traded her body for coin.

Disbelief, pity and revulsion warring with an awful fascination, she surfaced from her reverie to discover Laurie watching her, silently enduring Honoria's fascinated scrutiny.

The flush on her cheeks and the slightly defensive angle of her chin said Laurie must have figured someone had informed Miss Foxe she worked as more than a simple chambermaid at the Gull.

Honoria flushed, too, embarrassed to be caught staring and not wanting the girl to think she looked on her with disapproval, despite the occupation she'd been forced to. 'I'm so glad Eva will be able to attend. But we don't know the language of signs she developed with your mother. Can you give us some hints on how we might communicate with her?'

Laurie's brows lifted, as if surprised Honoria had deigned to speak to her. Finally she replied, 'Just tell her what you want her to do. She hears as fine as anyone. And her gestures are easy to figure out.' She smiled slightly. 'For a lady as understanding as you, Miss Foxe, I don't think you'll have no trouble.'

I understand more than you could ever know, Honoria thought. 'When she learns to read and write, she'll be able to let people around her know exactly what she thinks and feels, even if she never speaks a word.' Recalling the girl's obvious delight in flowers and the way she had looked back just at the moment Honoria was speaking to Father Gryffd about her, she added, 'She seems to sense and appreciate her world very well already. Maybe she'll be a poetess, able to describe the wonders of the Cornish sea and cliffs so people from far away can see them as she does.'

Laurie's lips trembled. 'I think she might be. She's so clever and good! Much better than me.'

'We're about to have tea, Miss Laurie. Would you care to join us?'

Even knowing Father Gryffd was a shepherd of the lost, Honoria was a bit startled that the vicar would bid a girl guilty of so notorious a sin to take tea in his parlour.

Her surprise was nothing to the shock widening Laurie Steavens's eyes. The girl inhaled sharply and gaped at him, as if she couldn't credit what she'd just heard. Tears gathered at the corners of her eyes before she dashed them away.

'That's powerful kind of you, Father,' she said huskily, 'but I couldn't possibly. Only imagine what your parishioners would think if they found out!'

'I should hope they would applaud my offering hospitality to a neighbour,' Father Gryffd replied.

'Thank you, Father. But it wouldn't be fitting. I must get back to the Gull, anyways. Afore I go, Miss Foxe, Ma asked me give you these. To thank you for your kindness to Eva—and to me.'

From her apron pocket she extracted a pair of knitted gloves and held them out tentatively, as if half-expecting Honoria to refuse them.

Honoria didn't need the vicar's urgent look to know she must accept them at once. 'It's not at all necessary, but how very kind of your mother.'

Holding them in her hands, Honoria immediately noticed the warmth of the thick wool. A closer glance revealed they were knit in a wonderfully intricate pattern of braids and knots. 'They are lovely! Your mother is very skilled.'

Laurie smiled. 'Pa always said Ma knits the handsomest gloves and sweaters in Cornwall! That's good wool, full of lanolin; they'll keep your hands warm even if the gloves get wet.'

'Please tell your mother how grateful I am, and how excited we are Eva will be able to come to school.'

'Just send word to me at the Gull when she needs to be here,' Laurie said. 'Glad you like the gloves, Miss Foxe. Good day to you both.' With another curtsy, she turned and walked back toward the inn.

Thoughtfully Honoria watched her walk away. Turning to the vicar, she realized he was watching Laurie with even keener interest—and an almost wistful expression.

Was the vicar, as she was, wondering how this lost sheep might be brought back to respectability? Or did he have a more personal interest in the lovely Cornish lass?

'I should like that tea now,' she said, recalling him.

Abruptly turning to find her watching him, probably with a speculative look on her face, he flushed and gestured toward the vicarage. 'I'll have Mrs Wells bring us tea at once.'

A few minutes later, when they were settled in the snug parlour, the housekeeper brought in a steaming pot along with some biscuits fresh from the oven. Honoria had just poured them each a cup when the housekeeper came back in.

'Father Gryffd, Mr Hawksworth is here, begging if he might join you. Should I show him in?'

'Of course. If you don't mind, Miss Foxe?'

Honoria felt a zing of excitement and a flush of warmth throughout her body. Hoping the sudden heat hadn't shown on her face, she said, with a calm belied by the sudden gallop of her pulse, 'As you wish, Father.'

Then *he* was striding in, bringing with him a gust of cool outside air and a sense of energy and vigour that was nearly palpable, along with a touch of the wildness of the sea itself.

Goodness, Honoria thought, hauling back on the flights of fancy. She was becoming as cast-away poetical as Tamsyn.

'Thank you for receiving me, Father. I must admit, when Mr Lowe mentioned he'd seen Miss Foxe's gig here, I stopped by hoping to catch her. After the distressing incident a few days ago, I wanted to make sure all was well.'

She coloured under the intensity of his gaze. It seemed to make her very skin prickle, almost as if she could feel it brush her skin, like a fingertip.

Though the thought was absurd, still it threw her so off-stride that she stumbled to find words like a maid as infatuated as Tamsyn. Sternly ordering herself to gather her wits, she replied, 'I'm fine, Captain Hawksworth. Thank you for your concern.'

'Incident?' the vicar asked, his brow furrowed. 'Did something untoward befall you after left the Gull? If so, I shall be most distressed for abandoning you!'

''Tis more what befell Laurie.' Quickly Honoria explained what had occurred on her previous visit to town.

The vicar shook his head, looking unhappy. 'There's no end of mischief gotten up in those beer shops. I'm relieved, Captain, that you were at hand to prevent something even worse from befalling the ladies.'

Gabe nodded. 'I, too, am glad I was near. Speaking of hands, that's a lovely pair of gloves you have, Miss Foxe. Locally made, I'm guessing.'

'Yes, by Mrs Steavens. Father, I've just been thinking. It's all well to teach the girls letters and numbers, but unless they leave to work in some factory, learning is not going to help them benefit their families. What if they could learn to construct gloves as fine, thick and heavy as these, in such intricate patterns? Couldn't they be sold in the larger market towns, even in London?'

'They are very fine,' the vicar said, looking thoughtful. 'Certainly it would be a boon to their families if they were able to bring in any money at all. But the women hereabouts, especially the fishermen's wives, have long knitted sturdy gloves and sweaters for their menfolk. I don't know where there might be a market for such goods.'

'I don't know anything about markets either,' Honoria said, 'but I know superior workmanship when I see it.'

There was a knock, followed by Mrs Wells's entry. 'Excuse me, Father, but could you come? There's someone needing your attention.'

The vicar rose at once. 'Thank you, Mrs Wells. Begin preparing the usual packet.' To Honoria and the captain he said, 'If you will excuse me a moment? '

They murmured assent and the vicar walked out. Honoria was more than a little nervous to be left alone with the captain, especially as his dynamic personality seemed to expand to fill the gap left by the departing vicar.

It made it deuced hard to concentrate, rendering a lady who, Honoria thought in disgust, had bandied words with glibbest gentlemen of the Ton suddenly too tongue-tied to produce a coherent sentence.

'Probably a beggar,' Captain Hawksworth said, breaking the silence that had fallen with the vicar's exit. 'It's widely known that anyone in difficulties will never be turned away. Father Gryffd is a man of God who truly lives up to his calling.'

Honoria thought of his kindness to Eva and Laurie. 'He seems not to judge the failings of others—a trait not as common as one might wish in clergymen.'

Suddenly she wondered uncomfortably how Father Gryffd might react if he knew the story of the lady he'd invited to advise his girls. Her conscience pricked; this business of false names was becoming more complex. She owed it to the vicar to confess the truth of her situation before she associated herself with his school. She'd no more wish for her scandal to bring harm upon the local girls than she would be to inflict it on her sister.

'You were talking about teaching girls knitting, then finding a market for their goods?' the captain asked, interrupting her solemn thoughts. 'It sounds like an excellent idea. Do you have any contacts who might help you in London? If not, perhaps I could assist.'

Honoria raised her eyebrows. 'I didn't know you had any dealings in legitimate goods.'

The captain grinned. 'Most hereabouts believe we deal more honestly than those who sell goods under a customs stamp, since the price they pay us is more reflective of the true cost. You may be wary of my…experience, but I promise you, I do know how goods must be funded, produced, delivered to market and sold. How would you go about doing that?'

'First, we would have to obtain superior wool, then ask Mrs Steavens to teach the girls how to knit articles worthy of sale. While they are perfecting their skills, we could approach shop-keepers to convince them to stock the items, then see about transporting them to the merchants.'

Hawksworth smiled. 'I think you might make a good trader yourself, Miss Foxe. Though someone from your background might not believe it, that was a compliment.'

If her mother heard her discussing the steps necessary to go into trade, she'd faint dead away, Honoria thought with slight smile. In fact, according to the Carlows, having her soil her hands in trade would probably be more scandalous than losing her reputation.

Her smile faded. She really did not wish to bring still more notoriety on the family name. But she would like to help the girls. Maybe Aunt Foxe knew someone in London?

Even as she thought it, the captain said, 'I have some London contacts. I could look into the matter, if you like, speaking to merchants about possibly handling the goods, inquiring about transport and the obtaining of wool.'

When Honoria hesitated, not sure she wished to launch upon an enterprise that would bring her in closer contact with him, Hawksworth grinned. 'They are quite legitimate contacts, I assure you. Last time I inquired, mittens knit by Cornish schoolgirls were not on the list of contraband goods.'

She smiled back. 'As you say, it's very early yet, but if it is not too much trouble to inquire, I would appreciate it. I shall speak with my aunt as well. Though she has lived in Cornwall for many years, she maintains an active correspondence with friends in London and elsewhere.'

The vicar returned, apologizing for his absence. 'Sorry to have abandoned you, but that latest poor wretch was hungry and cold.'

'Maybe he needed a wee nip of brandy to warm him,' the captain suggested, a twinkle in his eye.

The vicar looked uncomfortable. 'You're probably right.

Oh, I know Charles Wesley spoke most passionately against free-trading, but I confess I cannot see that it harms, more than it benefits, a parish.'

'But it's also difficult to persuade them to obey it, when it so greatly conflicts with what's in their best interest.'

'Still,' the vicar replied, 'One cannot deny, while the trade helps poor wretches earn a few more pence to ease their lives, importation of cheap gin from Ireland does encourage drunkenness of the dangerous sort Miss Laurie just experienced. Encouraging disobedience of the law is never wise.'

'Even if you partake of a drop or two yourself now and again,' the captain added with a smile.

'Shall we return our attention to mittens?' Honoria asked with a reproachful glance at the captain for his teasing of the vicar. 'I've just been discussing the project with the captain. He suggests we try selling the mittens in London.'

Father Gryffd brightened. 'It would be better, I think, taking them farther away. Most folk hereabouts know someone who can knit them, if they don't do it themselves. I'm not so sure about city-dwellers. And I have no connections in London. Do you, Miss Foxe?'

Honoria's conscience piqued her anew. She would confess her involvement in scandal to him this minute—but for the presence of Captain Hawksworth. 'The captain has just been saying he might know someone.'

'Merchants who deal in goods that are quite legal,' the captain assured him solemnly.

'Indeed, it would have to be,' Honoria added, giving him a severe look. 'No involving children in your...trade.'

The captain immediately sobered. 'I would never countenance involving children in that, Miss Foxe.'

Though she still wasn't sure she could believe everything he said, his avowal reassured her. 'I'm glad to hear it.'

Putting down her teacup, she looked up to see that disturbingly intense glance fixed on her. Then he smiled.

His smile seemed to coax hers forth by right. In fact, she felt the most curious sensation that some part of her soul, awakened from a long slumber, soared up and out to meet his.

She shook her head rapidly, breaking the hold of his gaze and trying to dispel the nonsensical notion. She succeeded merely in feeling dizzy.

The tea must be too strong, she thought, her emotions unbalanced by a touch of panic. She should remove herself now, before she felt or said anything idiotish. She rose abruptly.

'Thank you for tea, Father, and compliments to Mrs Wells for the excellent biscuits. But I must return to Foxeden.'

To her dismay, Captain Hawksworth rose immediately as well. 'I should be going, too, Father Gryffd. Add my appreciation to Miss Foxe's for your hospitality.'

If she'd thought to avoid him, she was disappointed, for abjuring the vicar to remain in his house, since a sharp wind was blowing, he escorted her to her gig.

Acutely conscious she had not managed to fully subdue the siren call of…of *something* that pulled her to him, she cast about for some topic that might lessen it. 'It wasn't kind of you to tease the vicar about consuming spirits. He's a fine man, one of best I've met in that role.'

To her exasperation, he immediately agreed. 'You are right, 'twas not well done of me. He is indeed a good man.' He laughed wryly. 'How difficult it must be for a Welshman to encourage adherence to English law! Especially one that does as much harm to Cornishmen as the customs.'

'They wouldn't be harmed if they just followed the rules,' she returned tartly.

'Perhaps, but if they obey them, how would the fisherman or day labourer earn the extra pennies that allow him to purchase tea—or a glass of spirits and a warm meal at Mr Kessel's inn? You can't hold it against a man to choose to do something that makes his hard life a bit more pleasant. Or expect him not to resent or flout authorities who try to prevent him from doing so, by force if necessary, merely to enrich a government in ways that do nothing to ease his lot at all.'

She shook her head in exasperation. 'You are an Irish devil! To hear you explain it, 'tis the most reasonable thing in the world to disobey the laws.'

'Because it is,' he returned promptly. Seeing she was about to object again, he laughed and held up his hands. 'Pax! I can see 'tis not a matter upon which we are likely to agree. And, you know, an Irishman has as healthy a disdain for English law as his Welsh cousins.'

'That I can believe. I expect you've always been a rabble rouser! Is that how you ended up in Cornwall?'

'It was a favour to a friend, actually. And I'll have you know I spent a very respectable career in the Army.'

'Where you made those *respectable* contacts in London, no doubt?'

His slow grin captured her again, warmed her from the face that seemed to glow under his gaze, all the way to her toes and deep within. It seemed her brain had shut down, for all she could do was gaze back, tingling with longing.

A tingling that turned to a shiver in every nerve as he grasped her gloved hand and brought it to his lips. 'I have appreciated our conversation even more than the vicar's excellent tea. I shall investigate finding markets for your mittens, Miss Foxe, and do my very best not to disappoint you.'

She was not sure how it happened, for her wretched mind seemed incapable of summoning coherent thought, much less speech, but suddenly her gig was beside them.

All she knew was his face angled down toward hers, his eyes staring intently, his slightly parted lips poised as if to descend to hers. Her pulse galloping like a winner at Newmarket, she waited in frantic anticipation for him to close that small gap between them and capture her mouth.

Her eyelids must have drifted shut, for in the next moment,

instead of his lips on hers, she felt the captain's hands at her waist, lifting her up to the seat.

Beneath her cloak, she felt each pad of his fingers against her ribs. The insistent pressure seemed to burn through her clothing into her skin, so that despite being fully dressed, with horse and gig and servant within a few feet of her, the touch seemed almost as intimate as if only the two of them stood there…alone in her chamber, he lifting her onto the bed.

The shocking image rattled her so much, only at the last moment did she manage to grip the rail and avoid falling ig- nominiously back on top of him. While the servant handed the reins into her numb hands, Captain Hawksworth bowed to her.

'I hope to report good news for you soon. Good day, Miss Foxe.' With a hand to his hat, he turned and walked away.

The groom set in motion the horse who, fortunately, knew the way home, since at the moment it seemed she was inca- pable of driving. Long practice kept the reins taut in her hands on the way out of town, until somewhere farther down the road to Foxeden, her mind finally cleared of its sensual haze and she tried to evaluate what had just happened.

Her first realization was that the captain was much more dangerous than she'd first thought him. He'd been able to almost persuade even her, who had family highly placed in government, that the laws against free-trading were flawed. He'd encouraged her to give shape to her sketchy scheme to help the girls and their families, thereby involving her in trading activities that would horrify her Ton relations.

Much worse, though, he tempted her. In him, she sensed the same turbulent, rebellious spirit that always swirled restlessly in her breast. He, like Hal, was an Army man, a man who'd been to foreign lands, tested his courage in desperate battles. Here was a man who welcomed challenges, be it against the sea, the revenue agents—or the establishing of trading contacts to sell mittens knit by schoolgirls. Here was a man who lived life vibrantly on every level.

Most dangerous of all was the call of sense to sense. In the past, she'd giggled at Minerva Press novels in which a heroine melted at the hero's touch, her thoughts scattered to winds by his nearness, her only desire to be wrapped in his strong, sheltering arms.

She wasn't laughing now.

She'd wanted those lips to descend and kiss her, more than she'd ever longed for a kiss from the several gallants she'd permitted that liberty. Anticipating those embraces had filled her with the zest of the forbidden, a mild and pleasurable sense of excitement—but nothing, nothing like this.

Her breathing suspended, her heart pounded, just imagining the feel of his lips on hers. She knew without ever having to experience it that kissing him would be more profoundly exhilarating than any touch she'd ever known.

The ferocity of her desire to experience it appalled her. She hadn't escaped ruination in London to flee here and let herself be drawn into a seduction that would get her expelled from the only haven she had left.

That realization finally broke the hold the captain had established over her senses. Hereafter, she must keep her distance. The free-trader bent on his illicit trade was intriguing enough. The free-trader turned honourable entrepreneur and partner, it seemed, was irresistible. And mere Miss Foxe could no longer count on Lady Honoria's elevated social position to distance him from her.

With the captain an expert in a game in which she was beginning to realize she didn't even know the rules, she'd do better to take her counters from the table and flee.

Chapter Ten

Thoughtfully Gabe watched Miss Foxe until her gig rounded the curve. He chose the long way back to the inn this time, needing the wind in his hair, the crash of waves in his ears to settle his pounding heart and agitated senses.

It might require a dip in the cold sea to settle another part of him.

He'd been relieved to discover Miss Foxe had regained her equilibrium after her fright at the hands of the miners. Despite his admiration for her fearlessness to going to Laurie Steavens's assistance, a swift and blinding rage had filled him at the thought that some ruffian might injure or frighten her.

Even a man who didn't chart his future past the next reef or the next month could still admire her, he told himself. By Heaven, he'd scarcely believed it when she took on that drunken lout outside the beer hut—delivering a blow that would have done credit to a masculine practitioner of the fancy. Was there no end to the surprises concealed in her?

Miss Foxe had been even more approachable today—maybe too approachable. Pausing beside the gig, he'd almost ruined everything by bending down to kiss the lips that seemed to beg for his touch, right there under the gawking servant's eye! Whatever had come over him?

Even worse, after putting his hands at her waist to lift her up on the bench, he'd had to struggle to make himself release her, so strong and fierce was the current flowing between them. He'd wanted to leap beside her, seize the reins, drive her to some isolated fisherman's hut, strip her clothes off layer by layer while he touched and gentled and inflamed her, then make love to her again and again while the sound of the surf roared in his ears as fiercely as desire was roaring through his veins.

And she would have gone with him. He was sure of it.

Almost.

Damn, but he wished he knew for certain whether she was a matron or a maid. If she were experienced and willing, he'd sweep her straightaway into a discreet dalliance that he already knew instinctively, given the enormous heat between them, would bring unprecedented pleasure to them both.

If it were possible to entice her without causing harm, he wanted to. But the more he encountered her, the more she surprised and impressed him, the stronger grew his sense of responsibility toward her. Fiercely as he wanted to possess her, he also liked her enormously. If there were a chance of redemption for her, he didn't want to jeopardize it. He'd have to proceed cautiously.

Because even if she were knowing, she was still gently-born and unmarried. Uncharted territory, that. His dalliances with ladies of quality had all been with widows or married ladies with indifferent spouses, if one didn't count the single objecting husband he'd had to sweet-talk out of pistols at dawn.

What had happened to ruin this maiden of quality—if, indeed, she had been ruined, a fate that was still only wild conjecture. She might be entirely chaste.

Though her presence here argued against that.

What would happen to her now, assuming she'd not been sent here as Miss Foxe's long-term companion? If she were indeed ruined, she might eventually be married off to someone obliging enough to overlook a loss of virtue in return for a sufficiently generous dowry. To a man who might never let her forget he thought she was soiled goods.

Or perhaps she'd end up an unpaid servant for her family, shuttled from one household to the next as births, illnesses or burgeoning nurseries dictated, her presence attended by whispers of past scandal, condescension, perhaps even covert, illicit offers by visiting lords of large appetite and small scruples.

His lip curled with disgust at envisioning such a sorry end for a lady of her spirit and wit. Whether ruined or chaste, she deserved a man who appreciated and valued her. Someone like— him?

That conclusion veered too close to the shoals of commitment, sounding the alarm bells again in his brain. Dalliance was one thing, but envisioning anything more permanent filled him with the need to trim his sails and tack off in the opposite direction.

Still, he was pleased to be able to involve himself in her scheme to sell the gloves made by her students. It would give him an excuse to talk with her, stay near her…though sea bathing would definitely be in order if he strayed too close. Even now, his fingers itched with a reprise of the desire to touch her cheek, bring her soft lips to his own.

He'd been far too long without a lady's intimate embrace— and was far too attracted to this lady. So attracted, in fact, that slaking his desire with some other female didn't really appeal, despite his need.

A shock went through him at that realization, followed by a vague sense of unease. Never had he fallen into such thrall to any one lady that he lost his taste for an agreeable substitute. His level of infatuation with and desire for Miss Foxe was disturbingly different from anything he'd previously experienced.

Uncharted waters indeed. Still, even if he had less inclination than usual to move on to another port, there was no need to ready the anchor chain. He couldn't envision any future beyond dalliance between Miss Foxe of Foxeden and the man she saw as a law-breaking free-trader.

Or could there be?

Damn, he was veering between one heading and another like a ship in capricious winds. Abandoning any notion of drawing a final conclusion about his relationship with Miss Foxe, he'd concentrate simply on acquiring some trading contacts for her, thereby earning her gratitude—and if it later turned out to be agreeable to them both and not harmful to her, maybe something more.

A short time later, Gabe entered the inn. Calling for a mug of ale, he sat over it contemplating remarks he could utter to a certain golden-haired lass that might make her blue eyes widen with enthusiasm—or turn them a stormy grey with annoyance. He was still smiling about the delights of teasing her when raised voices at the front of the inn pulled him from his musings.

In this isolated village, the arrival of a newcomer was novelty enough that he glanced over to take a look at the stranger now speaking with Mr Kessel. Something odd about the conversation caught and held his attention.

The exchange seemed more animated than usual, the newcomer gesturing broadly and inclining his head, from which he'd just removed a fashionable beaver hat, revealing a sweep of long, wavy dark hair. His garments were of good quality and cut: chamois breeches, dark coat, elegant boots obviously from a skilled London maker and polished to high shine.

Yet, there was something faintly exotic about him. Perhaps it was the exuberant fall of linen at his throat from which winked some ornate stone. When the man turned, Gabe saw he wore a gold earring in his left ear.

The newcomer gestured up the stairs to a boy following in

his wake, doubtless a servant of some sort, then followed him up, moving with the lithe grace of a dancer. His slightly olive skin and theatrical flair were most un-English. Did he spring from the tropics somewhere—India? The Caribbean? Was he maybe even a Gypsy, perhaps?

When Mr Kessel returned to the tap room, Gabe called him over. 'I see you have a new patron. An interesting-looking fellow.'

'Aye, he's unusual,' Kessel said with a grimace. 'A Gypsy, one of the Argentari.'

So his guess was correct, Gabe thought, trying to remember the name of the troop he'd encountered as a child. Seeking some of the famous Irish horses for trade, a group had camped near the sea at the outskirts of Hawksworth land the summer he turned ten, much to his delight and his father's disgruntlement.

'Comes a few times a year,' the landlord was saying. 'Buys copper and silver for his tribe. He's bought a cargo or two from Dickin in the past as well. Claims he deals in a variety of goods and has contacts with merchants in London, but being a Gypsy, one can't credit anything he might say.'

'Contacts in London?' Gabe repeated, his interest further piqued.

'So he claims. I know he paid cash straightaway for the cargoes; sent a crew of his own men to move it. If you're thinking of dealing with him, I'd proceed warily. He seems civilized enough, but there's an air about him. I wouldn't try to cross that one. Walking home some dark night, you might find yourself with a knife between your shoulder blades!'

With that cogent advice, Mr Kessel bustled off.

Should he approach the trader, Gabe wondered, sipping his ale thoughtfully. He had to admit, part of his urge to do so was a carryover from that fascination with Gypsy life he'd acquired as boy.

Warned by his father not to have anything to do with the foreign interlopers, he had, of course, run off to their encampment at the first opportunity. Kinder than his father, they'd not chased off the impertinent *gadje* child, but let him watch them as they tended fires, hammered out jewellery, or gentled their horses with an expertise he admired to this day. He'd even picked up a bit of language, enough to understand some of their sayings and the gist of the stories and songs sung around the campfire.

After a few weeks, they vanished as silently as they'd arrived. For the next few summers, he'd hoped they might return. They never did, but his curiosity about them remained.

The question about whether or not to approach the man was settled a few minutes later, when the Gypsy himself strode with a confident swagger across the tap room to Gabe and bowed.

'Captain Hawksworth,' he said, extending a hand to shake. 'Stephano Beshaley. You will allow me to buy a drink for the man whose fame I've heard celebrated everywhere since arriving back in Cornwall?'

When Gabe allowed that he would, Beshaley made another flamboyant gesture toward the bar. Flashing Gabe an irritated glance over Beshaley's head, Mr Kessel called, 'Sadie, where are you, girl? We've got customers to serve.'

A moment later Sadie came in. Visibly brightening when she spied Gabe and the Gypsy, she hurried over to the table.

'Sir, what a pleasure to see you again,' she exclaimed.

Beshaley leapt to his feet and made her an elaborate bow. 'The pleasure is entirely mine, lovely lady. Ah, how long we have been parted! My eyes have looked upon nothing but desolation, deprived of your beauty.'

Gabe thought the speech a bit extravagant, but appearing well-pleased, Sadie giggled and preened like a parrot. 'I do swear, Mr B, you could talk the bees from their honey. As if I don't know you been charming dozens of pretty girls since last you was here!'

'None so pretty as you, fair Sadie. Or so worthy of adornment.' Reaching up, he slid his fingers through her hair, pulled out a shiny gold clip and presented it to her.

'Why—how'd you do that? Oh, how pretty!'

Winking at her, he said, ''Tis magic, my sweet—a little treasure for one whose regard I treasure. Now, you will bring me a mug of ale and I will thrill to hold it, knowing it was warmed by your touch. And ale for my friend the Hawk, too, eh?'

He flipped her a gold coin, which she snatched in mid-air and tucked into her ample bosom. 'I'll get them drinks over here straightaway. Always a pleasure to help a handsome gent like you. Or you, Mr Gabe,' she added, as if belatedly remembering that, though generous, the Gypsy was transient and she ought not to neglect her regular customer—the usual target of her amorous glances.

Beshaley kissed his fingers to her. 'I rejoice in your good will, my angel, and carry the vision of your enchanting face in my heart.'

That flowery speech made Gabe rather ill, but Sadie beamed. 'I swear, Mr B, how you do talk!' Bobbing a curtsy, she waltzed away.

Both men watched her display of hips and bottom as she crossed the room. 'And how you do talk, my loose-lipped lass,' Beshaley murmured, the gallant tone disappearing from his voice. Looking back at Gabe, he said, 'A clever man knows goods offered too widely are of lesser value.'

'I'm well aware of that,' Gabe replied, wondering how many times Sadie had warmed Beshaley's bed, or how much information he'd prised out of her with gold coins and honeyed words.

Beshaley smiled. 'I knew you for a man of wisdom. Even goods of small value can be useful, as long as one does not pay more than their worth.'

A moment later, Sadie bustled back with their glasses, but unable to spark a revival of gallantries from either the Gypsy or Gabe, she soon retreated back to the bar.

Ignoring the girl now, the newcomer raised his glass. 'I did not come here to talk of loose wenches, but to make your acquaintance. Here's to you, a man of daring, whom I've heard commands his vessel like a great horse master does his mount, swift and responsive to his touch. To the confounding of King's agents and good custom for all!'

Gabe raised his glass and drank the toast. 'I've heard of you, too, Mr Beshaley. As a trader in copper, silver and sometimes other goods.'

Beshaley shrugged. 'I trade in such goods as interest me at the time. Though I have moved cargoes from Mr Kessel in the past, I deal in other things now.' He flicked a finger toward the gem winking in his neckcloth. 'Particularly beauties like these.'

'Diamonds?' Gabe asked.

'Aye, and other gemstones. I've a source in the Far East that provides high-quality uncut gems, as well as those already facetted and polished. I also buy and sell stones, both set and unset.'

'Rather a risky business, isn't it?' Gabe asked. 'Your goods are easily portable, but also highly pilferable. Do you not worry about losses?'

In one swift movement, Beshaley pulled a knife from his boot, then rolled it over his fingers and into his palm. '*In a village without dogs, farmers walk without sticks,* my people say. But in this world?' Laughing softly, he twirled the knife. 'No one bothers me—or I bother them, you see? If not with this slender blade, then with the power of my will. Retribution comes to all who cross me. You know the Carlows, sir?' he asked. When Gabe shook his head, Beshaley continued, 'A mighty clan who thought themselves untouchable. They know better now.'

The Gypsy cut a compelling, dynamic figure, Gabe thought. There was an intensity about him which made one believe he was the type of man one wanted on one's side in a pitched battle…and as the innkeeper said, not a man one would want to cross.

'You seem the sort who gets what he wants,' Gabe observed.

'So I do, my friend,' he replied. 'And so, I understand, do

you. There are many goods to be exchanged. I wonder, with your contacts among the gentry of Ireland, whether you would be interested in some trade?'

Somewhat taken aback, for he'd made no mention of his roots since coming here, Gabe said, 'And where did you hear that?'

'A man of enterprise has many sources. Many interests. And pays well to know of what's afoot.'

Gabe thought of the coin and the pretty words he'd tossed to Sadie. That artless girl probably would be a good source of information about everyone who came and went in the Gull and around the coast.

'By the bye,' Beshaley continued, 'if you have a mind to invest your profits in something easily portable which holds its value and is quickly convertible into hard currency, gems are ideal. If such a proposition interests you, we could talk. But not now! This is not for business, but to toast, as one enterprising trader to another. So you will drink with me, and perhaps talk of business later, eh?'

'Perhaps,' Gabe replied.

After draining his glass with a flourish—as he seemed to do everything—Beshaley said, 'I must go now and visit the mines. Perhaps I will see you when I return?'

'Perhaps,' Gabe repeated. 'As you can imagine, my schedule is…fluid.'

Beshaley nodded. 'One strikes when the time is right.'

'If I should not see you here, might I find you in London?'

Beshaley gave him a non-committal wave of the hand. 'I am in places from Calcutta to Flanders, Cadiz to Cornwall. And occasionally, London. As my people say, *A rabbit with only one hole is soon caught.* You also know the worth of that saying, lest the revenuers would have confiscated your ship long since. Well, I must go.'

Gabe rose with him and bowed. 'Thanks for the drink, Mr Beshaley.'

'My privilege, Captain.'

He strode out with the same fluid gait, exuding confidence and an air of command. He might be a man who'd hold his own in a fight, Gabe thought—but never one to trust.

He'd quickly abandoned his idea of asking about trading contacts. A man who dealt in gems and contraband would hardly be interested in handling a mundane item like mittens.

He'd just drained his ale when Kessel returned to the tap room. 'So, what did you make of him?' he asked Gabe.

'Interesting,' Gabe replied. 'And you're right; I'd be on my guard around him. Have you any specific cause to think him dangerous?'

'Did you see how he handled that knife?' When Gabe nodded, he continued, 'Usually he shows off that skill right away—to put others on guard, I suppose, or maybe scare them a little. One never knows what them Gypsy types be thinking, what with their spells and potions, their hatreds and vengeance. If you're considering a business venture with him, I'd be careful.'

'Anything more you can tell me of him?'

'He first came here…oh, five or so years ago. No sparklers then, dealing only in silver. Asked if we wanted any cargo moved, said he had a buyer in London. He made several runs— a shrewd bargainer, by the way. Don't know if he paid off the revenuers—or if he spooked them. We've not done business for some time. But he's bolder now, with more of a swagger. If you want my advice when you've not asked for it, stick to dealing with good Cornishmen and leave that one alone.'

Gabe nodded. 'It's best to know where the shoals are, before sailing into uncharted water.' Nodding, Mr Kessel walked back out to the kitchen.

An intriguing man, Beshaley, Gabe thought, who wore power and daring like a cloak and carried himself with the bearing of a natural leader. Gabe suspected he'd make an excellent pirate or smuggler, inspiring admiration and fanatical loyalty in his crew. But not an Army officer, who must follow rules and obey orders.

With regret, Gabe decided it was best to dismiss Stephano Beshaley and his offer.

He wished he could dismiss Miss Foxe as easily. She was taking up far too much of his thoughts. Itchy with inactivity, he had a strong urge to invent some excuse to see her. But as with gentling any wild creature, after one catches its attention, in order to lure it into letting down its guard, he'd found it was best to back off and let it follow him, rather than try to pursue.

So he wouldn't seek out Miss Foxe for a few days.

And if he wanted to keep that resolve, now might be a good time to put *Gull* to sea, sail toward a falling barometer and take her into a storm to test her new rigging, making sure her ropes would hold through the howling dark, high winds and rough sea that were the smuggler's natural ally.

And while he was gone, hope the tentative new line he'd strung to Miss Foxe would also hold and strengthen.

Chapter Eleven

A week later, Honoria sat at a table in the converted glass-house-schoolroom while Father Gryffd had the girls go over a page in their primer. In an astonishingly short time, the vicar had managed to convince the families of five girls, ranging in age from six to eleven, to attend school for several hours in the morning, before they were needed home to help their mothers with the chores.

He'd begun by teaching alphabet letters, then reading stories while they followed along, connecting word to sound. Numbers and sums came next, and then before lunch, Mrs Steavens came with Eva, who would go into the garden with Honoria while her mother helped the girls practice knitting. The older girls were already becoming proficient with the simpler stitches.

Since Eva could not sound out letters or respond verbally to words, the vicar used a different method with her. One might not always be able to tell whether or not she was comprehending, but there was no question about her level of excitement or intense concentration, clearly visible in her eager face and beaming smile.

Honoria, though pleased with the progress of her project, found herself still restless. After meeting the captain almost every day, she had expected him to turn up at the school, but she'd not seen him for an entire week. She missed the challenge he presented, the chance to match wits. Of course she missed his handsome face, his teasing banter and, Heaven help her, the potent sensual undertow that pulled her to him.

The prudent side of her warned, as it had on the ride home from the vicarage that first day she'd realized the power of his attraction, to beware his ability to tempt her to imprudence. But his absence and her solitude were hushing that voice.

Her restless, more wilful side replied that it was hardly necessary to be so careful, since she was ruined already. She had too much sense to allow things to go too far, so she might as well enjoy the much greater freedom she had in the country to talk and walk and bandy words with him, unfettered by the irritation of the trailing chaperone that would have been unavoidable in London.

Why not take advantage of her freedom to enjoy his company? Having been a reigning Belle, she'd grown accustomed to being surrounded by handsome young men; it was only natural she appreciated him providing a pleasure that had once filled so much of her life. She squelched the little voice pointing out that, during the month after her arrival in Cornwall before she met him, she had lived quite satisfactorily without being attended by handsome young men.

It was more difficult to suppress the woebegone feeling of missing a friend. Which ought to be reason enough for her to try to wean herself from the addictive pleasure of his company, the prudent voice reasserted with asperity.

'Well, Miss Foxe, shall we have some tea before Eva arrives?' the vicar's deep baritone interrupted the arguments.

Startled, Honoria turned to him, jolted further still to find the room now deserted. A guilty flush mounting her cheeks, she realized she'd been wool-gathering so intently, even the noise of the little girls' departure had not recalled her. 'Tea would be lovely, thank you. I believe I shall take a turn about the garden and watch for Eva, if that would be convenient?'

'It will do you good to stretch your legs,' he approved. 'I'll call when tea is ready.'

They walked out together, Father Gryffd heading into the vicarage, Honoria into the garden. Determined to put into practice the last, more prudent counsel to purge herself of longing for the presence of Captain Hawksworth, she set off at a brisk pace. She'd made two purposeful circuits around the kitchen garden when, in the distance, she spotted a single figure approaching.

Her pulse jumped in anticipation, until she almost immediately discerned the stranger walking toward the vicarage was female, rather than male. Impatiently stifling an immediate disappointment, as the newcomer drew closer, she realized it was Laurie Steavens, looking lovely in a smart new pelisse and bonnet.

Concerned, Honoria walked out to meet her. 'Is something wrong? Is Eva ill?'

'No, she and Ma are both fine.' Giving a furtive glance toward the vicarage, she continued, 'I'm glad to have caught you alone, miss. I wanted to let you know if you need me to tell Ma anything about Evie, you won't find me at the Gull no more, though you can still leave a message for me there.'

'Have you lost your job?' she asked in alarm.

'N-not exactly,' Laurie said, avoiding Honoria's gaze. 'I'm…with Mr John now. He didn't want me working at the inn no more, cleaning gentlemen's bedchambers.'

The captain's chamber? Honoria wondered. 'I'm surprised,' she replied carefully. 'He seemed to have an aversion to Eva, and I got the impression you didn't like him very much.'

Laurie gave her the flicker of a smile. 'But he likes me and don't mind Eva long as she keeps out of the way. He promised he'd be generous with his blunt, and he has. Been able to buy fine wool stuff for a new cloak for Ma and shoes for her and Eva. He sent around a whole haunch of beef from the butcher's, too. I can't recall when we last had meat, other than a stew Mrs K let me bring home sometimes from the Gull.' Finally looking up, she met Honoria's eye, in hers a plea for understanding. 'I...couldn't exactly refuse him.'

Honoria nodded. 'I don't suppose you could.' Honoria thought of the man's previous treatment of Eva. Something about Kessel's eyes and harsh line of mouth made her uneasy. 'Does he treat you well?'

Laurie shrugged. 'Well enough, I suppose.'

Honoria wasn't reassured; indeed, her feeling of foreboding deepened. 'If there is a...problem, will you promise to tell me?'

Smiling, Laurie shook her head. 'If there was a problem, miss, what could you do?' She straightened her shoulders. 'I don't mean to refine on it. What happens, happens. If this lets me take better care of Ma and Evie, I mean to do it while it lasts. You won't tell Father Gryffd, will you? I know, he'll find out soon enough, but I'd rather it be later than sooner. Foolish, I know, since it isn't any worse than what I already done and some might think better. Just...I'd rather he not know yet.'

Everything in her protested Laurie's situation. But the girl was right; there was nothing Honoria could do. Even Aunt Foxe, liberal in thinking as she was, was unlikely to upset her household by employing a girl who'd taken to Laurie's occupation. Nor had she any money to offer in compensation for Laurie's refusing to accept the landlord's son's protection. Besides, truth to tell, she had no right to interfere in whatever Laurie decided to do with her life.

Still, impotent rage flamed in her breast at the path Laurie had felt necessary to take. And she'd never felt more helpless.

'Well, I'll be going now, miss,' Laurie said.

When Laurie turned to walk away, Honoria impulsively grabbed her sleeve. 'All the same, will you let me know if there is trouble?'

Laurie studied her a minute, then shook her head. 'Kind of you, but it be best if you don't get involved. Mr John's got a wicked temper and he don't like nobody interfering in his business.'

She paused, then added in a wondering tone, 'I don't know why a lady like you'd be concerned about the likes of me, but I thank you for it. For watching Evie, too.'

'You're welcome. I wish…I wish I could do more.'

Laurie smiled. 'Mostly all we females can do is endure and survive. A good day to you, miss.'

She walked away, the jaunty feather in her new bonnet bobbing in the breeze.

Honoria watched her retreating figure, not able to shake that uneasy feeling. She wished she might confide in Father Gryffd, who had care for all his parishioners and seemed to have a special interest in Laurie. He was certainly in a better position to protect the girl—but she had specifically asked Honoria to keep the news a secret. She couldn't justify breaking a confidence just because she disliked the landlord's son.

The girl was out of sight when Father Gryffd appeared at the door, calling to Honoria that he was bringing tea and some macaroons fresh from the oven to the schoolroom—and Eva arrived.

Seeing the eager girl always lifted her spirits. Running to Honoria, Eva gave her a hug, and began the rapid series of gestures Honoria was just beginning to comprehend.

Laughing, she caught the girl's hands. 'Slower, Eva, slower! I'm not so clever as you!'

That earned her a look of surprise followed by a grin so big, Honoria's heart ached. How often in the girl's short life, Honoria wondered, had the intelligent mind Honoria knew was trapped within Eva's mute body been abused as backward and dull-witted?

Taking the child's hand, she led her to the schoolroom and poured tea. Another pang went through Honoria as she saw how, watching her intently, Eva mimicked the set of Honoria's fingers on her teacup, the curl of her finger, her upright posture sitting just at the edge of her chair.

Tea drunk, Honoria settled back to watch while Father

Gryffd worked with the child. Soon, she was overcome again with the feelings of restlessness that had afflicted her the last several days.

She'd already decided to stop on her way back to Foxeden and do some sketching. By now she'd about picked the spring garden clean and buried Aunt Foxe's rooms in floral arrangements and the stillroom in drying herbs. She'd found some charcoal and paper in her aunt's library, which her aunt had said she was welcome to use.

She hoped the pastime would absorb some of her energy and distract her, if only for a time, from the gnawing sense of uncertainty that dogged her more and more frequently as her distress over her ruination dissipated and her concern about the future increased.

With the vicar and Eva absorbed in work to which she could add nothing useful, Honoria was thinking to slip away early, when a knock sounded on the schoolroom door. Mrs Wells peeped in to announce that Mr Hawksworth had called, wondering if the vicar would allow him to visit the schoolroom.

A surge of gladness carried away Honoria's restlessness with the force and freshness of the sharp southeast wind on the Cornish cliffs. Her nerves hummed with anticipation and every sense seemed to heighten as he appeared in the doorway.

'Mrs Kessel told me upon my return this morning that you'd begun your school, Father. I thought I'd stop by and see how our prospective knitting venturers are doing.'

'Do come in! Though, as you see, most of our scholars have left for the day. If 'tis agreeable to you both, while I finish today's lesson with Miss Eva, Miss Foxe can acquaint you with our progress.'

Though Honoria didn't remember rising as he walked in, she found herself on her feet, her gaze locked on his face. He bowed and a guilty thrill made her heart hum as he gave her the smile she'd been trying not to crave for these last seven days.

'Miss Foxe, so good to see you! Though the *Flying Gull* racing through the sea is a pretty sight, 'tis nothing to the beauty awaiting me on land.'

'Ah, so that's why I've not seen—' Flushing, Honoria caught herself before she sounded as moonsick as Tamsyn. 'That is, nice to see you, too, Captain. I note the sea's saltiness has not leached the sweetness from your tongue.'

He grinned, blast him, as if he'd seen through her reply all the eagerness she'd been trying to mask. And whatever possessed her to mention 'tongue,' which immediately prompted her naughty mind to wonder what he'd taste like when she kissed him?

If. If she kissed him. Honoria shook her head, trying to clear it. But that was ridiculous, for she was *not* going to kiss him. They were going to talk about schoolgirls and mittens and commerce.

She was *not* going to note how his vitality and force and sheer maleness seemed to fill up the small room, forcing out air and making it more difficult to breathe—while making each breath more intense. How lips that spoke such honeyed words hinted how much sweeter they'd be pressed against her own.

'So school is well begun?' he was asking, jolting her back to the present. She blinked rapidly, noting that his expression had softened, as if taking pity on her speechlessness.

Heavens, what was wrong with her? Back in a London ballroom, she would have laughed behind her fan to see some other maiden so flushed and tongue-tied before a handsome young gallant.

Please, not 'tongue' again.

Angrily calling her wits to order, she said, 'The girls are making good progress on their letters and sums. Mrs Steavens has some of them already on the way to mastery of basic knitting patterns. It remains to be seen, of course, if any achieve the level of skill necessary to complete the complex designs we think more likely to be saleable. My aunt has agreed to write to some friends in London, asking their opinions of the possibility of marketing them there.'

The captain nodded. 'I will be interested in hearing their replies. I know you expressed concern about whether fashionable ladies would wish to purchase plain woolen mittens. But I've been thinking that, even if the Ton are not interested, London is full of maids and shop girls and governesses who care as much about comfort as fashion, who must go about in wet and chilly weather. Girls who would be delighted to purchase such necessities at a fair price, if they were available.'

Though it was impossible to truly ignore it, Honoria blessed him for distracting her from the disturbing force of his presence by making her picture the appealing notion of Mrs Steavens, Laurie and Eva, receiving enough blunt for honest labour that Laurie could retire from her current occupation, without leaving the family always teetering on brink of destitution.

'An excellent plan!' she exclaimed. 'Perhaps we could offer not just mittens, but scarves, caps, even reticules knit in matching patterns.'

He nodded, smiling at her enthusiasm. 'You do have a knack for trade which, as I said before, I find admirable, though I suspect neither your family nor mine would share that opinion.'

She tried not to feel a glow, knowing he approved of her.

'I'm going to go to London myself soon to see about the cost of transport and to find possible merchants to handle the goods. So, how is Eva doing with her knitting?'

'I'm afraid she's much more interested in learning her letters. Only look, see the glow about her when she's studying with Father Gryffd!' Honoria gestured toward the two.

As she noted, Eva was beaming as the vicar showed her how the story he'd just read was inscribed in the coding on that page. If she studied hard, he added, a whole world of stories would soon be open for her to discover.

'I suppose I should learn some knitting myself, so I might encourage her,' Honoria said, looking away from them with a smile. 'Father Gryffd says she hangs on my words and mimics everything I do.' She shook her head, sighing, as she recalled some recent events. 'Not always a wise idea, I fear!'

'Of course she watches you and copies. You possess a sparkling, dynamic presence that must make you a person of influence wherever you go. The knack of inspiring confidence in others is intangible, something that can't be taught.' He grimaced. 'As I have often observed, some men are incapable of leading, no matter how much gold braid and lace one layers on a uniform.'

'I would have liked to be a soldier, like my brother,' she said wistfully, almost absurdly gratified by his praise—before the new voice of caution reasserted itself, pointing out to her all she had lost by foolishly indulging the idea that she could live life on her own terms.

'But it's silly even to discuss it,' she said with an angry shake of her head. 'Only men have the freedom to go soldiering and exploring and to make what they wish of their lives.' Her thoughts going from herself to Laurie Steavens, she added bitterly, 'Women are everywhere hemmed in, constrained to narrow paths with few choices and punished if they stray from them.'

From somewhere deep within her, a swell of emotion rose, a chaotic mix of anger, disappointment, hurt, fear and despair. Terrified for one panicky instant that she might weep, she fought it down.

Suddenly she wanted to get away, to seize her sketchbook and flee to the cliffs where the fierce wind and roaring surf could work its soothing magic. She didn't need this impossibly tempting man luring her further toward the danger that had already destroyed her life—or tantalizing her with possibilities that could never be.

But before she could master her voice enough to announce her intention to depart, he caught her sleeve, forcing her to look up at him.

'I'd never thought about it before, for my sister seems happy enough to be a wife and mother, but you're right. Women are constrained. And it is unfair, isn't it?'

The sympathy on his face and in his eyes halted her even more effectively than his hand on her sleeve. Once again, she felt herself physically pulled toward him, drawn by a fierce spirit that seemed to mirror her own as it looked deep within her, both understanding and admiring what it saw. Even after he released her, she remained motionless, staring at him, the rational, protective half of her brain warring with the wild, instinctive part that urged her to reach out. To trust him.

Caution won again. 'Perhaps. But 'tis no point repining what cannot be changed. Father Gryffd, if it's all right with you, I believe I shall leave. I've promised my aunt some sketches of the coast and thought I'd attempt some today, while the weather is fair. Eva, I'll see you tomorrow, pet.'

'Of course, Miss Foxe. We're about done for today anyway, aren't we, Eva?'

The child bounded up and ran to Honoria. Tugging at her skirt, she made a series of rapid hand motions that looked something like water rushing toward a shore, the soar of a cliff and cawing sea birds before gesturing emphatically back to herself.

With a smile, Honoria said, 'You wish to come with me?'

As the child nodded enthusiastically, the captain said, 'You seem to have learned her language quite well.'

'We're becoming good friends,' Honoria replied before looking down to tell the child, 'Of course, you may come.' She might initially have wished to go alone, but she could never disappoint the eager girl.

Eva bounced once in excitement, then tilted her head to the side, drew her hand slowly down one cheek and pointed to Honoria.

'And what does that mean?' Hawksworth asked.

With a smile, the vicar answered for her. 'It means the cliffs are pretty—like Miss Foxe.'

While Honoria flushed a bit in embarrassment, the captain murmured, 'Clever child.'

Eva surprised Honoria by uttering a little giggle before turning to seize Captain Hawksworth's hand. Tugging at it, she made the sea and cliff gesture again.

'I think she wants me to come with you,' the captain said, sounding amused. 'I should very much like to go sketching, Miss Eva. If Miss Foxe does not object?'

Honoria hesitated, trapped. The strong surge of excitement that welled up at the idea of having his company ought to have been reason enough, her cautious side argued, for her finding some polite excuse to decline. But with the undertow of connection still running strongly between them, she didn't have the strength to resist.

Besides, she told the cautious brain, they would have Eva to chaperone—and what untoward thing could happen with a curious child in train?

'Very well, Captain, if you don't think you'd be bored.'

'In the company of two lovely and clever ladies?' he reposted immediately. 'Impossible! However, it might be possible to become rather sharp-set during a strenuous hike. If you ladies will walk with me to the Gull, I'll see if I can persuade Mrs Kessel to kit us out with some biscuits and cider, and obtain a gig to carry us there. Would you like that, Eva?'

Naturally the child nodded with great enthusiasm. Sighing, Honoria beat back the vague unease still troubling her and agreed that she would enjoy it, too.

She would enjoy it, she told her cautious side defiantly. Enjoy the company of the eager child, this highly attractive man and the beautiful setting.

How long it had it been since she'd been on an outing which promised only pleasure? *Too long,* she answered her own question. She would suppress all those tiresome voices of *what* and *why* and *should* and *shouldn't* and simply enjoy this day as the gift it was from benevolent providence.

Chapter Twelve

Three quarters of an hour later, Gabe helped the ladies into a gig and the little party set out. With a bit of entirely justified flattery, he'd induced a beaming Mrs Kessel to provide not just biscuits and cider, but some of her excellent ham and cheese along with a flask of ale and a blanket to spread upon the ground.

As they set out, Eva's urgent motions indicated she wished them to proceed to the south, toward Land's End. Acquiescing to her wishes, they proceeded several miles down the coast until she gestured for them to stop. She then led them to a large rock that formed a table-like structure set at the edge of a rocky point with breakers foaming below.

'It's a perfect place to spread out our provisions,' Miss Foxe exclaimed. 'What a clever girl you are indeed, Eva!'

'Shall we sample Mrs Kessel's fare before you begin sketching?' Gabe asked.

Slanting a glance at Eva, she replied. 'Yes, let's. Aunt Foxe tells me she sets an excellent table.'

'A fact I can confirm,' Gabe replied, handing Miss Foxe the quilt the landlady had lent him. While she and the girl spread the coverlet over the flat stony surface, he unpacked the repast and they all sat.

'I already knew her cider to be superior; the ham is delicious, too,' Miss Foxe remarked as she nibbled at the sampling Gabe offered her. Eva, however, hung back, not touching any of the feast he'd arranged before them.

'Please, have some, Eva,' he urged. 'The food and cider are for you, too.'

A worried frown on her face, the child looked over at Miss Foxe, as if seeking confirmation. 'Yes, Eva, the refreshments are for all of us,' Miss Foxe said.

Even so, Gabe had to encourage her again before finally, she took a small piece of cheese. A rapt smile crossed her face after she swallowed the morsel, and she made a rapid hand gesture that even Gabe could interpret meant 'good.'

'Try the ham, too,' he coaxed, meeting Miss Foxe's look of disbelief and consternation over the child's head. Who could have been so cruel, her expression asked, as to have fed themselves before her while forbidding a hungry child to eat?

Knowing that Laurie Steavens worked at the inn, Gabe had a grim suspicion just who it might have been.

It required a bit more encouragement from both of them before Eva relaxed and began to partake freely of the food. And when she did, they both effectively abandoned their own repast in the pleasure of watching the child's uninhibited delight.

Each bite was chewed slowly, each sip of cider savoured. Then she set them both to laughing when, at the bottom of the basket, she discovered an orange. After picking it up and rolling it between her fingers, she was winding up her arm to throw it to Miss Foxe when that lady cried, 'No, Eva, it's not a ball! You eat it.'

She took the fruit and held it up to the girl's nose, letting her smell it, then carefully peeled it, Eva watching wide-eyed through the whole process. After sectioning the fruit, she handed it to the girl. 'Taste some, it's delicious,' she urged.

The child looked dubious, but encouraged by her idol, took

a tiny bite. She looked startled, probably by the sudden spurt of sweet juice, but almost immediately closed her eyes and made a little humming sound, clearly enraptured by the taste.

After swallowing the first bit, she looked back questioningly at Miss Foxe, who handed her several more sections. 'Good, isn't it?' she asked. 'It's called an orange—like the colour. It grows on trees in warm lands far away.'

With even greater appreciation than she'd shown with the ham and cheese, the girl methodically devoured the orange pieces. After watching Eva for some minutes, Miss Foxe looked over to Gabe and mouthed 'Thank you.'

If he, who had only a glancing interest in the child, found it oddly moving to watch her enjoy this unprecedented treat, he imagined it must be even more gratifying for her mentor. A pleasant warmth filling him, he was glad he'd hit upon the idea of the picnic that was providing a deprived child—and the kind-hearted lady who cared about her—with such pleasure.

Indeed, so absorbed was Miss Foxe in watching Eva that not until the slices had almost disappeared did she recall she still held another segment of the orange in her hand. 'Excuse me,' she said to him softly. 'I almost forgot to give you your part.'

She held out the orange. He reached over to take it, but at the last minute, rather than simply pluck the fruit from her, he slipped his fingers beneath hers, brought her hand to his mouth and ate the orange off her palm.

In every sensitized nerve, he heard her almost imperceptible gasp, felt the tremor that shivered through her as his lips nuzzled and his tongue tasted. For long, lovely, slow minutes, he held her unresisting hand to his lips, even that miniscule contact sparking sensation to every nerve as with the brush of his lips and the slow exploration of his tongue he devoured the fruit, then licked up every drop of nectar.

He made it last as long as he could, well beyond any excuse he had for resting his lips there, before reluctantly releasing her hand. Her arm flopped jerkily back to her side, as if she had little control over its motion, while her eyes never left his face, now raised and gazing straight at her.

Cheeks flushed, eyes bluer than the dancing waves far beneath them, lips slightly parted, she looked startled, taken aback—and aroused. As he certainly was, the blood rushing thick and heavy in his veins, his body tightening with erotic tension while he went as hard as her lips looked soft and pliant.

He burned with everything within him to kiss them.

But if his orange-eating gesture had been impulsive, he wasn't idiotish enough to try to make love to her before the fascinated gaze of a ten-year-old. Nor, his instincts warned him, despite that firm evidence that the spontaneous gesture had evidently shaken her as much as it had disturbed him, was she yet ready for kissing.

Oh, but soon, he hoped! Else he'd need a great many more swims in the cold sea water.

His wits needed dousing to revive them, too, for his paralyzed brain couldn't seem to come up with some clever remark, or indeed, give voice to anything at all. It was Eva, pulling at Miss Foxe's sleeve, who finally broke the spell between them. Even then, the child had to tug for a full minute before Miss Foxe finally turned to focus on her.

Still holding her sleeve, the girl gestured at the sketchbook and then toward the cliffs. 'You want to show me something?' Miss Foxe asked, a bit breathlessly.

At the child's vigorous nod, Gabe finally recovered his voice. 'You two go along. I'll pack the basket into the gig.'

Still looking distracted, Gabe thought, Miss Foxe allowed Eva to carry her box of charcoal while she gathered up the sketchbook and followed.

Still more than a little distracted himself, as he walked over to stow the basket, he marvelled at the strength of the sensual response she sparked in him, that could fire him to a need so acute it approached pain with just one smoky gaze and a taste of her palm.

A need that only made him even more voracious to taste the rest of her, all of her, to suck and lick and savour every delicious inch from the arch of her instep to the curve of her ear. How readily he could identify with what Eva must have felt as a starving onlooker beholding a table full of savoury dishes she was forbidden to taste!

Oh, that soon, Miss Foxe might invite him to feast.

But though he'd made good progress in disarming her suspicion and luring her closer, instinct told him he hadn't quite drawn her close enough to try breaching the citadel. Besides which, damnation, he still didn't know her true status.

Much as he burned to, he wouldn't sample the nectar from an unplucked flower—or even further disturb one from which someone had already sipped, if there were a chance that taking such liberties might harm what he only wished to cherish.

Cherish?

He shied away from the implications of that word with the speed of a timid virgin stepping out of the path of a notorious roué. Putting the notion out of mind, he turned from the gig and paced off toward the horizon beyond which Miss Foxe and the girl were about to disappear.

To his surprise, Eva was leading Miss Foxe away from, rather than toward, the cliffs. He picked up his pace to keep them in view as Eva trotted along the edge of a deep ravine, skirting large boulders, then dropping out of sight again.

Quickly rounding the rocks, he saw just the top of Miss Foxe's bonnet as she descended a narrow trail into the ravine. A few minutes later, the trail grew narrower still as it doubled back on itself, passing around and under protruding rock formations. He was about to call out for them to halt and come back, as the trail was becoming ever more slippery and dangerous, when around the next bend the path suddenly opened up onto a vista of a cove sheltered behind a narrow inlet. He stopped, inspecting the place while Eva led Miss Foxe down the steep descent to the crescent of sand below.

The inlet was even narrower than the entrance to the cove where the revenuer had run his boat onto the shoal. Waves from the open sea beyond roared through the perilously skinny passage, then broadened out into a wide, shallow cove where the water lapped peacefully onto a flat, sandy beach.

An even more perfect spot to land a cargo than the other, Gabe noted, trying to recall the features of the coastline beyond and looking for some landmark that would alert him to the presence of the narrow entrance.

The ladies were already at the beach when he arrived, but since Miss Foxe had not deployed the sketchbook, he assumed they hadn't yet reached the destination Eva desired to show them. True enough, as soon as he caught up to them, she trotted off again, leading them toward what appeared to be a solid rock face.

Not until he was only a few feet from the wall did he notice the narrow cave opening, set obliquely to the beach so it was difficult to make out. Eva halted there, beckoning them to advance.

Miss Foxe gave the opening a dubious glance. 'Do you suppose it's safe?' she asked Gabe in a low voice.

'Eva seems to think so,' he answered. 'Do you want to stay here while I follow her?'

'And be thought a poor honey?' she asked scornfully. 'Never! I may not be very fond of low, underground places, but I shall manage.'

'Good,' he approved, noting that Miss Foxe was not one to let fear constrain her, a trait he admired—and possessed himself. 'Lead on, Miss Eva.'

At the back of the cave, they paused where Eva indicated to gather up and light a torch from a stack evidently left for that purpose. By its flickering illumination, Eva picked her way into a low squared passage that sloped gradually upward, whose roughly geometrical shape and the drainage channel to one side indicated it had been purposely excavated.

They followed the tunnel for some time, finally emerging inside a small stone hut. Outside it, the desolate, windswept moor extended as far as the eye could see.

'A smuggler's trail!' Miss Foxe exclaimed. 'Ending at this hut—a perfect place to receive and conceal goods until they can be carried off. Eva, what a wonderful place! How my brother and I would have loved to have discovered such a treasure when we were young. I'd heard such things existed, but thought them mere legend.'

'Not legend at all, as you've just seen,' Gabe replied, amused by her almost childlike delight. 'There are others even more clever—passages that lead into the cellars of public houses, into private homes more elaborate than this humble structure— even into the crypts of churches.'

'Into churches?' she asked, eying him narrowly, as if wondering whether this was just another smuggler's tall tale.

'Quite true,' he confirmed with a smile. 'In another village, there's a tunnel leading to the stables used by the town coroner, who kindly allows his hearse to be borrowed to transport goods farther inland.'

She shook her head and laughed. 'I begin to believe your claim that all Cornwall is involved in the trade! Was there anything else you wanted to show me, Eva?' she asked, turning to the girl.

While the two walked the area around the hut, Eva pointing out various grasses and wildflowers, Gabe put a professional eye to evaluating the surroundings.

By his estimate of the distance they'd travelled south from Sennlack, this place must be several miles from the village, yet not on the main road, if one could dignify the rough track that more or less followed the coastline by so elevated a title. A flattened area in the mix of coarse grasses and low-growing plants suggested that cargo might have been moved over it in the past, though the absence of wagon tracks said no goods had passed here recently. Across the moors, a tor in the distance served as an excellent landmark.

Making a mental note of the surroundings, Gabe walked over to rejoin the ladies.

'Though the flowers here are lovely,' Miss Foxe was telling Eva, 'I think I should prefer sketching the cove, where the high cliffs overhang that narrow inlet. Shall we go back?'

Apparently content after having shared her secret passage, the child followed docilely as Gabe relit their torch and led the little party back to the beach. While Miss Foxe searched for the perfect spot from which to sketch, he climbed the narrow trail back up the point where it emerged from the ravine. For a few moments, he stood there, studying with a seaman's eye the configuration of the rocks that formed the narrow inlet, the characteristics of the waves washing through it and the direction of the prevailing wind.

His inspection complete, Gabe returned to the sun-dappled beach to find Miss Foxe seated on a rock, Eva sprawled on the sand beside her, watching avidly while she sketched. The pose, as if staged by some artist intent on painting a study of a mother and child, was somehow both tender and moving.

He stopped short, surprised by his reaction. He couldn't recall having been touched by such a scene before, certainly not while observing his sister with one of her squalling brats. Perhaps it was the obvious connection between the mute fisherman's daughter and the gentlewoman, who in the eyes of the world would seem to have so little in common. Yet in their intensity, their exile from society and their uninhibited joy, both were so alike.

That delicate but tenacious sense of cherishing wrapped its tendrils around his heart again. Though he still yearned to possess Miss Foxe, he was drawn almost as powerfully by the fierce spirit that championed a child her own community had rejected, fearlessly rushed to attack a drunken miner abusing a lone woman and waded neck-deep to try to save a drowning stranger.

Who would rescue her?

His runaway thoughts jerked to a sudden halt. He had no

certain knowledge yet that Miss Foxe needed rescuing. But he couldn't deny that, though he'd enjoyed playing the role of dashing captain thrust upon him by the admiring local community, he wished even more to act the part for her, to be in truth a valiant knight whom *she* could depend upon, admire and appreciate.

From that realization, it was a short leap back to recalling the most satisfying way she might express that appreciation. This time, instead of reefing the sails of imagination as he had previously whenever his thoughts had blown him in this direction, he allowed his mind to fly free.

He envisioned bringing her to the cliffs on another such glorious day when the sky formed a cave of blue above them. He'd kiss her as it seemed he'd been longing to forever, arouse her with strokes and touches, then lower her onto a blanket of tiny wildflowers and make love to her, warmed by the sun, caressed by the sweep of the wind across the moors, serenaded by roar and hiss of the surf.

He imagined she would respond with all the uninhibited fierceness and passion that had sent her wading into a cold sea or chasing after an abusive drunk. A passion he yearned to ignite and inflame and enjoy.

The two were becoming inextricably linked, he realized: admiration for her fierce spirit leading to desire and desire for her deepened by his admiration. Which was quite unique, since he'd previously placed 'admirable women' and 'desirable women' in two entirely separate categories.

The prospect of having both meet in one woman was disconcerting. He wasn't at all sure what to do about it, but as he made his way to the ladies, one thing he did know for certain: winning such a bright soul cloaked in such a sensual body was well worth taking as much time and effort as necessary.

He crossed the beach toward them, but absorbed in their work, with the sound of his footsteps lost in the murmur of wind and shushing of waves, they didn't notice his approach.

Not wishing to startle them, he halted a short distance away and said, 'Forgive me for interrupting! *Let me not to the marriage of true minds admit impediments*.'

Miss Foxe looked up from her sketch and smiled. 'Very prettily said. Shakespeare, wasn't it?'

'Yes, from the sonnets,' he replied, wondering, as he seated himself on a broad rock behind her, if she recognized the rest of quote—and how it described the passionate, unshakeable love of two kindred spirits.

Setting down her sketchbook and charcoal, she said, 'Did you study with the Bard in one hand and the ship's wheel in the other?'

He smiled at the image of trying to read a book while conning a ship through a rough sea. 'No, in the Army, actually. There wasn't much to do in winter quarters in Portugal. Some of the lads had brought books, which I borrowed.' He chuckled. 'An action that would have astonished some of the harried clerics who attempted to cane some knowledge into me as a boy.'

She nodded an agreement. 'As a child, I hadn't much use for books either, being much more interested in horses, dogs and tagging after my brother. Oh, I read a few of the more fantastical novels in London, along with the daily newspapers and *La Belle Assemblée*. Aunt Foxe, bless her, even ordered some fashion periodicals to be sent here.'

Her smile faltered. 'Though I haven't much use for the latest fashions now. But Aunt has coaxed me into reading some of her favourite novels and poetry, which to my surprise, I am enjoying. Not as much, I suspect, as Eva will, once she is able to read them.'

She glanced back at the child, to discover her busily plying a stick of charcoal over a blank page in the sketchbook, her face a study in concentration. When she gazed back up and saw them watching her, she dropped both charcoal and sketchbook with a little inarticulate moan of distress.

Springing to her feet, she backed away, hands up as if to

ward off a blow, shaking her head, her expression a study in remorse and apology. After throwing him a look of consternation over what Eva's response told them about how the child had been treated, Miss Foxe spoke to her gently, reassuring the girl that everything was all right and that she was welcome to borrow the materials.

While Miss Foxe soothed the child, Gabe picked up the charcoal and righted the sketchbook, which had fallen facedown on the sand. Turning the book over, he drew in a sharp breath.

'Miss Foxe, look at this!'

She glanced over at the page and gasped. 'Why—that's me!'

'And an excellent likeness it is,' Gabe confirmed, staring in awe and disbelief at the sketch the child had jotted off in the short time the two had been chatting. A head-and-shoulders portrait of Miss Foxe in profile, it caught perfectly the outline of her nose, the curve of her lips and cheek, the arch of her brows, even the hint of the lace at her throat and the little tendrils tugged loose from her coiffure by the wind.

'That's amazing,' she breathed, wonder in her face. 'Eva, your sketch is very, very good!'

For a moment the girl remained still, as if not believing Honoria's words. Then, her face still entreating, she went off in a flurry of hand signals.

'What is she telling you?' Gabe asked.

'I'm not altogether sure, but I think she's saying she is sorry and that she loves the beach, because there she can draw in the sand as much as she likes. If I got that right, Eva?'

Still apparently not convinced she wasn't going to be punished, the girl nodded tentatively.

The idea for a new, even more attractive venture began shaping in Gabe's mind. 'Do you like drawing, Eva?'

The child's vigorous affirmative nod was his answer.

'Do you like to draw the beach and the coves, as well as pretty ladies like Miss Foxe?'

The girl gestured with her whole arm, encompassing both Miss Foxe and the rest of the scenery.

Turning to that lady, he said, 'If Eva can create drawings this skilful of the cliffs and sea, the coves and harbours, churches and fishing boats, she could produce something probably much more saleable than woolen mittens. Many of my Army comrades used to purchase sketches just like those in Spain and Portugal, to bring back as souvenirs for their wives and sweethearts. I wager that ladies and gentlemen of leisure in town, or at least at their country estates, would appreciate just as much having skilful renderings of the wild Cornish coast to decorate their parlours.'

Miss Foxe immediately reflected his excitement. 'I've seen such drawings times out of mind in the homes of family and friends! Sketches in colour might sell even better—especially of garden scenes or flowers. Eva,' she said, turning back to the child, 'would you like to make pictures with paints or pastels?'

When the child stared at her uncertainly, she exclaimed, 'Heavens, what am I asking her? She's probably never seen a paintbox nor a set of pastel chalks in her life! But we shall change that at once. Perhaps Aunt Foxe has some, and if not, I'll order them from London.'

Turning back to Eva, she took the girl's hands and said, 'Eva, you make wonderful pictures. I'd like you to make lots more of them. Would that please you?'

A slow smile started on the child's face. As if finally daring to believe what Miss Foxe was telling her, she bobbed her head enthusiastically, then launched herself at Miss Foxe's waist and hugged her.

Miss Foxe returned the child's embrace just as fiercely. Though happy for them both, Gabe was feeling a bit envious of Eva, held tightly against Miss Foxe's bosom, when that lady turned on him a smile so much more radiant and intense than any he'd coaxed from her previously that he forgot everything in a dizzying wave of surprise and delight.

'Thank you for driving us here, Mr Hawksworth—else we might never have discovered Eva's talent. Do you truly think we could sell her drawings?'

Still riding that breaker of delight, he would have agreed to anything she proposed. 'I've seen comrades buy much less skilful drawings of places not nearly as attractive as this coastline—and ladies not nearly as beautiful.'

Blushing a little, Miss Foxe clapped her hands in sheer excitement. 'If only we might create a market for Eva's sketches! I have no notion of what price such an item might fetch, but unlike knitted goods, which the girls will need time to learn how to perfect, Eva could have drawings ready for sale at once! Again, thank you so much!'

Staring into her radiant face, Gabe felt just a bit like that perfect knight. A layer of satisfaction, warm and sweet as honey, spread itself over the heady sensual pull that had drawn them together from the first. Gabe couldn't help returning her grateful, confident smile—and wishing this magical moment might last forever.

But the seaman in him had already subconsciously noted the change in the wind and the way the shadows in the cove had lengthened. Though the afternoons were longer now as summer approached, this one was nearing its end.

Reluctantly he said, 'As delightful as this interlude has been, I fear we shall have to leave. It must be fast upon four of the clock.'

Miss Foxe looked around her quickly. 'Heavens, you are right! The sun is so low, nearly the whole cove is in shadow. We must return at once, or my aunt will worry. I can hardly wait to tell her about Eva's skill and all our plans!'

Giving the child one more impulsive hug, she turned to Gabe, her arms still loosely about the girl. 'We both thank you for today, don't we, Eva?'

Burrowing back into the safety of Miss Foxe's arms, the child nodded and made another hand movement.

'She says "thank you", too,' Miss Foxe said softly.

'My pleasure, ladies—to you both.'

And so they gathered up the sketching supplies and climbed back up the narrow track to the gig while the sun waned and the clouds in the western sky began to burnish gold and purple. Before he helped Miss Foxe up into the vehicle, though, Gabe stayed her with a touch.

'One more thing before we go.' Pointing to the sketchbook he was carrying, he said, 'Might I keep your drawing, Miss Eva? With your permission, of course, Miss Foxe.'

Eva nodded gravely, while, blushing slightly, Miss Foxe murmured, 'If you wish.'

I'd rather keep the original, he thought, nearly voicing the comment aloud. To distract himself from blurting out something equally unwise, after helping the ladies into the gig, he occupied himself with carefully removing the drawing from the sketchbook. Then, handing the book up to Eva, he climbed up to the bench, released the brake and gave the horses the office to start.

An hour later, Gabe arrived back at the inn. Miss Foxe was safely on her horse headed back to Foxeden, and Eva had been escorted to the track leading to her house. Gabe ordered a mug of ale and took a chair, idly sipping at the brew while his mind filled with speculation about cargoes and trading routes and contacts with legitimate businesses in Bristol, Gloucester, Bath and London.

It was more important than ever now that he go to London, so he might check at galleries and print dealers, see what was being bought and sold, at what prices. If Miss Foxe's aunt didn't possess any, he needed to purchase pastels and oils for Eva to try. Miss Foxe was right; since coloured sketches and portraits would probably sell better and certainly command a better price than charcoal sketches, it would be prudent to discover if she could produce works in those mediums with the same natural skill so strikingly present in her charcoal sketch.

He also needed to check into dry-goods dealers, drapers, dressers and modistes who might be interested in offering an assortment of knitted gloves, scarves, hats and reticules of superior weave and design.

And he wished to find a frame for the sketch of a certain young lady that now lay neatly rolled on the table before him.

Smiling, he spread it out, feeling somehow closer to her, as if by holding this brief image of her likeness, he possessed some small part of her. Lovely as the silhouette was, if Eva proved to be as talented with a brush as she was with charcoal, Gabe intended to have her do a portrait of Miss Foxe as he remembered her from this afternoon—framed by cliffs and blue sky, smiling for him.

He seemed compelled by some driving need to try to inspire more dazzling smiles from Miss Marie Foxe. Smiles that, along with her enthusiasm, unquenchable spirit and loveliness, were burning her likeness into his mind and heart. Maybe forever.

As a man who'd always resisted being compelled to stay in any one place doing any one thing for very long, that thought ought to terrify him, send him speeding to weigh anchor on the *Gull* and sail out of Cornwall as quickly as his father's controlling hand had propelled him from Ireland.

But somehow, this time, he did not feel inclined to run.

Chapter Thirteen

Honoria galloped back to Foxeden, arriving sufficiently in advance of sunset that neither the staff nor her aunt appeared to have grown uneasy about her absence. She was relieved her aunt would be calm when they met at dinner, for after her interlude with Mr Hawksworth and Eva, Honoria was unsettled enough for both of them.

She went up to her room to prepare for dinner, then changing her mind, sent Tamsyn off with a request that her aunt meet her in the library before the meal, where they might talk privately. Honoria didn't want the whole staff buzzing about her plans for Eva before she determined whether or not they were feasible. After finishing her evening toilette, Honoria repaired to the library to wait for her aunt.

Matrons of a more conventional turn of mind might view with disfavour the idea of dealing with such a child, or dismiss the entire project out of hand. But Honoria knew Aunt Foxe would not prejudge Eva or her skill, but thoughtfully consider before giving her opinion on the concept's value and probability of success.

Anxious as she was to find a way to guarantee a decent income for the Steavens family and make it possible for Laurie to escape the protection of the unsavoury John Kessel, Honoria knew that was not the true reason behind her excess of nerves—but her fraught interlude with a mesmerizing free-trader.

For a moment, she wished the exceptional sketch Eva had produced this afternoon had been a likeness of the captain, so she might have something tangible to remember him by.

Though what could she do with it, if she had obtained one? Hide it in her room, pretending it was just a pleasant example of Eva's skill? Trying to deny the powerful mix of admiration, desire, curiosity and longing Captain Hawksworth inspired in her?

She hardly needed a portrait of him to prompt her memory or induce sighs, so indelibly seared into her being were his image and actions.

She could scarcely touch her palm against the door handle without a reminiscent shiver—and would probably never be able to eat an orange again without heat suffusing her body. Even envisioning the fruit now without its peel led her to inappropriate, erotic thoughts.

How fortunate that Eva had accompanied them that afternoon, she thought as she entered the library. She'd been attracted to the captain from the first—but never with such powerful intensity as today. Had he kissed her after eating that orange from her palm, she would not have objected. Nay, had she not been so conscious of Eva's curious gaze upon them, she would have surrendered to the compelling urge to throw her arms around him and pull him close, ravenous to feel his arms around her, his hard, lean body next to hers.

Ravenous for more. She'd burned to explore other, more hidden places—those manly parts she'd seen often enough when swimming with her brother, who'd never troubled to hide his nudity when they were both children. Parts he hadn't begun masking from her sight until he'd become a young man and caught her staring in fascination at that which had once been small and dangly and was now long and thick.

The thought of exploring Captain Hawksworth's manly

parts made her flushed and a little dizzy. Since she and her mother were not close enough to comfortably discuss intimate issues, she'd been relieved that the shortness of her engagement had spared her receiving from that lady what would doubtless have been an awkward and embarrassing description of the wedding night. Being country-raised, she knew well enough what the coupling of animals entailed and could extrapolate how the human species accomplished the same.

During that brief engagement, she had given some thought to what married life with Anthony would entail. Only a few years her senior, he was generally accounted a handsome, well-made man, and she'd speculated with a mild sense of titillation about exploring his body, having him explore hers. The flurry of excitement and anticipation such thoughts engendered were similar to the sensations she experienced when he kissed her.

The feelings engendered by thinking about kissing the captain were a hundredfold more intense. More acute and breathtaking than the heightened sense of pleasure she'd felt on a few occasions before her engagement, when she'd allowed one of the more dashing bucks to kiss her, the naughtiness of her behaviour and the need to conceal it adding spice to the encounter.

In short, her response to the captain was so markedly more intense than anything she'd known previously that it seemed her knowledge of passion fell into two halves: everything she'd experienced before coming to Cornwall, and the sensations he inspired in her.

If the touch of his hand on hers, of his lips against her palm, worked upon her so strongly, she wasn't sure kissing him was wise. She very much feared that any control she intended to maintain over her subsequent behaviour would disintegrate within seconds—if she indeed survived the initial brush of his lips against her own without fainting or having her rapidly accelerating heart simply beat its way out of her chest, like a sea osprey taking flight.

Just thinking about kissing him made her heartbeat race. As she looked at her palm, halfway expecting to find some trace of him engraved there, her hand tickled and burned. She pressed it against the cool surface of the library table with a sigh.

What was she to do about Captain Hawksworth?

If she feared she could not behave with modesty and decorum around him, so rapidly was her curiosity about, admiration for and desire for his touch and taste growing, prudence dictated that she avoid him.

But she didn't want to avoid him.

Every sense within her that spoke of life and joy and adventure and desire shrieked to be with him again, to experience to the fullest everything his daring, seemingly kindred spirit could offer her. The resulting din of demand was drowning out the calm voice of reason so effectively that she had to struggle more and more to hear its whisper.

Plain and simple, she wanted him. She wanted to touch and kiss and fondle him. She wanted him to touch and kiss and fondle her—and possess her, in every sense of the word.

It was madness.

What difference would it make? the seductive, cunning little voice whispered. *You are ruined already, with a reputation that can never be restored.*

True, the acerbic voice of reason answered. But a ruined reputation damaged only oneself. Giving her body to Captain Hawksworth might result in a child who would be condemned for life by the taint of being born a bastard.

Had the captain laboured under such a stain? It might explain how a man whose speech, dress and such details as he confided about his background, which all suggested a noble upbringing, had ended up at the helm of a Cornish free-trader.

No, disgrace imparted enough of a disadvantage; never would she knowingly extend the damage by inflicting such a burden upon an innocent child.

So honour dictated she avoid him, no matter how much her heart and spirit, as well as her body, clamoured in protest.

Unless he was not only as mesmerized by her as she was by him, but was prepared to make her an offer.

And if he should offer marriage, how would she respond?

Marriage with a free-trader, about whom she knew virtually nothing other than that he had been well educated, served in the Army, was handsome, alluring and seemingly possessed of strong principles of which she approved?

How could she even consider marrying a man who was so wholly a stranger?

But he's not a stranger, a little voice said. *In him, you are coming home.*

There you have it! the rational part of her replied in triumph. Could there be anything more illogical than this instinctive, insidious sense of connection to a man she knew so little? She must wean herself from it!

But logical or not, she didn't want to.

Enough, she would think no more on it! Exasperated, she began to pace the room, from the hearth to the window and back to the bookcases. Halting, she ran her restless fingers along the shelves, straightening and arranging, although in her aunt's well-ordered household there was scarcely anything to straighten or arrange.

She did find one volume whose title seemed to indicate it had been misfiled, tucked as it was among tomes about botany and science. Pulling out a book entitled *Aristotle's Masterpiece,* she was about to return it to the section containing the works of the Greek philosophers, when the subtitle caught her eye.

'The Secrets of Nature Displayed,' she read off the frontispiece. Idly flipping it open, she realized with shock that the book had nothing at all to do with classical philosophy. Instead, beneath her scandalized and very interested gaze appeared a detailed description of the appearance and function of those very manly parts she'd just been contemplating.

A well-brought-up, genteel young maiden like Verity would have slammed the book shut. Fascinated, titillated, Honoria read on.

In precise detail, the book described each part of the masculine apparatus, how it worked and how its performance led to pleasurable coupling. She lingered particularly over the description of that most essential part called the 'yard', a long, smooth cylindrical shaft, sensitive to its tip, which the writer described as 'soft and of most exquisite feeling'.

There followed an equally exhaustive discussion of a woman's parts. Hers began to throb as she read feverishly on, noting those places subject to arousal like a man's, places that that 'close with pleasure upon the yard of the man'. Then, in the poem designed, the writer said, to stir the appetites to a more joyous coupling, the poet urged the lady to take 'his rudder' in her 'bold hand…like a try'd and skilful pilot' and 'guide his bark in love's dark channel, where it shall dance…'

Oh, how she burned to follow that admonition and feel the captain's 'tall pinnacle' within her, ready to 'ride safe at anchor and unlade the freight'.

Though no fire burned on the grate, the room seemed overwarm. Fanning herself, Honoria was turning the page to the next section when an amused voice interrupted her.

'Find some instructive reading, my dear?'

Startled, Honoria dropped the book with a thump and looked up in consternation into the grave face and smiling eyes of Aunt Foxe.

Her aunt righted the volume and closed it carefully. 'A fine, plainly written explanation of the intimate workings of the body. How I wish such information, so readily available to men, could be disseminated as widely to girls! It would make the passage from maiden to matron much less mysterious and frightening for many a bride. Did you find it illuminating?'

'Y-yes,' Honoria stammered, knowing her face must be as scarlet as the hangings at the library windows.

Her aunt chuckled. 'You mustn't feel missish talking with me about it, child. Of course you are curious about such things! You were about to be married, after all; you must have thought about them. Or did Anne ever—'

'No,' Honoria interrupted hastily. 'Mama never said anything.'

'I don't doubt it,' Aunt Foxe said drily. 'How are girls supposed to know what to expect, pray, if no one explains? Though perhaps the best explanation is a demonstration by a loving bridegroom.' Her aunt arched an eyebrow. 'And since I'm still unmarried, you're probably wondering how I came to possess such a book.'

'I wouldn't be so presumptuous,' Honoria said.

Aunt Foxe smiled. 'No, I suppose you wouldn't. Such a kind and discreet child, for all your passion and spirit. But I think perhaps it's time I told you the whole story. Sit down, child.'

Still more than a little unsettled at being discovered mired in lust, Honoria followed her aunt to the sofa. For a long moment, that lady stared silently out the window toward the distant vista of the sea. Honoria began to think Aunt Foxe had reconsidered revealing anything, when at last Aunt turned back to face her.

'Many years ago, while your mother was still a girl, I made my debut. My portion being one of the largest of any maiden then on the Marriage Mart—though it wasn't yet called that— I was much sought-after. But I longed for a man who wanted more than my dowry and a connection to my prominent family. I wanted someone who would appreciate the unconventional spirit in me, the longing for something different and challenging that had always driven me, despite my mother's best efforts to exterminate it.' She paused and looked at Honoria. 'Sound familiar?'

'Why, yes!' Honoria cried, surprised to find how much her aunt's feelings had mirrored her own.

'One day as my chaperone and I were headed for Bond

Street, another vehicle tried to pass ours too closely and locked wheels. Over the protest of my governess, I climbed out to watch as they were disentangled. While the respective coachmen shouted, each blaming the other, a handsome young man in a naval uniform stepped over, called one of the grooms to assist him in disengaging them, then ordered the coachmen to proceed, as they were blocking the street. Since I was standing practically in his path when he walked out of the road, he bowed and I curtsied.'

'And you thanked him for his intervention?'

Aunt Foxe laughed. 'I would have—but after that quick bow, he walked right past me!'

'How disappointing!' Honoria said, expecting a much more exciting denouement.

'I quite agreed,' Aunt Foxe said, a twinkle in her eye. 'So I followed him into a haberdashery and thanked him there. At first he was hesitant to speak with a young lady of Quality to whom he had not been introduced.' Her aunt gave a roguish smile. 'You may not credit it, seeing me now, but in those days I was rather strikingly attractive and possessed of a certain charm.'

'Indeed, I can easily believe it!' Honoria said.

'I persuaded him not only to make my acquaintance, but to accompany me and my chaperone for some ices, where, with some skilful questioning, I discovered he had just been made captain of his first ship.'

She paused, smiling dreamily off into the distance. 'Members of his family had long followed the sea, and though gentry, were far beneath the Foxes socially. But after just that one meeting, I knew he was the only man for me. He was equally enthralled, though because of the difference in our stations, for a short time he resisted the attraction.'

'But you soon persuaded him otherwise?'

'Naturally. My mother, informed of the attachment, for I made no attempt to hide it, was predictably horrified. With my dowry, wit and beauty, she expected a great match for me—an earl, if not a duke. After ringing a peal over me and my poor chaperone, she forbade me ever to see Captain Phillip Manning again. Of course, I disobeyed her as soon as I could get a message to him to meet me the next day. On one of our secret rendezvous, looking ahead to our marriage, he bought me that book.'

Honoria tried to imagine Anthony presenting her with such a gift, and failed utterly. 'Captain Manning truly was as unconventional as you!' she said with a laugh.

'Oh, we were perfectly matched in every way! At first, Phillip had hopes of bringing Mama around, for he was after all a gentleman by birth and so not entirely ineligible. Papa, I think, might have given his consent, but Mama, declaring Phillip nothing more than a jumped-up fortune-hunter, for everyone knew naval officers sought to marry heiresses solely to advance their careers, would have none of him. Convinced it was hopeless and with Phillip's ship receiving sailing orders, since he'd declared his willingness to marry me even if I came to him penniless, we ran away, headed for Gretna Green.'

'But you were discovered?'

Aunt Foxe nodded. 'Mama's brother forced Phillip at pistol-point to give me up. I was sent to the country in disgrace and Phillip went to sea with his ship. Despite my ruined reputation, Mama still hoped, with the inducement of my large dowry, to bring some gentleman up to scratch, but by this time *I* would have none of it. Sent to the most remote family estate in Northumberland, I declared I would neither return to London nor marry anyone but Phillip. When she locked me in my room to try to subdue my spirit, I escaped out the window, broke into the estate agent's office and took some money, disguised myself as a boy and set off for Portsmouth, determined to engage lodgings and wait for Phillip's return. Or to book passage on a ship that would take me to him, if I could determine where that might be.'

'And did you?' Honoria asked, enthralled.

Aunt Foxe shook her head. 'Papa found me first and persuaded me to return to Northumberland, promising to prevail upon Mama to reconsider. My parents' marriage was not a happy one. Papa, who'd always had a fondness for me, did not wish to have me sold into the same sort of arranged, loveless union that family duty had forced upon him, regardless of the shrewish behaviour he would endure from my mother for opposing her.'

Her smile faded. 'But his powers of persuasion were never put to the test. Phillip's ship went down with all hands in a storm…' she pointed out the window toward the wind-tossed sea '…somewhere out there, rounding the coast of Ireland. When I recovered enough from my devastation to think, I begged Papa to bring me to Land's End, so I might go as near as I could get to the last place Phillip had been alive on this earth. We spent several weeks at the inn in Sennlack. Somehow, being here by the sea was comforting, and while I struggled with my grief, I fell in love with the sea, the cliffs, the coast. Convinced I would never marry, I determined to settle here.'

'And your Papa permitted it?'

'Not at once. Mama, of course, was appalled, but Papa remained adamant that if, after a year, I was still as set as ever upon that course, he would grant my wish. So a year later, he settled half my dowry on me, giving me complete control of it with no trustees to interfere. I built this house, and except for a few visits elsewhere, have lived here ever since.'

'And you never met anyone else you wished to marry?'

'No one for whom I was willing to give up the independence Papa had so kindly granted me.' She smiled. 'Until I settled here and assumed the direction of my own life, I never fully realized how restricted I'd been by the conventions Society places upon girls of good family. Another characteristic I believe we share?'

Honoria thought of the times beyond number she'd wished

to have the freedom, the opportunities, the challenges permitted Hal. 'Indeed!'

'However, though I set my face against marriage, I still experienced the urges of the body, for which that handy book, and a few others like it discovered later, served as useful guides. Just because I didn't wish to marry, doesn't mean I wanted to permanently deny myself all the pleasures of the flesh.'

'You mean that you...Aunt Foxe!' Honoria gasped.

'Come now, why so shocked?' her aunt reproved. 'Do you think your elder brother came to his marriage bed untouched? Why should women be censured for indulging desires Society gives men the freedom to savour? Desires that, if I'm not mistaken, you've experienced yourself, or you'd not have found Mr Aristotle's tome quite so fascinating. Am I right?'

There seemed little reason to deny the truth. 'Yes.'

'I also suspect those desires have been inspired by a certain dashing young captain. Who, I believe, is equally enthralled by you. I trust you had a very fine walk on the cliffs with Captain Hawksworth and the child?'

Honoria blinked. 'You knew about that already?'

'Tamsyn is the daughter of the innkeeper at whose establishment the captain resides. She takes a very personal interest in keeping track of him.'

Honoria groaned. 'I hope that won't cause problems among the staff.'

'Oh, I expect not. She's always seen the captain as a dashing hero far beyond her touch. And she likes and admires you. The question is, what do you intend to do about this...partiality?'

Honoria shook her head. 'I don't know.' The new, insistent little voice that whispered of a future prompted her to add, 'Do you know anything of Captain Hawksworth's family?'

'Not a thing. He's gentry-born, I suspect, but not of a degree comparable to the Carlows.'

Honoria sighed. 'So I suspect as well. Even worse, he's a

free-trader! It's a connection that would horrify Papa, Mama, Marcus—probably even Hal.'

Aunt Foxe shrugged. 'Family connections can be highly overrated if they separate you from the one man you will ever truly love. Is Captain Hawksworth that one for you?'

'I don't know!' Honoria said, all the insecurity and indecision and longing and confusion she'd been trying to suppress bursting free. 'I admire and respect him. He possesses a sense of honour and uprightness I would have never had suspected in one who is basically an outlaw.'

'Ah, but not an outlaw in the eyes of a Cornishman,' Aunt Foxe reminded her.

'So he keeps telling me,' Honoria replied ruefully. 'Beyond his character, I feel an…extraordinary attraction. A fascination, admiration—and, I admit, lust. He touches me, pulls me to him more intensely, more completely, than any man I've ever met. He…he might well be the one,' she said, admitting that possibility to herself for the first time. 'But though I know he finds me attractive and enjoys bandying wits with me, I have no firm indication that he intends more than flirtation.'

'So what are you going to do about him—and your future?'

Honoria shrugged her shoulders helplessly. 'I know what I don't want…but I haven't yet figured out what I *do* want, or if it would even be possible to attain it. I know I don't intend to return to London. Nor, like you, do I wish to marry an amenable someone found by Marcus or Mama who graciously deigns to accept to wife a girl of tarnished honour but large dowry.'

'I understand Narborough is too ill to take much of a hand in things, but your brother Marcus always struck me as a fair-minded lad. I don't think he'd force you into something you didn't want, no more than my father did me. By the way, I've just received a letter from Marcus addressed to you, if you'd like to read it.'

Honoria wasn't sure whether she was ready to read something Marcus had written or not. 'So he tracked me down. I didn't think it would take him long.'

'Oh, I expect your coachman told him straightaway where you'd gone as soon as he returned to London.'

A more dismaying thought occurred. 'You accepted a letter—for me? So do the servants and the postmen now know—'

'Heavens, child,' Aunt Foxe interrupted her agitation, 'do you think me a dimwit? When Mrs Dawes brought me the letter, she ventured to observe that perhaps Lady Honoria would be coming to join Miss Foxe. I agreed that was very likely, and would inform her of when the visit was to occur. So your secret is still safe.'

Honoria sighed in relief. 'Thank you, Aunt Foxe. I shall never be able to thank you enough for your kindness, first in taking me in, then in allowing me to perpetrate such an outrageous lie.'

'We sheep of similarly dark hues must flock together. But while you decide what you do wish to do for the future, be careful. The desires discussed in that book—' she angled her head toward the volume still lying on the table '—are very strong. And that book, by the way, was written to instruct midwives and young married couples on the best way to insure conception. Not, perhaps, the best reference for what you have in mind.'

Honoria sighed. 'I'm trying to resist having in mind what I have in mind. But I must confess, the prospect of having no reputation left to lose makes resisting temptation much more difficult.'

'If you are interested, I possess other volumes that discuss ways to avoid conception. However, it would be best for you to first decide what your—and perhaps Captain Hawksworth's—intentions are. Although I would certainly assist you in every way possible, you would not wish to harm an innocent child, especially a child of your own body you could never keep. So don't be foolish.'

She rose and walked to the window, her gaze once again on the distant sea. 'On the other hand, as I can attest, love is a rare gift. The young believe they have all the time in the world. They don't.'

She turned back to face Honoria. 'Though I caution against proceeding recklessly, I would also advise you not to miss the opportunity to experience something precious, something that for some of us comes only once in a lifetime.'

Honoria sat silently, mulling over her aunt's words. 'If you were to do it all over again…would you do the same?'

'Do I regret loving Phillip? *Never.* Would I have run away with him again? *Without question.* Should I have opened myself up more to the possibility of finding another love? On that point, I admit, I'm not quite so sure. I have sometimes been lonely.'

She walked back over to take Honoria's hands. 'But I know I am much happier than I would have been had I allowed myself to be coerced into marrying a man I did not love. My father, to my infinite gratitude, made sure that would never happen to me. And if Marcus declines to do the same for you, I promise I will.'

Feeling the burn of tears in her eyes, Honoria jumped up and hugged her aunt. 'Thank you,' she whispered.

'You are welcome, my dear,' her aunt replied, releasing her, her own eyes suspiciously moist. 'Your presence here has been an unexpected gift to me, too, you know. Imagine discovering after all these years there is someone in the family whose company I truly enjoy! Please know that, if you choose to, you are welcome to stay here at Foxeden permanently.

'Now,' she said, turning toward the door, 'I believe Dawes has been holding our dinner, which we ought to go eat before the roast dries out. And should you decide you wish to consult those…other references, let me know and I will point them out.' Giving Honoria's hand another pat, she walked from the room.

Though she was no closer to a decision about what to do

with her future, knowing she had her aunt's support—and affection—made the queasy knot of uncertainty that had sat in her gut for more than a month ease a bit. If nothing else, she could end her days as her aunt's companion, sharing that restless vista of sea, walking the cliffs, planting herbs—and maybe helping little girls like Eva.

Eva! In all the flurry after discovering the book and her aunt's revelations, she'd entirely forgotten to tell her aunt about Eva and her unexpected talent. She must do so after dinner, so she would know whether her aunt had paints or colours she might borrow to take to the school.

Would Captain Hawksworth come tomorrow to see how Eva's drawing progressed? Her whole being thrilled at the idea of seeing him again, discussing the plans for Eva's future.

As for her own, she might not know yet where the handsome captain fit in, but she did know with a deep certainty that her future could not be settled without resolving her attraction to him. Which left her with both disturbing—and arousing—possibilities.

Friendship? Stolen kisses? A scandalous affair?

Marriage?

She cast another glance at the volume Aunt Foxe had placed back on the table. As mesmerizing and titillating as the information contained within its pages, she had no need of the graphic text in *Aristotle's Masterpiece* to warn her about the power of the urges it described.

Just a short time alone with Captain Hawksworth had been enough for her to discover their potent, mind-dazzling force.

She would have to be very sure she could cope with the results if she permitted herself to allow those appetites free rein. And since Captain Hawksworth had proven himself capable of igniting her desire to a pitch of urgency she was not at all sure she could control, until she had decided how she meant to proceed, she'd better make sure she saw him only in company.

No matter how much her spirits and her senses yearned for him.

Chapter Fourteen

In late morning the next day, Gabe found himself walking toward the vicarage. The purported intent of his visit was to discover from Father Gryffd the current whereabouts of William Darby, the parish clerk, who in Sennlack, as in many Cornish towns, was also the quill master, or keeper of the books, for the smuggling operations.

He wondered for a moment whether the vicar was aware of his clerk's intimate involvement in the enterprise. Confession being good for the soul and confessions heard by clergy being privileged under the law, Gabe concluded he probably did.

Dickin's father the innkeeper, Perren Kessel, who functioned as the venturer by gathering orders and payment for William to record, had told him just this morning that he had collected enough of both to alert their contacts in France to prepare the next shipment. Soon, Gabe would be taking the *Flying Gull* back to sea.

The prospect of matching his wits against wind, wave, storm and possible pursuit always energized him, but this time did not, as it normally did, push all other topics from his mind. Not that the voyage itself concerned him; he'd long ago consigned whatever happened on these ventures to God and fate. If he were meant to be hauled up by a revenue cutter somewhere on dark reaches of the stormy water between here and France, no amount of worry would prevent it, and worry was therefore useless.

However, without being arrogant, he felt confident there was no cutter captain afloat who could capture the *Gull* on the high seas with wind in her sails and him at the helm.

But for the first time, there was someone back in England whose opinion of his ventures mattered. Someone he wanted to think well of him, someone he didn't want worrying about his fate. Unlike the Cornish, Miss Foxe did not possess the contempt the locals had for customs laws or their blithe disregard for the consequences of breaking them.

Doubts about the wisdom of undertaking this enterprise, niggling at him from the first, had needled with increasing force in recent days. Miss Foxe's knight, though perhaps forgiven his flouting of custom laws to the benefit of the poor or lowly, should have an equally noble but more legitimate goal.

The longer he dealt with smuggling operations, the clearer it became that, though Dickin and his father were men of integrity, not all those in the trade were as concerned about the welfare of their neighbours as they were about lining their own purses. Some were bullies with no compunction about hurting anyone who got in their way.

The image of Dickin's brother John came to mind.

Shoving that thought aside, he turned to wondering what, for him, might a more noble pursuit be? He knew he'd won Miss Foxe's approval by undertaking to establish a buyer for the goods produced by the schoolgirls.

But a close involvement with trade, however respectable, would be viewed with almost as much abhorrence by any genteel family—including his own—as a career as an outlaw.

Despite Dickin's encouragement to establish a permanent partnership, he hadn't from the beginning seen this as anything more than temporary, an exciting interlude that returned a favour to a friend while it bridged the gap between recovery from his wounds and—something else. Much as he'd kicked against traces of parental authority as a boy, after viewing the results of the lawlessness unleashed within French-conquered Spain and the necessity for discipline in the Army, he'd developed a new respect for the usefulness of order and regulation.

If his thoughts about the future hadn't been murky enough, along came Miss Foxe to further muddy the waters.

His intentions had been simple enough at first: indulge in an agreeable flirtation with a lovely lady to pass the time and discourage pursuit by some of the bolder local girls. When had that straightforward aim begun to complicate itself into such a compelling...what? Obsession? Infatuation?

He only knew he went through his days inspired to smiles or desire or longing when some act or event triggered memories of her. That when he went to his bed, dreams of giving and receiving pleasure from her warmed his night. That he woke, often hard and aching, to begin thinking of her all over again.

Never with any woman had he considered anything more permanent than dalliance. If—only if—this craving for her didn't fade, as had his craving for every other woman he'd ever fancied, and if he decided he wanted something more lasting, what did this knight have to offer his fair maiden?

The disconcerting conclusion was: not much. He had no profession, no land, not much income. He had expertise as a sailor, but no more interest than Dickin in living his life as a deep-water Navy man. And though he was glad to have contributed his part in ridding the world of the dictator Bonaparte, he'd seen enough of hunting men for prey that a permanent career in the Army did not appeal either.

For most of his life, he'd been driven to escape the bonds that pulled him into becoming a dull country gentleman like the father and brother whose strictures he'd sought to evade. He'd longed for adventure, and in the Army he'd found adventures aplenty. But a nagging imperative, building like a hard lump of indigestion in his gut, said that it was past time for him to decide on a calling and find a place for himself.

One he might be able to share with someone other than a short-term fancy woman.

He smiled, envisioning the real reason for his walk to the vicarage. Miss Foxe should be there, encouraging little girls at their primers and perhaps observing Eva make her first attempt in paints.

It would be easy to become quite fond of having Miss Foxe's palm to lick citrus juice from of a morning, after a night spent pleasuring her in his bed, to be followed by a day going about his work energized by her needle-witted commentary, inspired by her sometimes surprising and always uninhibited interests.

He still could not decide whether he wished to make that pleasant dream a reality. Nor, having no occupation that would support a wife, did he know how he would be able to do so if he did decide upon it.

But then, he wasn't compelled to decide right this moment. He had months yet to sail the *Gull*. It was another fresh spring morning, entirely too glorious to burden his spirits with such weighty reflections. For now, all he need do was anticipate the pleasure of chatting with Miss Foxe. Giving in to the need that pulled him toward her as relentlessly as the needle of the *Gull's* compass sought north, Gabe turned down the lane to the vicarage.

In addition to inquiring about William Darby, he did need to check on Eva, he told himself. Though he'd need to consult some print dealers to be certain, he'd bet the coloured sketches Miss Foxe had proposed having her do would sell more quickly than charcoal ones, and for a better price. If the elder Miss Foxe hadn't had any supplies on hand, he'd have to nip up to London immediately to talk with those dealers and obtain the art supplies needed before the *Gull* was called back to sea.

He was pacing through the garden, heading for the glasshouse schoolroom, when he saw Miss Marie Foxe with the vicar's servant, who was leading out her horse.

His gaze devoured her, lovingly noting each detail. The dark blue riding habit that brought out the sea hue in her eyes. The trim, graceful figure. The intricate arrangement of braids beneath her riding hat, gleaming honey-gold in the sun.

He knew the exact moment she noticed his regard. As if by some unspoken signal—for he hadn't said a word, nor had the horse or servant yet remarked him—she turned. Her rose-pink lips parted in a slight bow of surprise, then curved into the same brilliant smile that had blazed straight to his heart on the moor.

In an instant, he was transported back to the cliffs, to that fraught moment they had gazed at each other: the scent, the taste of her, and oranges sweet and heady in his nose, on his tongue, his every muscle primed to kiss her.

As if mesmerized, he walked to her, took the hand she offered, and brought it to his lips, barely repressing a groan as he brushed his mouth against her gloved fingers. His eager ears caught her whisper of a sigh, his eyes the quick inhale of breath that lifted her breasts closer to his chest.

So entirely focused was he on her, her smile, her nearness, that Father Gryffd's voice behind him made him jump.

She must have been equally entranced, at least he hoped so, for she startled as well.

'...Captain,' the vicar was saying, 'I expect you wanted to check on Eva's progress? I regret to say you just missed her, but I'm sure Miss Foxe can acquaint you with the details.'

'Y-yes,' he answered, befuddled by her nearness. Shaking his head in bemusement, he tried to clear his muzzy brain. 'Indeed, Miss Foxe, I meant to ask you about Eva straightaway. Did your aunt have any paints you were able to borrow?'

'No paints, unfortunately, but she lent us an old set of pastels and Eva demonstrated she could soon become just as skilled in their use as she is with charcoal. Shall I show you her sketches from this morning? Father, if we may?' She gestured toward the schoolroom.

Father Gryffd shook his head. 'Regretfully, I've some parish business I must attend to. But you are both welcome to return to the schoolroom and view Miss Eva's work. Shall I have Mrs Wells send over some tea?'

'Thank you, but I mustn't linger,' Miss Foxe replied. 'My aunt is expecting me home early today.'

No leisurely tête-à-tête? Gabe thought in disappointment. But if a brief chat was all he could get, he'd take it.

'I would like to view the sketches, if you can spare that much time, Miss Foxe.'

To Gabe's surprise, she looked unexpectedly uncertain. As her silence stretched on, he even began to fear she might refuse. The smile he'd surprised from her a moment ago had been as brilliant as yesterday's. What could have produced the sudden chill?

He had no doubt she'd felt the connection—and the potent desire—between them yesterday as keenly as he. Had the power of it disturbed her? Though possessing none of the same reservations about acting upon that attraction that might afflict an unmarried maiden, he supposed he could appreciate her uncertainty about how to handle so potentially dangerous a temptation.

Somehow, he'd have to reassure her that he would never take advantage of her partiality for him to lure her into something she would later regret.

And make sure his eager body understood that promise.

Finally, to his relief, she nodded. 'I expect I could remain a bit longer. Shall we go, then?'

Through their walk to the schoolroom and initial inspection of the drawings, her manner remained constrained, as if she were uneasy about being alone with him. But thankfully—for her hesitance and the retreat back to the cautious, reserved politeness with which she'd first treated him dismayed him more than he wanted to acknowledge—her enthusiasm for Eva's pastel sketches eventually dissipated that constraint.

The drawings were well worth her enthusiasm. Though in the blending and choice of colours, it was obvious the girl was still experimenting, equally obvious was the fact that she displayed a natural aptitude for capturing the hues of light and shadow that rivalled her ability to render line and form.

After showing him the last sketches depicting Eva's cove and the moor with its granite tor beyond the smuggler's hut, she asked, 'Do you truly think we could find someone to handle them?'

'I believe so,' Gabe answered, absurdly pleased that 'we' had returned to her vocabulary. 'I shall have to consult with some dealers in London. I expect the largest number of interested purchasers would be found there.'

Her lovely forehead creased in a frown, Miss Foxe looked away, seeming suddenly uneasy again. Finally, with a sharp sigh, she turned to him. 'This is hardly a topic of genteel conversation, but finding another source of income for Eva's family has become more important than ever.' Though her cheeks reddened, she continued gamely, 'As you may already know, her sister Laurie has accepted an arrangement with John Kessel. I cannot help but worry he will not treat her well. And he dislikes Eva.'

A shock went through Gabe. 'Are you sure about this?'

She nodded. 'Laurie confirmed it yesterday. When I expressed my concern, she told me not to worry—and in any event, that there was nothing I could do. I'm afraid she's right, as long as she is under Mr Kessel's power. But if the family had some other source of income…'

He hesitated, wondering how much to tell her. Finally deciding she deserved the truth, he said bluntly, 'I fear your concern is justified. John Kessel *is* dangerous. The man Laurie was struggling with at the kiddleywink—the one you rescued her from—was found yesterday floating face-down in the bay. The talk was that, stupid with drink, he'd fallen in during the night and drowned. But if John Kessel has made Laurie his woman… He's quite capable of disposing of someone who tried to trifle with a female he fancied.'

She paled a little. 'Then the matter is even more serious than I feared.'

'Probably not at this moment,' he said reassuringly as his mind raced ahead, trying to figure out how he might safely pry Laurie Steavens free of John Kessel's clutches. "Tis early days, so Kessel will likely still be too pleased with her to treat her roughly—and Laurie is too shrewd to do anything that might anger him. But you are right; her sister's situation does add urgency to the quest to discover whether Eva's art work is saleable.'

It also solidified a decision already half-made. In the short period before he must take the *Gull* to sea again, he'd journey to the metropolis. In fact, he'd set out as soon as he reviewed with his first mate the final details necessary to have the *Gull* fully prepared.

Maybe while in London, he could look up some of his Army friends, make some inquiries toward discovering what he might do upon quitting Cornwall. Activities that might allow him, at some point in the future, to legitimately support a wife.

'I would be grateful for anything you could do to help secure Laurie's safety. And now, I suppose I ought to return home,' she concluded with a reluctance that seemed as sincere as his own, easing his fears that he might have inadvertently frightened her away before he'd been able to determine how long he wanted to keep her close.

Certainly he wished to delay her now. He was casting about for some plausible excuse to achieve that when a brilliant idea occurred.

'Eva showed you her favourite place on the coast yesterday. May I show you mine? 'Tis on the way back to Foxeden, so will not delay your return overmuch, and it's at least as lovely as Eva's. I think the location would make a wonderful subject for her landscapes. I know I would purchase a likeness to remember it by.'

The shadow of a frown crossed her face. 'When you leave here, you mean?'

'Yes,' he replied, pleased to have this opening to assure her that he didn't plan to remain a free-trader forever. 'My tenure as skipper of the *Gull* was intended from the first to be limited, until the permanent skipper recovered from injuries suffered during a previous voyage. And you?' he added, thinking he might as well try to discover more about her plans as well. 'Do you expect to make a long stay with your aunt?'

'I'm not sure,' she said evasively. 'I really should be getting back.'

Very well, no more probing, he thought, alarmed by the abrupt chill in her manner. Determined to lure her back before she could retreat too far, he said, 'Why don't I ride with you and point out the spot on your way home? 'Tis quite close to the main road, which isn't surprising, since it features a very early Celtic church.'

She'd seemed on the verge of a refusal, but at the mention of the ancient dwelling—and perhaps its purpose, for one would have to be a very great rogue indeed to try to seduce a maiden in a house of God—she hesitated.

'It won't take long,' he coaxed. 'The church, though no longer in use, is surmounted by an ancient Celtic cross. The inlet beneath it, concealed behind a tumble of boulders, leads through a narrow passage to a small beach overhung by lichen-covered crags. Up on the cliff, I feel as though I can see to Ireland and the New World beyond, while when one is seated on the beach, one can almost breathe in the peace and tranquility.'

She gave him that sceptical look he so loved that said she suspected his eloquent description might be a trifle overstated. 'Very well…if it is indeed on the way.'

An upsurge of delight washed through him. 'Excellent. Give me just enough time to obtain my horse from the inn and we'll be off.'

She agreed, and after chatting with Mrs Kessel over a mug of cider while he fetched his mount, they rode out in the direction of Foxeden. Some half an hour later, the road curved around some granite boulders, beyond which a track led out to the rocky promontory.

'We go the rest of the way on foot,' he announced, pulling up his mount. He tried to keep his touch as impartial as a groom's as he helped her down, despite the tingling surge of warmth in the fingers that held her.

'I discovered these cliffs soon after arriving,' he continued, forcing his mind back to the view he'd brought her to witness. 'As the rocks face north, toward Ireland, rather than west to the ocean, I called them my Irish Cliffs. But now, you must see the church.'

After tethering the horses to a bit of gorse, he led her to the low, round-roofed structure perched near the cliff edge. Built of irregular, un-mortared stone that looked as if it might come apart any moment, it had been constructed with enough care to have withstood the gusts and storms off the sea for some seven hundred years.

'What a marvellous vista!' she cried, gazing out over the magnificent expanse of sea. 'You are right; with the church, the cliffs, the view, it is a most impressive spot.'

He gestured toward the path. 'Wait until you see the cove.'

She set off; he followed, then stood expectantly as she halted where the rocky trail spilled out onto the sand.

'It is lovely—almost enchanted!' she cried. Pacing down the pristine pale expanse, she stopped near a large, sea-smoothed boulder to gaze through the needle of inlet out to the sea. ''Tis almost as I'd imagine a beach in the Caribes; waves lapping a golden shore, water a brilliant azure-turquoise. How I should love to have Eva capture the scene! I'd like a drawing of it myself.'

A wistful look replaced her initial expression of delight. 'You were right; it would be restful to linger here.' She patted the rock beside her. 'Far from observing eyes, lulled by the warmth of the sun and the murmur of the surf while a gentle breeze blew all the cares from my mind.'

The melancholy chord in her voice touched him. *What troubles did she wish to commit to the wind?* he wondered. That powerful need to comfort and protect stirred in him again.

'Have a seat now,' he invited.

She smiled at him. 'Perhaps I will.'

And she did, scrambling onto the rock, seating herself with her skirts tucked around her knees, even removing her bonnet and angling her face into the wind and sun.

Gabe levered himself up beside her, content for the moment, since her eyes remained closed, just to stare at her.

But as his eager gaze examined her, more elemental needs began rising. He struggled against the burgeoning lust, reminding himself that he'd promised if he managed to get her alone, he would not try to seduce her.

But the scent of her, that alluring line of bare skin from neck to throat as she arched her head back, the pert tip of her nose, the bits of burnished-wheat hair pulled loose by the wind…all of it made his hands itch to touch and his lips burn to nuzzle, as desire chipped away at his noble intent.

What would be the harm in one simple kiss? a little voice argued. Kiss her, as he'd longed to since forever, and he might discover if her taste, her touch affected him as profoundly as it had when he'd licked the drops of orange from her palm.

Probably it wouldn't. Probably he'd discover his long time without a woman and the heightened sense of anticipation built by his continual teasing and tempting of her had exaggerated his previous response all out of proportion. One little kiss would set things back in perspective, would demonstrate that her effect on him was no more unique than that of anyone before her, that there was no need to change his life and rush a decision about his future, in order to make a place for her in it.

If during the kiss, he forgot himself and became overzealous, she was perfectly capable of slapping a sense of propriety back in him.

And if she didn't…

The reasons he'd previously enumerated against taking her here and now were growing dimmer by the second.

Suddenly he realized, as his eyes traced lovingly down the line of forehead, nose, lips, that he'd unknowingly leaned so close that his face was mere inches from hers. He continued to watch her, mesmerized by the play of light and shadow over her lips.

Sunlight gave their perfect rounded surface a sheen like the satin of a lady's gown, while when the sun retreated behind a cloud, the appearance changed to a velvet plush.

Which texture would their touch more resemble?

He felt the warmth of her breath on his cheek and realized he'd placed a hand on her shoulder.

Her eyes opened in a flare of surprise, then comprehension—before she leaned up to receive his kiss.

As his mouth touched hers, cider and sweetness and warmth exploded upon his senses, sending a stab of desire straight to his loins. Groaning, he deepened the kiss, his hand clutching her shoulder while he wrapped an arm around to bind her closer, intoxicated by the feel and taste of her, wanting more.

Suddenly, she was pushing violently against his chest. It must have taken a few seconds for that reality to penetrate the rampaging lust dulling his brain, for when he finally realized her invitation had changed to resistance and he let her go, she leapt away from him as if scalded.

She landed on the sand and stumbled a few steps backward, hands to her lips, trembling all over.

The sight of her retreating from him dispelled the warm sensual haze like a slap of cold seawater. After promising himself he'd make no attempt at seduction, had his impetuous action made her fear he intended to force himself on her? The idea filled him with horror.

Before he could order his incoherent thoughts enough to apologize, she burst out, 'Sorry! I'm so sorry. I didn't mean to tease! But when you pulled me close, it brought back memories. D-disturbing memories.'

Her eyes focused on the distant horizon and a tremor went through her. Shaking her head, she laughed a bit hysterically. 'I'm so sorry,' she said again. 'You must think me a complete bedlamite.'

'Not at all,' he assured her, concern and regret pulsing through him. ''Tis I who am sorry. Never would I wish to frighten or repulse you!'

Her attempt at a smile didn't convince him, given the distress that still clouded her eyes. 'You didn't. Indeed, it is my fault entirely. I wanted you to kiss me! I've been wanting you to kiss me practically since the afternoon we met. And when you did, at first I was ecstatic, but then...I never expected...oh, forg-give me!' Her voice breaking, she turned and walked away from him.

While she gave her garbled explanation, Gabe's mind, finally cleared of the last foggy bits of lust, had been racing faster than the *Gull* in a fresh breeze with her topsails set. All that he knew of Miss Foxe—her beauty, her innocent yet knowing allure, his suspicions about the reasons behind her sudden arrival at such an odd time of year in such a remote place, coalesced in one dismaying conclusion.

In two paces he reached her, halted her with a gentle touch to the shoulder. He swore under his breath as she flinched before turning back to face him.

'Did he hurt you?' he demanded, the anger flaming up from deep within him making his voice rough. His rage intensified as shock, then shame, filled her eyes, telling him he'd guessed right.

For a long time she didn't answer, merely stared at him as if unable to break away from the fierceness of his gaze.

Then, after swallowing hard, she said, 'N-no. Not really.' From the moisture welling at the corners of her eyes, a single tear spilled down her cheek.

This time he couldn't restrain an oath. 'Damn the man!' he cried. 'I'd kill him for you if I could.'

She uttered a shaky laugh. 'That's very chivalrous of you, but as the damage done is irrevocable, it doesn't really matter any more.'

'If remembering him makes you recoil at my touch, it matters to me,' Gabe answered hotly.

She gave him a short nod, as if in thanks. 'Sometimes I think about killing him myself,' she said in conversational tones, strolling back from the waves toward the lichen-covered crags beyond.

She paused to pick up a driftwood stick; he trailed behind her. 'Some moonless night,' she continued, 'out the dark of some dim alley, I'd strike—' she brought the wood up like a sword and jabbed it against the rock '—like this. And this and this and this!'

Her voice rose as she jabbed the stick at the unoffending rock again and again, until the soft wood splintered into fragments. Letting go of the shattered hilt, she put her head in her hands, dropped to her knees in the sand and began to weep.

His first, masculine instinct was to retreat and give her time to compose herself. But the sheer anguish in her sobs stopped him in his tracks before he could flee.

Fury engulfed him at the thought that, indifferent to the consequences, some bored or unprincipled or careless rogue had lured her to some secluded place and forcibly seduced her, frightening and wounding that proud, fierce spirit, sending her into shame and exile. As deep and intense as his anger, but more unexpected, came an overwhelming need to offer comfort.

Halfway expecting her to strike at him, gently he gathered her in his arms. To his gratification, though, instead of resisting, she clung to him.

The warmth and scent of her plastered against his body was like the beginning of his favourite daydream, the one that concluded with him removing her garments one by one and gradually acquainting himself with her lips and limbs and breasts. He was rather proud that, except for the inevitable male response to the so-long-anticipated feel of her pressed against him, desire to console continued to triumph over desire of a more carnal sort.

To take advantage of her distress, regardless of whether or not his caresses ultimately gave her pleasure, would be an unforgivable violation, placing him on a level with the reprobate who'd trifled with her. Though while she was still too lost in weeping to notice, he couldn't restrain himself from stroking the silk of her hair and kissing the top of her head.

He wanted her no less than before. Indeed, after clasping the soft curved length of her against him, he wanted her all the more. But if he was to feel the touch of her lips or the intimate embrace of her body, he wanted that to be a choice she made joyfully, while in full possession of her usual high-spirited confidence. Not numbly allowing him to offer mindless comfort in the midst of despair.

So, when her wracking sobs eased to shudders and then ceased altogether, regretful but resigned, he let her go.

She rose on wobbly legs and walked away. He watched her, speculating that having admitted her shame and then lost her composure, she'd be embarrassed, his fierce lady. He'd probably need to reassure her that he thought no less of her for what she had revealed.

That speculation was confirmed when she turned back to him, shamefaced. 'I beg you will excuse me. I suppose females always protest after such a display, but truly I don't normally weep.'

He thought of her flinging herself into sea, launching off to attack a lecherous drunk. 'I know you don't. I feel…privileged that you allowed me to witness how deeply you've been wounded.'

'I expect, after having wetted your cravat and waistcoat, I

ought to explain the whole. It will be…liberating to confess it at last, I suppose.'

'If you want to tell me, I would be honoured to hear it.'

After a sigh so forlorn it made his heart ache, she gestured for him to return to the rock bench they'd shared. Seating herself beside him, she began, 'I left London so precipitously, as I'm sure you've guessed by now, because of a scandal. 'Tis a long, involved story, but I'd quarrelled with my fiancé and, still angry with him, told my elder brother that I intended to show Anthony that if he didn't care about pleasing me, other men did. But to my disgruntlement, he wasn't present at the ball we were both to attend that night to watch jealously while I flirted with my other admirers.'

Gabe felt both a niggling sympathy for the erstwhile fiancé—and a ferocious jealousy.

'Later that night, one of the footman gave me a verbal message, saying Anthony wished to meet me in the hostess's garden. Confident that he wanted to apologize, I hurried out to meet him. But it wasn't Anthony I found waiting for me.'

Her lips twisted in a grimace of revulsion. 'At the far end of a pathway as shadowy and isolated as one of Vauxhall's Dark Walks stood one of the worst reprobates of the Ton. Thinking I'd stumbled on an assignation, I backed away, but before I could regain the path, he grabbed me.'

She shuddered again. 'In what seemed like an instant, he'd bound my hands in a noose of silken rope, declaring he was delighted that I'd decided to indulge in a little illicit play before committing myself to my dull fiancé. When I protested I had no idea what he was talking about and struggled to free myself, he…he said if I liked it rough, he would be pleased to comply.'

'The devil you say!' Gabe cried, unable to restrain himself any longer. 'Only give me his name and I'll put a bullet through him!'

She shook her head. 'Bad as he is, 'twas not completely his fault. I…I had acquired a reputation for being rather fast, daring to pull pranks more conventional young ladies would never consider. Nothing truly scandalous, but I can understand why he might have believed the note sent to him, purportedly from me, to be genuine.'

Gabe frowned. 'He received a note, you say? From whom?'

'I don't know. The note inviting him to dalliance and enclosing the rope asked him to attend the ball and wait for a footman to bring him word to join me in the garden. Apparently a liveried footman did so, just before giving a similar message to me.'

'Your hostess had a part in this?' he demanded in disbelief.

'I don't think so. I believe whoever set this up employed someone dressed like a footman to deliver the messages. For though it seemed I struggled with the rake for an eternity, it couldn't have been too long after that my brother, Anthony and some friends came running down the pathway. Marcus later told me a footman brought him a message, too, supposedly from one of his friends who'd seen me slip away in company with the rake, urging him to fetch Anthony and come find me.'

'And so they rushed to your rescue?'

She smiled grimly. 'Oh, they came—but by then, it was too late to salvage my reputation. You see, once h-he—' Her voice broke and she wrapped her arms protectively about her torso.

'Enough,' Gabe cried, gripping her shoulders, outraged and agonized by her distress. 'You needn't say any more.'

She shook her head vigorously. 'Please, I want…I need to continue. If I may?'

Too outraged to trust himself to words, Gabe merely nodded.

She took a deep, steadying breath. 'Once he had me immobilized, he no longer seemed even to hear my protests. I fought him off as best I could, struggling, kicking, biting, but that only seemed to inflame him more. By the time we were discovered, he'd ripped the front of my bodice and torn my skirts.'

'And your brother didn't kill him on the spot?' Gabe demanded in disbelief.

'I expect he was more interested in hurrying me away before the crowd of gentlemen with him got a closer view. Besides, when Marc challenged him, the rogue proclaimed loudly that I'd invited him to meet me—and surely a gentleman ought not to disappoint a lady? He'd released me and tossed away the rope as soon as he saw the crowd approaching, and from the titters at that remark and the leers on the men's faces, I could tell they believed him.

'Those faces,' she repeated, her voice fading to a whisper while her eyes, wide and anguished, gazed sightlessly at the horizon. 'I shall never forget them.'

'Then your brother led you away?' Gabe demanded, approving at least that part of her sibling's conduct.

'Y-yes,' she replied, returning to the present. 'Marcus lent me his coat and walked me through the crowd of men…all still watching me.'

'But once he'd gotten you safely away, didn't he go back and deal with the rogue?'

'He was too furious. He knew I'd been angry with Anthony and believed that, in an ill-judged fit of pique, I had indeed asked the man to meet me. When I tried to protest my innocence, he refused to believe me, saying it was incredible to suppose anyone else would have had either reason or means to construct so bizarre a plan. He chastised me,' she continued, her voice growing bitter, 'for trying to evade the blame for embarrassing the family and creating so appalling a scandal.'

She hopped off the rock and paced down the beach. 'Bad enough that Marc thought me stupid enough to have concocted such a mutton-headed, dangerous scheme,' she said, halting to look back at him, hurt and indignation in her voice, 'but then to accuse me of *lying* about it! Whatever silly stunts I'd pulled, and I admit, there'd been a few, I'd never given him reason to doubt my word.'

The anger seemed to leave her as swiftly as it had come. 'I left London at once, of course, but not for our country estate as Marc commanded. Being somewhat displeased with the men of my family, I chose to seek refuge here, with my mother's Aunt Foxe. She's a bit of a rebel herself, as you may have heard,' she added with a slight smile. 'She was kind enough to take me in. So here I remain, a ruined and abandoned woman.'

'Your fiancé did not stand by you?'

She uttered a derisive sniff. 'No. His was one of the outraged, leering faces the night of my disgrace. He couldn't wait to rid himself of me.'

'Then his behaviour is only marginally better than the rogue's,' Gabe declared, disgusted by a man who would fail to support the woman to whom he'd been promised, at least until he could uncover the whole truth of the matter. 'You deserve better!'

She waved a hand dismissively. 'Perhaps. Anyway, I appreciate your indulgence in allowing me to recite my sad little tale.' She gave a mirthless laugh. 'Though instead of an understanding shoulder to weep upon, perhaps you should have given me a quick slap to the head. I expect we'd best be leaving now.'

She turned toward the path to the cliffs. But Gabe was not about to let her brush off the harrowing experience and walk away, diminishing what had so deeply wounded her, what she'd trusted him enough to share.

'It's not too late, you know,' he said after her.

She stopped and raised a quizzical eyebrow. 'Too late?'

'To find out who was responsible for bringing you and the rogue to the garden, then alerting the others. Not too late to find—and punish him. I'll even lend you a sword—although you may have to arm-wrestle me for the privilege of running the wretch through.'

For a moment she stared at him through lashes that were still wet with tears.

'Are you suggesting we—'

'Look further into this? Find out who planned and executed it? Yes, I am. Damnation, someone went to a very great deal of trouble to ruin you. Even if you don't want to exact revenge, don't you at least want to know who—and why?'

She stared silently at him for a long moment. 'You would...do that for me?'

He made her a bow that would have done a courtier proud at a Queen's drawing room. 'Consider it a matter of honour. Now, with whom, besides your fiancé, had you quarrelled recently? Who might stand to gain from your disgrace? Who was present in the garden that night? Tell me everything you can remember.'

Chapter Fifteen

Hesitant, her heartbeat racing, Honoria stood motionless, staring at Captain Hawksworth. She ought to feel humiliated, after having just laid bare before the man whose admiration she most wished to retain the whole tawdry tale of her ruin. Instead, though, she felt...free.

He had offered her comfort, even after the absurd way she'd behaved, pushing him away like a prim dowager outraged by a tipsy roué's attempt to steal a kiss. Pushed him away, after all her lusty imaginings over the shape and size and feel of his masculine parts and how he might ply them and how she might assist him.

Still, the wave of fear and revulsion that had swamped her when his arms closed around her—completely unanticipated and without warning—had been irresistible. Panic lending her strength, she'd felt she would suffocate if she didn't get free, get some air, put some distance between them.

Obviously the attack by Lord Barwick had wounded her far more deeply than she'd suspected. Perhaps she'd been wrong to repress the memory and refuse to acknowledge her distress over it. Perhaps it was inevitable that eventually her tight-fisted grip over those events would weaken and the whole flood of anguished memories would come pouring forth—as they had today.

Having revealed all the sordid details that until now she'd hidden from everyone, she felt curiously washed clean. And contrary to her expectations—expectations partly responsible for her reluctance to confess to anyone what had happened—instead of looking at her in disgust, as Anthony had that night, Captain Hawksworth had been outraged on her behalf.

More precious than comfort, he was now extending to her something not even Aunt Foxe, who believed her story and sympathized with her plight, had offered: a chance to discover who had done this to her and why.

She felt a surge of energy and excitement. Instead of being simply a hapless victim, a tool of some unknown master hand, she might fight back. And if obtaining justice were not possible, she might at least hope to look with cold contempt into the face of the person who had destroyed her life.

Humbled, grateful, she said, 'I'm not sure what I remember.'

'Then since your aunt expects you shortly,' he replied, gesturing toward the rock, 'you'd better sit down and get started.'

She climbed up beside him again and cast her mind back to the events of those last days in London. 'With whom had I quarrelled?' She sat silent a moment, thinking, then shrugged. 'I can't recall a serious argument with anyone but Anthony. As for who might profit from my disgrace, I don't know that my downfall would benefit anyone. Oh, to be sure, there were young ladies jealous of my success among the gentlemen, but as I was already engaged, it's not as though I had just stolen a duke or marquess from under some damsel's nose. And even if I had, what female would have the resources to accomplish a scheme as complicated as this? Even after the relatively limited contemplation of it I've been able to endure, reviewing the events led me to conclude it must have been a man's doing. But for what reason, I still cannot imagine.'

'Had you any jealous suitors who might have wished to strike back at you for choosing to wed another?'

'I'd considered that. But though I had a great number of

admirers, some of whom professed themselves devastated by my engagement, I believe their protestations were mere gallantry. Most were dashing bucks who much prefer flirtation to treading a path toward the parson's mousetrap. Nor can I remember slighting anyone who might feel so spurned as to justify taking such a revenge, or repulsing anyone at all who appeared calculating enough to create so elaborate a plan. Unless he were playing a very deep game indeed.'

Captain Hawksworth nodded slowly. 'What of your family—might they have any enemies who sought to strike back at them through you? Someone with a sister seduced? A married woman whose affair embarrassed her husband or her family?'

Though her initial response was to laugh at the absurdity of such a notion, Honoria made herself consider the possibility. 'I don't think so,' she said after a moment. 'My father has been in uncertain health for years and, in any event, is devoted to my mother. My elder brother is the epitome of uprightness; I can't imagine him taking advantage of a woman, maiden or married. Now, my younger brother...'

'The Army man?'

'Yes.' She smiled, her heart warmed, as always, by thinking of Hal. 'He's accounted a rogue and a rake, but as far as I know—such escapades are usually screened from maidenly ears—his excursions among the fair sex have always been limited to willing widows and ladies of broad experience.'

'Anything else you can recall? A quarrel between families?'

She paused a moment, grasping at a thin shred of memory. 'There was some sort of scandal that occurred back in my father's day—though I'm not sure I'd even been born yet when it occurred. There was some trouble about it again a few months ago, but it all died down. We children were never told very much in the first place, and what little we were told I no longer remember.' She shrugged her shoulders. 'Perhaps I could ask Aunt Foxe.'

He nodded. 'That might be helpful, or further details may

occur to you later. Let's move on to the night of the ball. Who, besides your brother and fiancé, do you remember from that night?'

She sat back, scanning a series of memories in her mind. 'Papa wasn't feeling well, so Mama remained at home with him. Our former governess, Miss Price, had run off and married and Mama hadn't yet engaged another one, so my sister Verity and I were escorted by my brother Marcus. Lady Dalrington's ball was attended by the usual set. No one who seemed to be watching me. No one who seemed angry with me.'

She shook her head again, frustrated by her inability to recall anything out of the ordinary. 'I'm sorry; none of this can be of much help.'

'Who besides your brother and fiancé came to the garden?'

Clenching her teeth, she forced herself to remember—and found most of what occurred after Lord Barwick released her to be a nightmarish haze. 'That I truly don't remember well. Some of Anthony's friends, I suppose.' She shuddered as one figure detached itself from the fog. 'Viscount Keddinton, an associate of Father's I've never liked—he has the sort of pale eyes that look right through one.'

'Could there have been a disagreement there?'

'I don't think so. He still advises the family. Indeed, he's my sister's godfather.' One who, as they'd grown to woman-hood, looked at both her and Verity with something in his eyes they'd found disturbing, though since his behaviour remained impeccable, neither had ever mentioned that fact to their brother.

'Marcus probably asked him to come lend his support,' she continued. 'Besides, even if he disliked me for some fault of which I was unaware, I can't imagine what benefit my ruin would afford him.'

'No one else you can remember?' When she shook her head, he said, 'What happened after your brother arrived?'

She scanned her memory, the process a bit less agonizing

this time, though she had little more success identifying the sequence of events than she'd had in attaching identities to the pale faces leering out of the darkness. 'After fighting desperately, suddenly I was free. Marc was there, ripping off his coat and thrusting it around me. Shouting an exchange with the rogue, then hurrying me down the pathway to the coatroom. I stood shivering while he fetched my wrap, handed him back his own coat after I'd pulled the cloak over the tatters of my gown.'

Suddenly the other memory occurred. 'My cloak! I didn't discover this until days later, on the journey out of London, when I took my handkerchief from the little pocket I'd had made in its lining—and found a curious piece of glass. Though not unique, such interior pockets are uncommon enough that someone, doubtless the perpetrator, must have made a special effort to find that place to hide the stone, intending for me not to find it until later.'

The captain angled his head at her. 'A piece of glass?'

'Yes—with a meaning that was easy enough to decipher as soon as one examined it: facetted and polished on one side, rough and unfinished on the other. A reminder that I, who had been accounted a *Diamond* of the Ton, was now no more valuable to society or my family than a worthless lump of glass.'

The captain had been shaking his head in bemusement when suddenly his body tensed and his eyes widened. 'Facetted like a *diamond,* you say? Does the family name of Carlow mean anything to you?'

Shock coursing through her, she stared at him, speechless. Had he guessed her identity? If so, how?

Uncertain what he knew, she said cautiously, 'I am…related to the Carlows. Why do you ask?'

'I met a Gypsy trader at the inn here by the name of Stephano Beshaley. He said he specializes in diamonds, had important London connections—and claimed that he'd gotten the better of a prominent London family named Carlow. Tall, slender, elegant fellow, dressed rather flamboyantly. English features, but with a bronzed skin and faintly foreign air that spoke of his Gypsy heritage.'

While the captain described the trader, a shadowy recollection crystallized in her memory. 'A gem trader? Yes, I remember encountering such a man at the jeweller's the day Anthony and I quarrelled! He had provided the stones for a parure the jeweller showed us, one I liked very much, for the design was lovely and set with very fine diamonds indeed. The dealer bowed to us when the jeweller acknowledged him, though I don't believe we were ever given his name.'

Just then another image filled her head—a detail she'd not previously noted among the fog of events that awful night. 'He was there, too, that night in the garden!' she cried. 'At the edge of the crowd. A dark, slightly foreign face I didn't recognize until just now. Perhaps he planted the stone in my pocket.'

'Could he have engineered the whole scheme?'

Honoria shook her head. 'What possible reason could he have for doing so? A man not even of my world? But he was certainly there in Lady Dalrington's garden. I suppose he might have been hired to place the stone in my cloak by the same person who engaged the false footman to deliver messages. The man who did plan and set in motion the whole.'

'You are sure he's not more immediately involved? If he's part Gypsy, he'd believe in revenge, if one of your family had done him or any of his clan an injury.'

'I suppose it is possible, but I can't imagine who or why. My mother owns some exquisite jewellery, but mostly family pieces passed down through generations. Marcus probably bought some things for his bride, and most assuredly Hal needed baubles for his various *chere amies*, but I can't imagine either of them not offering fair value or failing to pay in full. And what if they had? Even for a Gypsy, the ruin of a sister for the failure to pay a debt seems a bit extreme.'

He smiled. 'You're right. We had a tribe camp on family land one summer, and though they could be a hot-blooded, argumentative lot, very careful of their horses and their women, they had a scrupulous sense of honour, according to their lights. Still, you are sure there was a slightly foreign gem trader in the garden that night.'

She nodded. 'Yes, I'm certain.'

'Then we shall start there. Though I should like to have a word with your brother! Had he started an inquiry immediately, we'd not be looking at a trail that's had more than a month to cool.'

'I wouldn't have thought it possible a few weeks ago that I'd be defending Marcus, but I see much more clearly now why he behaved as he did. With his new wife in an interesting condition and my father so delicate, he would have been frantic with worry about the deleterious effects the scandal might have on their health. And outraged over how the debacle would adversely affect my younger sister's prospects.'

She paused a moment, recalling Marc's letter, still sitting unread on her desk, and forced a small, painful smile. 'If I hadn't been so heedless and unmanageable, so often involved in small scrapes of one sort or another, perhaps he would have given more credence to my protests of innocence. As it is, I can understand how, angry and worried as he was, he would find it easier to believe that I'd foolishly set these events in train than to think that some unknown someone, possessed of no motive we've yet been able to determine, had devised so outlandish a scheme.'

And after all their discussion, the only clue she had produced to find the perpetrator of that scheme was a Gypsy gem trader who probably couldn't be traced. Her initial excitement fading, she admitted, 'I have a hard enough time giving it credence myself, and I know absolutely it is true.'

He nodded, smiling wryly. 'Sometimes the truth *is* incredible.'

Was he speaking of her or himself? she wondered. 'In any

event, I don't fault Marc for sending me away. He was justified in being ashamed of my conduct and in chastising me for the damage it could do my sister's prospects.'

His arresting blue-eyed gaze holding her own prevented her from dropping her eyes. As the embarrassment of having admitted her shortcomings reddened her cheeks, the captain shook his head.

'Heedless in your behaviour or not, your brother should have trusted more in your honour.'

His confidence in that honour touched her deeply. Blinking back a sudden burn of tears, she said, 'I was not unwilling to leave London, if doing so quickly would help contain the damage. My sister is so earnest and proper, she often drove me to distraction, but she is also loyal and sincere. I recognize now that I never valued her as I ought.' She sighed. 'Perhaps one must lose something before one appreciates what one had.'

'Like place and privilege?' the captain said, an odd faraway look in his eye.

'If you only knew how little I value those! But one's honour, one's secure, familiar place in the world, things one has taken for granted all one's life…You cannot imagine beforehand what a blow their loss will be.'

He looked struck by that comment, as if realizing for the first time its simple truth. Giving his head a little shake as if to clear it, he said, 'I suppose you will not tell me the name of the rake?'

'I will not. Despite my earlier words, what good would it serve to try to punish him? Not that his behaviour was any less offensive, but in this scheme he was just as much a pawn as I was.'

'Except he got away unscathed.'

'Such is the way of the world,' she replied with a shrug, too conscious of that truth to feel more than a brief flare of resentment. 'The lecher escapes, for to prosecute him would only further publicize the scandal, without bringing to light the one who is truly guilty.'

'I suppose,' he said grudgingly. 'Though a hard-fought match with a foil would do a great deal to relieve one's frustration with that truth.'

She smiled. 'If this mystery is ever solved, I might claim that prior right you mentioned and avail myself of one.'

She lifted her face to see his sombre gaze still on her. And then, as if by her confessions she'd peeled away the ragged, frayed edges of her anguish just as she'd stepped out of her ruined gown that infamous night, the sharpness of her sadness and despair eased. Rising above the diminishing distress, she felt the renewed physical pull of his nearness—and a new, fragile sense of trust.

Here was a man who had listened to her most shameful revelations and not turned away. A man who appeared to believe in her more completely and resent the wrongs done to her more ferociously than any of her blood kin, save her aunt.

A man who had held her as implacably as Lord Barwick in the garden—and desired her no less, but who had released her from an embrace she had invited without a word of reproach. Who had offered comfort, holding her close, his embrace gentle and devoid of any hint that he might try to take advantage of her distress and proximity.

As she gazed up at him, his face once again so near hers, desire coiled in her belly. This time, however, trust and a sense of gratitude augmented the affection she already felt for this man, intensifying the sensual tension between them with a complex emotional layer.

Suddenly she wanted to kiss him again. Not just to savour the feel of his lips on hers, though most assuredly she wanted that, but even more to prove to herself and to him that she could give herself into his arms without fear.

'Thank you for believing in me,' she said softly.

Lost in the mesmerizing sparkle of those blue, blue eyes, at the last moment, she leaned up until her mouth met his.

Chapter Sixteen

Though all his instincts assured him of the truth of it, at first Gabe couldn't quite believe, after the distress she'd so recently suffered, that Miss Foxe would once again offer the kiss he'd been burning to give her. Even after the first soft contact with her lips sent a glorious explosion of sensation racing to his every nerve, it required an instant for his jangled brain to conclude that what he was experiencing was real and not just a vivid fantasy.

In the last bits of lucidity before his brain switched off and he gave himself up to pleasure, a profound sense of awe and gratitude suffused him at the trust she displayed, a tribute to his honour more profound than any he'd ever before received.

This time, he would not betray that trust. He would handle her with so light and undemanding a touch that the nightmare of struggling to escape another man's unyielding grip would remain buried in the past. He'd make new memories to replace the old, memories of such purity and tenderness that she neither could nor would ever wish to forget them—or the man who created them.

So, though she'd initiated this embrace, this time he held himself rigidly still, hardly daring to breathe, locking his fingers together behind his back to resist the urge to wrap his arms around her and pull her closer. Robbed of the feel of her against him, he concentrated all his passion and artistry instead on that single point of contact: his lips against hers.

He brushed them softly, nuzzled their fullness, alternating between a feather-light slide and a warmer, deeper pressure. Delight as well as desire expanded in his chest, set his heart-beat roaring in his ears. But though he was as achingly hard as he had ever been, he found himself strangely content with this limited, leisurely exploration, able to hold the ravening need for fulfilment under control with unexpected ease.

Dimly, he noted her breathing coming more quickly, saw that luscious bosom rising and falling so temptingly close to his chest. Encouraged by her response, he allowed himself to open his mouth and apply a wetter brush against her lips, then used his tongue to trace their outline from one dimpled corner to the other.

Though his arms shook with tension in their locked position, he told himself he could go on kissing her forever, taking no more than she was willing to offer, the poignant sweetness of her response enough in itself, though he knew he would not be able to fully slake today the desire she enflamed.

Then she moaned and opened her mouth to him.

He groaned as well, almost overwhelmed by the need to plunge his tongue inside and plumb that velvet softness. Sweat breaking out on his forehead, he probed just a little deeper. Just to give her a taste and a promise of how much more there could be.

Gradually he deepened the kiss, exploring her mouth and enticing her with light, teasing touches of his tongue. To his delight, she joined in, pursuing his tongue with her own, engaging it in a delectable series of thrusts and parries that pushed him almost to the brink, though still they touched only with their lips.

Until she leaned close and wrapped her arms around his neck. Slowly, so as not to startle her, he brought his own arms around to cradle her against him. Though his heart was thumping against his ribs with the force of the waves slamming his ship's hull in a gale, he made himself keep each movement slow and gentle.

Then, with a breathless sigh, she fitted herself against him, and he knew he must move away or be lost. His body screaming in protest, trembling all over, he forced himself to step back.

To his gratification and delight, she looked as confused and bereft as he by his retreat, her eyes glazed and uncertain, her mouth lush and red from his kisses. It took all the will he possessed not to succumb to his body's demand that he resume kissing her—and this time, take her all the way to completion.

Instead, his breathing ragged, he leaned over to nuzzle the tip of her nose. 'Now 'tis my turn to thank you,' he said, his voice as unsteady as his breathing.

'I think that thanks should be mutual,' she replied in a shaken voice.

'You cannot begin to imagine how much I'd like to persuade you to remain here with me, but you should get home before your aunt begins to worry.'

'I suppose I must,' she said on a sigh, looking gratifyingly regretful. 'Thank you again for being so kind—and so prudent.' She laughed. 'As you've just learned, prudence has not previously been a virtue of mine.'

'Nor of mine. Perhaps we can improve each other.'

'I like the sound of that.'

He offered his arm. 'Shall we get started, then?'

Still bound in the intensity of the moment, they climbed back up the path to the stone church in companionable silence—if one could term *companionable* a state in which every instinct screamed at him to halt, pull her back into his arms and resume where they'd left off. But for now, restraint was preferable, until such time as Miss Foxe herself indicated she was ready to lead them further.

Reaching the tethered horses, he helped her up. Ah, how he savoured the zing that raced through him when his hands clasped her waist, lifting her slight weight!

'You intend to investigate?' she asked as she wheeled her horse toward Foxeden.

'Yes. Locating the gem dealer would be the first step. What was the name of the jeweller's, by the way? The one where you first encountered the dealer?'

'Phillips, on Bond Street.' Hesitating, she stared at him a moment as if to speak before finally saying, 'If you should get to London, you won't attempt to contact the Carlows, will you? As you might expect, I'm not in very good favour with them at the moment.'

'No, I'll not try to communicate with your distinguished relations without first asking your leave. Certainly not until I have more than unsubstantiated suspicions to offer them.'

Looking relieved, she said, 'Thank you. I suppose I shall reconcile with them in time, but for now, I'm not ready.'

'If their support was anything like that given you by your brother,' he said with a grimace, 'I can understand your reluctance to contact them!'

'I can assure you it was exactly like his,' she replied drily. Her mare danced impatiently, and with a quick move, she quieted her. 'I suppose there is nothing further to say now but to thank you again for your kindness and for showing me this splendid place! If you do not object, I shall certainly bring Eva to sketch here.'

'Please do so! I should love to see the results of her work. And *I* shall try to have some results for you very soon.'

Though she looked highly dubious, she smiled at him before, with a little wave, she touched heels to the mare and cantered off.

Holding his own mount motionless, Gabe watched her until horse and rider disappeared around the next bend. Why did he have the ridiculous feeling that his heart rode with her?

Setting his own beast in motion, he rode toward the *Gull,* scarcely noting the wild beauty of the cliffs as he ticked off the list of tasks he must complete for his journey.

The conversation had cemented his intention to leave for London immediately. If he set out at once, he might complete the transit by mail coach in no more than a week.

Gabe smiled wryly. In his preoccupation with Miss Foxe, he'd entirely forgotten his intention to consult William Darby about the *Flying Gull's* next voyage. Well, that would have to wait.

Miss Foxe had mentioned asking her aunt about the old scandal. Perhaps he, too, should consult with her aunt before he departed. Having spent little time in London, he was not well-acquainted with the prominent families there and would probably not have access to anyone who might know about the affair—or be willing to speak of it if they did—to one wholly unconnected with the Carlows.

He'd go to Foxeden tomorrow, call on her Aunt Foxe and discover whatever she might know that would help him in his quest.

Though the highest-born lady in the neighbourhood had always treated him cordially when they met at church or she took a glass of cider at the inn, Gabe had no illusions that she would receive him like a guest—or welcome a connection between him and her niece, however tainted her current reputation. From what he'd observed, however, she appeared very fond of her kinswoman, and when he explained his intent, would probably be willing to give him as much information as she possessed to assist in discovering who had wronged Miss Foxe.

She'd not be quite so disapproving of his friendship with her niece if he were to reveal his true status, but the fewer people in Cornwall who knew about that, the less likely any whisper of his activities would get back to his brother. Nigel, if he found out Gabe's current occupation, would probably have no compunction about calling out troops to track him down and haul him back to Ireland before his capture on the high seas or imprisonment brought scandal upon the family.

Knowing how strong was his yearning for Miss Foxe's company, if he wished to avoid the temptation to linger at Foxeden, he'd better pay his call in the morning, when he knew she would be assisting Father Gryffd at the schoolhouse.

With a rough outline of what he intended to do next clear in his mind by the time he reached the inn, Gabe turned the horse over to a stable boy and set to work.

After toiling well into evening to settle the last details with his crew aboard the *Gull* and pack up his belongings, Gabe waited until mid-morning to set out for Foxeden, wanting to be sure his Miss Foxe had already left for the school and that her Aunt Foxe would be up and able to receive him. On the ride out, he amused himself wondering how the elder Miss Foxe would settle the difficult protocol of where to receive a local hero who was nonetheless, as far as she knew, well beneath her rank socially.

His curiosity was satisfied when, after being cordially bid welcome by the butler, he was escorted by a pretty, blushing maid he recognized as Dickin's sister Tamsyn into a small back parlour. Probably the same room in which she received solicitors and tradesmen, Gabe figured.

Aunt Foxe impressed him by not keeping him waiting. 'Although I am flattered to have my company sought out by such a handsome and well-thought-of young man,' she told him, walking in a few moments later, 'since you have been some time in the neighbourhood without calling previously, I conclude that your visit today concerns my niece?'

After bowing, he replied, 'It does, ma'am. As you are probably aware, Miss Foxe and I have become acquainted through our work at Father Gryffd's school. I am privileged to have been offered her friendship, and yesterday, she further honoured me by informing me about the events that brought her to Cornwall. Information that I am sure disturbed you as much when you learned of it as it did me.'

'My niece—Miss Foxe—told you how she came to be in Cornwall?' Aunt Foxe asked, eyebrows raised in surprise.

'Yes, ma'am. I feel, as you certainly must, that she has been disgracefully used! As a man of honour outraged by injustice, I believe someone should attempt to rectify the wrong done to her, or at least to try to discover the identity of the person or persons responsible. I'm asking for your help in doing so.'

For a long moment, Aunt Foxe studied him, as if weighing what he'd just said. Finally she replied, 'What did my niece tell you?'

Gabe appreciated her caution; Aunt Foxe was a shrewd lady, not about to be flattered by a handsome man's visit into rashly betraying a confidence.

Briefly Gabe related the facts Miss Foxe had revealed to him: the quarrel, the summons to a garden rendezvous, the waiting rake, her discovery in a compromising position by the crowd of gentlemen that spelled her ruin.

Aunt Foxe nodded as he listed each point. He then added the additional information about the Gypsy gem trader Miss Foxe had recalled for the first time during their discussion yesterday.

'You have quite obviously won my niece's trust, Captain Hawksworth—a considerable feat, given her recent experiences,' Aunt Foxe said. 'Just what do you intend to do with it?'

'At the least, I'd like to uncover the circumstances that led to this foul attack upon her and track down the perpetrator. I haven't enough legal background to know if she has any remedy in law, nor enough familiarity with London Society to know whether, if her innocence could be proven, she would be restored to her former position. But I intend to do what I can.'

She nodded. 'You are correct in assuming I was as appalled as you were when she first revealed to me the circumstances behind her flight to Cornwall. I would be happy to assist your investigation in any way possible. What did you want of me?'

'It appears the Gypsy might have been hired by the perpetrator, and tracking him down must be my first task. Miss Foxe cannot think of anyone who would feel such animosity toward her as to feel moved to bring about her ruin. I tend to agree, and believe there must be some other explanation, perhaps someone who had a disagreement with her family. She mentioned that there had been some sort of scandal involving her Carlow relations during her father's time, an event about which she has no clear memory. Do you know anything of it?'

'A scandal involving her…Carlow relations?' Aunt Foxe asked. When he nodded, she continued, 'It never occurred to me that what transpired a few weeks ago might be connected to that earlier event.'

'What happened, then?' Gabe asked eagerly.

'I'm sorry to say I know almost nothing,' Aunt Foxe admitted, 'other than that my niece Anne—miss, ah, Marie's mother, was most upset over it. To escape the gossip in London, she brought the children here on one of their rare visits. Living so remote from the London social world, I'd not heard much about it, and not being upon terms of intimacy with Anne, I never inquired, nor did she offer any detailed explanation.'

Gabe's initial hopes dwindled with her admission. 'Well, I shall post up to London in any event. Is there anyone there with whom I might speak who might remember?'

Aunt Foxe's eyes lit. 'I can send you to my good friend, Lady Alicia Porter. She resides in London and knows everyone of consequence. If some great scandal occurred, Alicia would surely know of it—or know someone who does. If you can wait a moment, I will write you a note of introduction.'

'Of course,' Gabe replied.

'I shall be back directly.'

Wondering with growing hope and excitement what information her friend might possess, in the few minutes until Aunt Foxe's return, Gabe paced the room.

'I appreciate this exceedingly, ma'am,' he said, walking over as she entered to take the sealed note she held out.

'My niece is very dear to me,' she replied. 'I would do anything in my power to assist her. May I ask, Captain Hawksworth, why *you* are doing this for her?'

'Because I admire her. Because so flagrant an injustice perpetrated against an innocent outrages me. Because even if the wrong cannot be righted, if I can offer her a reason for it, she may find living with the consequences a bit easier to bear.'

'You admire her, you say. Do you realize that, should your quest be successful, her innocence proven and her position in Society restored, you would be returning her to a life that would distance her from you, probably resulting in the permanent loss of your friendship?'

'You mean that Miss Marie Foxe, a connection of the influential Carlow family, would be far above the touch of a Captain Hawksworth of the *Flying Gull*?' Gabe asked bluntly. 'Yes, I realize that.'

'I think perhaps you more than just *admire* her,' Aunt Foxe said softly.

Just how deeply engaged his emotions were, Gabe didn't truly know yet himself. He did know he cared passionately about Miss Foxe's welfare and that resolving her predicament had inspired him to the fervour almost of a holy quest, one he simply had to pursue.

Of course, with his true position in Society being a good deal more elevated than Aunt Foxe was aware, he had hopes that even should her niece's reputation be restored, as long as he left Cornwall without destroying his own, he might entertain some hope of a future for them.

However, since he wasn't prepared to reveal any of this yet, he said simply, 'What man could encounter such a brave and vibrant spirit and fail to fall under her spell?'

'She does possess a brave and vibrant spirit, one that has already been gravely wounded. I should be as angry as you appear to be now if some…careless rogue intent on his own pleasure were to wound her again.'

Gabe recognized a test—and a threat—when he heard one. 'I promise you, ma'am, upon my most solemn oath, that I desire only your niece's welfare.'

Once again Aunt Foxe studied him. He returned her steady gaze unflinchingly.

Finally she nodded. 'I believe you do. Then I must wish you luck, Captain, in all your endeavours.'

'Thank you, ma'am. If you would be so kind as to convey my compliments to your niece? As my presence will be required back in Cornwall shortly, I intend to leave for London today and so will probably not have occasion to take leave of her.'

'You will not be speaking with her again before you journey to London?' Aunt Foxe said in surprise.

'No, I mean to depart almost immediately.'

'I see,' she replied, frowning.

'Is something wrong?' Gabe asked, sensing some anxiety in the older woman. 'Some reason I should not go now?'

After a moment, Aunt Foxe shook her head. 'N-no. It's not my place to intervene; anything else that needs to be said should come directly from my niece. So, you wish me to convey to her only your compliments?'

Gabe thought about what he might say—wished he could say, but neither the place nor the time were yet right. He had a mystery to solve, at least one more shipment to transport and a future to determine before he could make any decisions—or declarations—regarding Miss Marie Foxe. 'Tell her I thank her for the honour of her friendship, and will do my best.'

Aunt Foxe offered him her hand. 'If you should find this varmint, Captain, I would appreciate your landing him another kick in the teeth for me.'

Gabe gave her a wolfish grin. 'I would be most happy to comply.'

She escorted him to the parlour door, then hesitated, her

wise eyes studying his face. 'I do hope you are prepared for whatever you might discover.'

'If Miss Foxe could endure what she has been forced to endure, I expect I can face whatever truth my quest might reveal.'

She smiled slightly. 'Thank you for being such a friend to my niece. She is worth every bit of your effort and devotion.'

'I know,' he replied softly, and walked out the door.

Chapter Seventeen

In the early afternoon little more than a week later, Gabe waited in an elegant anteroom in a Mayfair town house to be received by Aunt Foxe's London friend, Lady Alicia Porter.

Too restless to remain seated now that he was so close, perhaps, to obtaining the information he needed to identify the blackguard who'd injured Miss Foxe, Gabe paced the room, mulling over what he'd accomplished since leaving for London.

Wishing to travel as quickly as possible, he'd booked passage on the mail coach rather than travelling post. After departing from the Ship and Castle in Penzance, and with the extravagance of booking two inside seats so as to not be crowded by some onion-breathed farmer, he arrived at the Bull and Mouth at St Martins-le-Grand in London a little more than thirty-six hours later.

After repairing to the inn to sleep and bathe, he'd presented himself at Lady Alicia's town house that same afternoon, only to meet with the disappointing intelligence that her ladyship was out of town visiting a friend and would not return for another three days.

Deciding to delay searching for the Gypsy gem dealer until after he'd learned what Lady Alicia could tell him about the

Carlow scandal, he turned his efforts instead to investigating merchants who might be willing to handle the schoolgirls' knitted goods.

After strolling Bond Street, inquiring at several shops that dealt in lady's furnishings, he learned as expected that the discriminating clientele who patronized these shops preferred gloves fashioned from a variety of fine leathers. Except perhaps for cotton net gloves for summer wear, the merchants there weren't interested in stocking knitted goods.

On the recommendation of the innkeeper's wife, he'd next stopped at a variety of stalls in the Shepherd's Market area. Here he had better luck, finding several who admired the intricate patterns in Mrs Steavens's handiwork and allowed that they might be willing to accept some for sale.

His inquiries among the art dealers had been even more promising. After paying his shilling admittance to the European Picture Gallery in Haymarket, which contained oil paintings by well-known artists as well as prints and sketches, he sought out the proprietor. Mr Avery was most impressed by the charcoal drawing Eva had made of Miss Foxe, and when Gabe told him she would be producing landscapes of Cornish scenes, he grew even more enthusiastic.

One of England's rising young artists, a Mr Turner, the proprietor told him, had spent some months at St Ives, completing there a series of Cornish landscapes that had created a great stir among collectors. He had many knowledgeable clients who admired the Turner canvasses and would be very interested in acquiring similar works. If the artist Gabe represented could provide him with drawings or paintings of the same subjects rendered with the level of skill demonstrated by the charcoal sketch he'd just seen, Mr Avery assured Gabe he would have no trouble selling them. The price he named, Gabe felt sure, would put a smile on the face of Miss Foxe—and might go a ways toward getting Eva's sister away from the unsavoury John Kessel.

He had just reached that satisfying conclusion when the

butler bowed himself back into the room. 'Lady Alicia will receive you now, sir,' he said, motioning for Gabe to follow.

He escorted Gabe into a drawing room of even greater magnificence. Seated on an elegant divan near the hearth was an older lady dressed in the first stare of fashion.

He bowed before walking over to kiss the hand she extended. 'Thank you, Lady Alicia, for receiving me.'

She inclined her head regally. 'I'm delighted to offer hospitality to a young man recommended to me by one of my dearest friends. Living at the end of the world as she does, I seldom get to see Alexandre. But I note that the passage of years has not robbed her of her discerning eye, for I make no doubt, you are a handsome rogue!'

While Gabe felt his face redden, she laughed and said, 'So, Captain Hawksworth, how can I help you? Alexandre mentioned you were searching for information.'

'Yes, your ladyship. It concerns a scandal that occurred some twenty years or so ago, involving a prominent family named Carlow.'

To Gabe's delight and rising excitement, her eyes widened and she leaned forward. 'The Carlows? My, yes! No one then living in London will ever forget it! The most delicious scandal, with accusations and counter-accusations, illicit affairs, the attainder against the convicted man's family. Though, unlike the recent scandal, I should have said the earl's friends were more nearly involved in it than he.'

'The earl?' Gabe repeated. When Lady Alicia raised her eyebrows, he said apologetically, 'I'm not well acquainted with London Society.'

'George Carlow, head of the family, is Earl of Narborough. Won't you have a seat, Captain, and let me call for refreshments? This shall require some time to recount. How kind of Alexandre to send you to me, for I do so love telling a good story!'

After allowing that a glass of wine would be delightful, Gabe seated himself. His first, startled reaction was that Miss

Foxe was much more well-connected than he had imagined. Although he probably shouldn't have been surprised. The more elevated her connections, the greater her disgrace would have been, and she'd already admitted to him that she'd been one of Society's Diamonds.

His next thought was that he'd better resign himself to a long interview. Difficult as it would be to restrain his strong urge to press Lady Alicia for a short, succinct summation of events, so he might learn what he could and be on his way, her initial speech indicated that such a request probably wouldn't answer. Unlike her friend, the very discreet Aunt Foxe, it was apparent that Lady Alicia found gossip the food and wine of life and was neither reticent about conveying it nor anxious to do so quickly.

With as much good grace as he could muster, he answered her inquiries about her friend Alexandre's current health and activities. Finally, a pot of tea being provided for her and a glass of wine for him, the butler withdrew and Lady Alicia began her tale.

'It must be nearly twenty years now since that scandal transpired. George Carlow, Earl of Narborough, and his closest friend, William Wardale, Earl of Leybourne, both worked for the Home Office—apparently on some sort of spying activity. Also involved was Christopher Hebden, Baron Framlingham, a brilliant but rather unsteady man.

'It was said that Leybourne vehemently opposed Framlingham's involvement in the work, telling Narborough the man was too boastful and indiscreet. It wasn't just over business that the two clashed; Leybourne had courted Framlingham's wife Amanda before their marriage and objected to the way that gentleman, a rake both before and after being wed, treated his former sweetheart. As well he might; one later discovered Framlingham had fathered a bastard son with a Gypsy woman and forced his wife to keep the brat!'

While Lady Alicia paused to sip her tea, Gabe's mind worked furiously. If Gypsies were involved, having one of their clan exact some sort of revenge into the next generation was entirely believable. Impatiently, he waited for his hostess to continue.

Setting down her cup again, Lady Alicia said, 'As if the disagreement weren't already bitter enough, Leybourne had begun a discreet affair with Amanda. The exact turn of events was never entirely sorted out, but it is known that the two men had a terrible quarrel just days before the murder.'

'*Murder?*' Gabe burst out.

'Yes, murder!' Lady Alicia said with relish. 'On the evening in question, the three were to meet at Narborough's home over some matter of business. Narborough arrived late, to find Leybourne and Framlingham in the garden, struggling, Leybourne with a bloody knife in his hands! Framlingham died before he could be questioned, but with Narborough seeing the whole, there seemed little doubt about what had happened, even though Leybourne swore he was innocent.'

She paused again for a sip of tea and, desperately anxious to have her complete the tale, Gabe restrained himself from making any comment that would delay her resuming it.

'However, as Leybourne could produce no alibi for his whereabouts that night nor any clue to the identity, or even existence, of some other murderer—for he admitted he'd seen no one else in the garden with Framlingham, whom he claimed to have found already stabbed and dying—the jury swiftly convicted him. Leybourne's title was attainted, his lands seized by the crown, and he was hanged. All the while, his best friend Narborough did nothing to assist him, even though Leybourne continued to swear he was innocent.'

'A tangle indeed,' Gabe said, shaking his head. Here was a matter serious enough to produce the sort of vindictiveness from which Miss Foxe had suffered. Could someone from the disgraced Wardales have revenged himself upon a Carlow relation in payment for the earl's not defending his friend?

But why choose Miss Foxe? She seemed too far removed from the original events to make such a reaction credible.

'But there is more,' Lady Alicia broke into his reflections. 'On the day of the hanging, Framlingham's Gypsy woman, apparently deranged with grief, cursed all the families involved in the murder of her lover and then hanged herself out a window!'

'Rather dramatic,' Gabe murmured. Was the gem trader related to Framlingham's Gypsy mistress? If he were a member of the same clan, that could be reason enough for him to seek revenge on those who had driven his kinswoman to suicide—and a Gypsy might very well consider anyone with a connection to the responsible families an acceptable target.

But a Gypsy merchant would hardly have entrée to mingle freely at a Ton party. Could one of the Wardales, perhaps living on the fringes of polite society, have colluded with the Gypsy to exact a joint revenge?

His conviction growing as the tale continued, Gabe felt nearly certain that what happened to Miss Foxe must be somehow connected to this ancient scandal, and that the gem trader was involved.

Then another thought struck him. 'What happened to Framlingham's Gypsy son?' he demanded.

'Lady Framlingham was with child when all this transpired. Already in uncertain health, the grief and distress of her husband's murder caused her to collapse. Her family, the Herriards, took her in and while she was still prostrate, sent the Gypsy brat to a foundling home, which later burned to the ground, killing all the inmates.'

So much for his idea that the gem trader might be Framlingham's half-Gypsy son. But he could still have a connection to the Gypsy woman. Someone who believed in William Wardale's innocence and burned with hatred for George Carlow, the man who had let his best friend go to the gallows without trying to exonerate him, could have engaged a relation of the wronged Gypsy woman to exact vengeance for them both.

'What happened to the Wardales?'

'The widow withdrew from Society, of course. There was some talk that George Carlow had attempted to assist her and had been refused. The children should be grown by now, but I have no idea where they are or how they get on.'

'Is there anything else you can remember about the affair?'

Lady Alicia considered a moment, then said, 'I don't believe so. After the hanging, the scandal gradually subsided. The Wardales disappeared; Amanda Hebden remarried—a scholarly man, I believe, who didn't figure much in Society. George Carlow continued in government service until his health began to fail.'

She angled her head and looked at him curiously. 'Surely you don't think that old scandal is related in any way to the recent one? From what I've heard, 'twas the girl's own fool-hardiness that brought about her ruination.'

'Actually it was not; she was persuaded to go to the garden under false pretences, a matter I am trying to prove. Although I admit, it does seem rather far-fetched that someone would have concocted the elaborate scheme used to discredit her because of a long-distant scandal to which she had only the most tenuous of connections.'

'She was lured to her ruin, you say?' Lady Alicia echoed, much shocked. 'Are you sure of this?'

'Quite sure,' Gabe replied. ''Twas a monstrous injustice, which I should like to redress.'

'Gracious, I would think so!' she declared. 'For someone to deliberately *arrange* the ruin of Carlow's daughter—why, I've never heard of such wickedness! Lady Honoria must have been hardly more than an infant when those events took place.'

Confusion swirled in Gabe's head. 'Lady Honoria?' he repeated.

'Yes. That is what you were referring to, isn't it? The dreadful contretemps a month or so ago when Carlow's eldest daughter, Lady Honoria, was caught in the garden at Lady

Dalrington's ball, virtually *in flagrante delecto* with that infamous lecher Lord Barwick?'

Even as the truth of it slammed into him with a sick conviction, Gabe tried to deny it. 'I…I thought the compromised lady was a Miss Foxe.'

'No, no, you're confusing the names, probably because of the girl's connection to Alexandre. You did say you weren't familiar with London Society! Lady Honoria's mother—Anne—was a Foxe, niece to my friend, but the chit is a Carlow. I'm assuming Alexandre asked you to inquire about her? I believe she always had a fondness for her great-niece. I expect the girl is at Stanegate Court now, the Carlow country estate in Hertfordshire. 'Tis the most likely place that Carlow's eldest son Marcus, Viscount Stanegate, who has virtually assumed the running of the family since George's last attack, would have sent her to rusticate until the furour died down.'

Marcus. My elder brother, Marc. 'I—I suppose I did confuse them,' he said, his tone full of an irony lost on Lady Alicia.

'I do feel for the girl, poor thing, even though it's said she was wild to a fault. After having been ruined so thoroughly, and with her fiancé Lord Readesdell repudiating her after the scandal, it's unlikely that she'll ever marry.'

While Lady Alicia continued to rattle on, deploring the Carlow girl's loss of reputation and prospects, Gabe scarcely heard her. Ringing over and over like a death knell in his head were those three words: Lady Honoria Carlow.

After the first shock, anger blazed through him. He could somewhat understand why she might have concealed her identity upon coming to Cornwall. When the mighty have fallen—and this would have been a fall of gargantuan proportions—they'd naturally prefer not to have a host of idle bystanders pointing and smirking at the wreckage.

By why had she not confided her true identity to him, especially after he told her he intended to come to London? She must have known when he did so, he would inevitably discover the truth.

Aunt Foxe's odd look and final warning made more sense now: 'Anything else that needs to be said should come directly from my niece; it's not my place to intervene' and 'I hope you are prepared for whatever you might discover.'

Prepared, indeed! So much for his pretty daydreams of a future with Miss Foxe—no, Lady Honoria.

Lady Honoria.

He almost laughed at his idiocy. Once his tenure as the *Flying Gull's* captain was over, he'd had some hope of continuing their friendship, even with a well-connected Miss Marie Foxe. He was a gentleman's son and his brother, Sir Nigel, was thought to have made an excellent match when he wed the daughter of an Anglo-Irish viscount.

But to attempt a connection to the *daughter* of an *English* earl, a man important in government circles?

His heart protested that despite any difference in rank, there was a true connection between them, both physical and emotional. She felt it as keenly as he, that kinship of minds and yearning of the senses. A link such as he had never felt with any other, a bond that was rare and priceless.

Perhaps important back in Cornwall, common sense told him. In the eyes of the wider world, however, even for a respectable Gabriel Hawksworth returned to take up his position as the landless younger brother of an Irish baron, such a connection meant nothing; one to a Cornish free-trader less than nothing.

He was mad even to dream of a future with her.

No wonder Aunt Foxe asked him if he were prepared for what he might find.

Out of a sick feeling of despair, his anger resurged. Why, he raged again, had Miss Foxe—no, *Lady Honoria*—allowed him to come to London without warning him?

Maybe she felt his claim of pursuing vindication for her was only an idle boast that might never come to anything. Or that, even if he acted upon his intentions, he would be unable to turn up anything to vindicate her.

Well, to be fair, he hadn't made it clear that he intended to leave for London immediately nor that he was going to consult with her aunt. Without the connection Aunt Foxe had provided to Lady Alicia, he might well have never discovered the circumstances behind the old scandal—or stumbled upon her true identity.

Grudgingly, he admitted he could understand her not wishing to disclose her real name if nothing could be done to ameliorate her position. And after all that had happened to her, she'd certainly earned the right to be cautious.

Not that it mattered. There could not be anything between them now anyway.

Unless…unless her reputation could not be restored, and she was irretrievably banished from Society. In that case, they might create a world of their own—one where she was not above the touch of the younger brother of a man of small title—even a free-trader. He tried to push the ignoble hope from his head.

He'd push it all from his mind. He still needed to track down the Gypsy and force him to reveal who had hired him to assist in her downfall. And then confront that man.

A righteous anger sizzled in him at the satisfying thought of being able to deal with both the Gypsy and the disgusting, worthless maggot who had deliberately set about to destroy the reputation and honour of an innocent woman.

'Mr Hawksworth, are you all right?' Lady Alicia's concerned voice recalled him.

Gabe shook himself back to the present. 'Quite fine, your ladyship,' he responded. 'Just pondering my next step.'

'You spoke of trying to redress the wrong done to Lady Honoria. You mean to pursue that?'

'I do, ma'am.'

'A lofty aim, sir. Though I fear I have told you nothing that might assist you in that endeavour.'

'On the contrary, Lady Alicia, you have been most helpful. Thank you again for receiving someone who was wholly unknown to you.' After draining his wine glass, he rose and bowed to her, indicating his intention to take his leave. After an exchange of politenesses and a promise to let her know what eventually happened in his quest to exonerate Lady Honoria, Gabe fled from the room.

The disturbing news of Miss Foxe's true identity adding fuel to his frustration and anger, Gabe decided to go immediately to discover what further information he could glean from the jeweller at Phillips, hoping it would be enough for him to track down the Gypsy.

A short hackney ride brought him to Bond Street and Mr Phillip's establishment. As he would have expected of a shop frequented by a Lady Honoria Carlow, he thought, his lip curling, the premises were large and elegantly furnished, with a tasteful assortment of well-designed and undoubtedly expensive jewellery on display.

He walked in, telling the clerk who came to assist him that he had private business to discuss with Mr Phillips alone. Fortunately for his state of restlessness and general irritation, he wasn't kept waiting long. A tall, slim, officious-looking individual, Mr Phillips appeared soon after, escorting him to his office when he repeated that his business was confidential.

'With what might I assist you, Mr...' the jeweller began.

'Hawksworth,' Gabe supplied. 'I recently encountered a gem trader who encouraged me to invest in some diamonds. They appeared to be fine stones, but as I'm no expert, before purchasing any, I wished to consult someone who was. He claimed he had done business with you. A tall, slim, elegant man, slightly foreign in appearance. A Mr Ste—'

'Steven Hebden,' Mr Phillips interrupted. 'Yes, I've bought any number of stones from him.'

At that wholly unexpected name, Gabe's heart stopped,

then kicked back into motion. Shocked to his core for the second time in a day, Gabe said, 'Hebden is his name, you say? Steven Hebden?'

'Yes, that's right. I can understand your caution, for he does have a slightly—unusual air about him, but I've never known him to deal in any but the highest quality gems. Resides on Bloomsbury Square, I believe. I've sent him notes there on several occasions, when I wished to purchase more gems.'

The jeweller gave him an ingratiating smile. 'You're interested in investing in diamonds, you said? Might I suggest that acquiring stones already set would constitute an equally sound investment? I presently have some very fine diamond pieces, guaranteed to please the most discriminating taste.'

'I'm somewhat pressed today; perhaps another time,' Gabe replied, still struggling to assimilate the astounding news. 'Do you recall which house on Bloomsbury Square?' He placed a guinea on the man's desk.

Swiftly pocketing the coin, the jeweller said, 'Check with my clerk. He's the one who delivered the notes.'

'Thank you for the information, sir,' Gabe said, and bowed himself out. After a brief consultation with the clerk, he exited the shop and paced quickly to the nearest hackney stand.

After giving the jarvey the direction to Bloomsbury Square, Gabe let his mind turn over the startling news he'd just received. Hebden! The Gypsy used the name Hebden? Why would he do that…unless the murdered baron's son had not perished in the foundling home fire after all!

Lady Alicia said that the Gypsy woman—perhaps Hebden? Beshaley's mother?—had cursed all the families before leaping to her death. Having seen the Gypsy temperament at close hand, Gabe had no trouble believing that the grown son of a murdered father and a mother pushed to take her own life would believe himself to be the instrument to exact vengeance upon the families she had indicted in her curse.

Would he have acted alone? Was he solely responsible for destroying an innocent girl's life?

Whether or not the Gypsy felt justified in his vengeance, Gabe had a very different notion of honour—and he was about to demonstrate it to him, underscoring its vehemence with his fists.

The London streets seemed more crowded, the transit more dawdling than ever. Gabe was about to stick his head out the window and demand the jarvey pick up the pace when, in a shriek of brakes and squeal of leather, the coach jerked to a stop.

'This be the house, guv'nor,' the jarvey announced.

Tossing him a handful of coins, Gabe leapt from the vehicle and headed for the entry.

A slow-burning anger, fired to a hotter flame by irritation, anticipation—and the heartache he was trying to suppress over the revelation of Miss Foxe's true status—made Gabe ply the knocker with more than customary vigour. As he stood, nearly prancing in impatience to confront the Gypsy and find some answers at last, the door slowly opened, revealing a tall, swarthy man in a green coat of oriental cut, his head concealed beneath a turban.

'I wish to see Mr Hebden—or Mr Beshaley—immediately, on a matter of great urgency.'

Making no reply, the tall Indian studied him, remaining silent long enough that, piqued and insulted, Gabe's anger surged higher still. Inspecting him back, Gabe noted the dagger with a jewelled hilt tucked into the sash beneath the man's Bengal coat.

'A thousand apologies, Sahib, but Master Stephen Sahib is not here,' the man said at last.

'Not here—or not receiving guests?' Gabe demanded.

'Not in the house.'

'Indeed?' Gabe asked, not at all sure he could believe the man. How like Beshaley, to employ this exotic Eastern hulk of a butler! 'How about I have a look around, just to be sure.'

The Indian shrugged. 'The Sahib may try to have a look. And I will stop him.' He moved one hand to the hilt of his dagger.

The butler appeared well-conditioned, light on his feet and looked as if he knew how to use that dagger. All the irritation, impatience, fury and despair churning in Gabe's gut fired him to enthusiasm at the prospect of a good fight. The blood lust roaring through his veins, his fists tingling, he could almost taste the satisfaction of letting fly.

But his cause wouldn't be advanced by having the constable called on him for brawling at a gentleman's home, nor would it recommend him to Miss Foxe's—he really must stop thinking of her as Miss Foxe—distinguished family, if he ever met them, which didn't appear likely.

Regretfully, he made himself step back. 'When do you expect your master to return?' he bit out, irritated further at having to deny himself a good, satisfying row.

'I do not know, Sahib,' the hulk responded.

'You must have some indication,' Gabe responded angrily. 'Later today? Tomorrow? Not until next week?'

Totally impassive in the face of Gabe's anger, the turbaned man simply shook his head. 'I do not know, Sahib,' he repeated.

'Or more likely, you will not say,' Gabe muttered. It would be useless to leave a message; if he wished to confront the Gypsy, he would have to return and try to catch him later.

'Very well,' he told the man. 'But I will be back.'

The Indian gave him a glimmer of a smile. 'You would be a worthy opponent, I think, Sahib. Perhaps another time?'

'Perhaps,' Gabe said, amused despite himself, and he turned to walk away.

He'd accomplished a great deal today: discovering that the woman who fascinated him was far above his station, that her ruin might have been engineered by the half-Gypsy bastard of a long-dead English lord, and that a dagger-wielding Indian servant considered him a suitable opponent.

But despite all his anger, impatience and urgency, he was not going to be able to solve today the mystery of Lady Honoria's disgrace.

Chapter Eighteen

A week later, Honoria set out in the morning for Father Gryffd's school. She ought to be excited and hopeful, and truly she was, for Eva was making great progress with her pastels and Honoria was finding working with the girls to be quite satisfying.

Who could have imagined such a thing? she asked herself wryly. The impatient Lady Honoria, who'd been barely able to tolerate a two-hour session with her governess, spending her mornings as school mistress to a handful of village girls. If any of her London acquaintances heard of it, they'd dismiss the account as sheer fabrication.

Still, a restless dissatisfaction and a deep yearning she couldn't seem to conquer kept crowding in on her determined cheerfulness. A restlessness and yearning that was directly connected to the absence of one Captain Gabriel Hawksworth.

Though she knew after their discussion at the cove that he intended to do some investigating, she'd been surprised and dismayed to discover he'd left Cornwall without a word of goodbye. She'd been even more dismayed—and just a tad jealous—when Aunt Foxe revealed that he had, however, called upon *her* before his departure.

Her aunt had quickly reassured her that she had not divulged

Honoria's identity, even after the captain stated that he meant to go to London. Her real name, Aunt Foxe asserted, was a fact that her niece probably should have revealed to the captain at the same time she trusted him with the other details about her circumstances. Since she had chosen not to, Aunt Foxe had not felt it her place to enlighten him.

However, as he sought information about the old family scandal, she had referred him to her friend Lady Alicia. By now, most likely he had learned everything there was to know about those events—and been given Honoria's real name.

Aunt Foxe had added that she would not be at all surprised if the young man were angry and perhaps hurt, injured by Honoria's failure to trust him with that final bit of information. For she was certain the captain had a decided *tendre* for Honoria.

Did he? Honoria wondered for perhaps the thousandth time as she urged the mare to a canter down the road toward Sennlack. And if he did, would that warmth of feeling survive discovering she had been less than honest with him about her status?

Her uncertainty over that answer added another layer to the growing sense of impatience and anxiety she was trying to suppress. She kept thinking back to that moment in the cove when, after revealing everything else about that most shameful episode of her life, she'd teetered on the brink of giving her name as well.

But a caution forged of painful experience had restrained her. Would time show that to have been a dreadful mistake? If she'd known he'd be leaving immediately for London, would she have had the courage to confess her deception?

Far more important to her now than solving the mystery of her ruin was retaining the good opinion of the man who had held her so tenderly and kissed her with such fierce passion in the crystalline cove beneath the stone church.

She'd had more than a week to ponder the nature of her feelings for the captain and realize how very unique and powerful they were. Never had she felt so strong a connection to any other man.

Never longed for his company. Never sat dreamily recalling an expression, a word, a smile. Never woke in the night with the memory of his mouth on hers making her whole body tingle with awareness and need.

Never wanted to put into practice the instructions she'd been clandestinely reading in books slipped out of Aunt Foxe's library.

Though even as recalling those suggestions set desire coiling in her belly, a troubling doubt hovered at the back of her mind. If she ever had the opportunity—and could summon the boldness—to touch him in the manner those books suggested, would the fear and distress burned into her soul by Lord Barwick's attack recur and strike her unawares, as it had the first time she'd kissed him? Make her shrink away from him again, embarrassing, disappointing and frustrating them both?

Well, she concluded testily as the vicarage appeared in the distance, at this rate she'd probably not need to worry about that. The captain must not be missing her as keenly as she was missing him, for he'd already been gone nearly two weeks, ample time to have posted to London and back, and there was still no word of his return.

In fact, Tamsyn had confided to her this morning that the *Flying Gull* had left her moorings over three days ago. Which meant the captain must have quit London to meet his ship at some other port. *To make another smuggling run?* she wondered, anxiety of a different sort filtering through her pique.

Tamsyn had brushed aside her inquiry about what might happen if his ship were captured, saying there weren't no way the Hawk could ever be taken by sea, such a fearsome good sailor he was. However, Honoria's experiences having taught her even the powerful could be brought low, she couldn't share the maid's blithe optimism.

Oh, enough! she told herself as she rode into the stable yard at the vicarage. After putting off the expedition in order to wait upon the captain's return, she'd decided to take Eva to Captain Hawksworth's cove to sketch today. Hopefully the fresh sea air and the beauty of the spot would inspire not only Eva's drawing, but herself to a more positive frame of mind.

Though how that could be possible, when every colour and wave, boulder and crag would remind her of the intimacy they'd shared and the kiss that had rocked her to her soul, she wasn't sure.

A kiss that, given his long absence, obviously hadn't had the same world-shaking effect upon the captain.

With a sigh, she dismounted, handed the reins to the waiting servant and paced to the classroom.

She checked on the threshold, for the room was deserted. Surprised and a bit alarmed, she proceeded on to the vicarage, where the housekeeper answered her rap.

'Good morning, Mrs Wells,' she began. 'Did I forget today was to be a holiday?'

'Oh, miss, you ain't heard the news? Let me call the Father, then, afore he sets out!'

Even more alarmed now, Honoria paced the parlour while the housekeeper fetched the vicar. He hurried in a few moments later, an anxious expression on his kind face.

'What's amiss?' she cried. 'Has something happened to the children?'

'No. One of the miners rode down from the coast to say he saw free-traders transporting a cargo this morning in broad daylight! I thought after the last time, when there was that altercation with the new revenue agent, the local entrepreneurs had agreed 'twas too dangerous to do so during the day, but certain of them must have decided to proceed anyway. I'm very much afraid the riding officers may have caught wind of it and there might be a confrontation.'

He looked at Honoria apologetically. 'So many of the families, men and women, are involved in carrying the cargo off the beach that the girls stayed home this morning.' He paused, frowning. 'Although that doesn't explain why Eva has not come. Perhaps she heard of the excitement and wanted to go watch.'

'Might that not be dangerous?' Honoria asked. 'Especially if the riding officers do turn up?'

'Dangerous indeed,' the vicar replied. 'That's why I intend to ride out. If it appears there might be bloodshed, perhaps I can try to prevent it.'

'And get your own head blown off in the process?' Honoria asked, thinking darkly of John Kessel. She doubted the innkeeper's son would hesitate to shoot a clergyman if he stood between Kessel and making a profit on his run.

'I expect I'm not musket-proof,' the vicar conceded with a smile, 'but I'll leave that up to the Almighty. I just know I must go and do what I can to help.'

A sudden thought struck dread in Honoria's gut. 'Is…is Captain Hawksworth landing goods, do you know?'

The vicar looked at her with concern. 'I'm sorry, lass, I don't know. Tamsyn did tell me the *Flying Gull* left the harbour several days ago, so it's quite possible his ship is involved in this run.'

Fear more intense than anything Honoria had experienced save the night of her ruin constricted her breathing and clawed a gash in her stomach. 'Then I'm coming, too,' she announced.

'My dear, that certainly wouldn't be wise—' he began.

She cut him off. 'I'll trail behind if you don't want me riding with you, but coming I am. I'm not a fool; I've no intention of involving myself with the landing party and will choose a safe observation spot behind some rocks or something and watch at a distance. But if Gabe—Captain Hawksworth is involved, I must be there to see what happens.'

The vicar must have read the resolution in her eyes, for he simply nodded. 'Very well. Let's get the horses.'

'Do you know where the cargo is to be landed?' she asked as they paced toward the stables.

'South along the coast. There's a tor on the moor and beyond it, an old stone hut. During the first wave of free-trading in the last century, someone dug a tunnel from the beach up to the hut. The place hasn't been used for quite a while, which is why the lander chose it this time, thinking the riding officers might not know about it.'

Trying to dissipate some of the fear clogging her mind, Honoria was about to joke that the reverend knew an uncommon amount about the transport of smuggled goods when it clicked in her mind that the place he'd just described sounded uncannily like the spot reached from Eva's beach.

Another wave of fear clenched in her gut, sharper than the first. 'Who is the lander?' she asked urgently.

The vicar hesitated, but apparently deciding that having already displayed such extensive knowledge of the run, it would be rather silly to profess ignorance now, he replied, 'John Kessel. He's the lander on most of the runs for his brother's ships.'

They'd reached the stables now. Collecting her mare, Honoria exhaled a shaky breath and tried to tell herself there was no connection between Eva's failure to appear at the vicarage and the fact that her sister's lover was directing smuggled goods to be brought ashore through an area that sounded very much like Eva's secret tunnel.

They mounted swiftly and rode out of Sennlack, heading south. With the day overcast and a stiff wind blowing that would have carried their words away, neither attempted to converse. The wind's force, Honoria thought, would also drive the waves higher, so that the breakers bearing the ships through the narrow cove opening would be particularly dangerous.

Would revenue agents be waiting on the beach or beyond the tunnel to confront them, ready to fire on the free-traders if they offered any resistance? Which, with John Kessel in charge, they almost certainly would.

Was Gabe one of the captains who'd be fired upon?

The miles seemed to creep by under the hooves of their horses. While foreboding took up residence in her mind and dread occupied her stomach, Honoria realized the truth that she'd been trying to evade for the last week and more.

She loved Gabriel Hawksworth—a free-trader, a man about whose family and past she knew almost nothing, whose future over the next several hours might include anything from a sackful of gold coins as profit on the venture, capture and imprisonment in some dank prison before going on trial for his life, or a ball between the eyes from the pistol of a determined riding officer.

She also realized that, whatever his birth or current occupation, in the depths of his soul he was a gentleman, possessed of more honour, compassion and concern for his fellow men than a ballroom full of high-born Corinthians. That her position as Lady Honoria, earl's daughter, was nothing compared to the fierce joy that flooded her at the idea of being able to share her life with the man she loved, whatever his position.

If he cared for her as she cared for him, she could wish for nothing more glorious than making a life with him, wherever he wished to go, whatever he wished to do.

Though she devoutly hoped he'd meant it when he said that his time as a free-trader was nearly done. She wanted to enjoy his teasing wit, his incisive commentary, his intense blue-eyed gaze and bone-melting kisses for a very long time without having to worry that around the next bend waited a revenue agent with a levelled pistol, or somewhere beyond the next cove sailed a Royal Navy ship eager to force his vessel onto the rocks.

Though her hopes and desires were leaping ahead of reality as quickly as a smuggler's lugger outrunning a revenuer cutter. She knew the strong connection—and potent desire—between them was mutual, but whether the captain was interested in anything more permanent than a brief liaison, she had no idea. If he cared about her enough to journey all the way to London to try to find evidence to exonerate her, that must mean he entertained some strong feelings for her, mustn't it?

Or might it only mean he was once again displaying that deeply engrained sense of fairness that was so much the hallmark of a true gentleman?

Had she ruined any tender feelings he might hold for her by withholding the secret of her name? But surely, if he cared for her, he would be willing to forgive her that one bit of caution.

Those doubts, fear of what they might discover at the landing sight and a wild euphoria at admitting her love for Gabe cycled endlessly through her mind as they rode south. But though she thought she'd worried over every contingency they might encounter, she was still not prepared for what she perceived when they rounded the crest of the next hill and made out the ant-like line of men and women laden with casks and barrels, emerging from the stone hut and loading their cargo onto farm carts.

By the door of the hut, guarding access to the tunnel, stood Eva.

At the sight, Honoria's resolve to remain hidden dissolved. Appalled and furious that the child was involved—and certain she knew who had involved her—Honoria touched her heels to the mare's flanks and spurred her toward the distant hut at a gallop, heedless of the vicar's warning cry behind her.

Within moments she reached the hut, and dismounted as an eager Eva ran up to her. Reins in one hand, Honoria gave her a one-armed hug. 'I'm taking you home,' she said urgently. 'It's not safe here.'

Distress on her face, Eva was signalling that she must stay, when the door of the hut opened and John Kessel emerged, stopped short and stared at them.

'Here now, brat, what are you doing?' he growled, ignoring Honoria. 'Get back to your post!'

'She's not going back,' Honoria said evenly. 'She's going with me.' With difficulty, cognizant of how dangerous the man could be, she refrained from telling him exactly what she thought of him involving a child in his illegal operations.

'Just what right do you have to interfere, missy? Her mother knows she's here and will be happy to have the blunt I'm paying her. Happy, too, I'll wager, that someone finally found a way for her idiot daughter to be useful. If the revenuers do appear, they won't be able to get much information out of her, will they?' he asked, with a bark of laughter.

His speech containing too many points with which she disagreed to begin rebutting them, she simply said, 'It's not safe for a child here. Find someone else to stand your lookout. I'm taking Eva with me.'

His levity vanished beneath a menacing frown. 'This be none of your business, girl. You just ride that pretty little mare home to your aunt's and go back to your tatting. And if you know what's good for you, if you encounter any riding officers along the way, you'll forget what you seen here.'

A rising fury burned away all caution. In John Kessel's determined face she saw another evil man bent on accomplishing his own selfish plan, uncaring of the innocents he harmed. English law was harsh, too harsh, probably. Children not much older than Eva had been transported for less than the capital crime of smuggling, and Honoria was not about to let Eva become another helpless victim.

'I'm sorry to be disobliging, Mr Kessel, but Eva cannot stay here. Let's go, Eva,' she said calmly and coaxingly to the child, who stood regarding them both, confusion and anxiety on her face. 'You shall ride behind me on my beautiful horse. You'll like that, won't you?'

With a snarl, Kessel grabbed Eva's hand and yanked her back toward the hut. 'And I says you're taking her nowhere until she's finished here. You understand me, girl?'

'Or what?' Honoria snapped back, almost quivering with fury. 'You'll beat me? Strike an unarmed woman smaller than you, like the great loathsome bully you are?'

With a growl, Kessel dropped Eva's hand and strode toward Honoria. She was backing away, ready to tell Eva to make a run for it as she desperately scanned the area for something she might use as a weapon, when the first shot rang out.

Chapter Nineteen

Overwhelmingly anxious to be back in Cornwall after foul weather and breakdowns of the coaches delayed his arrival by nearly five days, Gabe rode the horse he'd hired in Penzance back into Sennlack. Before taking the lathered beast to a well-deserved rest at the Gull's Roost stables, however, he'd ride by the harbour and check on the *Flying Gull*. With the unanticipated delay in his return, and the details of their next run to France already nearly complete when he'd departed almost two weeks ago, he knew he'd probably be taking her to sea immediately.

Though before he left, he would somehow carve out the time to visit a certain lady. He had a tale to relate he knew she'd find interesting, though until he tracked down the Gypsy—a task that, maddeningly, he would have to leave until after this next voyage—he wouldn't be able to offer her the full story.

How would she react when she realized he knew the truth, all of the truth?

How would he, facing her again now that he knew it?

He'd ruminated over their next meeting for most of the long, boring, frustrating journey from London. He was no closer now to deciding how to handle the situation than he'd been in the shocked few moments after first discovering her identity.

Pulling up before a vista of the harbour, chopping waves under a sky of scudding grey clouds, Gabe mulled it over yet again.

Should he maintain a polite, respectful distance, as befitted a lowly younger son addressing the daughter of an earl? Sweep her into a passionate embrace as demanded by a man who'd been invited to her touch, revelled in her taste, had her voice and scent and essence too deeply imbedded into his soul to let her go?

Once she knew he knew, would she return that embrace or slap his face for effrontery?

Gabe was frowning over the possibilities when it dawned upon his distracted senses that the *Gull* was not at her customary anchorage. Shaking his head free of the distracting Miss Foxe—no, Lady Honoria—he leaned forward and peered through a patch of drizzle, but that space remained empty.

The *Flying Gull* wasn't in the harbour.

Fury raged through him as he wheeled his mount and guided it in the direction of the inn. Who had dared take his ship to sea without him in command? Given his unexpected delay in returning, the answer that bubbled to the top of his consciousness added to his rage—and a sense of betrayal.

That foreboding was only enhanced when he leapt from the saddle at the Gull and no stable boy appeared to take the reins. His ire burned hotter when he stalked into the stable to find it, too, deserted.

That state of affairs not being the poor nag's fault, he delayed long enough to remove the saddle and give the animal a quick brush-down before continuing into the inn.

Which, as he'd feared, was also deserted.

Though there were normally few customers during the middle of the day, there could be only one reason for the establishment to be totally empty. Pacing behind the building to a narrow platform that overlooked the cove, he found Old Jory sitting in his accustomed corner, smoking his pipe as he gazed with mostly sightless eyes out to sea.

'Where are they landing it?' he demanded, too incensed for an exchange of civilities.

'Flatland about four miles south of town,' the old sailor replied. 'There's a tunnel cut from the cove to an old stone hut. You'll see the craggy tor that marks it on the moors as you ride in.'

From the location and description, it sounded like Eva's cave and tunnel, Gabe thought with a jolt of unease.

After a quick thanks, Gabe hurried to the stable, glad there was at least one fresh horse left.

Some half hour later, he was approaching the summit of a rise, the craggy tor in the distance, when he heard a sharp, popping sound that, after years as a soldier, he recognized as musket fire, as surely as he knew the whine of the wind in the *Gull's* rigging when it was time to come about.

Spurring the job horse to greater speed, Gabe topped the hill and reined in to reconnoitre the scene below. Only a green recruit rode hell-bent into battle without first taking the measure of the ground.

His resolve to honour that timeless wisdom shattered, however, when he saw in the distance a slender figure in a deep blue riding habit, crouched behind the small stone hut which was indeed the structure concealing the opening to Eva's secret tunnel. In the shock of that instant, he also recognized the fleeing horse as Aunt Foxe's mare. And beside Miss Foxe cowered a child who could only be Eva Steavens.

In face of the danger threatening her, whether she ultimately received him with passion or disdain mattered no more than the adage of analyzing the field. Kicking his horse into motion, Gabe descended the slope at a full gallop.

Pushing his mount to cover the ground as quickly as possible, Gabe wished he was on his old cavalry saddle, a pair of pistols primed and ready in their holsters and his sword in hand. As it was, he carried only a small pistol that gave him a single shot.

After reviewing his weapons, he noted that there appeared to be only four or five revenue agents firing at the men driving the loaded farm wagons. They must not have received word of the landing in enough time to summon the troop of infantry garrisoned nearby to assist them.

He also thought he could make out, leading the group, the zealous young revenue officer he'd pulled half-drowned out of Sennlack Cove. Perhaps the revenuer was so keen to be avenged for his previous dunking—and failure to seize that particular cargo—he had chosen not to wait on reinforcements.

It required no reflection at all to determine who would be foolish, and arrogant, enough after that first near-disaster to call for another daylight landing.

Hadn't he warned Dickin about his brother's recklessness? And how could his friend have allowed John to order the *Gull* to sea—his ship, his crew—in his absence?

Now that he was closer, Gabe could hear the shouting of the free-traders, those nearest the structure running their tubs into the stone hut and doubtless back into the tunnel. Once there, they could close and bar the exit door behind them, making it nearly impossible for the revenuers to break through and trail them back to the beach.

The customs agents must have realized that, too, for they concentrated their fire on the men engaged in loading goods onto the carts. Those individuals had taken cover behind their wagons, some frantically pulling out an assortment of blunderbusses, muskets and pistols to return fire, while others wielded picks, clubs and shovels, ready to defend their cargo.

Gabe noted approvingly as he approached that in the mêlée, Miss Foxe had grabbed Eva and dragged her away from the hut, sheltering with her behind a nearby outcrop of rocks. If he could work his way behind the hut with the revenuers still concentrating their efforts on the cargo wagons, he might be able to lead them back along the cliff edge to a position where he could safely mount them on his horse and send them out of danger.

Then he could return and confront the Kessel brothers.

He glanced back toward the wagons. At the moment, the struggle between the revenue agents and the free-traders seemed a stalemate, the King's officers possessing more fire-power, but the free-traders having superior numbers and better cover.

As Gabe returned his attention to the stone hut, John Kessel himself stepped out the doorway and peered around the struc-ture to gage the progress of the struggle over the cargo. Spotting him, the revenue officer Gabe had saved wheeled his horse and headed for the hut at a gallop, levelling a pistol as he approached.

Less than a hundred feet more, Gabe thought, pressing his skittish mount, who was not at all happy about heading toward, rather than away from, the firing. Then to his horror, as he watched helpless to do more than utter a furious curse, before he could reach the woman and child, Kessel sprinted to the rock and grabbed Eva. Pulling the child in front of him, he forced her back toward the stone hut, using her as a shield between him and the revenuer's pistol.

'You've only one shot, whoreson,' he shouted at the man. 'Take it and you hit the brat.'

The revenuer pulled up his horse, irresolute, his pistol still levelled at Kessel. Though the child struggled, Kessel held her easily, keeping her thrust before him. 'I suggest you ride away before my men turn on you.'

At that moment, Laurie Steavens, a livid bruise on her cheek, emerged from the hut. 'Let her be!' she screamed, running toward her sister.

While the revenue agent looked about wildly, unwilling to fire upon the child or the girl, Gabe leapt from his horse and raced over. After jerking Eva away from the distracted Kessel and shoving her toward her sister, he tackled the smuggler, knocking him to the ground.

'Take her and run!' Gabe shouted at Laurie as he untangled himself from Kessel. While the girl scrambled away, her sister in tow, still on his knees, Gabe looked up at the revenuer. 'Let the females go. You've no quarrel with them.'

At the far side of the stone hut, numbers were winning out over firearms. As the revenuers ran out of ammunition, small groups of free-traders advanced, wielding clubs and sticks. They circled behind the revenue agents and then laid into them. One agent had been cornered against a wagon and was being beaten about the head and shoulders by two of the smugglers.

On this side of the hut, their leader aimed his weapon at Gabe, then at Kessel, his face contorted in anger.

'Don't do it,' Gabe urged. 'You only have one shot. I've been a soldier; trust me—you haven't enough men. Save your weapon to get your troopers away, before fools drunk on power and free whiskey—' he jerked his chin in the direction of the men attacking his agent '—cause a serious injury.'

After another fraught moment, with a roar of impotent rage, the leader kneed his mount and charged the wagon where the knot of smugglers were abusing his man, firing his one shot into the group. While the smugglers scattered, the leader pulled the injured man onto his horse. In the confusion, the four other King's men backed away to find their mounts and rode off, the free-traders jeering and shaking fists at them as they retreated.

Gabe scrambled to his feet and ran over to Miss Foxe. 'Are you all right?' he asked anxiously, his eyes scanning her for possible injury.

'I am fine!' she assured him. 'How can I thank you and Laurie enough for intervening? If you hadn't distracted Kessel, he might still be holding Eva. But what of you, sir? You are bleeding!'

Gabe glanced impatiently down, noting the scrapes and cuts on his hands where he'd hit the rocky soil when he knocked Kessel down. ''Tis nothing. Take my horse, please. Deliver Eva home and then get back to Foxeden. If you hurry, you should manage to arrive not too long after your aunt's horse and spare her worrying that you've been thrown to your death.'

She'd been about to protest, he could tell, but at this, she checked. 'You are right; she will worry when Mischief returns riderless. But I did so wish to speak with you! There's so much I need to tell you.'

'And I, you. A very great deal!' Now that the danger had passed, he allowed himself a moment to gaze hungrily at her lovely features. 'But here is not the time and place. I've a reckoning to settle with Mr Kessel.' His gaze narrowing, he glanced toward Dickin's brother, who had hauled himself to his feet and was hurrying over to join the cheering men at the wagons. 'Will you come to the school tomorrow?'

'Tomorrow?' she echoed, dismay and disappointment in her tone. 'Y-yes, I suppose I can wait until then.'

He permitted himself one final pleasure—pressing her hand, a contact that immediately submerged the sting of his assorted cuts and bruises in a tingling warmth. 'Good. Eva will need comforting, I suspect, before you take her home.'

'We'll bring her back to the vicarage first,' Father Gryffd's voice interrupted him.

Gabe blinked, startled to see the clergyman leading his horse toward them. Apparently he'd missed the vicar in the confusion, for Miss Foxe did not look at all surprised by his presence. 'Thank you for bringing me here, Father,' she said, confirming Gabe's impression.

''Twas a brave, bold thing you did, lass, getting the child away from Kessel,' the vicar said. 'I just praise the Lord you're both unharmed.'

Holding her sister's hand, Laurie joined the group. 'I tried to stop him from taking her, Father,' she said, tears choking her voice. 'But he wouldn't listen.' She laughed, a touch of hysteria edging the bitter sound. 'He never listens to any but his own counsel now. Dickin argued against transporting the goods by daylight, but John called the men out anyway.'

Unconsciously she fingered the bruise on her cheek. 'I…I'm going back home with Eva. He said he'd kill me if

I tried to leave, but I don't care any more. I won't go back to him.'

Father Gryffd nodded, his gentle eyes lighting with compassion and a fervour that, on another man, might have been rage. 'You must both stay at the vicarage. Yes, and your mother, too. Eva can continue her schooling and you'll be safe, until you decide what you want to do next.'

Laurie's eyes widened, hope lightening them for a moment before it dulled. 'No, it wouldn't be right. 'Tis powerful kind of you, Father, but I can't involve you in my quarrel.'

'You are one of my lambs; it is my quarrel,' Father Gryffd replied softly. 'Besides, you think John Kessel would dare to attack a man of God?'

Gabe didn't doubt it. Apparently Laurie didn't either, for she said, 'I believe he thinks he is above God.'

'No one is above God, and all our fates lie in His hands,' the vicar said. 'But since the Almighty also helps those who help themselves, let me assure you that there's no Cornishman alive who can best a Welshman when his ire is up. I wasn't born a priest, you know. I insist that you stay. For the child's and your mother's protection, if nothing else. You know John Kessel, may the Lord yet rescue his black soul, would think nothing of threatening them to force you to his will.'

No one present doubted that fact. One tear leaking down her battered cheek, Laurie nodded. 'We'll stay, then. How can I ever thank you, Father?'

To Gabe's shock, the vicar actually gave her a wink. 'Oh, I shall think of a way,' he said before turning to Miss Foxe. 'With Miss Steavens here to reassure Eva, why don't you take the captain's horse and go directly to Foxeden? He is right; the mare will doubtless return straight to her barn, and I should not wish for your aunt to worry.'

'Well…if Eva has her sister, I suppose she doesn't need me,' Miss Foxe said.

Eva darted from her sister's side and threw her arms around

Miss Foxe's waist, hugging her fiercely. 'Oh, I think she does need you, Miss Foxe,' Laurie said. 'But she can see you at school tomorrow. Can't you, Eva?'

Nodding, the girl released Miss Foxe, who gave the child's head a quick caress; her eyes were suspiciously bright. 'But, Captain, if I take your horse, how will you get back to town?'

He shrugged. 'I must find Richard Kessel and settle some business first. I'll claim a ride back to the inn with him.'

'Very well, then. Father, Captain, Eva, Laurie, I suppose I'll see you tomorrow.'

Gabe indulged himself in one more opportunity to touch her as he helped toss her into the saddle, just that brief contact firing the desire always simmering within. Then he stepped back to savour the view of her trim ankles emerging from the froth of petticoats, since, as the mare with the sidesaddle had galloped off, she was forced to ride astride. Pulling his gaze from that distracting and delectable sight, he murmured. 'Until tomorrow, *Miss Foxe.*'

Her eyes widened, telling him she understood from his subtle emphasis that her true name was no longer a secret. She gave him a quick nod, doubtless in appreciation for his not revealing it to the others. 'Until tomorrow, Captain Hawksworth.'

After watching the arousing spectacle of her trim posterior bouncing on the saddle as she rode off, Gabe set his jaw and walked off to find Dickin. Since neither he nor the elder Kessel had been at the inn, they were probably down at the beach, supervising the unloading.

John Kessel approached him as he walked to the stone hut. Brushing off his clothes with an elaborate gesture, John said coldly, 'Make no mistake; I'll see you pay for your interference.'

'Truly,' Gabe said, within a hair's breadth of taking out his frustrations by pummelling that smug, arrogant face. 'Just how do you think to manage that? I'm not a little girl a fourth your weight and size.'

Kessel inhaled sharply and curled his hands into fists. Gleeful at the possibility of a satisfying fracas, daring the man to try to strike, Gabe glared at him.

Kessel looked away first. 'We'll see about that,' he muttered.

Gabe felt an itching premonition between his shoulder blades as the man strode off. He'd have to be vigilant. Kessel was more the type to strike with a knife in the back out of some dark alley than with fists openly raised in a fair fight.

He ducked into the hut and swiftly followed the tunnel to the cave. Emerging onto the beach, he spotted his friend immediately, directing the unloading of a small boat that was retrieving tubs moored along the cliff wall.

'Ah, Gabe, my lad,' Dickin called out as Gabe walked over, 'will you plant me a facer first or let me explain?'

'Explain. But it had better be good.'

Dickin nodded. 'I don't blame you for being angry, but you knew the order was almost complete when you hared off to London. After Dubois sent word that all was in readiness, we needed only the right weather to make the run. I delayed as long as I could, but when a perfect, sweet little storm blew in from the southwest, with Johnnie arguing we should go at once, at length I had to give way. Conan Willes skippered the *Gull* before you; he is nearly fully healed, and after five months on shore, was itching to get to sea. So I let him. He and Will Glasson both had a most successful voyage.'

'And the landing?'

Dickin flushed. 'I thought Johnnie had agreed not to bring in another cargo in daylight. 'Twas already in the works when I found out, too late to call a halt. But after today, I'm sure he'll not try it again. Jake Dawes took a ball in shoulder, the men tell me, and there were other injuries.'

'Aye, from a group of three, kicking and beating a single

revenue agent,' Gabe said, angry all over again as he recalled the incident.

'The boys do get carried away sometimes,' Dickin said noncommittally.

'The *boys* take their cue from their leader. Dickin, your brother is beyond controlling. Nay,' he said as his friend raised a cautioning hand, 'I'll not be silenced. It's not just the cavalier confiscating of my boat and crew. Johnnie has no care for the danger into which he puts his men or the pain he inflicts. Did you notice the bruises on Laurie Steavens's face?'

Dickin's flush deepened. 'I did caution him about that.'

'And how did John respond?'

Dickin looked even more uncomfortable. 'He said she was his whore and he would do what he liked with her.'

Fury scoured Gabe. 'She's not a whore, damn your eyes for doing nothing! She's Mrs Steavens's daughter, Eva's sister, a maid who worked for your father for years! Are you going to wait to restrain Johnnie until after you find *her* floating face-down in the harbour some morning, like you did that miner who crossed him?'

'We don't know that Johnnie did that!' Dickin defended hotly.

'Dickin, he's your little brother. You don't see him clearly. If you could have looked into his eyes as he held Eva before him, his hands cutting into her thin bare arms, hurting her, liking that he was hurting her, daring that revenuer to shoot...'

Dickin looked away. 'He's young; he'll grow out of it,' he said at last. 'I can bring him back to heel.'

'Can you?' Gabe asked softly. 'I'm not so sure. Even if you can, I fear more men will die before it happens.' He shook his head. 'I can't be part of that, Dickin.'

'Oh, posh,' his friend responded. 'Your Irish feuds are much deadlier than anything we Cornishmen get up.'

Gabe laughed. 'You don't know my oh-so-righteous brother! Maybe there's something I can agree with Nigel about after all. I'll honour my pledge and serve out my six months. But then I'm leaving, Dickin. For the sake of your safety—and your soul—I urge you to get out of it, too.'

'And leave it to Johnnie?' Dickin shook his head sadly. 'Nay, my friend, I've Da and the inn to run, Tamsyn and all the family to support. What, I should try to eke a living out of the sea? Live on fish and the promise of next season's catch? But you've fulfilled your bargain. Conan came through the voyage well, despite the sea being so rough. I think he's healed enough to resume captaining the *Gull*. You're free to go whenever you wish, Gabe. With my thanks—and the reckoning between us made even.'

Gabe smiled. 'Nay, we'll never be even. There's no reckoning you can figure to repay the man who saved your life.'

'If we can part friends, then that will be payment enough. But—' Dickin gave him a curious glance '—what will you do?'

Gabe stood silent a moment, reflecting. 'I've never liked the lawbreaking part of free-trading—the scent of shame and the gallows luring around each bend. As the Gypsies would say: *You cannot walk straight when the road is bent.* But I do love matching my wits and my ship against the sea. Watching moonlight sparkle on the wake while the wind sings in the rigging. I've also discovered I like bringing goods to people who need or want them. I think I'd like to acquire a ship and keep on trading—lawfully this time.'

Dickin nodded. 'You'll settle in London then, or Dublin?'

'I don't think so. My family would be only slightly less scandalized by my setting up as a merchant than they would be if I were carted off in irons for free-trading. Perhaps I'll live aboard ship. I imagine the fingers of American maidens would appreciate the warmth of Cornish mittens just as much as those of London shop girls. There's Bruge for lace, Ghent for tapestries, Brussels where art dealers may be as interested as London ones in having Cornish landscapes to trade.'

'When will you leave?'

Gabe's thoughts winged instantly to Miss Foxe—no, Lady Honoria; he *must* start accustoming himself to referring to her by that name. 'I have some personal business to settle. A few days, at any rate.'

Dickin grinned. 'Give that *personal* business my best, and if she is too much a fool to hang on to you, half the wenches in Cornwall would be happy to take her place!'

A man called to Dickin about a problem with the towlines. Turning back to Gabe, he said, 'I'll see you at the inn later?'

'If I can borrow a horse. I lent mine to Miss Foxe.' It was a blessing, really, that her identity was not yet generally known. For a few more hours, anyway, he could go on pretending they inhabited the same world.

'With most of the cargo inland, we can spare a horse. Tell Will Glasson I said to give you the freshest one.'

The two men clasped hands. 'Thank you again for your help, old friend,' Dickin said. 'And good luck, in all your endeavours.'

Gabe felt curiously light, now that the decision to leave Cornwall had been made. But that decision had been the easy one.

His next task, the interview tomorrow with Miss Foxe, would be much harder. In the face of danger, the small deception over her name had seemed trivial. He couldn't seem to work up any indignation over it any more.

He knew he would willingly have taken a bullet for her today. Emotion welled up in him, expanding his chest, constricting his breathing, filling him fuller than the headsails on the *Gull* in a tearing wind. If he'd been a sloop he could have sailed all the way to the Americas on the power of it.

He might as well admit it; he, who had meant to avoid female entanglements for another decade or more, had fallen in love with Miss Foxe…who had turned out to be Lady Honoria, a woman so far above his touch that he would never had given her more than an admiring glance, had he known her true identity when they met.

Now it was too late.

However precious she was to him, there was no escaping the fact that Gabriel Hawksworth, even as a respectable merchant and trader, could never begin to offer Lady Honoria the comfort or position in society that were her birthright as the daughter of the Earl of Narborough.

A man of noble character would find the Gypsy, uncover the truth that would free her from an unjust exile, then walk away and leave her to live out her much more magnificent destiny.

Was he noble enough to do it?

Thrusting that question out of mind, he headed for the tunnel and his ride back to town.

Chapter Twenty

Waking before dawn after only a fitful sleep, Honoria detained the startled tweeny, who came in to relight the fire, long enough to assist her in donning a riding habit. With the pale pink fingers of early morning just creeping into the eastern sky, she walked to the breakfast room, unable to remain in her chamber a moment longer, though it would be hours before she could hope to see Captain Hawksworth at the school.

She'd paced like a caged beast all last evening, too, uninterested in her dinner, too restless to settle on any activity, impatient and so testy she'd had to apologize several times to Aunt Foxe after uttering some sharp remark. Almost, almost she'd been tempted to slip out to the stables, saddle Mischief and ride into town to accost the captain at the inn, so anxious was she to learn what he'd discovered.

How he now felt about her.

He knew her real name, for certain. She hadn't missed the subtle emphasis he'd given her alias on the moor yesterday. But, she recalled, brightening a bit, neither had he seemed furious about it. Perhaps she hadn't mangled things between them irretrievably after all.

Actually, accosting him in his bedchamber sounded as appealing by morning light as it had at midnight. The knowledge acquired from her aunt's naughty books burning in her, she was most eager to put it into practice.

She'd wanted him even when she told herself the attraction between them was little more than lust. But as the emotional connection strengthened and now, after admitting she loved him, the caution keeping her from giving physical expression to the joy that bubbled up in her at the mere sight of him had steadily eroded until it now restrained her from acting by the thinnest of threads.

Even the terror of yesterday's ambush hadn't wholly muted that joy or done more than reduce to a simmer the passion that made her yearn with ever-increasing fervency for total union with him.

That deliciously wicked poem from *Aristotle's Masterpiece* ran through her head again. Indeed, she thought of it often, for with its sea-going metaphors, it seemed as though written expressly for her and the captain. She couldn't look at him now without thinking of the admonition to take his 'rudder' in her bold hand 'like a try'd and skilful pilot' and 'guide his bark in love's dark channel…'

Her channel liquefied at the thought. She closed her eyes, imagining what it would be like to run her fingers down the solid length of his 'yard,' to explore and caress the soft and sensitive tip and navigate it within her…

From time immemorial, women had captured and held their men using the power of those navigational tricks. Might she, like a modern siren, lure the captain onto the shoals of delight and keep him there…until he no longer wished to leave?

Though a tiny niggle of doubt stirred, she was nearly certain that this time, given the opportunity, she would be able to invite his caresses without being seized by fear or panic.

She was startled from her thoughts by the entrance of Tamsyn with a tray of cups and saucers. As the maid checked on the doorstep, doubtless surprised at seeing Honoria dressed and down for breakfast a full hour earlier than normal, Honoria noted that the girl had been weeping.

Anxiety raced through her. She'd left the moor before the free-traders finished moving their cargo, without knowing the outcome of their confrontation with the King's men. There'd been shooting aplenty. Had any of Tamsyn's friends or family been injured? Had the revenuers returned with reinforcements?

Was Captain Hawksworth all right?

'Tamsyn, what's wrong?' she asked.

'Oh, miss, the most awful news! Truly, I don't know how I shall bear it!'

'What news?' Honoria demanded, even more alarmed.

'It's the Hawk! He and my brother Johnnie had the most dreadful row last night and now he's…he's leaving! Leaving the Gull, leaving Cornwall! Oh, my heart is like to break!'

While Tamsyn fell into a new fit of weeping, Honoria's own heart hammered in sudden panic. The captain was *leaving?* Everything in her being protested the thought.

What was she to do? And how long did she have to do it?

Frantic to find out, she grabbed the girl's arm. 'When, Tamsyn? *When* is he leaving?'

Halted in mid-sob, the girl looked up at her. 'I d-don't know. D-dickin just said "soon". Conan Willes, that was skipper of the *Flying Gull* before the Hawk, is going to take her back. But it won't be the same. Nothing won't ever be the same.'

Honoria cast a frantic glance at the mantel clock. Though it was still too early for anyone to be at the school, suddenly she couldn't bear remaining in the house another minute.

She'd saddle Mischief now, ride along the cliffs, gallop over the moors, then proceed to Sennlack and pace the vicarage garden until the captain appeared.

She knew he would not leave without seeing her. But after he saw her, would he leave anyway?

The prospect of having him walk out of her life—and perhaps never return—filled her with a sick horror. Though there was nothing she could do to make him stay, if he was truly set on leaving.

But that thought being too awful to contemplate, she put it out of mind. Striding past the snivelling Tamsyn, she made for the stables.

The animal saddled and ready, she set off, giving the mare her head, the rush of wind past her face as the horse galloped across the moor not working its usual soothing magic. When the mare tired, she reined in and proceeded at a slower pace toward Sennlack, her mind pulsing with anxiety, longing and dread.

She'd thought she would have time—weeks if not months— to try to entice the captain into staying forever. How could she exist without the hope of a future with him?

Before long, she reached the bend in the road where a track led out to his Irish Cliffs. The site drew her as irresistibly as the tide running back to the sea. Here she had laid her soul bare, shared with him her deepest shame, explored with him a passion more powerful than anything she had ever imagined.

Surely he couldn't just turn his back and walk away from the connection she was certain he felt as intensely as she did.

Drawn by the hope that the cove, which held such vivid memories of the two of them united, might bring some peace to her troubled, fearful soul, she dismounted and took the track down the trail to the church. Then stopped, her heat stamping with gladness and panic as she saw a horse tethered near the structure.

She didn't recognize it, but the captain rode a variety of different mounts out of the Gull's Roost stables. Certain it must be his, she darted onto the trail leading to the beach, slipping and sliding in a heedless rush down the narrow, rocky path until she reached the bottom where it spilled out onto the beach.

There she halted, her heart soaring upward like one of the heaven-bent gulls circling overhead, for sitting on the rock where they'd talked—kissed—was Gabriel Hawksworth.

She hurried across the sand and stopped behind him, heart hammering, hesitant now, hungry, aching.

The joyous smile that lit his face when he turned and saw

her poured a healing balm on the cruel cuts anxiety and doubt had scored on her heart.

Then she was seated beside him, he taking her hand—ah, the luxuriant bounty of his touch!—and kissing it.

'Lady Honoria,' he said, a touch of reproach in his tone. 'So you couldn't wait either?'

'No. I nearly rode to the inn to see you last night. Please, you must tell me straight away—'

'What I discovered?' he interrupted.

'No, no!' she said impatiently. 'Whether you forgive me for not telling you everything, including my name.'

'Why did you not tell me?' he asked softly, recapturing her hand and tucking it in his own.

'I was afraid,' she confessed. 'Afraid you would be angry over the deception I'd practised. And ashamed,' she added in a lower voice. 'After what happened in London, the name Honoria sounded too much like a mockery. So I gave you my second name, Marie, instead.'

'Honoria,' he repeated. 'It suits you. I would wager no one who knows you well would ever doubt that.'

'My own brother did,' she reminded him, her tone still bitter. 'You do understand why I chose not to use my real name? I didn't wish for scandal to follow me here and taint Aunt Foxe, just as I wanted to leave London so that it would not further stain my sister. You…know all about my family now, I suppose.'

'Yes. But don't you want to know what else I know?'

'Nothing matters as much to me as knowing I've not lost your…friendship,' she asserted, shying away at the last moment from daring to say the word 'love.'

After all, she was the only one who'd yet acknowledged that emotion. But he was smiling at her so tenderly that some of the icy shackles of fear loosened and fell away.

'I'm not angry,' he confirmed. 'Now let me tell you what I learned.'

For the next few minutes, he related to her an almost unbelievable tale: the three friends and spymasters, the fight, the murder, the Gypsy curse, the hanging of his best friend that her father did nothing to prevent even as Leybourne protested his innocence. And finally, the most intriguing news: that the gem trader she'd seen in the garden, the Gypsy Gabe had met at the inn, was the long-missing son of the murdered Baron Framlingham.

'No one knows what happened to Leybourne's family,' he told her. 'I think it highly probable that one of his relations who believes in his innocence and blames your father for not trying to exonerate him may have hired the Gypsy, who has reasons of his own to seek vengeance, to find a way to strike back at him. And you provided the means.'

'An innocent man's murder is certainly grave enough to justify the extreme measures taken against me,' she said thoughtfully. 'But after nearly twenty years, how could one hope to prove a connection?'

'I must track down the Gypsy trader, Stephano Beshaley— or Stephen Hebden, as the jeweller called him. He is the only link in the story we know for sure was present the night of your ruin—the one who must hold the key to the *why* of what happened. I mean to compel him to give it to us.'

The fear that his nearness and his smile had set in abeyance returned with a vengeance, like a punch to the gut. 'And then…you'll be leaving Cornwall for good?'

He gave her a sharp look. 'How did you know?'

'Tamsyn.' She tried a smile that didn't quite succeed. 'She was distraught to think of you leaving. I…I am distraught, too.'

Whether or not she would have had the courage to baldly confess her love, she had no opportunity to discover, for he put a thumb to her lips, stilling them—and distracting her so effectively that for a moment, she could think of nothing but the scent of his skin and the feel of his callused finger.

'Don't say anything. Not yet. Let me discover what I can,

see if it's possible for Lady Honoria's honour to be vindicated. To give you back a choice of what to do with your future.'

She shook her head sadly. 'Honour is not redeemable.'

'You don't know that,' he argued. 'You have passion and intelligence, spirit and fire! You deserve so much more than to be exiled to a quiet backwater, shunned by Society.'

As he spoke, he rose from his place beside her on the rock. 'I suppose we'd better go back now.'

Every particle of her protested his loss. Casting about desperately for a means to make him stay, she recalled the siren on the rocks. Could she tempt him, lure him to remain with her? Seize with both hands what she wanted—what she knew he desired as well, even if he might not love her? Use every trick she had read about to create one unforgettable memory of a passion that, if she did not seize this chance, she might never experience?

And perhaps, in this one last encounter, bewitch him as he had bewitched her?

Her heart already pounding with nervousness and anticipation, she grabbed his hand before he could walk away. 'I do deserve more. A man willing to defend me from revenuers' pistols and Gypsy traders' lies. One who believes in my honour and honesty even more than my blood kin, who's willing to search until he finds the truth that could clear my name. I deserve it and I want it. I want you, Gabe. Only you.'

One hand still holding his wrist captive, as she spoke she slid her other hand up his coat, from his chest to his cravat, then traced a single fingertip along the bare skin of his neck to his chin.

In a flush of joy and triumph, she felt the pulse leap at his throat beneath her questing finger.

He brought one hand up, as if to pull hers away, and instead clasped it over hers, holding her finger against his skin.

'This is madness,' he whispered hoarsely. 'I mean to restore your reputation, not destroy it.'

'It can't be restored—regardless of what you discover. But

having no reputation can be liberating. It means I have nothing to lose, nothing to prevent experiencing what I most desire. I think—I hope—you want it, too. Don't you…Gabe?' she whispered.

He swallowed hard, still resisting, though the molten blaze of his blue eyes and the frantic pulse at his throat testified how difficult he was finding it. 'I don't want to steal your innocence.'

She almost laughed at the irony: she had nearly been raped in a countess's garden by a nobleman the Ton called a gentleman, while this free-trader, whose company the men in that ballroom would probably have disdained, was too honourable to accept what she offered, what he clearly wanted.

Perhaps one more little lie would be justified to free them both. Tracing his face with her fingers from his temples down to his jaw, she said, 'I have no innocence left to lose.'

'I thought…your brother had arrived in time.'

'The damage was already done.' Which was true, although not in the way she was inferring.

But she'd been right; just the suggestion that her virginity was already forfeit made desire flame hotter in his eyes. 'You are sure?'

In answer, she leaned up and captured his lips.

Chapter Twenty-One

With every bit of nobility he could summon, Gabe tried to resist her, while her hands caressing his face steadily sucked away his will, swamping him in desire like the surf undercutting the sand beneath one's feet on the beach.

His heart was already thundering against his ribs, his pulse roaring in his ears. His skin felt so hot, he wondered that his shirt didn't smolder, while need built and built, bubbling up until it threatened to overflow, like a cauldron of caulking pitch left over too hot a fire.

He felt her hands against his face, scorching as a brand, and knew he must back away before the remains of his control snapped like a bowsprit in a high wind. She was the storm, a gale blowing away all sense, all reason, sweeping him into a whirlwind of passion that would carry away every lifeline that tied him to his careful, solitary existence. Until, in the blinding force of that gale, he could see and feel and sense only her, only him, only now.

And then her lips touched his and he knew he was lost, no more able to resist her than his ship could defy the power of the sea.

She teased his mouth as he had teased hers. Brushing, nuzzling, nipping at it, until she electrified him by trailing the moist wet blade of her tongue along the outline of his lips.

When he gasped at the rush of sensation, she slid her tongue past his parted lips, into the willing warmth of his mouth.

And then he was kissing her just as hungrily, revelling in the taste of her, renewed shocks of sensation jolting through him as she captured his tongue and sucked it lustily and everything within him melted and crackled and burned.

Dizziness swept through him and he took a faltering step backward, nearly falling. Laughing softly, she broke the kiss.

'Shall we go somewhere safer?' she asked. 'I don't want to fall into the surf and drown.'

Her willing slave now, he would have agreed if she'd wanted to strip him naked on the sand. Instead, she led him back to where the crags overhung the beach, the continual dampness softening the stones here with a carpeting of moss and lichen. Tossing down her cloak, she pulled him down beside her, her mouth already on his again as she urged him to sit, his back against the sloping, vegetation-covered rock.

Her touch now was deft, unhurried, and he gave himself up to it utterly, giddy senses swimming as with lips and tongue she made love to his mouth in every variation possible, nipping, licking, sucking, penetrating deeply, then withdrawing to lick teasingly with the lightest of touches around the very edges of his mouth. It didn't seem possible he could be pushed to the very brink of climax merely by a kiss, yet he had to fight to keep from going over the edge, though she touched him only with her mouth.

His erection straining almost painfully against his breeches flap, he could have gone on letting her simply kiss him forever… But then he felt her hands at his chest, pulling loose the knot of his cravat and thrusting the cloth aside, plucking open the buttons of his waistcoat. Plunging her tongue deeply again in his mouth, she tugged the tails of his shirt out and worked her fingers under the fine linen, rubbing and stroking along his belly and ribs until her questing fingertips reached his nipples. There she raked her fingernails across the sensitive tips in rhythm to the thrusts of her tongue.

Just when he thought he could stand no more without exploding, she swept her fingers downward. Withdrawing her tongue, she gave him the lightest of tiny butterfly kisses along the outline of his lips, over his chin, his eyelids, while very, very slowly she edged her clever fingers down the taut skin of his belly, then lower still, beneath the waistband of his breeches where his erection throbbed, thick and heavy.

He was barely able to breathe now, every muscle tensed, but instead of taking him in her hand, stroking him as he quivered in expectation, her fingers sought instead the smooth curve of his hipbone, the hollow where leg met trunk, excruciatingly close, yet not touching, the plump rounds and rock-hard shaft.

Then, still giving him feather-light kisses, she removed her hand entirely. While he moaned an incoherent plea, she began plucking open the buttons of his trouser flap, until in a turgid rush, his shaft sprang free.

A shiver of sea air blew across the exquisitely sensitive tip, dewed now with the desire he was the thinnest of threads from losing all control over. And when at last, at last, she took him in both hands and stroked from the base down to rub her thumbs over the moist aching tip, he exploded in a mind-melting burst of sensation that sent ecstasy rushing to every clenched muscle in his body.

He hadn't recovered wit enough to feel shamed that she'd brought him to the peak alone, when, dazed, dazzled, he realized she had laid her head against his sweat-soaked shirt, her cheek over the wild beating of his heart. A purity of joy he could never imagined suffusing him, he wrapped his arms around her and cradled her to his chest.

They sat together for some time, the wind whispering a blessing and the surf humming a little song of gladness, before he finally felt he could trust his brain enough to summon words. But when he opened his lips to speak, knowing he couldn't begin to express the peace, joy, wonder of being here with her, she pressed a finger against his lips.

'No talk now. Only loving.' And kissing him again, she reached down to cradle his flaccid member in her hands.

Good lad that it was, it began instantly to rise back to full attention. This time, she let him use his lips to make a leisurely exploration of her cheeks and brows, nose and ears, shuddering as he licked inside the delicate shells and nibbled on her earlobes. While he ministered to her, she rapidly rekindled desire from a slow simmer to a boil, gripping him lightly with both hands and sliding them from the hilt to the tip; tracing that same journey with a barely perceptible touch of one fingertip. Caressing just the taut skin of the head.

This time, however, he didn't intend for her to be a mere spectator. While he kissed her and she stroked him, he slipped a hand under her skirts and gradually worked up her legs, over the silky smoothness beneath the anklebone, around the lush fullness of calf to the tender skin behind her knee, then to the velvet of her inner thighs.

He delighted as her breathing went to little panting gasps that grew sharper as his fingers played across her thighs, creeping ever closer to the centre of her desires. She squirmed on the cloak, parting her legs wider for him, but he refused to be hurried, tasting the salty tang as the skin of her neck dampened and she moved urgently against his fingers.

She cried out when at last he parted her moist folds and delved within, running a finger tip over the plump ridge in a series of light strokes that pulled moans from deep in her throat.

But though he knew he'd not last much longer, before he readied her, his shaft swelling at the thought of the hot wet channel it would soon chart, he simply had to taste her. He tugged up her skirts to give him access, glorying in the sight of her pale naked limbs gleaming in the sunlight.

She played the wanton for him, letting her legs fall apart, gifting him with a full view of her soft, blonde-tufted mound and the pleasure-swollen lips beneath. Urging her sideways so as not to lose the feel of her fingers against him, he leaned down to ply her sweet depths with his tongue, echoing the pattern he'd created with his stroking fingers. She strained against him, uttering incoherent breathy sounds of pleasure.

Finally she pushed him away, urged him back to a sitting position. After bending to take him briefly in her mouth—all soft pressure and exquisite heat—she rose on her knees to straddle him.

While her mouth sought his again in greedy abandon, she lowered herself on his waiting shaft. After a brief, initial check, her hands clutching his shoulders, she moved lower, slowly, slowly taking him deeper while he vibrated with tension and delight. Finally she began to move against him, rocking him deep, setting off with each stroke little explosions of delight, each a precursor of the culmination to come. Until finally, clenching his shoulders again, she cried out and tensed around him, while he exploded in another brain-melting scorch of heat that sucked from him breath, thought, wits.

Sometime later, his brain focused to the delightful reality of his lady reclining on his chest, her intimate moistness still cradling his satisfied member. He sighed deeply, thinking despite the sharpness of the rocks behind and beneath him, he could recline here forever, cradling her body and wrapped in her luxuriant heat.

Knowing his time to do so was rapidly running out, as she dozed against his chest, he caressed the softness of her naked thighs and bottom. It would be worth a smuggler's boatload of gold, he thought dreamily as his fingers stroked and gentled, to wake every morning like this, with Honoria, his Honoria, dozing on his chest, his shaft nested deep within her.

Except she wasn't *his* Honoria. He'd meant what he'd told her earlier. Though he guessed what she'd wanted to say—the same words that his heart cried to speak—it would be better if nothing were said, or promised, until after he'd finished untangling the mystery of her ruin. Though he would never be able to bring himself to regret loving her, it had been unwise. And if he could produce proof of her innocence and win her a chance to reclaim her former life, what they had shared here today would remain his cherished secret.

Even though he now began to suspect she'd deliberately misled him about that innocence. Though she had been as ardent as he could have imagined, as his brain gradually resumed functioning, he recalled her gasp and the sudden bite of her nails into his shoulders when she first welcomed him into her body. With a little frown, he realized he had almost certainly been the first to breach her maidenhead.

Should he take her to task over it? he wondered, nuzzling his chin against her hair. She'd understood him well enough to know he would have resisted her every attempt at seduction, had he believed she was still untouched.

That sense of awe and humility welled up in him again, that she not only desired him, but had entrusted him with such a gift. It also spoke to how little faith she had in her chances of vindication.

Which only made him that much more determined to obtain it for her. No matter how desperately he wanted her future given into his hands.

If she had a family worthy of the name, they must respond to evidence of the vile trickery perpetrated against her by mounting an all-out campaign to restore her to her rightful place. He'd deliberately refrained from voicing his feelings to forestall her making promises she'd later feel compelled to keep. If he made much of being the first to claim her, she might feel honour required that she not accept her family's assistance, even though she'd hardly be the first maiden to go to her wedding couch no longer a virgin.

So he would say nothing. He'd bend every effort to giving her back a choice over what she wished to do with her life…and try to ignore the little voice within pleading for her choice to be him.

She woke then and stretched lazily, the movement creating a delectable caress of his nether regions that caused them to stir enthusiastically once again. Best that they both get dressed before the intoxicating elixir of desire she concocted so effortlessly bewitched him into taking her yet again.

'Though I'd rather stay here all day, we should go back. Father Gryffd and Eva will be worried if you do not appear at the school.'

''Tis early yet,' she whispered, her kiss-reddened lips impossibly seductive. 'Once we arrive at the school, our time will be over. No—' she put a finger over his lips '—don't say anything. Most especially, don't apologize or make me any noble speeches. You said it best: we will talk no more about this until after you've found the Gypsy. Now, I ask just one more thing.'

He would give her the moon to hang as a pearl broach at her throat, if she wanted it. 'What, sweeting?'

She started unhooking the clasps of her habit's jacket, each tug moving her against him in a series of small gliding motions that sent pulses of pleasure through his rapidly hardening member. Pulling off the jacket and tossing it aside, she shucked her shirt, then said, 'Undo my stays. I want to feel your mouth on my nipples.'

As she arched her head back to give him access, fully erect once again, he bent to comply.

Chapter Twenty-Two

Three weeks later, a grimly determined Gabe rode back into London. After questioning everyone in Sennlack who'd been acquainted with the Gypsy, he'd worked his way from Penzance to Falmouth, Truro to Bodmin, Launceston to Exeter and from Cornwall along the route to London, finding evidence of Beshaley's trading with jewellers and merchants, but not the man himself.

He'd searched out Gypsy encampments, too, and although one could never be sure they would give a straight answer to a *gadje*, he was reasonably certain none of them were harbouring the man. Which meant, unless he had overseas connections—Gabe recalled the massive turbaned butler—he must be in London. This time when he paid a call on Bloomsbury Square, Gabe would refuse to accept 'not home, Sahib' as an answer.

Much as he tried to concentrate only on his quest, Honoria's lovely face kept recurring in his mind's eye, the echo of her laughter murmuring in his ear. Speculation about where she was and what she was doing crept back into his consciousness whenever he relaxed his vigilance. Each time his disobedient thoughts returned to her, he ached with longing—probably a hopeless longing—that she might one day be his.

In the dark of the few hours he allowed himself to sleep, dreams invaded his mind, transporting him back to the cove. He awoke to vivid images of reclining once again on a bed of moss-covered rocks, joined with her, her soft body straddling his, her cries of pleasure thrilling him as he emptied himself into her.

A wave of guilt flooded him. It truly had been madness to succumb to her. If a child were to result, she might have no alternative but to throw in her lot with him, forfeiting the opportunity to regain her former life he was working so hard to give her.

However, after three weeks of fruitless searching, an insidious little voice had begun urging him to give up the quest, acknowledge the Gypsy was not to be found and accept there was nothing further he could do. It urged him to return to Cornwall, inwardly rejoicing that, with Honoria still disgraced, her highborn family might actually countenance the suit of a commoner like him.

Thinking of the vast gap in rank between the Earl of Narborough and titleless, landless Gabriel Hawksworth, he smiled grimly. But just what position did a disgraced gentlewoman occupy?

Perhaps one *not* so far above his, that same voice whispered.

Impatiently, he shut it out. He would think no more of the future until he had tracked down the Gypsy. If Beshaley were not now in London, he would almost certainly return there sometime. Gabe could wait—what else had he to do, now that the *Gull* had been taken back by her previous captain? While he waited, he could look into purchasing a ship of his own, establish trading contacts, contemplate where he might set up his business so as to have ready access to his sources—mittenmaking schoolgirls and a certain precociously gifted artist—without embarrassing his family.

But even if he were eventually successful in proving Honoria's innocence and seeing her restored to her former status, a growing sense that they belonged together, strengthened a hundredfold after lying with her, had started gnawing away at his resolve to do the honourable thing and walk away. A certainty welling up from deep within had begun asserting that they were as inextricably linked as a ship and the sea. Despite the fact that he could never offer her the advantages that were hers by birth, he was growing less and less certain he could, or should, leave her without first confessing his love.

Truly giving her a choice between her old world—and his.

But first, he must find the key to the past that only the Gypsy possessed.

Not bothering to check in first at a hotel, Gabe rode directly to Phillips Jewellers on Bond Street. Anticipation and excitement mounted in his chest when the proprietor confirmed he had indeed dealt with Mr Hebden recently. In fact, he'd just purchased some exquisite gems—if Gabe cared to see them?

Gabe did not. Thanking the man and promising to return upon another occasion, he reclaimed his horse and set off for Bloomsbury Square.

By the time he reined in before the modest town house, blood lust, frustration, longing and righteous rage had him primed and more than ready for a fight. If that butler did try to fob him off, he intended to discover just how good the Indian was with his dagger.

The same turbaned servant answered the door. 'Is Mr Hebden at home?' Gabe demanded.

After looking him over carefully, the butler replied, 'I regret, but the Master Sahib is not at home.'

Shouldering past him into the house, a feat possible only because the Indian had clearly not anticipated he would attempt such a move, Gabe said, 'I'm sorry, too, but that's not good enough. You will please tell "Sahib" that Gabriel Hawksworth is here to see him on behalf of Lady Honoria Carlow. If he truly isn't at home, I shall wait. You are, of course, welcome to try to prevent me.'

Shifting his weight onto the balls of his feet, hands fisting at his sides, Gabe waited expectantly for the Indian to reach for his dagger.

Before the man could move, however, a voice behind him said, 'Stay, Akshat. I will receive Captain Hawksworth.'

Garbed in an immaculate black coat, spotless cravat and tight buff breeches, seeming, but for the lilt in his voice and the slight exotic darkness of his skin, every inch the English gentleman, Stephano Beshaley—Steven Hebden—walked into the entrance.

'Won't you come into the library, Captain? Akshat, bring wine.'

'There's no need,' Gabe said curtly, not at all pleased at being robbed of his chance to have a go at the butler. 'I've come on business, and it will not take long.'

Hebden inclined his head. 'As you will.'

He escorted Gabe into the room, a modest space with a modicum of leather-bound books on mostly empty shelves behind a large desk. 'I take it this visit does not indicate a desire to invest in diamonds?'

'No.'

'Clever of you to have tracked me down. You come on behalf of Lady Honoria Carlow, you said. Just what is your connection to the lady?'

'I should rather ask you that. I met her in Sennlack under the name of Miss Marie Foxe.'

He had the pleasure of seeing surprise flicker on Hebden's face before the expression of amused hauteur settled over it again. 'Marie Foxe? Posing as a relation of old Miss Foxe of Foxeden? How interesting.'

'Perhaps, though I'm more interested in the part you played in sending her there. What happened the night of Lady Dalrington's ball? Who hired you to assist in luring Lady Honoria into the garden? I'm willing to pay for the information—or beat it out of you.'

Hebden wrinkled his nose in distaste. 'Please, Captain, your offer of payment is insulting. I'm not a common tradesman. And I'm no man's hired lackey.'

The Gypsy's last comment struck him. 'If you weren't hired to assist at the ball, why were you there? Did one of Wardale's kin put you up to it?'

'Ah, you know about the scandal? Perhaps I underestimated you, Captain. Something others have often done of me, to their eventual sorrow.'

He looked at Gabe condescendingly, the self-satisfied smugness of his expression making Gabe yearn to plant him a facer. 'The plan was such a marvel of perfection, I see no need to deny my part in it. Indeed, I wasn't approached by Wardale or anyone else; the design was entirely mine from the start.'

'*Entirely* yours?' Gabe asked incredulously.

'You have difficulty believing that?' Anger flashed in Hebden's eyes. 'I see I shall have to explain. It all began with my father's murder.'

'So you *are* Framlingham's lost son!' Gabe cried.

Hebden inclined his head. 'Yes. Hebden's Gypsy brat, his half-breed by-blow. The son who, upon his father's brutal murder, was ripped from everything familiar and sent to a foundling home. Have you any notion what life is like in a foundling home, Captain?'

'Far less comfortable than in a nobleman's house, I imagine,' Gabe replied.

Hebden laughed shortly. 'Far less *comfortable*.'

'I thought the building burned to the ground, killing everyone within it,' Gabe said.

'A few of us escaped. There followed some edifying years living on the street, then the voyages to foreign lands that led to my trading in gems. But always, I knew one day I would fulfill my mother's destiny by punishing those who caused my father's death.'

'Your mother cursed all the families involved,' Gabe remembered.

'And everything is now unfolding as she foretold. Guilt *is* eating them alive. Have you met Lady Honoria's father, the earl?' Hebden asked, malice in his eyes. 'In very poor health—as well he should be. And, as my mother predicted, the children will pay for the sins of their fathers, till justice destroys the wicked.'

'Justice!' Gabe cried. 'What kind of *justice* is it when someone entirely innocent is made to pay for her father's supposed crimes? Lady Honoria was but a child at the time!'

'As was I, when the Herriards cast me out!' Hebden retorted. 'The symmetry is quite perfect, do you not agree? In return for a Hebden son losing his home and his place, a Carlow daughter loses hers.'

'And you arranged this?' Gabe asked, incredulous that any sane man could justify such a travesty.

Looking pleased with himself, Hebden nodded. 'I was at the jeweller's the day she quarrelled with her fiancé, Lord Readesdell. A spoiled, selfish chit already known to be wild to a fault! The merest slow-top could have predicted she would seek to punish him. Quite amusing to involve Lord Barwick, who'd been sniffing around her skirts for some time and been roundly snubbed for his efforts.'

'How did you involve him?' Gabe asked, trying to control his rage long enough to ferret out the truth.

He'd thought he might have to coerce Hebden into revealing it, but with pride in his tone, the man replied, 'Quite easily! Wardale, formerly Lord Leybourne, was hanged with a silken rope, the usual practice for convicted peers. 'Twas another reason to choose Barwick, whose amorous perversions were well known. A silk rope dispatched along with a note on Carlow letterhead, requesting that he meet Lady Honoria for a little, ah, *restrictive* love-play, and it was done. All that remained was to hire a footman to give first him, then her, a message to meet in the garden and arrange for them to be discovered. Very neatly handled, if I do say so.'

'How could you coldly ruin an innocent girl—you, who know what it is for the guiltless to suffer!'

'Oh, she wasn't so innocent. If she hadn't already made herself a byword for behaviour just short of scandalous, Barwick wouldn't have believed she sent the note, nor would her sanctimonious brother Marcus have imagined her capable of arranging the rendezvous. A just God, whose instrument I am, ensures that only the guilty come to harm.'

Hebden laughed, further incensing Gabe. 'Did the jade feed you some pathetic falsehood about her purity?' Hebden made a scornful noise. 'The hot-blooded wench probably enjoyed Barwick's attentions!'

The memory flashed into Gabe's head—Honoria, jerking out of his embrace, white-faced and trembling. The anguish in her eyes as she haltingly described what Barwick had done to her.

With a growl of rage, he charged Hebden, fists raised.

But before he could land the first blow, Hebden doubled over with an anguished cry, both hands clutching at his head. While Gabe halted, puzzled, Hebden staggered backward, stumbled blindly into a chair and went down.

Gabe stared at him, mystified and disgusted. Much as he thirsted to feel the Gypsy's face bleeding under his fists, there was no way he could strike a downed man.

In the next moment, the library door burst open. Dagger raised, the Indian charged in, a murderous gleam in his eyes, two more men following on his heels.

Gabe wheeled to meet the butler's attack, arms up to deflect the first slash. From the corner where he'd fallen, Hebden moaned, 'No…Akshat. Just get him out.'

The butler checked his blow, while the other two cornered Gabe and grabbed him roughly by the shoulders.

'Don't worry, I'll leave in peace,' Gabe told him. 'Who

gave you the power to judge anyone's innocence or guilt, you contemptible muckworm? You can't right a wrong by perpetrating further injustice! I'd be careful about trying to strip vengeance from the Almighty's hands, lest that righteous God you claim to represent strike back at *your* kin!'

Jerking free of the two men restraining him, Gabe gave Hebden one last disgusted look and stalked from the room.

As he exited the town house, he noted that it was barely past noon. Possessed now of all the facts, with plenty of day light left to track down his final quarry, he vaulted into the saddle and directed his horse toward the Carlow residence on Albemarle Street.

The butler who answered the door tried at first to fob him off, saying that neither Lord Narborough nor Lord Stanegate were receiving visitors. But when Gabe curtly told him that he came on business related to Lady Honoria, the servant's manner abruptly changed. Escorting Gabe to a small ground-floor receiving room, the butler told him he would inform Lord Stanegate of his presence.

'See that you do,' Gabe said, barely repressing the rage simmering in him.

As he waited for Honoria's brother to appear, Gabe paced the room restlessly, noting the handsomeness and quality of the furniture and hangings. Finally he halted by the window, which overlooked a small back garden, where roses were blooming.

A melancholy longing pierced his restless anger. Vividly he recalled the day he'd met Honoria, approaching her aunt for an introduction and then audaciously bearing her off to view the roses in the vicarage garden. From the first moment he'd seen her striding into the waters of Sennlack Cove, she'd captivated him. His Miss Foxe.

But this was the domicile of Lady Honoria. The room—nay, the entire building—had the look of understated elegance and impeccable taste that spoke of distinguished pedigree and old wealth. *Here* she'd walked the halls; strolled in that garden, received her admirers—gentlemen of birth and fortune who had doubtless been escorted to the main reception rooms.

His certainty about the rightness of his bond with Honoria wavered. What made him think he could offer her anything to equal what he saw all around him, the opulence and comfort she'd enjoyed her whole life?

The door opened and a tall, well-muscled man walked in. Gabe scanned his face, looking for echoes of Honoria's countenance, and found little resemblance. Where in her eyes grey mingled with a laughing blue—like the sea in shadow and in sun—Lord Stanegate's were dark grey and cold. The golden strands that reflected the light in Honoria's hair were entirely absent in her brother's thick dark locks.

Gabe bowed stiffly, aware that those cold eyes were subjecting him to an equally intense and measured inspection.

His simmering rage revived. This tall, forbidding stranger was the man who'd compounded his sister's humiliation and anguish by refusing to believe in her.

Perhaps he had more to offer Honoria than the Carlows after all.

'Captain Hawksworth,' Marcus Carlow said, his voice imbued with the authority of one born to privilege. 'I don't believe I've had the honour of your acquaintance. I'm Stanegate, of course. Wellow tells me you've come on some matter regarding Lady Honoria? Just what are your dealings with my sister?'

Viscount Stanegate's forbidding manner might have cowed a lesser man, but four years of commanding soldiers through the blood, dirt, terror and danger of battle had forged Gabe into a man not easily intimidated.

'More supportive of her than you, sir,' he replied. 'I met your sister in Sennlack, where, by the way, she goes by the name Miss Foxe. Having become acquainted through her aunt, we developed a friendship. I soon came to greatly admire your sister's spirit and character.'

'If this is a declaration,' Stanegate interrupted him, 'you may spare your breath. I will not countenance—'

'My lord, I would ask that you refrain from leaping to conclusions, apparently a frequent failing, and hear me out before you make a reply,' Gabe cut him off acidly.

Anger flared in Stanegate's eyes, but as Gabe expected, discovering the mission of someone who came bearing news of his sister was important enough for him to overlook, for the moment, Gabe's insolence.

'Excuse me,' Stanegate replied, his tone irony dripping. 'Pray, continue.'

'As I said, your sister and I grew close enough that she confided to me the circumstances under which she came to be in Cornwall. Though her story apparently was not convincing enough to be believed by her immediate family, and despite knowing her but a short time, I was immediately certain that she had been the victim of a dreadful conspiracy. I set myself the task of uncovering the truth. And today, I accomplished that.'

Stanegate's expression went rapidly from irritation to surprise to avid interest. 'Please, Captain,' he said. 'Tell me everything you have discovered.'

'At Lady Dalrington's ball, Honoria said she was approached by a footman who told her that her fiancé, with whom she had quarrelled earlier, wished to meet privately in the garden to apologize. Anxious to settle the disagreement, she hurried out—only to find herself accosted by an infamous rake, who bound her hands in a silk rope—'

'A silk rope, you say?' Stanegate interrupted. 'I saw nothing of the sort when I found them!'

'Barwick untied her and tossed it away when he heard gentlemen approaching. Then asserted, worthless reprobate that he is, that he'd been invited to meet the lady in the garden. By Heaven!' Gabe burst out. 'How could you let the man say such things of Honoria without blackening his eyes where he stood!'

'She was terrified and trembling, her gown torn, her bodice gaping open!' Stanegate retorted. 'At that moment, all I wanted to do was shield her from lecherous gazes and get her home. Of course I sought out Lord Barwick later, prepared to call him out! But though he apologized for embarrassing my sister, he protested his innocence most vehemently, declaring he had received a note from Honoria on paper bearing the Carlow crest, begging him to meet her in Lady Dalrington's garden. The note further instructed that she'd send a footman to alert him when she could slip away. At the ball, a footman did just that. Barwick may be a loathsome toad of a lecher, but he doesn't lie.'

'Nor does your sister, Lord Stanegate,' Gabe said evenly.

Stanegate flushed and ran a hand through his hair. 'I know,' he admitted. 'The whole affair was a disaster! Even you must admit how bizarre it sounded. My wife was in a delicate condition, my father's health dangerously fragile, my innocent younger sister has yet to contract an eligible marriage. Having Honoria spring another of her ill-judged, crack-brained schemes upon us at just that moment…well, I lost my temper. Almost immediately I regretted the immoderate manner in which I'd addressed her. I intended to beg her pardon, but with Parliament in session and the press of estate business, by the time I came to see her, she'd already left London. When I discovered she'd gone to Cornwall instead of Stanegate Court, I knew she was seriously angry with me. I've written her since, but received no response.'

'But now,' he said, turning back to Gabe, 'you tell me you have *proof* that someone deliberately set up the rendezvous in the garden to ruin her—and have discovered the identity of the person who perpetrated this outrage?'

'I've just come from speaking with him. He admitted—nay, he *boasted!*—of concocting the whole elaborate ruse, showing not a particle of remorse for the harm he'd done. In fact, he seems to see himself as a sort of instrument of fate.'

'Stephen Hebden,' Stanegate said quietly. 'If there was a silken rope involved, it must have Hebden. Or was he calling himself Beshaley?'

'He goes by both. He has attempted to harm your family before?' Gabe asked. When Stanegate nodded, he said, 'Then by Heaven, why have you not had him clapped in irons?'

'We hoped we had seen the last of him. And in Honoria's case, on what grounds could we press charges? Barwick told me he burned the incriminating note as soon as he'd read it. What would be the point of trying to bring him, or Hebden, to court in a case which I doubt any solicitor could win, at the same time reviving a scandal best buried and forgotten as quickly as possible?'

'You'd rather save the family embarrassment than vindicate your sister's honour?' Gabe spit out contemptuously.

Fury hardened Stanegate's face. 'You obviously know nothing of London Society, sir, else I should call you out for such an insult! Have you no idea what a trial would mean to Honoria? Seeing her caricature in every press-shop window, hearing herself the focus of scurrilous speculation by every rogue and reprobate in London? Blackening her reputation so thoroughly in polite Society that her chances of returning there would be ruined, even were she proven innocent!'

'I'll allow you know the probable reaction of the London Ton better than I,' Gabe replied, somewhat mollified.

'If you have proof of Hebden's involvement, I can try to restrain him, though I shall probably have to operate outside the law. Where did you meet with him?'

'He keeps a house in Bloomsbury Square,' Gabe replied.

Stanegate nodded. 'I shall check with my contacts at Bow Street and get some men on it immediately.'

'Once you've dealt with him, I hope you intend to make every effort to restore your sister to her rightful place.'

'Despite what you seem to think, that has been my inten-tion from the beginning. I've only been awaiting the best moment to start.' Fixing Gabe again with that intimidating stare, Stanegate said, 'Just what is your interest in this, Captain?'

'I'm a friend of your sister's. I'm also outraged by injustice and would like to see it punished.'

Stanegate raised an eyebrow. 'And that's all?'

It was all Gabe intended to reveal to her brother, at least at this point. 'That's all. Can I trust you to do the right thing by her?'

'I give you my word.'

Gabe stood and offered Stanegate a bow. 'Then I have accomplished all I set out to do.'

'Thank you for efforts on her behalf,' Stanegate said as he walked Gabe to the door. 'And you're right. You have been more a friend and protector to my sister than I. For your care of one whom, though you may not believe it, I cherish, you have my eternal gratitude.'

With a stiff nod, Gabe went out.

Suddenly, the fatigue of his many days and nights on the road swamped him. Bone weary, he mounted his horse and rode to the Clarion, where he bespoke a room and some dinner.

He'd rest, then return to Cornwall and report to Lady Honoria. The idea of seeing her again sent a heady, reviving flush of warmth through him.

What would he do about her? Much depended on what action her brother took. Gabe would say and do nothing until Stanegate had time to make good on his word.

Well, maybe he'd do one thing. Since he was in London anyway, he might as well return to Cornwall prepared.

Pulling his horse up in front of the hotel, he half fell from the saddle, handed the reins off to a waiting groom, and stumbled inside.

Chapter Twenty-Three

A week later, Honoria knelt in her aunt's garden, taking out her loneliness and frustration by uprooting weeds and savagely beheading the fading pansies. Captain Hawksworth had been gone nearly a month and she'd heard not a word.

Cornwall had slipped from late spring into glorious early summer, swept fresh by a brisk southwest wind, its moors covered with a colourful carpet of thrift, campion, gorse and squill, while playful dolphins chased each other in the turquoise waters, falcons and kestrels soared with gulls overhead, and finches chattered away in the newly leafed trees.

The season's surge into summer only emphasized her stationary position, frozen in time between who she had been and who she might become. As the days dragged on, frustration was increasingly tinged with fear and a touch of despair.

She tried to tell herself it was only natural that it would take time for the captain to run down the Gypsy and wrench out of him the truth about that dreadful night. Then he would return and tell her what he'd learned.

Whether he felt more for her than a friendship compounded with lust, he would return, at least long enough for that.

While she waited, she was discovering that seizing what you want is not always wise. She'd been drawn to Gabriel Hawksworth already, but having tasted his body, experienced with him the indescribable pleasure and intensity of union, she couldn't see ever giving herself to any other man.

Even if he managed to redeem her reputation, making her Lady Honoria of the large dowry and important family connections once again. Even if her brother were horrified at the notion of her misalliance with a free-trader. She'd rather remain here, living in a cottage, tending vegetables in her garden, waiting for him to return from the sea, than marry some titled lord and live in ease without the man who had now left his mark upon her body as well as her soul.

She only wished she knew how the captain felt. Surely he didn't now see her as a wanton, a loose woman to be enjoyed and then left behind?

Her trug full of dried pansies and wilted weeds, she got to her feet. Anxious as she was, would she really prefer to have behaved with the circumspection of a Verity, restraining her passion and waiting until her brother awarded the captain her hand, something Marcus was very unlikely to do? Prefer to have never experienced the joy and ecstasy Gabriel had given her on the mossy ledge beneath his Irish cliffs?

No, she rallied herself. Despite the passage of nearly a month, she would not be so weak-spirited as to doubt the strength and purity of what she felt for him. Of what she was nearly certain he felt for her.

She would just continue to wait, trusting in his affection, confident of his return.

She sighed. Patience had never been one of her strong suits.

Then a thought occurred that sent excitement licking through her veins. If the long delay meant he was finding it difficult to find the Gypsy and impossible to prove their suspicions, retrieving her position might be impossible. And that could be a blessing.

Gentleman of character that he was, he might possess some foolish but noble scruples that said a union between himself and Lady Honoria would diminish her. But there would be no impediment to a union between him and a mere Miss Foxe.

And if he were still uncertain, teetering on the brink of deciding whether to claim her or continue his solitary bachelor ways…she'd found the role of siren most satisfying. Since she was a fallen woman in truth now, she might as well make the most of it. Rather than waiting on the gentleman, she could make the first move.

She recalled the heady sense of literally having him in her hands, at her mercy, trembling and needy before her. She smiled, letting her mind recall in loving detail every glorious, wonderful moment of seduction and surrender. If keeping him at passion's edge would keep him near her, with or without marriage lines, would that be enough?

Sighing again, she continued on toward the manor. She must put on a good front for her aunt—though from the sympathetic looks and attempts to engage her in cheerful debate, and the appearance at meals of all her favourite dishes, she suspected Aunt Foxe knew exactly what had recently transpired.

Oh, would he never return? she thought, kicking an unoffending pebble out of her path.

As she exited the walled kitchen garden, Myghal, her aunt's old gardener, shuffled toward her and doffed his cap. 'Beggin' pardon, miss, but there be a gentleman to see you.'

Her heart flew straight to her throat. 'Captain Hawksworth?' she demanded.

'Dinna say, miss,' the man replied. 'He's awaiting you in the south parlour, Dawes told me.'

Gabe! It must be Gabe. Joy and anticipation streaked through her, launching her spirits skyward like the spray from storm-swollen breakers colliding against the cliffs. And goodness, here she was in her oldest gown, dirt smudging her cheek and under her nails, her hair thrown up carelessly under an ancient chip-straw hat, looking like a milkmaid after an overlong encounter with her herd!

Before going to the south parlour, Verity would have washed her face and hands, tidied her hair and had Tamsyn lace her into her prettiest dress.

Honoria picked up her pace, ran up the entry stairs and headed straight for the south parlour.

She did pause by the hall mirror long enough to brush a dirt mark off her cheek. One glance was enough to conclude her hair was a hopeless tangle and nothing short of a stiff scrub brush could do anything about her nails. Her heart thudding against her ribs with delight and sudden shyness, she hurried to the door of the south parlour, threw it open and rushed in.

Her joyous words of welcome died in her throat. 'Marc!' she cried. 'What are you doing here? Is Papa all right?'

'That's hardly the warm welcome I was hoping for after journeying all the way from London,' her brother said, walking over to give her a hug. 'All the family is fine. Are you?'

For a moment, she leaned into his embrace before stepping back. 'You'd best keep your distance!' she replied, ignoring his query. 'You've caught me just in from the garden. I thought you were someone else, or I would have delayed meeting you until I made myself more presentable.' With a bitter edge to her smile, she added, 'So here I am, looking the hoyden as usual, I suppose you'd say.'

Marc sighed and shook his head. 'I see you didn't read any of my letters.'

Honoria thought of them, lying still unopened in her chamber. 'No,' she admitted.

'If you had, you might have been happier to see me, for I apologized over and over. But since my sister declined to communicate with me, I realized if wanted to be reconciled with her, I'd have to come to Cornwall. So here I am. Will you forgive me, Honoria?'

Her heart squeezing on a tremor of pain and remorse, she realized all she really wanted was to have him say those words.

'Of course I forgive you.'

'Honoria, I'm sorry I doubted your word. I regret that I let you go away, still thinking me angry at you, still believing I'd abandoned you and your future. I'm sorry I lost my temper and wounded someone who's been dear to me since the day she first opened her lovely eyes that, even then, looked on the world with passionate curiosity and determination.'

Honoria felt those eyes brim with tears. It meant more than she could put into words to learn that she had not, as she'd believed, forfeited her brother's respect. 'When did you decide I was not dissembling?'

'Almost immediately. I intended to apologize at once, and had Papa not charged me with an urgent errand at the Home Office, would have done so first thing the next morning. By the time I returned, you had already left London. Once you were gone, there seemed no reason to recall you while I set investigations in motion. I questioned Lord Barwick that same evening, finding him much in his cups—doubtless worried I was going to put a bullet in him.'

Honoria shrugged. 'Like me, he was only a tool.'

'Tools have we all been,' Marcus said soberly, 'suffering retribution for crimes we never committed.'

Then his expression lightened and he laughed. 'Speaking of retribution, your Captain Hawksworth came to see me. Gave me quite a bear-garden brawl for the way I'd treated you! He was so offensive, I would have challenged him to fisticuffs, if he had not been correct in almost all his accusations.'

'Almost all?'

'He seemed to think I'd done nothing about your situation, which is not at all the case! It would probably still be better for you not to return to London yet, at least not until Verity is settled. But even if you were at fault—' he held up a hand '—and I don't believe you were, you are a Carlow. London is your world and your right.'

Though warmed by her brother's support, Honoria shook her head. 'Not any longer. I should remain out of Society so as not to compromise Verity's chances any more than I already have.'

'She charged me to carry a letter to you, by the way,' Marc said, pulling a folded missive from his waistcoat pocket. 'She misses you, as I do. We want you to return, as soon as it is safe for you.'

She blinked, confused. 'Safe for me?'

'Yes. We need enough new *on dits* to occupy Society that the scandal sheets don't go after you upon your return. Then, Mama will have Lady Jersey and some of her other friends quietly reintroduce…'

His words trailed off as she shook her head. 'No, Marc, I don't want to go back. I'm not the same girl I was last spring. Better, I hope. I want something different now.'

Marc frowned at her. 'What?'

She looked away. More prudent not to tell him what he probably wouldn't want to hear until she knew for sure what she meant to do—and that she wouldn't know until she saw Gabe again. 'I can't speak of it yet.'

'Am I correct in assuming it involves a certain impassioned young captain?'

She slid him a glance under her lashes, but his expression told her nothing. 'And if it should?'

'I'd never stand in the way of your happiness. Whatever you decide about your future.'

'Thank you,' she said softly, another weight lifting from her soul. Regardless of where her path took her, she didn't really want to walk it estranged from her family.

'Since you did mention it, I expect you will want to do some tidying up. I'll go settle into my chamber and then visit Aunt Foxe. Shall I see you at dinner?'

She nodded. 'At dinner, then.'

He gave her a grin and a quick kiss on the forehead and walked out. Honoria drifted into the entry hall after him, but though reconciling with Marc had soothed some of the ache in her heart, with dinner still hours away, she felt too restless to be cooped up in the house.

Since she was muddy and windblown anyway, she'd take a walk on the cliff path, read Verity's letter and mull over what Marcus had said.

Tucking the note in her sleeve, she fetched a cloak, slipped out the door by the kitchen and set off.

Some half hour later, Gabe rode up to Foxeden. He had extended his stay in London by another day in order to talk with investors about the buying of a ship and to consult Mr Avery at the gallery, who received Eva's new pastel drawings with all the enthusiasm he had hoped. There was still much to be done to launch himself upon a trading career, but it had been nearly a month since he'd seen Honoria and he couldn't wait a moment longer to be with her again.

His talk with her brother had convinced him Stanegate intended to restore her to Society. He was glad for that and wished the viscount success, but during the long ride back from London, he'd also decided he would not nobly stand aside and send her away. Though neither as smuggler nor as tradesman would he be considered remotely eligible as a husband by her family—or his—he would not let her return to her old life without trying to convince her to be his wife.

She might prefer a position in Society to embracing him and what he could offer. But he didn't think so. Filled with that hope, his last stop before leaving London had been at the office of the Archbishop of Canterbury, where he harried the poor clerk into issuing him a special license in record time. If he could persuade Honoria to have him—Gabe grinned, envisioning some of the spots upon which he would concentrate his efforts at kissing her into agreement—he intended to marry her at once and bring her with him as he embarked upon his trading enterprise.

Trying to master his nervousness at knowing he would soon

be putting his whole future happiness to the test, he knocked at Foxeden's front door. He was returning the greeting of the butler who admitted him when, to Gabe's astonishment, Honoria's brother strode down the stairs from the parlour.

Stopping short, Gabe bowed. 'Stanegate. I didn't know you'd planned to come to Cornwall.'

'Since my sister would not come to me, I was obliged to go to her,' the viscount said, bowing back. 'Though I'm not at all surprised to see you here.'

Gabe looked squarely at Stanegate. 'I intend to ask Honoria to marry me.'

'And you seek my permission?'

'No. I'm simply informing you, as a courtesy. She's of age and can wed with or without your leave. Though I've been a free-trader—'

'I understand they are held in high esteem here,' Stanegate inserted.

'I am gentry-born. My brother is—'

'Sir Nigel Hawksworth, of Ballyclarig Manor. A magistrate who also sits at the Assises for County Cork. Married the Honorable Miss Chastain, daughter of Lord Chastain of Parnell Hall. You served for four years in the 3rd Regiment of the 27th Inniskilling Foot, attaining the rank of First Lieutenant, before being wounded at Orthes.'

Gabe stared at him. 'How did you—'

Stanegate shrugged. 'My secretary is very efficient. I know you think I'm a shabby sort of brother, but when an unknown young man turns up, rattling his sabre at me, ready to gallop off to defend my sister's honour, I do take notice.'

Flustered, Gabe tried to pick up the threads of the explanation he'd mentally rehearsed to give Honoria's family, if she consented to marry him. 'My family owns some of the prettiest acres in Southern Ireland, but I've long known I would never be content overseeing one of my brother's holdings. My recent time as a free-trader confirmed that the sea's in my blood, and though I don't wish to remain in the trade and risk making Honoria a widow before she's scarcely been a wife, I do mean to continue at sea.'

'You'll seek a naval commission?'

'No, I had my fill of regimentation whilst in the Army. I've interested a small group of investors, and with their blunt and some of my own, I intend to purchase a ship. Just a small sloop at first, but sound enough for ocean sailing and commodious enough to carry a good cargo of legitimate goods. Art, woollen goods, artefacts. Spices from the Indies; pineapple from the tropics. I'll sail her wherever there are desirable goods needing transit from their place of production to a market with willing buyers.'

'And you want to bring my sister into this vagabond life?'

'If she'll have me. She may prefer returning to the life she's always known, the life you can offer her, conventional marriage to a respectable society gentleman. Love her as I do, I could never be that. But I can give her moonlight on the sea, the ship's wake a phosphorescent glow in the blackness. The pearl of dawn, when out of the shadowy greyness the sky slowly distinguishes itself from the sea. Tropic beaches gleaming in the sun, the great endless green stretches of hardwood forest in the Americas. I intend to be very persuasive,' he concluded, having no intention of telling her elder brother what other, more intimate techniques he meant to employ.

Stanegate smiled. 'You're convincing me. Is Sir Nigel one of your investors?'

Gabe laughed at the thought. 'My brother would rather throw his gold into the sea than have it used to sully the name of Hawksworth with trade.'

'Would you be willing to let me buy in? By the way, I think you and my sister are a pair, Captain. Honoria has chafed at the confines placed upon gently-born maidens the whole of her life. Always she's wanted to have a man's freedom, a man's adventures. When you return to London to complete your negotiations, come see me. After all, if my sister is going to be living in a captain's cabin, I'd better make sure the ship is top-of-the-line.'

'You won't object?' Gabe asked, scarcely believing he could be hearing correctly.

'No.' Stanegate walked over and offered his hand. 'You certainly don't need it and probably don't want it, but nonetheless I give you blessing. I wish you joy with my sister, Captain. She'll lead you a merry dance.'

Dazedly, Gabe shook his hand. 'Good luck to you, too, my lord. Did you find Hebden, by the way?'

Stanegate's jaw tightened. 'No. By the time my agents arrived at Bloomsbury Square, the house was deserted, the knocker already off the door. I intend to keep hunting. If he remains in England, I shall run him to ground.'

'Good,' Gabe said, nodding. Recalling Hebden's strongly expressed sense of being an instrument of destiny, Gabe warned, 'I don't think he's done yet.'

'I'm afraid you are right,' Stanegate replied, looking grim.

Just then Dickin's sister Tamsyn walked in through the servant's door and stopped short. 'Captain Hawksworth!' she cried, awe in her voice.

'Miss Tamsyn,' Gabe said, giving her a bow. 'I've come to call upon Miss Marie. Will you tell her I'm here?'

'She's not in the house, Captain. She left not half an hour ago, walking toward the cliff path.'

Gabe glanced back at Stanegate. 'I'll see you later, my lord. It appears I'm going for a stroll.'

Chapter Twenty-Four

On a flat rock overlooking Sennlack Cove, Honoria sat, face to the brisk wind, Verity's letter secured in both fists. Upon unfolding it and seeing the familiar script, she'd been struck by a wholly unexpected longing for her little sister, that paragon of perfection she'd so often found annoying when they occupied the same house. Something, Honoria recognized sadly, they were unlikely to ever do again, despite the wish Verity expressed in her letter that Honoria might soon return to them.

Verity missed Honoria acutely, she wrote, her intelligence, her wit and her insightful observations on the events and personages in London. As for the scandal, truly she had never heard overmuch about it, and nothing at all this last month.

Marcus had advised her to make no comment if anyone discussed it, and though he must know best—Honoria rolled her eyes at this—it had often been very hard to remain silent. Whatever reason her sister had for going to meet Lord Barwick, Verity knew it must have been a good one. If anyone wished to cut her acquaintance over the matter, she was quite willing that they do so, since if they wanted to condemn Honoria, Verity did not wish to know them anyway.

Honoria halted, tears making the words blur. She felt both

a pang of guilt and a wave of affection at her little sister's fierce loyalty.

Swiping a hand over her eyes, she resumed reading, then exclaimed with concern at discovering that Verity's childhood friend, soldier Rhys Morgan, had been badly wounded. When Honoria returned, Verity went on, perhaps they could visit and cheer him, poor man, since Marc had said the injuries were so severe that Rhys would not be able to return to soldiering. Verity hoped Lord Keddinton, who was godfather to them both, might be able to find a position for him somewhere in the government.

As a girl, Honoria recalled, her sister had been quite infatuated with Rhys, though she claimed to have outgrown it. Had she? Was the noble soldier the right man for her sweet, innocent, courageous little sister, who saw the best in everyone and fiercely defended the people she loved—even flawed mortals who'd often failed to appreciate her, like Honoria?

Certainly Verity deserved to find a fearless, principled man who would cherish her with the same passionate abandon Verity offered up to all whom she loved.

Suddenly a realization brought her up short, a truth so essential it seared straight through all her doubts and confusion to resonate in the depths of her soul.

Alluring as it might be to play the siren and seduce Gabe again, passionate abandon without true love to enrich it wasn't enough. In time, a bond fuelled only by passion's fire would burn low, leaving behind the ash of disillusionment and regret.

She wanted to be loved with the same purity and fierceness, nobility and honour that Verity loved her family. Nothing less would last. Nothing less would do.

Even if it meant she had to stand aside and watch Gabriel Hawksworth sail away, leaving her behind on the cliffs, for ever looking out over the sea at a love that had tacked just out of reach, as Aunt Foxe's had.

The turbulence of her feelings calmed as the rightness of

that decision settled over her. With a sigh of regret, she let go the image of the siren on the cliffs.

Would the captain be able to offer her devotion as well as passion? Oh, that he might return so she could put an end to this wretched uncertainty!

She was folding the letter when a shadow fell over it. Startled, she glanced sharply up—and he was there.

In a flash, Honoria leapt up. She was about to throw herself into his arms and pull his head down for a kiss, when she recalled she'd just decided she wanted more than passion. She would be cherished, too—or have nothing.

'Captain Hawksworth!' she said, dropping her arms back to her sides. 'How wonderful to see you!'

'Miss Foxe.' Smiling tenderly, he reached out, running his hand over her cheek, then drawing a fingertip across her lips, which quivered and burned. 'It's delightful to see you again, too.'

Honoria had to concentrate very hard to remember why she'd decided not to play the siren. Needing to focus on something other than the urge to suck his finger into her mouth while she brought a hand up to stroke…something else, she said, 'Please, tell me everything you discovered in London.'

Gesturing at her to resume her seat, he propped a boot against the rock. 'I discovered everything we could wish! Stephano Beshaley alone planned your ruin. He seems to think himself divinely appointed to carry out the curse his mother placed upon all the families involved in his father's murder. Once he realized the identity of the lady arguing with her fiancé at the jeweller's, he immediately saw an opportunity to strike back at the Carlows by destroying your life, as his had been destroyed—an innocent for an innocent. He sent the note to Barwick, hired the footman to summon all the parties to the garden—then watched with satisfaction as his scheme unfolded just as he'd designed.

'I alerted your brother,' he continued, 'and he has hired

agents to track Hebden down, thus far without success. Stane-gate also promised to turn his efforts to restoring your reputation and returning you to Society.'

'Yes, so he told me. Except I don't wish to go back, even if Marc could arrange it. I love Cornwall: the cliffs, the vista of an endless, restless sea. I like feeling useful, helping the girls and Eva.'

'Ah, yes, Eva! I showed her pastels to Mr Avery, the owner of the European Picture Gallery, who was most enthusiastic. He bought them all and wants more.'

So distracted was she by his presence, she'd forgotten to tell him the news that had shocked all of Sennlack. 'You won't imagine what happened with Laurie! After the ambush, Father Gryffd insisted on bringing her, Eva and their mother to stay at the vicarage to protect them from possible retribution by John Kessel. The vicar, who apparently had always admired Laurie, asked her to marry him! Though she protested that such a thing was impossible, in the end he convinced her. Knowing folks hereabouts would have difficulty treating her with the respect due his wife, he announced last Sunday he's accepted a position with the Methodists to preach in the Americas. Since, of course, Laurie wouldn't go off and leave her mother and sister behind, they are moving to America, too.'

'I'm so glad they will all have the chance for a new life together—and I can see that to bring Eva's art to the world, I'm going to have include a stop in the Americas among my voyaging. Now, what of you? You truly don't intend to accept the new life your brother wants to offer you?'

She shook her head. 'Even if I wanted to return, I don't see how I could without my presence reviving the scandal and hurting Verity. That I can never do.'

'Could you be happy living apart from Society?'

'I think all my happiness requires is the reform of a certain smuggler. After that attack by the revenue agents, I fear for all the free-traders. You have decided to give up the trade, Tamsyn said?'

'Yes. I've turned the *Gull* back to her former captain. My days as a free-trader are over.'

She'd hoped that would be true, but having him confirm it removed a huge weight of anxiety. 'Wonderful! What…shall you do, then?' she asked, trying not to sound too anxious.

'I shall stay with the sea, but as a legitimate trader, buying, transporting and selling goods to willing customers. I shall sail wherever the wind takes me, from the tropics to the Orient, the sandalwood coast of Brazil to the timber-rich forests of America, acquiring and bringing back treasures.'

He directed that intense blue-eyed gaze at her, which set her stomach fluttering, as it always did. 'Your brother seemed to think you would find such a life exhilarating.'

He might only mean that Marcus had told him she'd always yearned for adventure. But he'd given her a perfect opening, and summoning all her courage, she replied, 'I would find such a life perfect, if a certain captain invited me to sail with him.'

He studied her closely. 'Are you saying what I think you are saying?'

'I'm telling you what I would have said that day at the cove, when you forbade me to make promises I might later regret. I'm telling you my happiness lies not in places or titles or position, but in being with you. Aunt Foxe once advised me that love is a rare and precious gift; if one is lucky enough to find it, one should seize and savour it. I love you, Gabriel Hawksworth. I want to seize and savour life with you.'

For a moment, while her heart trembled between hope and despair, he said nothing. Then he grabbed her hands and began covering them with kisses, and she laughed with the sheer exuberant joy of knowing he loved her after all.

'So, too, do I want to seize and savour life with you! I can't offer you anything to compare to the position you'll forfeit in choosing me over your family—but I offer myself. All my heart, all my loyalty, all my devotion. I'll work my whole life to be worthy of you. Will you marry me, my heart?'

She shook her head, tears misting her eyes, hardly daring to believe the wonder of it. Out of humiliation and disgrace, she'd found a perfect love for all time.

'No, 'tis I who must work my whole life to be worthy of *you*. A man who believed in me when my own family did not. Who sought out my enemies and vanquished them, giving me back my honour. I want to spend my life with the man who loved me not for being an earl's daughter but for who I am, who taught me the world I've always known is well lost for the chance to be a smuggler's lady.'

'Nay,' he said, pulling her into his arms. 'To be a sea captain's wife.'

* * * * *

COMING NEXT MONTH FROM

HARLEQUIN®
HISTORICAL

Available August 31, 2010

- **HIS DAKOTA CAPTIVE**
  by **Jenna Kernan**
  (Western)

- **CLAIMING THE FORBIDDEN BRIDE**
  by **Gayle Wilson**
  (Regency)
  Book 4 in the *Silk & Scandal* miniseries

- **CHIVALROUS CAPTAIN, REBEL MISTRESS**
  by **Diane Gaston**
  (Regency)

- **SURRENDER TO AN IRISH WARRIOR**
  by **Michelle Willingham**
  (Medieval)
  The MacEgan Brothers

Other nations understand
that we are a christian nation
Surely do those who flee to us
Try to make a thing for us

their ungodly lands a mess
for all are respected
We will tolerate your faith
But dont change what made
us great

REQUEST YOUR FREE BOOKS!

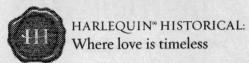

HARLEQUIN® HISTORICAL:
Where love is timeless

2 FREE NOVELS PLUS 2 **FREE GIFTS!**

YES! Please send me 2 FREE Harlequin® Historical novels and my 2 FREE gifts (gifts are worth about $10). After receiving them, if I don't wish to receive any more books, I can return the shipping statement marked "cancel." If I don't cancel, I will receive 6 brand-new novels every month and be billed just $4.94 per book in the U.S. or $5.49 per book in Canada. That's a saving of 20% off the cover price! It's quite a bargain! Shipping and handling is just 50¢ per book.* I understand that accepting the 2 free books and gifts places me under no obligation to buy anything. I can always return a shipment and cancel at any time. Even if I never buy another book from Harlequin, the two free books and gifts are mine to keep forever.

246/349 HDN E5L4

Name _____ (PLEASE PRINT)

Address _____ Apt. #

City _____ State/Prov. _____ Zip/Postal Code

Signature (if under 18, a parent or guardian must sign)

Mail to the Harlequin Reader Service:
IN U.S.A.: P.O. Box 1867, Buffalo, NY 14240-1867
IN CANADA: P.O. Box 609, Fort Erie, Ontario L2A 5X3

Not valid for current subscribers to Harlequin Historical books.

Want to try two free books from another line?
Call 1-800-873-8635 or visit www.morefreebooks.com.

* Terms and prices subject to change without notice. Prices do not include applicable taxes. N.Y. residents add applicable sales tax. Canadian residents will be charged applicable provincial taxes and GST. Offer not valid in Quebec. This offer is limited to one order per household. All orders subject to approval. Credit or debit balances in a customer's account(s) may be offset by any other outstanding balance owed by or to the customer. Please allow 4 to 6 weeks for delivery. Offer available while quantities last.

Your Privacy: Harlequin Books is committed to protecting your privacy. Our Privacy Policy is available online at www.eHarlequin.com or upon request from the Reader Service. From time to time we make our lists of customers available to reputable third parties who may have a product or service of interest to you. ☐ If you would prefer we not share your name and address, please check here.

Help us get it right—We strive for accurate, respectful and relevant communications. To clarify or modify your communication preferences, visit us at www.ReaderService.com/consumerschoice.

HH10R

HARLEQUIN®

A Romance

FOR EVERY MOOD™

Spotlight on

— Heart & Home —

Heartwarming romances
where love can happen
right when you least expect it.

See the next page to enjoy a sneak peek
from Harlequin Superromance®,
a Heart and Home series.

*Enjoy a sneak peek at fan favorite Molly O'Keefe's
Harlequin Superromance miniseries,*
THE NOTORIOUS O'NEILLS, *with
TYLER O'NEILL'S REDEMPTION,
available September 2010
only from Harlequin Superromance.*

Police chief Juliette Tremblant recognized the shape of the
man strolling down the street—in as calm and leisurely
fashion as if it were the middle of the day rather than
midnight. She slowed her car, convinced her eyes were
playing tricks on her. It had been a long time since Tyler
O'Neill had been seen in this town.

As she pulled to a stop at the curb, he turned toward her,
and her heart about stopped.

"What the hell are you doing here, Tyler?"

"Well, if it isn't Juliette Tremblant." He made his way
over to her, then leaned down so he could look her in the
eye. He was close enough to touch.

Juliette was not, repeat, *not* going to touch Tyler O'Neill.
Not with her fingers. Not with a ten-foot pole. There would
be no touching. Which was too bad, since it was the only
way she was ever going to convince herself the man standing
in front of her—as rumpled and heart-stoppingly handsome
now as he'd been at sixteen—was real.

And not a figment of all her furious revenge dreams.

"What are you doing back in Bonne Terre?" she asked.

"The manor is sitting empty," Tyler said and shrugged,
as though his arriving out of the blue after ten years was
casual. "Seems like someone should be watching over the
family home."

"You?" She laughed at the very notion of him being here
for any unselfish reason. "Please."

He stared at her for a second, then smiled. Her heart fluttered against her chest—a small mechanical bird powered by that smile.

"You're right." But that cryptic comment was all he offered.

Juliette bit her lip against the other questions.

Why did you go?

Why didn't you write? Call?

What did I do?

But what would be the point? Ten years of silence were all the answer she really needed.

She had sworn off feeling anything for this man long ago. Yet one look at him and all the old hurt and rage resurfaced as though they'd been waiting for the chance. That made her mad.

She put the car in gear, determined not to waste another minute thinking about Tyler O'Neill. "Have a good night, Tyler," she said, liking all the cool "go screw yourself" she managed to fit into those words.

It seems Juliette has an old score to settle with Tyler.
Pick up TYLER O'NEILL'S REDEMPTION
to see how he makes it up to her.
Available September 2010,
only from Harlequin Superromance.